"Among the many things I love about reading a Sandra Byrd novel is knowing that her words will transport me to another place and time, that she will win me over with intriguing and complex characters, and that I'll savor every word. *Mist of Midnight* is no exception. I loved this book! Sandra Byrd could belong to the writing group of the Brontë sisters if they'd had one. *Wuthering Heights* and *Jane Eyre* along with crumbling mansions, mysterious distant cousins, and one woman's journey to prove who she really is are just few layers that ripple through the mists. Bravo, Sandra! Another winner."

—Jane Kirkpatrick, award-winning author
of *A Light in the Wilderness*

"From the first word to the last, *Mist of Midnight* is a completely absorbing romantic, and mysterious, novel. Ms. Byrd's writing is splendid, and her characters are so complex and endearing that they leap off the pages. I couldn't put it down. An absolutely irresistible read!"

—Anne Girard, author of *Madame Picasso*

"Sandra Byrd's trademark attention to historical accuracy combines with an eerily building intrigue to envelop readers in a sense of dark foreboding that hinges precariously between hope and desperation. *Mist of Midnight* is a subtly haunting, beautifully atmospheric, and decadently romantic Victorian tale that will find a comfortable home among the best Gothic romances of days gone by."

—Serena Chase, author of *The Ryn* and contributor
to *USA Today*'s Happy Ever After blog

"Once again, Sandra Byrd delivers a richly layered story that will leave you eagerly awaiting the next book in this brand-new series. *Mist of Midnight* has it all: intriguing and memorable characters—including a central female protagonist who is both complex and inspiring—a plot chock-full of mystery and suspense, and a Victorian gothic setting, impeccably researched and artfully and evocatively relayed. Prepare to be transported!"

—Karen Halvorsen Schreck, author of *Sing for Me*

"*Mist of Midnight* is a beautiful, haunting tale. Sandra Byrd masterfully weaves together both romance and suspense among a cast of mysterious characters. I was immediately swept into the wonder of this story, and I loved unraveling all the secrets and discovering exactly what happened at the old Headbourne House."

—Melanie Dobson, author of *Chateau of Secrets* and *The Courier of Caswell Hall*

"Not since *Jane Eyre* have I read a Gothic romance that has captured my heart so completely. From the exotic India to an English estate shrouded in mystery, Byrd's eye for detail shines through on every page. Romance lovers are sure to devour the tale of Rebecca Ravenshaw and her search for the truth behind the mysteries of Headbourne House and the handsome young captain who lives on the estate."

—Renee Chaw, reviewer at Black 'n Gold Girl's Book Spot

MIST
of
MIDNIGHT

A NOVEL

SANDRA BYRD

HOWARD BOOKS
A DIVISION OF SIMON & SCHUSTER, INC.

NEW YORK   NASHVILLE   LONDON   TORONTO   SYDNEY   NEW DELHI

Howard Books
A Division of Simon & Schuster, Inc.
1230 Avenue of the Americas
New York, NY 10020

First Howard Books trade paperback edition March 2015

HOWARD and colophon are trademarks of Simon & Schuster, Inc.

For information about special discounts for bulk purchases, please contact Simon & Schuster Special Sales at 1-866-506-1949 or business@simonandschuster.com.

The Simon & Schuster Speakers Bureau can bring authors to your live event. For more information or to book an event contact the Simon & Schuster Speakers Bureau at 1-866-248-3049 or visit our website at www.simonspeakers.com.

Designed by Jaime Putorti

Manufactured in the United States of America

10 9 8 7 6 5 4 3 2 1

Library of Congress Cataloging-in-Publication Data

Byrd, Sandra.
  Mist of midnight / Sandra Byrd.
    pages cm
    1. Young women—Fiction. 2. Inheritance and succession—Fiction. 3. Great Britain—History—Victoria, 1837–1901—Fiction. I. Title.
  PS3552.Y678M57 2014
  813'.54—dc23
                            2014007378

ISBN 978-1-4767-1786-9
ISBN 978-1-4767-1787-6 (ebook)

. . . man he made and for him built
Magnificent this world, and earth his seat,
Him lord pronounced; and, Oh indignity!
Subjected to his service angel-wings,
And flaming ministers to watch and tend
Their earthly charge: Of these the vigilance
I dread; and, to elude, thus wrapped in mist
Of midnight vapor glide obscure, and pry
In every bush and brake, where hap may find
The serpent sleeping; in whose mazy folds
To hide me, and the dark intent I bring.

—*PARADISE LOST*, JOHN MILTON

LATE FEBRUARY 1858

BOMBAY

They were gone now, every last one of them. Gone, but not completely gone.

I still saw them at midnight.

I surrendered too, by leaving. The ship pulled from the shore whilst I beheld the distancing plumage of saris—azure and emerald and flame the soft brown arms, necks, and noses circled with gold, like exquisite birds of paradise. A threadbare charity dress the Lord Mayor of London had provided, to me and to all survivors who had nothing of their own to claim, pasted to my skin with a familiar fine grit of dust and sweat.

The dress was black, for mourning.

I clutched the rail, my ears tuned to the rough symphony of a dozen dock languages: half Eastern, half Western, smattered into a whole. My eyes were hollow, my legs frail as a Hindu holy calf's after nearly eight months at the Residency with other survivors.

"We'll soon be home, lassie." Mrs. MacAlister lifted one hand from the ship and put it on mine as she faced into the salt-spiked breeze.

We'd met but a month earlier and I knew little about her, but she'd agreed to be my chaperone for the eight-week journey.

I was already home. Home was India. Home was with my parents, my brother, my friends, although now I was deprived of them all.

"England for ye, of course, and Scotland for me; civilization," she continued. "Then ye shall have peace and happiness. Security ever after." She nodded and smiled, but her eyes were flat—weary and restless like the driftwood the ship's wake pushed aside.

Peace and happiness. Security. All that was mine until the Indian mutineers rode in; they said they wanted to reclaim their land, we said we were innocent: sent to serve, not steal. There was truth and misunderstanding on both sides. They'd killed my parents, they'd smothered my hopes. Instead of robbing me of my dreams they'd warped them until I could barely sleep three steady hours without hearing the gurgling of blood in the throat of a man shot off his horse, or recalling pitched insanity in the eyes of a woman who'd witnessed her husband struck down.

Had my mother looked like that before they cast her body, with Father's, into a dry well?

I had discovered, in those starless nights, that I had lost not only my family but the affections of the Lord as well . . . *he giveth his beloved sleep*, the psalmist promises.

I slept not.

Were the dreams memories? Fever fancies? Whichever, they could not be banished no matter what I tried. Perhaps I would be afflicted with them forever. Perhaps they would rob me of my rationality. Perhaps they already had.

Mummy. I miss you.

I looked a thousand miles southward, where my brother Peter rested beneath the fertile earth of Tamil Nadu, his body having been yielded up as a living sacrifice some years earlier via cholera. I closed my wet eyes and summoned an old memory to blot the fresh ones at hand: Mother, clutching four-year-old me in her arms as she sailed unwillingly from England nigh on twenty years earlier, at the command of my father, who'd been driven to serve. Mother had not kept England's horizon in view as long as possible. Instead, she'd refused to look back, fearfully recalling, perhaps, Lot's wife, turned to a pillar of salt for despairing of losing her home against the command of God's angels.

I, however, opened my eyes and kept my beloved land in view till India's hand slipped from mine.

If the only gain to be had in exchange for having my home stolen was security, then I determined to find it, grasp it, keep it. Security would have to satisfy; peace and happiness, one suspected, had fled for good and I would not risk losing the permanence of the former to gain the transience of the latter.

My heart and mind would not survive another deathblow.

CHAPTER ONE

LATE APRIL 1858

Dusk had begun to smother daylight as we walked down the cool street, peering at the numbers above the doorways, one after the other, skirts gathered in hand to keep them from grazing the occasional piles of wet mud and steamy horse muck. It was with some relief that I finally located the right building just before closing time and opened the creaking door. I let Mrs. MacAlister in first.

"May I assist?" An older woman stopped bustling as we entered the Winchester office of Mr. Walter Highmore, Solicitor. She peered at us from beneath thick pelts of white eyebrow.

"I am Miss Rebecca Ravenshaw," I introduced myself. "Here to see my father's solicitor."

"Oh!" She drew her breath and steadied herself on the back of a worn upholstered chair. "Why, that can't be. That's not right of you to claim, neither." Her mouth grew firm, a notable contrast with the loose flesh of her cheeks and chin. "Miss Rebecca Ravenshaw, why, she's late."

"Late?" I blinked. "I don't understand."

"Passed on." She gave me a hard look, the look one offered a ne'er-do-well. *"Deceased."*

Deceased? Ah! I now understood and rushed to reassure her. "Oh, no. You must have had word from the London Missionary Society; there has been a misunderstanding. Alas, my parents were killed in the Mutiny, but I was able to escape. I've been in northern India these many months, waiting for transport out, and I boarded one of the first ships bringing survivors from Bombay. My chaperone and I have just arrived." I offered a warm smile and expected, fruitlessly, as it transpired, one to be offered in return.

She gripped the chair back firmly enough to leach the blood from her fingertips, pinched by well-bitten cuticles. "I suppose you've read the published details in the paper then, young lady, as much as anything," she replied. "Available for any quick and clever charlatan. Miss Ravenshaw is gone. There is no misunderstanding, though she died here, of course, not in India. It's cruel of you to suggest different."

What did she mean? I had just explained the situation to her and yet she pressed more resolutely into her mistake, questioning my character in the process. I pulled myself up to my full height and spoke calmly. "I assure you, I am quite alive, standing here before you. Would you please have Mr. Highmore call upon me at his earliest convenience?"

She wouldn't meet my eye but she looked over my thin, threadbare dress. "Where shall I tell him he may find you?" she sneered. "Will you be staying at the Swan? After all, Captain Whitfield has once again taken up residence on the estate." She lowered her voice and muttered more to herself than to me, "Though not all hereabouts believe he came by it rightfully." I inclined my head but she rushed forward into the next sentence, speaking louder, perhaps to cover her earlier indiscretion.

"Dear young Miss Ravenshaw, buried there at the chapel, at peace, one hopes, though given the cause of death . . ."

"Buried at Headbourne?" If what she was saying was true, there was only one explanation—an imposter had come, claiming to be me, and then had died. How very distressing for all involved. My stomach quickened as I began to realize that the easy, warm welcome I'd hoped would be put forward might not be offered. I tried to grasp the circumstances. "What did the woman die from?"

"That's not for me to say."

"Well, who shall tell me, then?" My voice rose beyond ladylike but I was tired and frightened. I held my jaw together to keep my teeth from chattering in dread. What had happened to my home? It, and my father's accounts, were the only things left me.

Her lips remained pursed, her eyes veiled. That someone had posed as me, and was now dead, was truly startling, but I had been through much worse in the Uprising and I must not be deterred on this last leg of my journey or all would be lost. "I do not know Captain Whitfield or why he is in my home"—I steadied my voice—"but perhaps I should make his immediate acquaintance."

"You'll find him at home." She sniffed and wiped her nose on a dusty sleeve. "Headbourne House."

Headbourne House was our family home. My father's home. My home! Who was Captain Whitfield? Perhaps a second imposter claimant. The husband of this recently deceased young woman who had been posing as me.

"When he returns, I'll inform Mr. Highmore you called." She all but shooed us out the door and shut it tightly behind us, snapping down the blind.

Mrs. MacAlister gave me a sidelong look and tightened her bonnet against her brow. "How very strange." She stepped a foot farther away from me. How little I had left to prove who I was. Nothing, in fact. Anyone who knew me was thousands of miles away by sea in a country currently rent with strife and faulty communications.

I steadied my hands, which I'd just noticed were shaking, by clasping them together. "We shall soon put it right." I said it, but I wasn't sure I believed it. This situation was not only wholly unexpected, but completely unimaginable. I should think, later, upon how to deal with it, but I was still so very, very tired and needed my wits about me.

The hire carriages, which had swarmed the streets only minutes before, seemed to have been engaged to the last and none were to be found. I finally caught a glimpse of one, much farther down the rain-slicked way, and waved. It rolled, rickety, toward us. One wheel wobbled drunkenly and another had a noticeable chip in the frame along with a missing spoke. The coachman soon brought his team to bear. As the horses came closer I shied back from them but they, unlike most horses, did not shy away from me. Rather they seemed to lean in toward me so I leapt back from their hot breath and peglike teeth.

There were no other carriages in view. The night mists had begun to cause a light sheen on Mrs. MacAlister's face and she shivered. "Headbourne House," I instructed the driver without further consideration.

"That be quite costly," he said. He looked at me straight on; his eyes were milky and one wandered so that I was unsure upon which I should fix my gaze. I opened my purse and anxiously put a piece of silver into his hand. He kept it open and I reluctantly added another.

He didn't move, but I clasped my purse shut anyway. Mrs. MacAlister did not proffer a coin of her own, as might be expected, but turned her face from me. The driver nodded for us to get in but did not offer a hand. I hefted Mrs. MacAlister in first, then followed her. She was unusually quiet as the team jerked and clopped away.

"Are you quite well?" I asked. I was weary from the journey, still ill from months of internment, and had little patience to pry forth whatever hesitancy had suddenly overcome her.

"Certainly." She did not look up, but her forehead cleaved in a deep line of concern. Her voice was abnormally cool and uninvolved.

The coachman cracked his whip toward the team and they sped up. Mrs. MacAlister, who had known me and understood the suffering I had borne, no longer trusted me. Perhaps she, too, thought I was a pretender, learning of the Ravenshaw family's death before making my way to the Residency with the other survivors. It was true, no one there had known me, they'd simply trusted me to be who I said I was.

All the while, someone here in England had also claimed to be Rebecca Ravenshaw. She, too, had simply been believed.

"Ye have a deep knowledge of Scripture, certainly, as one would expect from the daughter of missionaries," Mrs. MacAlister murmured, reassuring herself, I guessed, before doubt over my identity snatched such guarantees away. "But then any well-brought-up young lady would. I didn't know much about ye when we first met among the survivors, naught but what you told me. Told everyone."

"I am the well-brought-up daughter of Sir Charles and Constance Ravenshaw, missionaries in South India these many years and, as you know, am returning to England. And you are . . . a Scottish doctor's widow?"

She scowled. "Ye know that I am."

And I am who I say I am, too. I looked out of the small carriage window at the street and town; the tall, narrow buildings made of stone and brick belched black smoke, smutting everything in sight. The cobbled streets were so different from the sunny yellow, compacted dirt boulevards I was used to. Melancholy and night dropped heavily one after the other like twin carriage curtains as we traveled out of town and into the deepening green of the countryside, receding into ivy and oak. Soon all colors bent to brown and I grew increasingly fearful. Did he know the way? Was he taking us to the right place? I shook myself to clear the gloom. Silly. Why wouldn't he be?

The air sharpened to cold and a collection of birds warbled weakly in the distance. An unwelcome thought shadowed my mind. If it had been so easy to plant a seed of doubt in the mind of a woman who, surely, must know who I am, how difficult would it be to convince those who had already known the pretender Miss Ravenshaw that I was, actually, who I said I was?

I clenched my hands so the nails would lightly pierce the flesh, keeping me fully present. The one and only thing I had assured myself of, with certainty, was that upon docking in England I would have a safe and permanent harbor. How could this now be at risk? I forced myself to take slow and steady breaths in time with the clopping of the horses to bring calm to my spirit.

"We'll be there soon, miss," the coachman called back. "Ten minutes."

I tugged at my cuffs to make certain they were straight. Who was Captain Whitfield? Some crusty old naval man, perhaps, with an eye patch and leathered skin, who had found a way to capitalize on my family's misfortune.

Dark had now entirely fallen. I rearranged my hair and awkwardly tightened my careworn bonnet, nearly tearing off one fragile string in the process.

How soon would I run out of money? Too soon, no matter how late it came.

"We should have gone to the inn first." Mrs. MacAlister's lips thinned and primmed. I did not respond because, truthfully, I agreed with her. The carriage bounced along up a lengthy, uneven drive that beckoned in my memory, though I recalled it as being wide and bright, not overgrown and rutted, as it was now. I felt, more than remembered, that this was my home. My homecoming, which should have been marked with joy and relief, was instead conspicuously concerning.

The house loomed in the distance, to the right of the drive, of course, which arced in front of it and then slipped off into a spur leading to the stables. I recalled the carriage house tucked behind and to the side. If it were daylight, I should be able to see the soft downs that thickly ribboned the property like a wrapped gift. As the carriage slowed, I saw the guesthouse farther in the distance.

I believe my grandmother Porter once stayed there.

Well beyond the guesthouse was the chapel and the family graveyard.

Where *she* was now interred. *"Dear young Miss Ravenshaw, buried there at the chapel, at peace, one hopes, though given the cause of death . . ."*

We pulled to a halt and the carriage rocked for a few seconds on old springs.

"Will I be waiting for you then, for a return trip?" the driver asked.

I nodded. "Yes, if you please."

He held his hand out once more and I plunked down another precious coin.

"I'll wait in the carriage," Mrs. MacAlister said. "Do be quick." She was perhaps contemplating abandoning me here and returning to the safety of town and inn. Her anxiety and mistrust traveled through the miasma and settled on my shoulders.

"Please don't leave until instructed."

The coachman nodded and this time, he helped me down. I began to walk slowly, wincing slightly, as my foot had not completely healed from the injury sustained as we'd fled the Mutiny. I passed through two stone lions on my way up the pathway, crumbling and partly obscured by moss. I suddenly recalled Peter and me roaring at them, and then laughing as they looked back, silently. Now, perhaps because of the angle of the moon, I saw only their toothy, menacing smiles. *We're still here, but you are not welcome.*

Rebecca! Take hold of yourself. Stone animals do not talk.

Scaffolding surrounded some parts of the house, but there were long portions completely ignored and shrouded in shadows. Lamps, like eyes finally opening, began to be lit in the front rooms. Whoever was inside certainly must have heard our arrival on this still, damp night. I walked up the many steps, but before I reached the door and could knock, it opened.

There stood an imposing middle-aged gentleman with a short tuft of gray hair.

"Captain Whitfield?" I asked.

"Indeed no," came the unsmiling response. He stepped aside and there, in the hallway, stood a tall man, perhaps five years older than I, with a close-cropped dark beard, his clothing well tailored, his boots highly polished. I looked up and caught his eye and as I did, he caught mine. He was young. Attractive and well cared for, I admitted, a steady contrast to the state of the property itself. Perhaps it was my fatigue or my shock at finding him to be so unlike my expectations, but I did not look away, nor did he.

"I am Captain Luke Whitfield," he said, as there was no one present who could properly introduce us to one another. "And you are . . . ?"

"I am Miss Rebecca Ravenshaw," I said, and as I did, I heard murmuring from the small assembly of servants in the great hall behind him. Captain Whitfield's countenance did not waver, although a tiny flicker of surprise crossed his face. "I have heard that some have said that I have died, but I assure you, I have not."

Captain Whitfield stepped aside and ushered me in. "All can see that you are clearly, vibrantly, alive."

Was he being forward? Or mocking me? My strength drained, my nerves twitching, I did not feel up to parrying either just then.

"Whether you are actually Miss Ravenshaw, however, that is, at best, unlikely, at least for those of us who do not believe that phantoms can be summoned. Landreth, please show the . . . lady into the drawing room."

I closed my eyes for a second and rocked back on my feet to keep from fainting. Whitfield didn't believe me, either. Of course, why would he? They all thought I was recently dead!

Who could assist me in righting my claim? My family had been gone from Headbourne House for twenty years, and before that we'd attended a sparsely populated dissenting church. There might be no one left living who would even remember me or recall what I looked like as a child, much less recognize me as a woman.

I opened my eyes and looked again at the captain, his straight back, his guarded smile. I froze for a moment, genuinely frightened for the first time that I might not be able to prove my claim.

I shall not allow it. I simply cannot because that would leave me homeless. . . . I cannot return to India. I have no fare for passage, nor support to live there.

He glanced out of the front door. "Has someone accompanied you?"

I nodded. "My chaperone, Mrs. MacAlister, waits in the carriage." She should have come inside with me.

A young woman carried a silver tea urn into the sitting room. I glanced after her, and at the sofa, and then remembered sitting on that very sofa as a child, feet kicking well above the ground.

"Miss?" Captain Whitfield called my attention.

"Forgive me, yes." I returned abruptly to the present. "My chaperone is waiting for us to return to town, after you and I have had a chance to speak together briefly. We'll be staying at an inn."

He nodded. "You've made arrangements?"

I shook my head. "We arrived late. But it has been suggested that we might stay at the Swan."

The young maid dropped a platter and the butler, Landreth, looked at her sternly.

Captain Whitfield responded. "That won't do. I'll send Landreth to ask Mrs. MacAlister to join us and you may spend the night in the guesthouse."

"Thank you. I appreciate your offer, but the Swan will suit us admirably."

He nodded, and I exhaled, relieved for the first time that evening. My father had often said that I could trust an English military man and Father seemed to have been correct.

I took the teacup, its blue-and-white pattern faintly familiar. I stared at my hand, which held the cup delicately by the handle, and blinked back tears. It looked so like my mother's hand, unexpectedly. Perhaps it was the china pattern that brought it all back. She had not left the teaching of taking tea to an ayah; as with all English customs Mother was keen to pass along, she'd seen to it herself. I steadied myself and affected a calm voice. "I hope to speak to Mr. Highmore, my father's solicitor, at his earliest convenience, and the situation will be resolved, of that I am certain."

"I shall ask him to visit with all speed," Captain Whitfield said. "I expect you will be tired. Cook will prepare some supper for you and my housekeeper, Mrs. Blackwood, will show you to the guesthouse."

"But . . ." I began, bewildered. And then Mrs. MacAlister appeared in the doorway, holding her small satchel in one hand and mine in the other. Before the front doors were firmly shut I caught a glimpse of the hired carriage retreating down the long, uneven drive and looked at the captain. I swallowed hard. "I thought I'd made it clear that we would return to Winchester for the night."

"I insist you remain here as my guests," Whitfield replied. "Until Mr. Highmore is able to, as you said, resolve the situation. At that point, the next step will become obvious to us all."

He spoke in a most gentlemanly way, but there was no doubt that his rounded words blunted a threat. Ideas ran through my mind. We were miles away from any other house, and even if I had the means and direction to make it to one of them, what should I say? I'm the long-lost daughter of the house along the road, thought dead, but truly not, slinking around in the countryside after dark with an elderly Scottish widow?

There was no possibility of posting a letter or a telegram, save through Captain Whitfield. But this was my house. I would not let him see the fear that coursed through me. I took myself in hand and tucked that fear deep inside, hoping it would eventually dissolve.

"That's very kind of you." I summoned a confident tone. "I'm certain we shall find it more welcoming than the Swan."

"I am relieved to hear that," he replied with a teasing smile and a focused gaze; to my dismay, I blushed at his attention. He took my gloved hand in his own and held it for the briefest of moments, warming me through as he did. I noticed the pause before the release. "I shall look forward to learning more about you soon." This time his words were softly spoken and I knew enough about human nature to maintain that he meant them sincerely. I let down my guard a little, too.

Later, as Mrs. Blackwood settled us into the guesthouse, I took time to thank her and then, before she left, to ask, "Why was Captain Whitfield relieved when I replied that we'd be better accommodated here than at the Swan?"

She busied herself with the candleholders, ensuring that the smallest drip of congealed wax was removed by her nail before responding. "The Swan is a brothel, miss. Good evening." She blew out all lamps but one and closed the door behind her.

A brothel! The audacity of that woman at Highmore's office.

I blew out the last lamp and settled into bed, knees drawn up to my chest; they knocked with chill and fear. What should I do if the situation was not able to be resolved? I had nowhere to go. How would I live? I had no profession. There was no charity available to returned missionaries; family was expected to care for them so that all new funds could be put toward fresh fieldworkers. But I had no family; my mother's mother and sister, of Honiton, had died some years previously. And my father's line had ended in a thin branch . . . or so I'd thought.

Did Captain Whitfield have a claim to Headbourne House through Father? How had he ended up here?

I sighed. Captain Whitfield, resident jailer; his insistence we remain put me ill at ease. And yet, there was something soft and genuine in his last smile. He had seen to it that our meal was not cold, as might have been expected, but warm and of the highest quality. I did not know what to make of him.

The moonlight filtered through the window. I was afraid to sleep lest I be visited by my loved ones in haunting dreams, so I got up to peer out of it. I found I could not see but two feet ahead of me for the mist, which obscured all. Was it possible for someone to come close enough to look in the window without my seeing them? I pulled the curtains shut and then chided myself for entertaining such a foolish notion. *I must be tired. Of course I was tired.*

I returned to bed and listened to the creaking of the house. After some time, I thought I heard footsteps. They grew louder and closer, seeming to approach my door. Then they stopped. I waited, barely breathing, for them to resume. Had I truly heard them at all or were they, too, foolish notions? Was my mind giving over to imaginings?

After some minutes of quiet, I quietly slipped from the bed and pushed the elephantine walnut dressing table in front of the door.

CHAPTER TWO

Early next morning, there came a knock at the door.

"Yes?" Light slipped through the crack between the tightly closed drapes; otherwise, the room remained dim.

"'Tis Annie, the day maid," a young voice called back. "Mrs. Blackwood has sent me to see to your needs and Cook has prepared a light breakfast. May I come in please, miss?"

I struggled up in bed, still swaying to the tempo of the sea. "Of course, Annie, please do." I tugged the sheets around me as I had but one thin nightdress in the goods that had been provided for us.

"Ah . . . the door is blocked, miss."

"One moment," I said. I had so wanted to make a good impression and I'd already started things off badly. I slipped out of bed and as quietly as I could pushed the dressing table to its rightful place before returning to bed and calling out, "It's clear now."

Annie entered and set a tray down on the dressing table, looked at it, then at me, then back at it again.

"I thought I heard footsteps last night," I admitted, feeling a little foolish.

She inclined her head. "None but the two of you slept here, miss."

"Perhaps it was a fancy from fatigue," I cheerfully suggested.

She walked to the windows and dramatically pulled the drapes open, freeing the brilliant morning sunlight.

"I'm not trained as a lady's maid, but there being no lady here requiring one, I'm the only one at hand to help you dress. If you'll have me, miss."

I smiled. "I've got on quite well without a lady's maid since the Uprising, thank you, but I'm grateful for your assistance."

"Miss Ravenshaw, she were a lady," she said. In other words, this was another clear indication that I was not only not a lady, but was not Miss Ravenshaw.

"Thank you for the compliment," I responded and she scrunched up her face, not having meant it to be a compliment, I supposed. Annie shook out my black dress and ran a damp rag over it.

"Did the woman posing as me have a lady's maid?" I asked, making my way to the dressing table and sitting down. I wanted to establish right away that she'd been posing, and I was who I said I was.

"Oh yes, miss!" She nodded enthusiastically. "She had her Indian maid, of course, and then a French maid from the dressmaker's in Winchester, who helped her find the finest gowns and slippers and boots. Mostly in black and gray, of course. She did not have the whitest of skin, though." She glanced up at my face then, still slightly brown from being exposed to the Indian sun.

"My browned skin along with my brown hair and eyes helped me escape with my life, disguised in a sari."

"I see," she said, her eyes veiled. "If that's so then your skin will go fair again soon, miss, won't it?" She brushed and plaited my thick brown hair and I determined to glean information from her whilst she was still forthcoming.

"Are there many Indian maids hereabouts?" I asked. Perhaps, if so, I could learn some information that might help me figure out just who this imposter had been.

"Oh no, miss," she said. "I'd never seen an Indian person before the maid arrived. I'm quite sure no one in my family has. Lots of us are in service, you see. But no one I know or have ever heard of has had an Indian servant before."

This was disappointing. I would have to approach it from another angle, later. "You mentioned there was no lady in residence. So there is no Mrs. Whitfield, then?"

Annie giggled. "Not yet, miss, though nowadays, there's plenty that wish they were Mrs. Whitfield. Him with this big house, now that she's dead, and all that money. A military man, well, you know how it is. Some ladies don't even care about the rumors!"

"Rumors?" I kept my voice quiet and my face free from expression.

She stopped and shook her head, perhaps realizing that she had said too much. "There, all done. Captain Whitfield has sent for Mr. Highmore and he should be here soon." She backed out of the room, and I was soon left to sit in the parlor, with its freshly beaten carpets and lemon-waxed wood, to wait for the solicitor.

I had not been waiting long when he arrived. Mrs. MacAlister showed him in, though her sour look toward me told me she did not approve of acting as housekeeper as well as chaperone. I offered a quiet apology. What could be done?

"Mr. Highmore. Thank you for driving out to see me."

He removed his hat and then bowed stiffly. "My pleasure, Miss . . ."

I sighed. "My name is Ravenshaw. Rebecca Ravenshaw. The only one I am aware of having ever existed. If you please . . ." I indicated for him to be seated. "I am confused why everyone seems to believe that I am dead when, indeed, I am not."

He set his hat next to him. "*Miss Ravenshaw* returned from India last summer, late last summer, after her parents were killed in the Mutiny," he said. "They'd left her with friends in Madras on their way north, and as soon as word got back to her of their untimely deaths, she fled, rightly so, to England, with her Indian maid, well before anyone could leave the fracas in northern India."

My face flushed. She had not only stolen my identity but my history as well, had implied that my parents would abandon me, and then sought to profit from the deaths so many had bravely faced.

I shook my head both to clear it and to show my disagreement. "I assure you, Mr. Highmore, I am Rebecca Ravenshaw and my parents did not, and would not, leave me in Madras regardless of what this upstart claimed."

Mr. Highmore stood, clearly taken aback by my language. "I beg your pardon, miss!"

I immediately recalled a proverb my father had oft repeated to me; apparently it had not yet rooted. *Seest thou a man that is hasty in his words? There is more hope of a fool than of him.*

"Please accept my apologies, Mr. Highmore," I said. "It has been a long journey and I am distressed to return home and find this upsetting situation." I would not show him how very disturbed I felt inside. I held myself together like a proper lady, tilting my head down in a submissive manner. It would not take much for these people to toss me into the street for good, with little to my name, if they had reason to suspect I was not the decorous missionary daughter I claimed to be.

Speak only after consideration, Rebecca. Act gently, Mother had oft said. *A gentle Englishwoman will speak her mind quietly, if at all.*

I'm sorry, Mother. My head snapped up. I should not be answering my mother, even in my head. It was . . . irregular.

Mr. Highmore cleared his throat, phlegm thickly catching over and over again before finally clearing. Then he sat down again, seemingly appeased. "We spoke with Miss Ravenshaw at length before her death, and she knew all about Sir Charles and his wife, Constance. Some with the London Missionary Society came and visited with her and she was at ease with all of their questions and they with her answers. She even had a few effects from Sir Charles's wife. I am convinced that she was, indeed, who she said she was. I am not easily fooled."

"I'm certain you're not," I soothed. "What kind of effects, if I might ask?"

"Items from the mission, I believe." I could see by the set of his mouth that he would say no more.

"How did this young woman die?"

He would not meet my gaze. "All knew the trials she'd been through—the loss of her brother, of her parents, of her home—so, although she tried very hard to cheer herself and overcome what had happened, it was a tragic ending. At Christmas, one thinks of family, so it was not completely unexpected, was it?"

"She was ill?"

He rubbed a thumb on the brim of his hat. "It was said to be self-murder, miss."

Said to be self-murder? The hair on the back of my neck prickled.

He glanced out of the window over my shoulder to the far distance where I'd seen the family chapel. "She's buried there.

Fresh grave. Toward the back. It struck us hard, miss, we all felt so kindly toward her. I'm not sure anyone is quite beyond it even yet. So when someone appears, claiming to be her, well, you can well imagine that this would not bring about sympathy and goodwill." He produced a pressed handkerchief from his pocket and blew his nose, whether from real sorrow or for effect I did not know.

"We all thought she might have come down with something from the East Indies, perhaps, a strange and foreign illness that came on and killed quickly. That, too, would have been understandable. But no. It was by her own hand. The doctor confirmed it." He glanced toward the door.

"I'm truly sorry for this young woman's death," I said gently, and I was, pitying her for whatever demons had prodded and pushed her to take her own life. "But the truth remains that she was impersonating me, which is a crime. Perhaps she'd overheard someone speak of our deaths at the Missionary Society in London and sought to make gain on our loss."

"There was news that the whole family had died. A telegram reached me from London. I reflected upon that this morning. Telegrams don't lie." He looked at me, holding my gaze, and I admit to withering a bit under the heat of his contempt. "Impersonation is most certainly a crime. Particularly if it's to gain property to which one is not entitled."

I addressed his unspoken charge. "But I *am* Miss Ravenshaw." My head pulsed in time with my frustrated heart. I spied a burly man in the doorway behind Highmore, someone I had not noticed before. Mrs. MacAlister crept farther away from us, toward the back of the room.

"If I may be permitted to do so, I would like to ask you some questions, questions that only the rightful Miss Ravenshaw could answer." Highmore glanced up again and nodded at the large man near the doorway.

I drew my chair closer. "Certainly."

"Do you know where your father had invested his funds? The money he'd made from the Burmese war?"

"Mr. Highmore, I assure you that my father did not talk about his investments with his family, unless it regarded the investment in souls, which he was notably, and admirably, given to." *Sometimes to the exclusion of all and everyone else.*

Highmore nodded and asked about our mission, then persisted with obscure details about my mother's ministries with lace and education. How often had any of us returned to England? Some of that information would have been public knowledge, I'd thought, but certainly not all or even most.

"Will this help?" I asked.

"Perhaps. I shall make arrangements for a visit from the London Missionary Society, who, I am sure, will also want to hear you recount your . . . tale. Now that communication is fairly reliable again, I shall additionally send further inquiries to the mission at Travancore who will be able to make the final decision as to your identity. Within three to four months I expect to have an answer verifying your identity. It's late April, so"—he counted on his fingers—"I would imagine by August."

"August?" I stood up. "Oh dear. What shall I do until then?"

"Unless you have family or friends who might be prevailed upon to take you in, you'll be at the charity of Captain Whitfield, or not, as he sees fit until that time," he said. "If he turns you out, please leave a forwarding address so I may be in contact. Until then, you will wait patiently and let me complete my work." He turned to me abruptly. "What was your mother's maiden name?"

"Porter," I replied without hesitation but with some shock.

Could he, could *he* have been implicit in this in some way? Could he be stalling, perhaps to cover up mismanagement of my father's funds?

"Mr. Highmore?"

"Yes?" He turned back toward me, his black coattails swaying, his proud demeanor an affront.

"The senior Mr. Highmore was my father's original solicitor. Perhaps you have a personal interest in how my father's funds are handled. Were handled."

I saw a flicker of fear. He *was* concerned that he had made a grievous error, as indeed he had. "I took over when my own father died some months ago. My integrity and reputation are well known amongst those from this area. When—if—I hand the documents over to you, there will be a full accounting from the day your father left for India. Good day." He placed his hat upon his head and left, taking Mrs. MacAlister with him to make arrangements for her forthcoming trip to Scotland. With the exception of Annie, I was now quite alone.

I took some deep, steadying breaths. "Who was that man at the door?" I asked softly.

"The big one?" she asked, and I nodded.

"Why that's the constable, miss."

I wheeled around. "The constable?"

"Yes. He's well acquainted with Mr. Highmore . . . and Captain Whitfield, naturally," she said. "They served in the military together."

"I see." And I did. My breaths quickened again. "Does the constable often come here?"

"Oh, no. I think the last time was about when, well, when *she* died. Mr. Highmore was called for, of course, and the captain sent for the constable and the doctor."

"I suppose the doctor is also well acquainted with Captain Whitfield."

"Why, yes, miss, he is." She seemed surprised I would know this.

My heart sank. It was understandable, Mr. Highmore had said, that Miss Ravenshaw had died. After all she'd been through, why, who would even question it? And if it could not be proved to have been a suicide, which they all had been convinced of, then a mysterious foreign illness would do as just cause.

For her. And perhaps for me, as well, if I were not careful? Was someone truly after my house and my inheritance? The spring damp clung to me and I shivered, then patted it off my forehead with a handkerchief.

Come now, I took myself in hand. *Let's not give in to fancies.* Before the Rebellion, in which all I knew was turned upside down, I had a calm and firm grasp on how things worked in the world. And then I saw Indian soldiers brutally cutting down English men, women, and children midstride and English soldiers blasting Indians with a viciousness calm demeanor denied. Conceivably anything was possible now, in the shadows. I'd been taken completely unawares then. Perhaps I was no longer a sound judge of reality.

I walked to the window, though I avoided looking toward the chapel and its burial grounds and its fresh grave with my name on it. Then I turned away.

In the near distance I could see the house, my house, very clearly now in the light of day. It was larger than I had remembered it, perhaps as many as thirty rooms all told, including those on the very topmost floor where things were stored and the live-in maids slept when we'd had them. Some windows appeared to be broken, and the moldings powdered. The vast gardens, leading to the soft green downs, were hopelessly tangled and overgrown, like the matted hair of an unloved and untended child.

I glanced at the second floor. I'd been young when we left, but I recalled that Peter and I had slept in adjoining rooms, with our governess's room connected to both. We used to sneak past her while she softly snored so we could play together late at night.

Had Peter not died, this house would be his and not mine. He would have taken care of me. *I must care for myself, and our family home, as it has been left to me to steward it. I shall have to be clever. I remain on charity till my claim can be proven. If it can be.*

I felt, more than saw, someone enter the room, and I turned. "Captain Whitfield." He stood near the door, dressed in magnificent riding clothes. I suddenly became aware that I was wearing the same secondhand black dress I'd worn the day before. Then I was irritated at myself that I cared if he saw me as fashionable or not. What did it matter?

"I trust I have not interrupted?"

"Not at all," I replied. Annie stayed near the back of the room, for which I was glad, as my chaperone had absented herself. Most irregular. It would not do to be alone with him, especially in light of my recent comments about the Swan. He indicated I should take the sofa, and I did, which left the chair for him.

"Mr. Highmore says there may be some merit in your claim," he started.

"Mr. Highmore will certainly confirm that I am the mistress of this house," I said, tired and overwhelmed with the events of the past year. Then, again aware that I was at his mercy till that came about, and that he had treated me very kindly indeed, I softened my tone. "I'm sorry, Captain Whitfield. I understand that, well, that this was unexpected for you as well. May I ask . . ." Suddenly I lost my nerve, aware again that I had no right to demand answers from anyone though they all had the right to demand explanations from me.

"How I came to be here?" He set down his gloves, black with an intricate crisscross pattern at the cuff, and his riding crop. His hands were, at once, smooth as a gentleman's and strong as those of a man not afraid of work. "Sir Charles's will provided that in the event that he died without a living heir, his property would be left to any remaining member of his family, traced patrilineally, of course. Although it was necessary to go back many generations, that honor fell to me. So that would mean, if you truly are Miss Rebecca Ravenshaw, we would be some sort of relations many times removed."

He smiled at that, and then ran his hand through his hair, which was longish and thick black with the exception of a streak of silver to the side of the parting. It made him look wolfish and dangerous, but when I let my eyes travel downward and connect with his, they were liquid brown, warm and edged with lines from sun and smiling.

Against my will, I smiled back at him. Perhaps he could be trusted. Perhaps.

"My household had been here less than a month, after having been notified of the Ravenshaws' deaths, when Miss Ravenshaw arrived to claim her property. I moved into the guesthouse, temporarily, whilst I looked for a property and then, well, then, with the death, finding a new home was no longer necessary."

Death by her own hand or someone else's? I couldn't help but wonder, as it had already been implied.

"As for the current situation, I've arranged for you to have access to resources for clothing, household purchases, and other personal matters while this is settled."

This was unexpected. Unexpectedly welcome and thoughtful. I thought back to my small store of coins, just a few more than the Bible's widow had held, and nearly burst out crying in gratitude. I impulsively stood, walked to where he sat, and threw my arms around him for just a moment, and while he didn't withdraw, he remained unyielding. I stepped back, mortified, and resumed my seat on the sofa.

A proper young Englishwoman would not prostrate herself so before a complete stranger! Or before anyone at all. I looked to the back of the room where Annie stared, openmouthed.

"I'm so sorry for that," I said, gathering my dignity from the corners to which it had scattered. He waved at me, gently dismissing the breach of protocol.

"I do not have anywhere else to go while this matter is concluded," I continued. "I'll certainly repay you everything spent for my care in the meantime. It should only be a matter of a few months. I'm terribly sorry for the inconvenience."

He nodded curtly. "I am sure *the Ravenshaws* would have preferred I be generous, and so I will be, though I will require a full account and reimbursement should the matter not be settled as you believe it will be."

The Ravenshaws. The implication was that I was not among their number. I was about to speak up when I recalled that Highmore had said that Captain Whitfield could dismiss me whenever he tired of generosity, up to the point when my claim was proved.

"I've asked Mrs. Blackwood to begin to prepare the house for your arrival," Whitfield continued, his tone cool and in command. "I've scheduled quite a few improvements to the property and buildings, and I'll continue to oversee them.

"I'll take my meals in the dining room, as there is only one cook; you're free to join me at will. I'll leave Landreth to oversee the house. My valet, Thornton, and I will reside at the guest cottage for the time being—I am often gone on business—and the day maid can tend our household needs." He seemed to have finished.

I stood. "I did not mean for you to have to immediately remove yourself from the main house."

He grinned, and when he did, I caught my breath at the beauty of his face. "Are you suggesting I remain in the house along with you in an irregular union?"

"Certainly not!" Then I saw that he teased me and I softened.

"Let it not be said that I would deny a *rightful* heiress her home, for any amount of time," he said, and his voice turned dark, as did his mood, because he stood up and abruptly took his gloves in hand. "I have arranged several social events for the next few months—the invitations have been sent and provisions made. If it wouldn't be too much trouble, I'd rather not rescind them as many of the invitees are back and forth from London during the season, calendars settled, and I'd hate to inconvenience. You are welcome to attend, of course."

"That sounds splendid, and I look forward to meeting my neighbors."

"I'm sure they will be most curious to meet you . . . although they may be forgiven for believing that they already have."

"About her—" I began.

"I'm sure you have questions, but perhaps they will be more suitably put after Mr. Highmore has completed his investigation, if occasion warrants."

He didn't believe me. None of them did. And yet, for some reason, he was willing to let me live in the house whilst he removed to the cottage. Chivalry? Perhaps. But he was certainly accommodating, though he alone had the most to lose by my claim. I should try to find out why.

"If you'll excuse me, I have an engagement." He nodded and left. He strode across the lawn, through the coach house, and to the stable yard, which were all well cared for, and was greeted by a stable boy. His gait lightened as he approached the young man and clapped him on the back.

The captain then rode out across the lawn and to the downs behind the house. Someone, on horseback, awaited him there, her long riding dress whipping about her legs, strawberry-blond hair slipping from beneath her pretty bonnet. An older woman trailed behind them, also on horseback. A chaperone, perhaps.

I turned and looked at Annie, who was still looking at me with a combination of shock and wonder.

"I don't normally embrace complete strangers," I offered weakly by way of explanation. "I was just so thankful."

She picked up her duster and began to work again. "You don't have to explain to me, miss, this or anything else. I'm the day maid. You're the mistress . . . for now. Anyway, all the ladies fall for him, even though they promise themselves that they won't."

I was about to object when a line from *Hamlet* came floating back to me. *The lady doth protest too much, methinks.* I decided to remain quiet so she would not get the wrong impression.

CHAPTER THREE

Within a day of our discussion, Captain Whitfield had removed his personal belongings from the house and I had moved in. On his way out I saw him linger in the music room, the centerpiece of which was a large and beautiful pianoforte of engraved rosewood. I faintly remembered that my father had played well, which was somewhat unusual for a gentleman. The portraits on the walls had been dusted, and the carpets beaten, though the curtains near the window showed their age, having faded from ruby to near pink. When I pulled one back, the deep folds exhaled dust and were found to be ruby still. While Mrs. MacAlister busied herself nearby and Annie polished the wood in the next room, I broke the silence. "Do you play?" I nodded toward the pianoforte.

He nodded. "Yes. I had this tuned recently, and it plays splendidly."

"I'd like to hear it," I said. "I've missed music."

He sat down on the bench.

"I hadn't meant that *you* needed to play," I said, immediately aware that it might be best if I stopped talking altogether.

He stood. "I hadn't meant to assume . . ."

"No, no," I said, and drew nearer. "I simply didn't want to impose. Please, if you like, play something."

He sat and played, from memory, a short, emotionally resonant piece that brought forth a portion of the melancholy I'd so carefully marshaled behind a wall in my mind, bringing a small release of pain. "That was beautiful," I whispered. "Who was the composer?"

He turned on the bench and looked toward me. "Why, Beethoven, Miss Ravenshaw. Surely you know that . . . having learnt to play the piano."

I knew from the occasional English visitors we'd had in India that all well-brought-up girls in England knew how to play the piano. My shoulders slumped. This had not started off well.

"I was very young when we left England, Captain Whitfield," I answered. "Although my parents raised us to be as English as possible, there were some customs and traditions that were contrary to our environment, or out of our reach. Pianos, for example, are difficult and expensive to acquire in southern India." I softened my voice. "All the more reason for me to appreciate this song. You must play it often, for you played it perfectly."

He sat, dumbstruck for a moment, which I took to be an unusual state of being. "I haven't played that for years," he said. "I'm not quite sure why I played it now."

He stood as if to regain his balance and sense of command. "Do you play an instrument?"

"I play the sitar," I said proudly.

His gaze rose and he looked me in the eye. "Then it is a shame, Miss Ravenshaw, that we are unlikely to find one in Hampshire so that you could practice and perform."

Prove myself, he likely meant. It was disheartening. I could collapse in a jelly less than a week into my homecoming, which is what I was tempted to do, or I could steel myself, which is what I did instead. "Yes, a shame." At least he was referring to me by name.

Landreth signaled to him, he nodded and turned back to me. "I have business to attend to in London for several days." He grimaced. *Unpleasant* business, I suspected. Did it have to do with me? With the imposter? With the house?

"Have a pleasant journey," I said as sweetly as I could. "Would it be all right if I availed myself of the carriage in your absence? Or shall I remain under home confinement?"

At that, he laughed with gusto. "No, Miss Ravenshaw, you are not under arrest." He smiled and shook his head. "You surprise me. I would have thought you'd known that home detainment is limited to disobedient wives."

Now it was my turn to be speechless, which I could see he rather enjoyed.

"You may use the carriage, and my horses, too, if you care to ride."

"I . . . I don't ride much anymore," I said.

"You don't play the piano or ride?" He seemed incredulous; two pillars of gentle English womanhood had been called into question.

"I rode till recently," I answered in explanation.

He nodded. "Why would you think you were under confinement?"

"Well, when the constable appeared the other day . . ."

I could tell by the quizzical expression on his face that he wanted to know how I'd recognized the constable, but he did not ask, and I was glad. I should not have liked to be compelled to reveal my source, and I could hear Annie pause in her duties in the hallway behind us. A new wariness in his face made me suspect my knowledge of the constable caused him to believe that I was local, and not, after all, recently from India.

"At Mr. Highmore's suggestion," he responded.

But with your approval. "In case our interview did not proceed according to his expectations."

He nodded and gallantly bowed a little. "Enjoy Headbourne House in my absence." It sounded positively proprietary.

"Thank you for your generosity," I said, and hoped he knew I meant it. As soon as he'd left the room, I spoke up. "Mrs. MacAlister?" I knew she'd be hovering nearby, and she was.

"Yes?"

"Would you kindly accompany me to Winchester this afternoon? I need to buy some clothes." Now that I knew I could access my father's funds, I could purchase some necessities.

"Aye. And we need to find a chaperone for you," she said. "I leave in four days, and it will not do to have ye here without one."

She spoke with conviction, but not with warmth. Although she was not exactly standoffish, my situation as it stood agitated her and I knew she was eager to leave for her home; truthfully, I was ready for her to depart. She offered much in the way of disapproval and meager helpings in the way of affection. "Will you make inquiries? Is there anyone you know who might help?"

"I've already begun inquiries, when I was in town with Mr. Highmore. I put in a word at the Presbyterian church."

Oh dear. I'd hoped for someone with . . . warmth.

"If I may . . ." Annie stepped forward and I heard Mrs. Blackwood stop walking in the hall just outside the room.

"Yes?" I responded gently.

"You'll also be needing a lady's maid, miss." She seemed apologetic. "Every *lady* has one, of course." She looked at me pointedly before continuing. "I have many other duties and it wouldn't be expected for me to waken two hours earlier than usual for much longer."

I spontaneously reached out and touched her arm, which took her aback. I withdrew my hand. I would not have felt comfortable touching my maid in India, because of caste. Perhaps there was a similarly understood rule here, too. "I'm sorry," I said.

"For what, miss?"

For making you uncomfortable, and for not knowing what was expected of me, I wanted to say, but didn't because it might call my identity into question. "For your hours of extra work on my behalf, which I greatly appreciate. Where shall I find a suitable lady's maid?"

"You could inquire at the milliner's," she said. "Or the dress shop. They often have lists of those nearby and recommended. Only . . . be wary." Mrs. Blackwood now walked to the edge of the room and glanced at Annie, who now looked fearful of overstepping again.

"Wary of what, Annie? Of whom?"

She looked uncomfortable and softened her voice. "It took me some time before I found this situation, miss. I rather like it here as it's nearby my family and I shouldn't like to have to move away to find another situation. But you do need a lady's maid. The French ones are best."

I understood. She worked for Whitfield. Perhaps it was Whitfield I needed to be wary of. But what had that to do with the lady's maid? I knew I could ask no more. "Thank you, Annie. I shall make an inquiry."

Her face flooded with relief as she realized I would press no further, and I thought, *Her situation is in some ways as delicate and insecure as my own.*

. . .

Some hours later I walked into the dressmaker's shop, and was unable to form a proper sentence at first. The room was populated with bolts of the most beautiful fabrics: silks and cottons and linens, lounging on their sides on the cutting tables like women on Turkish divans, leaning toward one another like friends gossiping, or standing set apart, like prima donnas. The walls were hung with trays of buttons and ribbons and trimmings of every sort. Because my mother had been an accomplished lace maker, we had always had lace to trim our simple gowns, but we had nothing like the array of goods currently beckoning. Mrs. MacAlister spoke up, as I had not yet overcome my childish awe. "We're interested in some dresses for the lady." She nodded toward me. "Mourning, at first, but also some for afterward."

"Certainly." An older woman bustled forward. "You are her mother?"

Mrs. MacAlister shook her head.

"Her lady's maid?" The woman clearly expected a young woman to be accompanied by one of those necessary women.

At that, I could not help but grin. Mrs. MacAlister an ayah?

"I am Miss Rebecca Ravenshaw of Headbourne House." I held out a hand, which was gloved in well-worn leather of a style some years past, I was sure. "I am recently returned from India, and am in need of a wardrobe."

"Miss . . . Ravenshaw." She recoiled. Had the entire town heard of the brief stay of the woman who had come before me? Winchester was rather large, but a suicide was, one guessed, uncommon and noteworthy. "One of our dressmakers, Michelene, worked at Headbourne House. She can help."

Ah, yes. I relaxed. Annie had spoken of a French lady's maid.

"Michelene." The proprietress spoke lightly but the shop was not large, and soon a lovely young woman of an age with me glided into the room.

"Miss Ravenshaw, Michelene d'Arbonneau. Michelene, this is . . . Miss Rebecca Ravenshaw of Headbourne House."

Mademoiselle d'Arbonneau didn't lose her smooth smile, I'll grant her that, but a tic flittered across her left eye. "I'm delighted to meet you, Mademoiselle Ravenshaw." Her hair was arranged in silky brown coils that tumbled below her shoulders; her dress was more finely wrought than any I had ever seen, sea-green silk that gently swelled as she walked. I felt dowdy, plain, foreign, and hopelessly out-of-date.

"I understand you worked at Headbourne House," I started. "Annie has spoken of you and the unfortunate woman here earlier claiming to be me."

She nodded solemnly. "Such a lovely girl. But a tortured soul. *Pauvre petite.* I am shocked to learn, now, that she was not who she said she was," she said, her eyes glimmering. "Who could imagine such a crime *terrible*?"

Self-murder a crime? Or did she mean the theft of my identity?

She held my gaze for a moment, appraisingly, and I held it right back. What did she know about the poser? Had she confided in her? Women became close to their lady's maids in agreement with or even against their will. Michelene quickly grew bright, perhaps falsely bright. "Where is the Capitaine Whitfield?" She leaned forward into the question. I thought it odd to bring him up so quickly, and noted it as so.

"At Headbourne," I replied. "In the guesthouse. However"—I turned back to the older woman—"I do have need of several dresses, some slippers, boots, gloves, and such like. I'll need them quickly." A look passed between them. "My accounts are being sent to Mr. Highmore, for the time being."

The proprietress smiled. "Of course we can assist you. You must be properly attired for a woman of your station. All will expect it."

Over the course of two hours, Michelene suggested several fine dresses in rich fabrics and with fine detailing, all of which could be very quickly made. Though black and gray would be required for the few months remaining in my official mourning period, we also found some so that I would be appropriately and beautifully attired when my year of mourning was completed, in about two months.

"Ah, you look beautiful in the claret, *non*?" She had me turn toward the looking-glass and I gasped. I would never have chosen this dress, and yet it was perfect. We shared coloring, so I guessed she'd know exactly what would suit. The rich tones of the dress made my skin look even whiter, as did the gold gloves. Encased in such a gown I no longer felt dowdy. I was lovely. I was strong. I was *English*.

"Indeed!"

Michelene brought out some linens and discreetly suggested some undergarments, corsets, silk stockings, and other confections. I had never felt so feminine; their softness slipped against my skin and I relished the delicate touch of it all. I chose some with wide hoops and crinolines, as was the fashion, but I insisted on some with less complicated, but still fashionable, forms, so I might walk more easily, as I had in India.

And one day, ride?

I pushed the thought aside.

Though I was still thin from the months interned at the Residency, I felt womanly again. My mother had loved pretty clothes and had long denied herself their pleasure, not wanting to take mission funds to adorn herself. Except for the lace, of course. No one had lace as beautiful as my mother.

I would wear these as much for her as for myself, but I must also exercise some restraint. I reserved half of the dresses Michelene had set aside for me—after all, I had nothing at all to wear and even my charity boots were a size too large—and kindly asked her to return the others.

As we made arrangements for the final deliveries, Michelene drew near. "You have need of a lady's maid?"

I nodded. "I believe that I do. Is there a list, perhaps, that I might review and make some discreet inquiries?"

Mrs. MacAlister's silent concern intensified from across the room as Michelene drew even closer and lowered her voice.

"I very much enjoyed working at the Headbourne House. What a pleasure it would be to care for a young woman such as yourself, *une belle jolie*, denied the pleasures of civilization for so long, and now, ready to be alive again, with Michelene to help revive her, *n'est-ce pas*? As to the list . . . well, that takes time, perhaps. Time for the lady to have inquiries made after her, time for her history to be verified, for interviews, for the checks of the references. Do you have someone who could act as lady's maid while these inquiries are made?"

I thought of poor, tired Annie, who would likely refuse even if asked. After all, it had been she who'd sent me here. Had Annie sent me here specifically, knowing Michelene? I dismissed the thought. Why should she do that?

A flicker of concern lit again. "No," I answered.

Mrs. MacAlister moved closer, within listening distance.

"*Voilà!* I would not need to make such focused inquiries,

which may or may not end well, having recently been in service at Headbourne. Nor would you."

It was probable, she implied, that my dubious identity in light of the recent tragedy at Headbourne would put off other suitable lady's maids, at least for the immediate future.

I nodded toward her employer. "Wouldn't she mind?"

She shook her head. "As you English say, it's every man for himself, *non*?"

She seemed full of life and I desperately needed someone to help me be well turned out for the social events Captain Whitfield had planned over the coming months and, really, for life in England on the whole. Perhaps, I hoped, she could shed some light on the mystery that now shrouded my home more ghoulishly than its regular mists. This alone was reason to employ her, in fact, for the immediate future anyway. "Please, come when you can."

"I require my own room, the day maid to care for it, and an equitable salary. Plus, the traditional perquisites of a lady's maid."

"Yes," I agreed, reluctant to show my ignorance by asking just what those perquisites might include. I hoped I should not regret this choice but, truly, what option did I have?

We left the shop, and Daniel, the carriage driver, came round to pick us up. On the way home, Mrs. MacAlister spoke up.

"And the devil take the hindmost."

I turned toward her, confused. Perhaps she, like me, did not sleep well and was now babbling. "I'm sorry, I don't understand."

"The rest of the phrase that Frenchwoman used. 'Each man for himself, and the devil take the hindmost.' I fear for ye, lassie. I leave soon and then ye shall be alone in a new place and at the hindmost, as you do not yet understand their ways."

I nodded and sank into the carriage, pulling my shawl tightly about me as we made our way home. I'd felt, in the past year, the devil breathing just behind me, hoping to take me, and I'd certainly felt as if I were the hindmost. I still did.

That night I turned down the lamp in my room, which overlooked the gnarled gardens, the groomed downs, and the guesthouse, which had gone dark. I locked my door, sat on the edge of my bed, and ran my hand along the smooth counterpane covering it.

Had this been mine as a child? I could not remember, though I squeezed my eyes shut and begged for a happy memory to step forward. Had my mother touched it? I ran my hand along it several more times, in case it had been so, as if to soak up some of her touch through my skin, and grieved quietly. I wanted her to embrace me. I wanted Father to take me with him on a visit. I wanted my brother, the cavalry, *anyone* to ride to my rescue.

My stomach clenched from the unusual heavy English food, and I ran to the commode and remained for some time before returning to bed. I yearned for curry and rice, and lush, soft fruits not decaying and disguised by brandy. I did not want to be here. At least, I did not want to be here by myself. I wanted reassurance that my mind was whole and would remain whole.

I'll try not to whine, Lord, or I promise to do so in private, just between the two of us, because You know how grateful I am to be alive.

I climbed into bed and listened hopefully in the dark for that still small voice of reassurance, which, disappointingly, did not come.

Lord Jesus, we are here together. But I still feel bereft, unutterably alone.

My lamp sputtered, dimmed, and went out, and I drifted into sleep.

. . .

"Mummy, come quickly, Peter is not well."

Mother followed me as I ran out of the house and into the garden where Peter had collapsed, unable to make it to the outdoor privy. His eyes were sunk deep into his skull and Mother held his hand, then pinched the skin, which was worryingly wrinkled. Father and Mr. Mead were able to carry Peter into the house, where he continued to let out his life by the quart. I'd never seen Father cry before, and when he did, I knew that Peter had passed into the arms of our Lord.

I bolted upright in bed, panting with anxiety, my gown wet with perspiration. I rolled over to ascertain where I was, yes, here at Headbourne. My breathing slowed, and I lay back in bed again, welcoming rest, but not sleep.

CHAPTER FOUR

Within a day, Landreth called for Mrs. MacAlister and me to come to the drawing room.

Mrs. Ross had arrived.

Her hair, the color of tarnished silver, was drawn back beneath a severe black bonnet; she wore a black dress with a firmly starched lace collar. The lacework was exquisite, and when she noticed me staring at it with frank admiration, she smiled. When she smiled, but only then, her dour Scottish countenance lifted and she warmed and filled with light. I had a faint wavering in heart and stomach, a signal in my senses, a fleet feeling we had already met somehow, somewhere.

Could we have?

She spoke up. "I'll be Mrs. Ross. The kirk sent me." She handed some papers to Mrs. MacAlister. "You're looking for a guardian for the young lady?"

"Yes, a chaperone." Mrs. MacAlister opened the papers and read through them. "Widowed, and recommended by the kirk and elders. Yes, yes, here is the name of someone I know. Godly man. And this one, too." She folded the papers and tucked them deep into a skirt pocket as if to silently assent. *You'll do.*

The housecat came round my legs, brushed up against me, and meowed once before looking Mrs. Ross over. I smiled. The cat was rarely seen, but she'd taken to me and I to her. I welcomed her comforting, curious presence as she sensed, perhaps, that no one else had accepted me.

"Miss Ravenshaw is the daughter of missionaries whose lives were taken in the Mutiny," Mrs. MacAlister offered in explanation.

Mrs. Ross nodded knowingly. "I'm sorry for your loss, lass."

"I will be returning to my family in Scotland in a few days' time, and she'll need a chaperone, of course," Mrs. MacAlister continued. "No well-brought-up young lady can be without a chaperone."

Shortly thereafter, Mrs. Ross came to stay. Mrs. Blackwood showed her to her room and I accompanied them.

"It's very near Miss *Ravenshaw's* room," she said as we walked the second floor of the long right wing. No member of staff overlooked an opportunity to press home that they believed me to be a false claimant soiling the name of a young woman they'd accepted and liked.

I glanced down the right wing, gloomy and unlived in, all doors closed and, perhaps, locked. The two halls were of even length, but the one to the right looked longer and projected farther, or seemed to, because the darkness made it bleak, a tunnel to the unknown. My heart skipped a beat. Perhaps dark deeds had occurred that had invited the gloom to visit, and then to tarry. I sensed that was true.

I spoke up. "What is down at the end of the right wing?" I reached into my memory. "Wasn't there a larger suite of rooms? Perhaps they would be better suited for my needs, especially as Mademoiselle d'Arbonneau will soon arrive."

"Oh no, miss, you cannot have those rooms." Mrs. Blackwood clutched her key ring in her hand to still the jingling. "Captain Whitfield has left strict orders that no one shall enter the rooms on that wing while they are under repair."

"How long have they been under repair?"

"Since . . . late December." She seemed reluctant to answer.

Late December. Just after her death. I shivered again. Had no one been in there since then?

"But we shall find you other suitable accommodations if you prefer them to the very nice area that has been specially prepared for you." She bent over to pick a small piece of lint off the lemon-polished floor and sniffed as she put it into her pocket.

Mrs. Ross was settled into her bright room and by the time I came to pay a call on her to check her comfort some hours later, the entrance to the right wing had been freshly, firmly blockaded.

At the end of the wing was a room with a closed door in front of which the young housecat, which did not seem to have a name, stretched. I had never noticed her sentried in front of any other room. "What room is that?" I asked Annie as she swept by me on her way to get coal for Mrs. Ross.

"That's where the woman claiming to be Miss Ravenshaw"— she lowered her voice—"*died*. 'Scuse me."

So the woman had died here, in the house proper. Had there been blood, was that why the room was closed off? A violent struggle? Surely, if so, someone would have had a care to have it cleaned by now. The mystery was as mazy and murky as the recesses of that right-hand passage. Was it a shrine? Hiding a crime?

I felt unanchored in my own home and wanted to become more at ease.

I went belowstairs and located Mrs. Blackwood. "Hello?" I

knocked on the open door of her sitting area. She popped to her feet, the great ring of keys clanging at her side.

"How may we be of help?"

"I'm sorry to intrude," I said. "I wondered if you might reacquaint me with my house. It's been some time, you'll understand."

"I understand very well why you don't know your way about." She wiped her hands, and I followed her to the front stairs. Before we began our ascent, she pointed to a wall of bells. "If you'll just ring for me from now on, miss, we can come to wherever you are."

Not "Miss Ravenshaw," as would be due the daughter of the house, but "miss." A woman without a name or a place. In one fell swoop Mrs. Blackwood had also politely informed me that the working area of the household was not a place I'd be expected or well received.

I nodded, and we walked upstairs. The cat followed me and I was pleased by her presence, missing the many animals that had lived near us in India.

We passed through the breakfast room, and then the drawing room.

"Captain Whitfield, he loves this room." Mrs. Blackwood pointed to the large, open music room.

"Does he entertain often?"

She beamed. "When we came to this house the first time, we were so pleased he'd have an establishment of his own at which to entertain."

"So you've been with Captain Whitfield for some time?"

"Oh, yes, many of us have, at the rented properties or London. Not Cook, of course," she said.

"No?" I asked. "When did Cook join you?"

She acted as though she hadn't heard me. Perhaps she hadn't.

"We were so glad when he came home. It is his *own* home, with a history that is his, *his own family*, owned and not rented. It's something Lord Frome cannot taunt him with any longer. Perhaps others round here must be kind to him now, too."

I opened my mouth to ask who Lord Frome was, but I knew she probably would not "hear" me again so I did not proceed. She was not engaged by or for me, and as far as she believed, this was not my house. Mrs. Blackwood closed the music room door and began to walk down the hallway.

We passed the dining room. "You'll not be taking your meals in here, of course, we're sure you're very comfortable dining in your own rooms, and Cook is happy to continue to send meals there." Her tone had a note of finality. We proceeded up to the second floor. "Of course, you'll know all about these rooms"—she gestured left—"as your rooms are here."

"But what about the right wing?" I asked. "What rooms are there?"

"There's the room where . . . the other young lady stayed," she said quietly. "Some other guest rooms. A linen area. And the large suite where Captain Whitfield was installed until recently, but only after the young lady had passed on, of course. He is a true gentleman. He removed to the guesthouse before then. As he has now."

Her demeanor made it clear that she thought that was due to his honor and not my merit. I looked down the right hallway again. "Renovations must have begun after I arrived?"

She pursed her lips. "They had been planned for some time."

She did not rush me, and I gazed down that long passage. The afternoon shadows had shifted and I could not now see the end of it. "If I remember correctly, the suite of rooms that Captain Whitfield had taken for himself once belonged to my parents."

She looked startled that I'd know that. "That may well be, miss. Is there anything else I may assist with?"

"Michelene d'Arbonneau will be here shortly," I said. "She requires a room with a carpet, and will someone attend to cleaning it."

"If you're sure that's wise, miss," she answered.

"Is there a reason it wouldn't be?"

"We did not say that it wouldn't be." Her lips pursed ever more tightly.

"Thank you, then." I sighed and returned to my room, keenly aware that the staff and servants were all Captain Whitfield's, and it was to him that they owed their loyalty. Well, Mrs. Ross and Mademoiselle d'Arbonneau were to be mine, not his. And with Michelene arriving the next day, I intended to have more answers about just what had happened here. In due course.

In reality, though, Michelene raised more questions than provided answers I sat in the chair in front of the dressing table, turned around so I could watch Michelene unpack the new dresses, hats, slippers, boots, and stockings she'd brought with her from the dress shop. "I will show each one to you, non, as I put them in the armoires?"

"Yes, please!"

First she showed me the mourning clothes; as I was in the final quarter of mourning, they were not as severe as they might have been. The fabrics still shimmered and the blacks were muted, but then highlighted with mourning jewelry, including hairpins made of jet.

I knew my official mourning would soon draw to a close. But I suspected the deep veil of sorrow would always shroud my heart.

"You can wear the jet pins even after mourning," Michelene said. "They are good for ladies with dark hair, *non*? To beautifully hold up the hair without being seen?" Michelene next pulled out a beautiful blue-gray silk. "This is very much like the one worn by Princess Victoria," she said, speaking of the Queen's oldest daughter.

A wave of concern crossed me. "I shouldn't like to be seen as pretentious," I said. "And I'm aware that for the moment I am spending money that is being withdrawn from my accounts, but overseen by Captain Whitfield."

"This is the most dear of all of them, and you shall need something to wear to Graffam Park, *ma chère*."

"What is Graffam Park?" I had not been invited anywhere that I was aware of.

"Why, it is the home of Captain Whitfield's mother and step-father, Lord and Lady Ledbury. They have been invited to his summer soirée, here, so etiquette will demand that they return the invitation. If you are still here." She let the last sentence drop like a stone. But then she pulled out the shoes, and showed them to me, pair by pair, so I was taken away again.

"I'm grateful you are here to assist me," I confessed. "There are customs and requirements of which I am seemingly unaware. My mother took care to bring me up as a proper young English-woman, but I'm afraid that our English community was rather small and she was also much occupied with assisting my father. There seem to be some gaps in my social education, and of course, having been away for twenty years, I don't always know where they are."

"Do not fret," Michelene said. "I am here to assist. I was happy to assist the . . . other young lady purchase her gowns and such for the months she lived here, and I'm happy to assist you."

"She dressed well, Annie says. You were able to help her with that?"

"But of course. She was a lovely girl, and everyone was quite taken with her. I think even Captain Whitfield. She had dark hair, very much like yours."

The pretender had spent my money on clothing. A thought occurred to me as I watched her with the dresses. "What happened to her many fine gowns after her untimely demise? Are they stored? Have they been sent to charity?"

Michelene did not turn from busying herself in the second wardrobe. "*Non*, not to charity. It is the custom for a lady's maid to receive, as a benefit of her services, the gowns and dresses her mistress no longer desires or needs. In this case, the *pauvre petite* had no further need for her gowns, and when I cleaned out her rooms I took them with me. As she would have wanted."

This was breathtaking to me, who had worn every dress let out and lengthened till it was no longer socially acceptable. I stared at the back of her fine silk dress. "I see." Was that one of the distinct perquisites she had mentioned? Had permission been overtly given? Had the imposter, too, purchased gowns of many colors and fine fabrics, anticipating her post-mourning period? I would make discreet inquiries about this practice.

"I assume jewels are not perquisites."

"*Mais non*," she said. "But the little one had no jewels."

She turned. "This one"—she took out a copper-colored dress with a rather daring neckline—"this is the one you should wear, after mourning, when you dine with Captain Whitfield."

"I do not dine with Captain Whitfield," I said. "I dine in my rooms. In any case, I would certainly not consider dressing to please him." A faint blush crept up, as I'd never been good at dissembling.

She raised an eyebrow and put the dress back in the wardrobe. "I understand. He's a Hussar. So very attractive, but a little dangerous, *non*?"

Ah, the Hussars—light cavalry regiments known for their loyalty, courage, and daring, but also for their womanizing, risk-taking, and a healthy view of their worth in the world.

"They fearlessly take what they want or feel owed," Michelene continued.

"Perhaps that is only the French Hussars," I said. "Not the English." But she'd put her finger on it. He was an attractive, but also a potentially dangerous, quantity. Certainly a man very much different from those I'd experienced.

In another context, time and place, set of circumstances, that would not have been altogether unwelcome.

Michelene continued on as if she hadn't heard me. "Hussars would scare many women, especially women who have been rather, what is the English word, protected?" She looked puzzled. "Coddled!" She clicked her fingers as she said it. "Now, I am very fatigued, and I should like to rest in my rooms for a while. I will be but a moment away if you need me, and will be back later this evening to undress your hair and help you prepare for bed."

"Thank you." I smiled. "But I do feel that the gray gown needs to be returned. If I am invited to Graffam, we can purchase a new gown then."

She frowned.

I continued softly, but with an effort to assert my authority, "That will be all for now."

She offered a patronizing, sophisticated smile and left. Instead of mistress of the house, I felt like an imperious little girl pretending to tell her governess what to do.

The next morning, after breakfast, a new silver salver rested on the large table in the main hallway, reflecting the glory of the mid-May sunshine. I looked questioningly at Landreth, who was supervising some workmen near the sitting room.

"That's the salver for calling cards, miss," he said. "I've taken the liberty of having it placed here again, as you will surely be receiving callers."

I nodded slowly. "Thank you, Landreth." I walked closer to him and lowered my voice. "I'm sorry to trouble you, but could you kindly inform me of the protocol for callers?"

"You don't know, miss?" His tone was bewildered and, perhaps, a little suspicious.

I shook my head. "If I had intended to adopt a false identity, surely I would have familiarized myself with the appropriate etiquette before embarking on such a deception."

"If you were of the right station, miss, then yes, you would have known to do so."

I looked at him and he at me, a standoff. "But you do not find me to speak in an uneducated manner, do you?" I gently put forth.

"No," he said. "But neither did she." We both knew whom he meant by *she*.

Had she not known calling protocol either? Or had she spoken more coarsely than he'd first considered?

I could see I'd need to share with him what I'd already told Michelene. "I assure you that my mother raised me in all ways as gently English born, from the taking of tea to the playing of instruments, such that were available, to the appropriate manner in which to interact with household staff," I said quietly, "caring for their comfort as well as my own. However, some customs seem to have held a different protocol among the English in India than the English at home—calling among them. I should genuinely appreciate your guidance."

He nodded, apparently satisfied with my explanation. "During the week, ladies come by to leave cards, and from time to time, once you know the environs, you shall do the same. You'll choose a day when you'll accept visitors and on all other days only your closet acquaintances will call."

I did not have any close acquaintances, though I yearned for some, even one. "Shall I need calling cards as well?"

He nodded. "Michelene can assist with that." I noted the unusually iron tone when he spoke her name as she approached from the stairway. They looked at one another with something short of disgust. There had been something amiss when she was here the last time, I was becoming certain of it. But a servant without discretion is soon a servant without a situation, so I could not expect Captain Whitfield's staff to tell tales.

"What day would you like to be 'at home'?" he asked.

I shrugged helplessly. Was one day better than another? "Monday?"

"Thursday would be an excellent choice."

"Thursday then."

"And," he continued, "there is a sliding passage in the sitting room." We walked to the room together and he showed me. "I will announce each visitor before she comes, and if you choose to be not 'at home' just then, you may slip through this passage into the breakfast room and disappear without causing distress."

I smiled. "Thank you, Landreth. You are invaluable. I shall thank Captain Whitfield when he returns for allowing you to continue to assist me." He didn't smile, but his cheeks pinked. It was enough, for now.

"Captain Whitfield will return on Thursday next, miss."

"Very good." I walked back into the hallway and saw Michelene standing very near the large new salver. She dipped her hand into it, which was rather bold, and pulled out a card.

"Someone has already been by?" I asked.

Landreth nodded and Michelene brought the card to me. "Miss Delia Dainley." Miss Dainley's card was subtly embossed. I looked up and noticed a look pass between Michelene and Landreth.

"What is it?" I asked.

Michelene spoke. "There exists at least one coddled young Englishwoman who is not afraid of Hussars. Miss Dainley."

CHAPTER FIVE

The next Thursday, after a small and leisurely lunch, Michelene helped me prepare for Miss Dainley's call. Several other women had also left cards, so I might expect one or two others to drop by as well. "It's very kind of them to call upon me so quickly after my arrival," I said with both nerves and enthusiasm.

Michelene continued to twist and wrap my hair around the back of my head, tying it off, and pulling some free into long curls. "Perhaps they want to see you quickly, wondering how long you'll be here."

I frowned at her. "What a thing to say! I plan to be here a good long while."

"*Oui*," she replied. "But I think that the woman claiming to be Miss Ravenshaw, who was here earlier, she believed so as well."

Had she meant I would be found out as a pretender? Or—my face cooled—that I'd be dead, like the first woman?

I reflected upon that for a moment. "What was she like?"

"Oh, I do not speak of the dead," she said, even though she had. She quickly crossed herself. "But I will say that she was beautiful and well cared for. Even after I came to serve as lady's maid, she kept her Indian maid close. They were like sisters, *non*? She did not like to be separated from her."

"Did you speak to her—the maid, I mean?" I asked. I was as curious about that woman, almost, as I was about the imposter.

"The maid did not speak English, nor French," she replied. "So we could not talk."

"What language did they speak?" I asked. This truly surprised me.

She shrugged. "It sounded heathen. You might ask Captain Whitfield. He seemed quite taken with her." She pulled some of my hair to the front and ran over it with an iron she'd heated in the fireplace grill.

"Taken with the maid?"

She shook her head. "With Mademoiselle Ravenshaw. Perhaps the maid, too. He seems quite appreciative of ladies, and they of him, which is perhaps why there is no Mrs. Whitfield. No one he's been willing to set others aside for. Though that's not necessarily a requirement of a happy marriage, *d'accord*?"

"What? But of course it is," I said. She tsk-tsked me in that characteristically French manner but said nothing further and indicated I should stand as she adjusted my dress front and back.

I thought about Captain Whitfield and his pull on me. I should have been more resistant to his charms than almost anyone, as he had, for the moment, appropriated my house and doubted my integrity. Was he capable of harming someone, her, me, to keep the house? Had he planned it that way, or was he as he seemed, a gentlemanly victim of circumstance, much like myself? If she had indeed been murdered, perhaps someone else had done it. Who else had motive? I should seek to find out. Cautiously.

I strengthened my resolve to remain focused on the visitor at hand. It made me quite jumpy. Would she like me? Could she become, I hoped, a friend?

"Tell me about Miss Dainley," I said. "What should I expect?"

"She's a mild young woman, at least on the outside. Sweet, like the cherries. But with a hard stone inside, *non*?" She pulled the top layer of the skirt of my dress up to one hip and hooked it there with a hidden clasp. Then she made certain that the buttons on the bodice of my dress were tightly closed and straight from neck to waist. "I understand she is to leave for India soon."

"Indeed! Perhaps this is why she wanted to meet with me." I could be useful!

"Certainly, this is true. She may wish to forgo her departure, if at all possible." She ran a finger over the fur ruffs on my three-quarter sleeves. I looked at them and smiled; they were so beautiful. She caught my glance and looked satisfied. "She sails with the 'fishing fleet' early in the autumn. Unless she can catch the big fish in England first."

"You said she was not afraid of a Hussar." I asked tentatively, "Would you be?"

Michelene smiled. "I would not be, *certainement*. It's been said that when the Hussars come, everyone begins running. The men away from them, and the women toward them." She laughed. "They are handsome, yes, and commanding, but also, they have been known to pillage and loot the spoils of war without conscience if they feel it belongs to them. And they adore women." She did not seem aware that she was nearly purring. She turned me to face the mirror. "*Voilà*. My handiwork."

I gathered my courage and looked at my reflection straight on. "Oh!" I was utterly thrilled with the lovely image that was, shockingly, me! I could face anyone now. "You have transformed me into an English lady," I said to Michelene, embracing her. She, being a Frenchwoman, accepted my embrace with ease.

"You already are an English lady," she said. "You simply needed a French touch."

A knock came at the door. It was Landreth. "Miss Delia Dainley has arrived. Shall I show her into the drawing room?"

"Thank you, Landreth. I shall be down directly."

"*Bon courage*," Michelene whispered as she nudged me toward the door.

Mrs. Ross had assured me that, as there would be no gentlemen present, I was free to receive Miss Dainley on my own. Landreth showed me in.

"Miss Delia Dainley, may I present Miss Rebecca Ravenshaw? Miss Ravenshaw, I give you Miss Dainley." He thoughtfully withdrew.

I instantly recognized her—even without the riding habit. She was the woman who had been riding with Captain Whitfield. "Miss Dainley, I'm so very pleased you have come to call and take tea with me."

Miss Dainley smiled and offered her gloved hand in response. I indicated that she should take the most comfortable chair in the room, next to the floor-to-ceiling, leaded-glass windows that overlooked the downs.

She wasn't interested in observing the downs, though; she was busy assessing me. I took from her look that Michelene had dressed me well, and a warm flush of contentment rose within me. She sat down and Annie soon appeared with a tea tray. It trembled in her hands like an unsteady cymbal. All three of us sighed little puffs of relief when it was safely settled on a sturdy side table.

"I'm very happy you were able to see me. After your *very long ordeal*, that is." She took a teacup from Annie with a practiced nod. "And journey?" Her raised eyebrows and the touch of asperity in her voice made it clear she, too, did not believe me to be who I said I was.

"Yes," I said. "It was long indeed. But faith saw me through and here I am now. In my own home."

She raised an eye to me at that and set her teacup down. She waved away the cake tray that Annie had offered. Preserving her figure, perhaps? She was a pretty woman, her long strawberry-blond hair finely curled around a creamy complexion, protected most days, I was certain, by a shadowing bonnet.

I took a sweet, so long denied to me after the Rebellion, and much to be enjoyed now that I was home. "Michelene, my lady's maid, tells me that you are planning to embark for India this coming autumn."

She nodded. "I am the fifth daughter in my family," she said matter-of-factly. "My brother is already in India, and he has recently assured me that, now things have quieted down and the country is firmly under British control again, it would be quite safe for me to go. He hopes to make introductions."

She was refreshingly direct and my heart softened toward her. It was a difficult thing to be a woman. Fortunately, an unmarried woman with property was accountable to no one but herself; this was the secure position I would soon find myself in, however temporarily tenuous this mystery had made my fate.

I reassured myself of this, anyway, over and over again, late at night.

"I hope that you will find India to be as welcoming and hospitable as I did," I said.

She flinched and a look of surprise crossed her face. "You would not be afraid to return?"

"Not at all. I spent many happy years there up until the one of . . . of horror." My hand shook as the abrupt memory of my rushed and disorderly flight ahead of the rebels came back. I felt, once more, the final embrace of my mother and father. We hadn't known it would be our last. Perhaps Father had known. He'd looked mournful. I pushed the memory back, afraid it would unsettle me. My real fear, I now admitted, is that one too many unexpected memories or fancies pushing their way in would unsettle my mind for good.

"How did you come to be in India?" Her voice softened.

"My father was a second son, and had fought in the Burmese War, and then traveled a bit," I said. "He returned home with distinction and, after his brother died from smallpox, my father inherited Headbourne House. He settled down, married my mother, and my brother, Peter, and I were born here. But he never forgot the people of the East Indies and some years later he put his investments into the hands of his solicitors and returned as a missionary."

She sat there quietly for a moment. "Did your mother wish to go as well?"

That seemed a rather personal question from a woman I'd only just met, but I sensed that she was asking as much for herself as anything else, so I answered, delicately.

"My mother did not want to leave England; she had envisioned herself here, in Hampshire, at Headbourne. But my father decided we must go, and so we did."

She nodded. "She made a way once there?"

"After sufficient time. The land is beautiful, of course, bluest of seas, and in the south, palm trees and fruitful soil that grows a veritable cornucopia. Even this"—I indicated my tea—"and coffee. We became inclined toward and grew fond of the people." I closed my eyes for but a second. "The scent of chickpeas being harvested—it smells of home to me." Was it possible to smell something that was not present? I smelled them, even now, as much as I smelled the bitter bite of the tea right in front of me, but I dared not share that. She'd think me mad.

"Chickpeas?" she asked. "Is that some foreign vegetable?"

"It is a legume common in India," I said. Miss Dainley sniffed and sipped her tea and Annie refilled it. I'd noticed Annie hovering in the background, close enough to listen. I could hear the footsteps of several other servants in the hallway just beyond, busying themselves with tasks that allowed them to eavesdrop.

"My mother suffered extreme melancholy. The day my father baptized his first convert, my mother, brother, and I remained in our small house with our ayahs whilst my mother wept."

Miss Dainley's eyes grew large and she signaled for Annie to bring cake to her after all. "But she recovered?"

"After some years, yes," I said. "She made her peace with it, and with my father, who was a good man at heart. Truly, what else could she do? And many, many Indians converted to Christianity after that. Tens of thousands in various places. Eventually my mother founded the first schools for girls in southern India. She made certain that girls of all castes, including slave castes and out-castes, had access to education. And she taught them to make lace. Salvation for both body and soul. I was her closest friend and assisted her ministry in every way."

"Lace! Why ever would that be of help?" Miss Dainley's nose wrinkled. A nickname came to me. I should have to be careful in future not to refer to her as Miss Disdain.

I smiled. "Ah, but it was. Great numbers of lower-caste women became skilled lace makers and made an income for the first time, ever. Their husbands became educated and were able to make money on the coffee plantations of Englishmen, as managers."

"What did they do with the earnings?" Delia leaned forward and now I sensed no reserve, just interest. I weathered the rush of homesickness and imagined my Indian sisters, smiling, chattering, sitting with me, bobbins and pillows on laps on the wide bamboo veranda, its corners concealing lime-green lizards. "They were able to pay their taxes, taxes imposed for things such as men's facial hair. Worse, lower-caste women were not allowed to wear clothing above their waists, denying them dignity."

Annie gasped and I could hear Mrs. Blackwood draw in her breath from somewhere out of sight, in the main hallway.

"They were . . . naked? Their bosoms? For all to see?" From the tone Miss Dainley used, I suspected she may have been more concerned for her future husband's view than for the humiliating plight of the Sudra women.

"Yes. My parents spoke to the rajah and the resident on their behalf. My mother loved Tamil proverbs. One was 'The word of the destitute does not reach the assembly.' So someone in power must speak on their behalf. The missionaries helped them win the right to clothe themselves, above the waist, too, and then gave them clothes and the skills to earn money to buy their clothes in the future."

I stopped, mortified. Why had I been rushing along like a poorly brought up girl, a verbal runaway cart on a first social call? Landreth would most certainly not approve.

"I'm terribly sorry. I apologize. Perhaps I have been a little homesick and have carried on overly long about myself." I took a deep breath and affixed a courteous smile on my face. "Please, do tell me about yourself."

Miss Dainley nodded. She seemed pleased to change the subject. Whether it was a relief to be done with my ill manners or that she did not want to learn more about India just now, I did not know.

"You'll be happy to learn there is an inspiring season of events planned, for the summer, during the periods when the others come back from London," she said. "A few of these events will transpire in . . . your home."

"You'll not be in London?" I asked. I knew it was the season for those well born, and well off, to attend social events in the city.

"No." She shook her head. Her discussion of her family's lack of resources made further explanation unnecessary. Even if I had arrived earlier, and had not been in mourning, I would not have known anyone to oversee a London season for me.

"Captain Whitfield has seen to the arrangements for entertainments to be held at Headbourne. He's a wonderful host if, perhaps, somewhat misunderstood of late. I believe he is to return today?"

I nodded. *Had she made inquiries? Or had he told her?* I chided myself. Why should it matter to me? "Misunderstood? And what kind of events?" I asked politely.

"Oh, nothing, really." She waved the topic away with her lace handkerchief. "As to events, musical soirées, shooting parties, dinners and balls, that sort of thing, of course, you will be invited to reciprocal arrangements. As long as you're still here, of course. The grandest of all will be the costumed ball at Graffam Park in autumn. Lord Ledbury spares no expense. The theme will be announced a month in advance and then it's a melee to come up with an appropriate costume and a suitable gift for Lord and Lady Ledbury."

"Something to look forward to. I do hope we can become friends, and I know I shall rely upon your wisdom until your autumn departure, as I reacquaint myself with English ways," I said. "I'm happy to be of help to you in any way I may, as to India."

She nodded, but she was no longer looking at me, distracted by the sound of an oncoming team of horses pulling a carriage.

Captain Whitfield had returned.

Miss Dainley stood and I stood as well. Through the front windows, we could see him drive toward the coach house and stable yard. I noted she had told me not about herself, but about the season's events.

"I look forward to calling upon you, and becoming acquainted with your family," I said.

For a moment, she did not take her eyes off the advancing carriage. Then she looked directly at me, voice firm once again. "I should much prefer to visit with you here. Such a jolly home, and Captain Whitfield's hospitality is so accommodating." She smiled. "You do agree?"

To what was I agreeing? That I had a jolly home or that Captain Whitfield was hospitable? Was she asking me to give tacit approval to whatever visits she planned to make here at Headbourne without offering the courtesy of a return visit? Of course, if I visited her, there would be no possibility of Captain Whitfield's accompanying me.

In any case, she didn't wait for a response. We walked to the door and she pulled on her bonnet, but very loosely, which allowed her hair to show to its best, glossy advantage. Landreth began to signal for her carriage, but Miss Dainley stopped him.

"Captain Whitfield would be happy to attend to this himself," she said.

Landreth nodded his agreement and, as she began to descend the steps, I could see Whitfield move toward her with ease and familiarity.

Landreth closed the door behind her but I could hear cheery conversation and then Whitfield's laugh. I turned toward Landreth. Had he suggested Thursdays for my "at home" day because he knew Miss Dainley would want to see the captain, and Landreth approved? Or was it merely a coincidence?

"Will that be all, miss?" he asked me, and I became aware that I should not be idling by the door.

"Yes," I said. I wavered, then gathered my courage to move forward with something I'd been recently considering. What pushed me to finally act? I knew, even though I barely dared admit it to myself. It was seeing Miss Dainley interact so familiarly with Captain Whitfield.

"Just one more thing. Will you please inform Cook that I shall accept Captain Whitfield's long-standing invitation to take the evening meal with him in the dining room this evening?"

CHAPTER SIX

On my way back to my room, I stopped at Mrs. Ross's quarters and knocked. "Yes?" she called out.

"May I come in?"

"Of course."

She sat in a chair, desk on her lap, Bible open in front of her. It reminded me that I had not yet found a Bible; I should set about that immediately. Whilst I had the comfort of many memorized scriptures, I desired to see the words themselves, living and active on the page.

"I'm sorry to interrupt, but I wondered if you could take dinner with me in the dining room tonight. Captain Whitfield has returned and I'd like to dine with him, as he'd earlier extended an invitation."

"Certainly, lassie." She looked at my face. "Why are ye so long?"

I sighed. "Miss Dainley took tea with me today."

"She wasna kind?"

"No, she was," I said. "It's just that, well, she has a mother and a father. And many siblings. She seems to know everyone hereabouts."

Mrs. Ross nodded, and thoughtfully did not point out that my response had little to do with her question but much to do with what was on my mind.

I realized that I knew almost nothing about her, except that she was Scottish, Presbyterian, and highly recommended by people whom Mrs. MacAlister knew. "Do you have children, Mrs. Ross?"

She shook her head. "Nae."

"Siblings?"

She shook her head again then looked down at her Bible, open, I could now see, to Hebrews, chapter 13, and she read it aloud. "'For he hath said, I will never leave thee, nor forsake thee.'" She, too, had cause to be lonely but was seeking solace with God.

"Thank you, Mrs. Ross. Of course, you are right. Half past eight?"

She nodded her agreement and I closed the door behind me. As I made my way into the hall, the little cat came alongside me, walking beside me, keeping right up against my skirt. I stopped, and looked down at it, and it looked up at me and meowed quietly. "Thank you, little cat," I said. "I know that I am not alone, but sometimes it feels that way. But for you." Where had she come from? Perhaps she was alone in this world and too small to be bothered with.

She stayed with me, in my room, till Michelene came to help me dress for dinner. As soon as she saw my lady's maid, the cat's hackles rose and she glanced at me before fleeing.

Somehow, it felt like a warning.

I stepped into the dining room at half past eight, and Captain Whitfield was already present, standing, as a gentleman would, until I arrived.

"I was delighted when I heard you would finally be joining me this evening," Whitfield said. His face was freshly tanned from, I surmised, his rides in the growing spring sunlight; he moved with more ease than the cat. Mrs. Ross, in her black cotton and lace collar, came into the dining room. Captain Whitfield struggled to control a frown and that made me struggle to control a smile. He had perhaps forgotten that she would accompany me.

"My chaperone," I reminded him.

"Ah, indeed, it would not do for the neighborhood tongues to start wagging so early on," he said.

"So early on? I shan't like to set them wagging later, either," I jested, and he grinned back. I got the feeling he did not mind wagging tongues. Or perhaps not on the surface, anyway.

He was dressed for dinner, impossibly impeccable. He wore black, as was right for a gentleman of his station who was not in uniform, with the exception of his shirt, which was cream linen. Michelene had told me that only wealthy gentlemen wore linen regularly as it was expensive and difficult to keep clean and pressed.

He came around and first helped Mrs. Ross to her seat, as she was older, and then he helped me into mine. He tried to be nonchalant, but I could see he studied me; I was dressed very differently now than before he had taken his leave. My dress, though black, rustled and shimmered in the candlelight, the fabric cleverly gathered at the small of my back to show my figure to its best advantage.

Landreth supervised the courses, and we talked.

"Are you quite settled?" he asked.

"Almost so." I looked at the first course being brought in. "Now that I have begun to accommodate myself to English cuisine, I've found the food exquisite."

"Have the staff made you feel welcome?" he asked.

"Indeed. Landreth has made a particular effort. He's greatly helped me with calling." I took a sip of soup and casually added, "In fact, you will of course have noticed that Miss Delia Dainley came to call today. Is she a friend of yours?"

He nodded. "Her mother has long been a friend to my mother."

Soup was over and the bowls cleared. "Miss Dainley mentioned that there would be a large costume ball at your parents' house at the end of the summer. As they are, of sorts, distant relatives to me, I would be delighted to learn more about them."

He didn't look up, and the staff present looked surreptitiously at one another, then back at the captain. Had I said something wrong? I hoped not. Landreth approached to refill our wineglasses. The captain used his napkin, then replaced it on his lap before answering. "They are distant to me, as well. There is not much to say. My father died when I was but a young lad, my mother married Lord Ledbury quite soon thereafter, and my brother Anthony, Viscount Frome, was born within the year. I was raised at Sandhurst, alone, while he was raised at Graffam Park, in the bosom of family."

The salmon was brought in.

"Please do tell me about *your* family," he said, turning it deftly from himself.

"As you know, my parents were killed in the Mutiny. I had a brother, too, Peter, who died about ten years ago, of cholera. When we were children, we preferred not to sit in this dining room, as I recall." I smiled. "Our governess would bring our meals to our room and we'd tell stories."

Whitfield grinned. "Better company."

"Yes," I said. "Once in India, we'd make up stories about the monkeys that lived near us. We'd name them and imagine their home lives, if they took tea, played croquet and the like when we couldn't see them." I blinked back some tears. "During the Uprising, when we all waited in the Residency for the government to free us, I told those stories to the children, to pass the time."

"A kindness," he said quietly.

"The least I could do."

He returned to his salmon, and I to mine. From time to time he seemed to be staring at the fork in my right hand, and I wondered if I was holding it incorrectly or if I'd chosen to use the wrong one. I looked toward Mrs. Ross. She was using the same fork, and in the same manner.

We spoke of lighter matters as the fowl was served and removed, and finally, the cherries and the sherries.

By that time, I'd eaten so much, I could barely breathe. I stood, and Mrs. Ross did likewise. Captain Whitfield came round to pull each of our chairs away as Landreth came nearby to escort us out of the dining room.

"Thank you for your companionship," he said. "I'm sorry I won't be at home often to enjoy it."

"Thank you, too, Captain Whitfield, for your hospitality." He nodded and met my gaze, and held it with an intimacy that was perhaps not yet warranted. It was not wholly unwelcome.

"Taking meals in the dining room is much more pleasant, this go-around," I said. I was rewarded with a warm, genuine laugh and a deep bow.

Michelene met me in my room within a few minutes and had to tug to help me out of my dress.

"I thought I told you to eat only a few bites," she said. "I will bring small meals into your room after you have retired for the evening."

"I'm afraid so much rich food may make me unwell."

She clicked her tongue. "Cook had said she'd continue to serve you many foods that you may not have eaten for some time."

"That is kind," I replied.

"I told her that was likely to make you unwell, but she did not heed me. Perhaps that was her goal."

I inclined my head. "Why wouldn't she heed you? Does Cook have some reason to want to make me feel ill?"

Michelene shrugged her shoulders. She helped me into my nightdress and then left my room, with only one lamp still lit.

I dearly wished for sweet dreams, but alas, I began to recall, just before slumber arrived, a particular young woman, a sweet mother of only eighteen years, who had died at the Residency, leaving her baby an orphan. I'd held that baby as I told the older children monkey stories.

I'd felt orphaned, too.

I went to my window and, as I looked out, I could see directly into the guesthouse; though it was some distance away, it was well lit from the inside. I blew out the flame of my lamp and let the dark encase me as I looked across the grounds. In the drawing room window was the silhouette of Captain Whitfield. I did not want him to think that I was hoping for a glimpse of him.

Even though I am, I acknowledged. I quickly turned away. Why did he unsettle me? I knew the answer. Although I hadn't wanted to, I'd succumbed, just as Annie had said women did.

I found him attractive. Compellingly so, somehow.

I closed my eyes, quietly praying for my friends in India: the Meads, and Penelope, and Violet and her father in Ceylon—so very happy that they in the south had avoided the Mutiny, which had taken place only in the north. I prayed for beloveds at the mission, for dear Musa, and last, for myself and for the wisdom and strength I'd require but felt I currently had in meager supply.

Before I went back to bed, I opened my eyes and could see, even through the rising night mists, that Whitfield had turned to face the window and was looking not at the house in general but directly back at me. I held his gaze for the second time that night, and then finally looked away.

CHAPTER SEVEN

The household buzzed, preparing for the following night's musical soirée, which I knew to be a gathering of friends for conversation, piano music, and singing. Perhaps I would make a start on finding friends, even though I could not play my home's piano. Whilst I waited, I wrote letters to India. Mr. Highmore had said that a packet would be sent shortly to further verify my identity, and if I would like to include any personal letters, he would be glad to see that they accompanied the official correspondence. I thought it was kind of him. Also, I knew he intended to use this opportunity to allow me to prove myself. I comforted myself that while I did not yet have friends here, I had them somewhere in the world.

First, I wrote to Violet, who had been like a sister to me until she moved to Ceylon some years back with her parents to a coffee plantation. Then to Penelope, who had been a lifelong friend and remained near the mission. Before the Mutiny she had been set to marry John Mark, a missionary's son who had hoped to become a translator.

Father had wanted John Mark for me and had been disappointed when I indicated that I did not feel for John Mark in that way. I wondered if they'd married; if, indeed, they were perhaps expecting the birth of a child. I wondered if I ever would.

I then wrote to Mr. Mead, my father's closest friend, who had been unhappily removed from serving with the London Missionary Society just a year or two earlier, though he remained in India serving in new capacities. I hoped that he would write back.

Captain Whitfield made his way into the room.

"I'm about to take a short stroll in the gardens, as the renovations I've already commissioned will soon commence. As you may have some vested interest in the property, I thought you might like to accompany me?"

"Certainly," I said, happy that Michelene had included a black but pretty cotton day dress in my repertoire. I sealed the last envelope and left them all on my bureau as Mrs. Blackwood bustled about the room. Whitfield offered his arm and I took it.

We passed through the stone lions and followed the cobblestoned pathway toward the back of the house, which looked out over the downs. "Take care," he said. "The stones are loose and need to be taken up and reset. I have arranged for that to be done fairly quickly, as there are some events scheduled in the gardens over the summer."

I nodded. "Thank you. I would have done the same, but you have set things in motion much sooner. I'll be very happy to repay you, once my funds are freed, for anything you've spent on the house and its upkeep, but I shan't be able to repay you for your thoughtful attentiveness, to the house, and to me."

He looked at me, his brown eyes perhaps slightly softer for only a moment. "It's my pleasure, Miss Ravenshaw."

I felt a little happiness unlocked from within me then. It was a welcome respite from heartache.

We walked through the tangled, untended flowers, perennials that had been planted with thought and care some time ago. I touched a lovely vine that covered the arbor as we walked through it. "What is this?"

"Wisteria. You've not seen it? I understood that most gently born women were amateur gardeners at heart, tossing off Latin names of this or that with one another in their drawing-room conversations."

"First, Captain Whitfield, it is bad form to compare one woman with another," I teased. "Second, I was more involved in assisting my mother in teaching young ladies to read and write and provide for themselves than in learning polite botany for gentle conversation."

I brushed by the wisteria and it had a lovely scent. "Sweet, but in an unassuming way," I said.

"Who is she?" Captain Whitfield jested. "Have I met her?" I couldn't help but tap him lightly with my fan. "Not who, what. The wisteria."

To my gratitude, he responded with a smile. "Ah, yes, wisteria does have its charms." He looked me in the eye. "It's a devil to re-locate an established one, though." That smile never left his face, but I sensed the warning nonetheless. Did he mean he had no intentions of leaving Headbourne?

We passed a large shrub. "This bush, however, I do know the name of. Rhododendron. It grows profusely in India. In fact, it makes a delightful wine."

"I hope not to see you out here at night gathering blossoms and passing them on to Mrs. Blackwood for the still."

"Although I am awake many nights, not being able to sleep well, I shall try to keep myself from prowling the gardens," I said. "Speaking of evening activities, I'm looking forward to your musical soirée tomorrow, and wonder is there anything I should know beforehand so I am not at a disadvantage and can help put your guests at ease?"

"Miss Dainley has agreed to come early for this very reason," he said. "She offered to do so, which I thought very kind."

"Indeed," I replied. "Miss Dainley." I wondered if Miss Dainley would be informed in advance on every event held at my home; if, in fact, she would be acting as actual hostess. I pulled up a large bishop's lace. "I shan't want these weeds, pretty as they are, to take root."

Captain Whitfield smiled; he knew what I'd meant.

After a few more discussions on the structured section of the gardens, he guided me back toward the house.

"Did you plan to replace some of the statues?" I asked.

He nodded. "Yes, I had such a thought. There are several fine statue suppliers near Winchester. I frequent one that does fine work."

I wondered why he frequented a statuary when he had not had a permanent home.

He continued, "Also, another day, when I am not preparing for guests, I'll show you the renovations I have planned for the interior of the house. The work will begin soon, and I hope that the changes will meet with your approval."

"I'm slightly concerned about those changes to the house," I said. "Perhaps they will be costly, and my financial situation has not yet been resolved, though I am confident that it will be, eventually. My father will have taken care to provide for Peter and for me."

He nodded. "The work I've commissioned thus far is not for aesthetic purposes," he said quietly. "Headbourne has gone unattended and unlived in for nearly two decades. The moldings are crumbling such that I fear large chunks of stone could fall on a passerby."

My eyes widened.

"The pipes sometimes send up rusted water."

I nodded. "I see."

"The chimneys need tending to so they do not stop up and cause anything to set fire."

I clearly saw the situation now. "Yes, I agree, Captain Whitfield. Please . . . proceed. And thank you."

He smiled. "I shall purchase the statues out of my own funds. The gardens, somehow, feel very personal to me."

I smiled back at him in heartfelt appreciation, put my hand on his arm again, and watched his face flush. I was happy to see I could have some effect on him as well. We walked back into the house.

"Captain Whitfield," I said as we looked toward the central stairway from the large front hall. There was a strong likeness of a commanding man, in uniform, a silver streak racing through the side of his dark hair. "Whenever did you have time to have your portrait painted?" I pointed to the large painting that was heavily framed and centered so that it was instantly noticeable. It was a mark of ownership, I thought, to display his self-portrait, and I hadn't sorted through what I thought of that.

He smiled wickedly. "Why, Miss Ravenshaw, that isn't me at all. It's the original owner of Headbourne House, Charles Whitfield Ravenshaw. I believe he would be our common ancestor, which confirms us as cousins, does it not? I have had it brought from storage and restored."

My blood drained. I had made a bungle and I responded too quickly, I knew, in an effort to recover. "Very, very distant cousins, one supposes, Captain Whitfield. However, the resemblance between the two of you is remarkable."

"Yes, yes, it is. There is no doubt at all about my relation to him, is there?" His implication was clear as he took my gloved hand in his own. The kiss he bestowed upon the back of my glove was cool formality, quickly withdrawn. "Until tomorrow evening."

I kept my poise and my smile till he withdrew, at which point I made my way to my room as quickly as possible, berating myself in harshest terms for being the Baroness of Blunder.

"What are you doing? Is the gown not clean?"

Michelene sighed, hovering around me with a damp cloth. She first sponged my face, and then my fine linen gown, at the bodice level. "It will cling a little more this way, just so, *n'est-ce pas?*" she said. "And it makes your skin look 'dewy.' Do you want Miss Dainley to have every advantage?"

"I am not in a competition with Miss Dainley."

"Then with whom are you in a competition?" she asked. Her voice took on a low note, replacing the jesting tone that usually undergirded her light banter.

I turned to look at her, subdued. "I don't know. The woman who claimed to be me? What am I competing for?"

"Ah, *chérie,* if you don't know that, you can never win." She raised her eyebrows but said nothing more before bustling back over to the armoire and fussing with the gowns. "These two dresses, I am sorry to say, I have made an error with." She pointed to one that was trimmed in a mustard-yellow ribbon. "You will look much too sallow in this when the time comes to leave the black behind. Sickly." She turned toward me. "Do you suffer from the malaria?"

I nodded. "We all do, and, in fact, I have wondered if I am having a recurrence. There is so much to do, the food is new . . . but still I feel peculiarly unwell."

"Are you sleeping?"

"Not much," I said. "I—I haven't slept well in quite some time, and I'm afraid it makes me more irritable than usual. Perhaps unsound . . ." I lingered and she looked alarmed. "Unsound in judgment from time to time," I finished.

"We shall think upon that, *non*? But now, back to the bustles, and the dresses. This one, and the lettuce dress, I am sorry, I think I chose unwisely. They do not flatter you. With your permission, I will order two new ones to replace them and they shall be ready by July."

I shrugged. I didn't see why we couldn't exchange them for ones that better complimented me. I had so little experience with these kinds of clothing that I wasn't sure I knew which flattered and which did not. I was concerned about the expense. But I was far from having an overbearing wardrobe yet, and if I was going to be in "competition," I certainly did not want to appear sallow or sickly. I must trust Michelene. I knew my mother had trusted her lady's maid, her ayah, in such matters when she'd been new to India, as I was newly returned to England. "Yes, indeed."

She clapped her hands. "*Bien.* I will order them, and what is needed to accompany them, next week." She turned me toward the looking-glass. "Now, I shall pluck your brows and place just a little bit of this"—she indicated a pot of gloss—"on your lips. And then you shall be ready to 'take the ridge.'"

I smiled at this. It was my home. She was right.

I could hear the piano being played. From the martial rhythm of the piece I knew Captain Whitfield was at the keys. With the exception of the one Beethoven tune with which he had graced me, all of the music I'd heard him play had been marches, all cheerful. A thought occurred—perhaps artificially cheerful? I recalled his sadness when speaking of his family. Wishing for the cover of crowd anonymity, I waited until the hum of guests had reached a swell before making my way downstairs.

Trays holding champagne and dainties were passed among the fifty or so guests. I wondered that there were no cakes, but perhaps they would be served later in the evening. Miss Dainley approached me, and after a few remarks of genteel conversation, pointed out a few of the less important guests, in her eyes, and then she introduced me to a few that she thought were of higher status than me. I could tell the difference by the tone of her voice. After a moment, she said, "Come with me."

She led me toward a man of about Captain Whitfield's age who stood at the center of a triangle of simpering women, each of them old enough to be his mother. Maybe one of them *was* his mother!

Miss Dainley waited until there was a break in the conversation and then introduced me. "Baron Lewis Ashby, may I present Miss Rebecca Ravenshaw."

Lord Ashby's face was smooth but for a spotty beard, his hair thinning and trimmed into a Roman style: short fringes atop a wide forehead. He took my hand and kissed it. "Miss Ravenshaw. We have all been looking forward to meeting you."

"In fact, we thought we already had," came a quiet voice from one of the three harpies; I turned but was not quick enough to see who'd said it.

I raised my chin and ignored it. "How do you do, Lord Ashby."

"I should very much like to hear about your recent experience in India," he said. Then he grew red and hastily added, "Before the Mutiny, of course."

I couldn't help but smile. If I were the Baroness of Blunder, here then was the Baron. His misstep put me at ease and I was thankful for it.

There was no trace of irony or sarcasm in his voice or on his earnest face. "I look forward to speaking with you about it." He offered his arm to me and led me to a set of seats near the edge of the music room and gestured for some champagne. We sat down and he began to talk of local properties, and horse breeding, which made me slightly uncomfortable during a first conversation with a gentleman. I responded in kind with some facts about the food in India and the weather, and answered his questions about how miraculous it was, indeed, to be able to wrap a long length of fabric into a sari.

"I suddenly feel a little dizzy," I said. "I think it may be the champagne. Perhaps I should walk outside for a while."

"The doctor is close by." Ashby pointed out a dignified man loitering near a table with several pretty young ladies. "Shall we ask him?" He motioned for the doctor to join us.

"No, please," I said. "I'm sure I'm fine. Just fatigue and . . ."

Too late. The doctor made his way over. "Hello, Ashby. And this lovely woman must be a guest of yours?"

Ashby shook his head. "No, indeed. This is the mistress of the house. May I present Miss Rebecca Ravenshaw? Miss Ravenshaw, Dr. Roger Floyd."

The doctor took a reflexive step back. "How curious." Beads of sweat lined his forehead like seed pearls. "A relative of the young woman who died here earlier this year?"

"Indeed no," I said. "I am the only Rebecca Ravenshaw. How do you do?" I held out my hand. "Perhaps you alone can shed some light on this confusing subject."

"Which is . . . ?" He drew his arms across his chest.

"The woman who was here, months ago, impersonating me. I'm most eager to learn who she was."

The doctor glanced across the room. I followed his gaze

until it met with Captain Whitfield's. They locked eyes for a moment and then Dr. Floyd took out a handkerchief. After blotting his forehead he said, "I'm afraid there is not much to share. The young woman arrived with an Indian maid. Some months later, she took her own life. I examined her, determined the cause of death, and signed the certificate. Captain Whitfield and the maids seemed to have the situation well in hand before I even arrived."

"The cause of death . . ." I started. But Dr. Floyd spoke up.

"That's all there is to share, Miss . . . Ravenshaw," he said. "Professional confidentiality. I'm sure you understand." He bowed curtly, closing off any further conversation, and made his way back to the young ladies whence he came.

Ashby looked at Whitfield, whose head was down, and then back to me. "More champagne, Miss Ravenshaw?"

"No, thank you, Baron, I cannot selfishly monopolize your conversation all evening; I shall take some cool air on the veranda."

"I shall look forward to speaking with you again soon, then," he replied.

I nodded with real affection, and after some moments on the veranda I heard a voice behind me.

"There's no telling what an impoverished baron looking for a wife will do to make headway with a pretty young heiress, is there, Miss Ravenshaw?"

I instantly tuned in to his voice. Had he come to see what the doctor had told me?

"Is that a confession, Captain Whitfield?"

He put his head back and laughed. "I do not, nor shall I ever, meet any of the aforesaid qualifications." He took a sip from his glass. "I'm sorry you won't be able to share in playing piano tonight," he said.

I noticed that, behind him, Miss Dainley glanced our way, moving forward, and trying, it seemed, to get his attention. "I've enjoyed *your* piano playing, though," I said. "Will we hear Beethoven as the night goes on? I do hope so."

He shook his head. "No. I am not certain what came over me when I played that for you. It was an extraordinary departure from my usual repertoire."

"I'm honored," I said. "And glad that such beauty was not denied voice."

He took a sip of his wine, then another. "Do you always speak so frankly, Miss Ravenshaw? So flatteringly?"

"Not always, Captain Whitfield. It seems I, too, have made an extraordinary departure from the typical," I said softly.

"Touché," he said, his eyes alight with fresh interest before he took a bow. Miss Dainley was nearly upon us now. "I must return to my guests."

I inclined my head and he moved on. I watched as he walked away. The doctor had definitely made eye contact with him, and a silent message had been sent and received. Did the doctor question Whitfield in the death of my imposter? Or was he passing Whitfield a message of some other kind? How had Whitfield, and the two maids, by whom he meant the Indian maid and Michelene, taken things in hand?

Shortly thereafter, the musical evening began. Within a few songs, Miss Dainley was cheerfully turning the pages for Captain Whitfield's rousing tunes, although I noted that a few other guests had shied away from him, ending conversations with him quickly, turning away from him and toward others if they appeared together in the party's small groupings, despite his seemingly friendly overtures and his position as host.

I made my way upstairs. I had an early start the next morning.

Mr. Highmore, the solicitor, was coming to call to bring me news from the London Missionary Society and to ask me to recount my experience.

Michelene had felt unwell earlier in the evening, so I told her I could prepare myself for bed that night. I made my way up the stairs, pausing to look down the corridor of the right wing before turning left to go to my own rooms. In contrast to the music and laughter below, the dark hallway pulsed with curious silence. The carpets were nearly invisible on the floor, the walls alongside the hallway seemed to tilt in strangely. I shook my head and blinked to clear my eyes. Far, far in the recess, eyes glowed.

Eyes glowed? I must be tired again.

No. They were there. For a moment it reminded me of the leopards of southern India, which hid in the grounds behind our house, waiting for a cow—or a child—to come along unattended. Fear rose in my throat and I swallowed its acidity.

The eyes blinked and I was brought back to the present. *Tiny eyes. The cat!* Why did she lie in front of that door all the time? Was she trying to draw me there? To tell me something? I felt so relieved. My mind was sound!

I made a kissing noise once, twice, and then the little cat scampered down the hall, mewled, and joined me. She'd never slept in my room, nor sought me in the evening, but that night she did and I could feel myself drifting into a deep sleep nearly the moment I slipped into bed. Was she the reason?

Perhaps—I delighted in the thought—it was instead the satisfaction of parrying in conversation with Captain Whitfield.

CHAPTER EIGHT

Mrs. Ross awaited me in the breakfast room next morning, lightly crunching a toasted crumpet smeared with gooseberry jelly and sipping a cup of tea, which Mrs. Blackwood continued to refill. "Guid morning, lassie. All set then, for your meeting today?"

"Thank you, dear Mrs. Ross, for remembering to be ready early today," I said. "Truthfully, I'm a bit nervous to meet them, and to speak of it again. Once I open the door it all comes tumbling back and there are some things I do not have answers for."

"'He shall direct thy paths,'" she quoted. "What do ye not yet have an answer for?"

I took a slice of toast from the sideboard and a cup of tea for myself. I sat down next to her. It had been attentive of the Lord to direct her to me, a kindly and wise woman, mature in her faith, someone I could understand and whom I felt comfortable putting questions to. After a moment, I spoke up, softly.

"Did He direct my mother and father's path northward, then, to coincide directly with the Rebellion?" *And send them to their brutal deaths*, I thought, but did not say it aloud.

"He did," she said quietly, but directly. "Or at least allowed it, unchecked."

It was like a kick to the stomach. "It is a hard truth." Pain constricted my throat. "Why now? There are so many, so many malingerers and loafers and those interested in naught but their own advancement. Why not one of them instead?"

She set down her crumpet. "I was nae aware that the Lord enlisted malingerers or loafers, nor the proud at heart as soldiers, lassie. To be on the field is to engage and to risk."

"Then perhaps I shall remain off the field." I could not afford this costly conversation just now, right before I was to meet the Missionary Society man. I set down my teacup.

She reached over and took my hand. "Doona be afraid to ask Him the hard questions. He oft poses them Himself."

I nodded my agreement and took a bite of toast before a small smile eased its way out as I envisioned Mrs. Ross in all her black girth, bonnet tight, engaged on a battlefield near kilted warriors. We made small talk about the musical soirée, which she said she had greatly enjoyed, and hoped I had, too. I told her I had because I wanted to cheer her as much as myself.

Landreth led us to the morning room, and shortly thereafter, Mr. Highmore arrived, joined, as he'd promised, by a fairly young representative from the London Missionary Society. He could certainly not have known my parents; he was little older than I. "Welcome, gentlemen." I tried to project confidence.

"Miss Ravenshaw, please allow me to present Mr. Giles, from the London Missionary Society."

I smiled toward young Mr. Giles. "How do you do, Mr. Giles? You were recently put in charge of arranging and overseeing support for the East Indies missionaries, is that right?"

Mr. Giles beamed. "Yes, that's right. I wish I had been able to correspond with your fine parents, but both time and postage are dear."

"Of course," I said. "Please, make yourselves comfortable." They sat down on nearby chairs and Highmore began.

"Mr. Giles wonders, well, as news has only filtered back indirectly, if you could affirm the situation as it unfolded in northern India," Mr. Highmore said. I did not know if he was asking me truly to inform those my father had corresponded with, or to prove my identity, but in either case, I did not mind.

"Please, spare yourself the uncomfortable details," Mr. Giles said.

"It's very simple," I said. "My parents and I set out from Travancore to travel northward to find a doctor for the mission. We had been without medical assistance, for the mission and for those we served, for some years, after Dr. Lawrence drowned."

Not only had Peter died for lack of medical attention, but dozens of Indian friends and converts, as well as the Hindu and Mohammedan villagers we sought to offer a cup of water to in the name of Christ. Father wanted care for all of them.

I drew myself back to the conversation. "My father made some inquiries, which were favorably received. We traveled north, but as you know, the timing could not have been worse."

Father should have insisted we stay home at home and he go alone! But Mother, well, she had been adamant, truth be told. And I had wanted to go, too.

"We arrived at Fatehgarh and then the troubles soon began, Indian soldiers rebelling against their English-led units, killing civilians, too. I was able to escape with another lady and the help of a native man who smuggled us out at grave risk to himself, through fighting and much difficulty, and in some cases, death."

Mother had said, "It cannot be so bad. But if it is, she must go, and quickly."

"It is so bad," Father replied. "Rebecca is leaving. You, too."

"No," she said. "You may, you must, send Rebecca away, but not me."

"More tea, miss?" Annie stood before me and I recalled again where I was.

"Yes, please," I answered before turning back to the men. "Ultimately, we ladies managed to reach the Residency and were given respite there with the others from Gwalior and other areas, whereupon we waited for assistance from England."

"We may have preserved our lives from gunshot or sword wound but now we shall die of disease!" a young woman named Miss Andrews cried out in madness only hours before she did, indeed, succumb to death.

Mr. Giles's voice brought me back to the present. "And you made safe passage?"

I drank the hot tea unfashionably fast, burning the middle of my tongue, so I could set the cup down. I did not want to draw attention to my trembling hand. "I left on one of the first ships out, and arrived here at Southampton with Mrs. MacAlister, a widow of the Rebellion."

"Your parents are . . ."

Mother embraced me, Father embraced me. Neither said that they loved me, nor did I tell them, for to do that would be to admit that this was, perhaps, the end. In any case, we knew where our affections truly lay, and that we would embrace again, if not here, then in the hereafter.

I choked a little and pinched my eyes together for a moment. "We learned that . . . after having been dispatched, they were sent with others to the bottom of a dry well."

At that, tears began to well up in Mr. Giles's eyes, too, and a great warmth emanated from the steadying hand of Mrs. Ross.

Afterward, Mr. Highmore spoke quietly to me. "Mr. Giles seems satisfied with the circumstances as you've relayed them, so, assuming the packet we sent along to India eventually comes back with affirmation, we can assume that you are who you claim to be." He looked puzzled. "Though I am quite at a loss as to who the first Miss Ravenshaw actually was, if your claim indeed proves true. And quite angry that she deceived me."

"She seems to have deceived everyone," I assured him. "Apparently a wicked drifter of some kind, as she has had no family to inquire after her. No morals, nor concern for my family, my home, myself, nor for any of you. It doesn't really matter to me who she was."

I wanted to know who she was, I did. But, for my own sanity, I refused to become obsessed with her. Obsession seemed too ready to answer any small encouragement I might offer it upon any topic.

"Indeed." Highmore went on, further lowering his voice. "There is some small concern over the amount remaining of your father's funds and investments. As you may have known, your father did not take support from the society, but funded his way with his own money and investments, wanting to save the support fully for those who had no other means."

I caught my breath. I had not known that. This could cause a predicament for me. Why hadn't father loved me enough to ensure I would be well taken care of if something happened to him—which, in fact, it had? It was in his nature to refuse money that might be used for missions. "What does this mean?" I asked. "For me, now?"

He put his hand over mine. "Fret not. I shall investigate and ascertain round and true sums for you, though it may take some months. I do not know how much he had invested elsewhere because, as I mentioned earlier, I have recently taken over from my own father. There are the expenses that have already been undertaken on Headbourne House, and of course, some monies have already been transferred to Captain Whitfield, who remains, for now, legal heir."

I nodded.

"Continue to have the bills sent to me, but perhaps review them first. All will be well, I am certain that this will end well." He cleared his throat, an action that belied his words. "Yet it may take some time to conclude."

Yes, the house and funds would soon be mine, would remain mine alone, and then I would be settled, secure, and safe for once. For always. "Thank you, Mr. Highmore, I am indebted to you."

"Did you have some letters you would like me to post along with the other correspondence?" he asked.

"Oh, yes." I walked to the bureau in the drawing room, but the small pile of letters I had painstakingly written to our friends had disappeared. I looked all through the bureau but could not find them. Where could they have gone? I was certain I had not moved them. Was it possible that I'd done something with them that I did not recall? I searched my memory but recalled nothing.

"Mrs. Blackwood?" I called out. She did not respond so I rang the bell, and she shortly arrived.

"Yes, miss?"

"Did you happen to notice what happened to the letters I left here?"

She shook her head. "No, Miss Ravenshaw. We shall ask around." She left and returned within five minutes. "We inquired of the maids, and anyone else who might have been in the room, and none remembers seeing them. In fact, Annie said when she dusted the bureau she wiped down the pen but there were no letters there."

"No, no," I said, searching my memory. "I believe that you were with me in the room whilst I sealed them." I wondered if I had written them another day and was, indeed, losing my rationality or at least my memory of this, and perhaps other, events.

"And yet," she retorted, "they are not here."

"Yes, you are correct." I sighed before turning away. Had she cause to steal them? What cause would that be? None that I could see. Perhaps someone else had entered the room after I'd left. I did not believe there was anyone who could profit, though, by my personal correspondence.

I returned to Mr. Highmore. "I'm disappointed, but the letters have disappeared. I'm afraid I'll have to forgo sending them for now."

Mr. Giles had not yet put on his hat, and indicated that he wished to have another word with me.

"Miss Ravenshaw," he began. "I do hope you won't think this inappropriate, but I wondered, have you had a chance to avail yourself of the Methodist church in Winchester?"

"I admit I haven't," I said. "I've just now begun to recover my strength, but I intend to very soon, as soon as transport can be arranged to the Methodist church."

"My dear, if not the Methodist church, begin to attend somewhere. Do not delay—for your own soul's sake. Perhaps, too, you shall find someone who knew your parents?" Was he looking out for my soul or looking for another way to prove or disprove my identity?

"Thank you, Mr. Giles." No matter his motives, he was right.

After Landreth had shown the men out I turned down the short hallway away from the stairs and put my hand on the knob of the door to a room I hadn't had more than a glance into during Mrs. Blackwood's tour. My father's library.

I pushed open the door slowly; the room was not as grand as many of the others in the house, but it was very personal. Perhaps this accounted for the reason I hadn't visited it before. I knew I'd "find" my father here.

I sat down at the desk in the corner and looked at the shelves. There were perhaps two hundred books in the room, some very old indeed and some, on the lower shelves, which appeared to be more current. The room smelt of leather and dust and I could see wear in the wood of the desk where my father's hand would have rested. I knew that the shelf I sought would be close at hand, and turned in the chair to the one just behind the desk. Yes, they were there. The Bibles.

There were several that they had left behind, and I pulled one at random to take with me to my room. I opened it, saw Father's handwriting inside, notes placed here and there. I closed the book and stood up, and as I did, I caught sight of another book very close to his desk. *Paradise Lost*, by John Milton. I took it in a trembling hand then held it close to my chest, with the Bible, on my way to my rooms.

Yes, Mr. Milton. I do very much feel like paradise has been lost.

CHAPTER NINE

A few days later I walked through the front door and down the long flight of steps, passed between the two stone lions, and began making my way across the path to the stable yard where Whitfield could often be found. Several boys worked the long, hay-strewn aisle which ran between the standing stalls. It smelt sour, of sweat—horse and man—and dry, green grass.

"Is the captain here?" I asked one of the young men. He stared at me. "I'm Miss Ravenshaw."

"So you say, miss," he answered. I steeled my face so it didn't show the frustration simmering within me. He skipped away and called out for Daniel, but Daniel did not appear, Captain Whitfield did instead. He approached, wearing his straight riding breeches and long boots, and had on another of his fine, thin, linen shirts, which had begun to cling to him in the day's heat.

He caught me looking him over and I blushed.

"Have you come to examine the horseflesh then?"

I let the baton lie where he'd thrown it. He'd caught me. There was no ladylike way to respond, so I attempted to steer the conversation in another direction.

"Good afternoon, Captain Whitfield," I said. "I've come to ask Daniel, and you as his employer, for some assistance. I should like to begin attending church. Mrs. Ross, of course, attends the kirk and some of its members come to collect her. I'm guessing that you and most of the household must travel to the village church in your carriage." Of course, there would have been no Ravenshaw carriages left unsold after my parents departed for India, nothing left of the estate but overwrought gardens, the crumbling house being devoured by brambles, and its neglected furniture within. I should have to buy a small carriage of my own when the estate was settled, for shopping, visiting, charity, and church.

I stopped and thought for a moment, anew, about church.

"Are services ever held here, on the grounds, at the chapel?"

He shook his head. "No. The chapel, too, has fallen into disrepair, on the inside, anyway, so it would not be fit for services in any case. I have secured the outside a bit. Cleaned up around the graves."

I shivered.

He drew near me. "You look wan. Do you suffer from malaria?"

I nodded. "I do. There was not much quinine at the Residency whilst we waited to be brought to England. I should, perhaps, ask the doctor for some."

"I, too, contracted malaria, whilst serving in the Crimea. Don't bother with the doctor. I've found Dr. Warburg's Tincture to be effective and regularly visit the military hospital in Southampton to acquire it," he said. "I'm happy to purchase a few bottles for you next time I'm there, if you'd like me to."

"I'm not aware of Dr. Warburg's Tincture, but if it will help me regain my health, then, yes, please do, and thank you very much."

"I find I am often away on Sundays and frequently miss attending church," he continued. "When I returned to England, I purchased a carriage, of course." He waved his hand toward it. "And my second carriage shall be delivered shortly. Then you will have the means to be able to attend the Methodist church if you like. I'll see that it's readied with all speed."

"Thank you," I replied. "That is very kind of you indeed. If there is any way to repay you . . ."

Daniel walked a horse by us then, jarring me from my reverie, and Whitfield spoke up. "No repayment is necessary but, well, would you like to see my horses?"

His voice sounded so boyish and earnest, and when I looked at him he looked as though he might be almost pleading and I found that I could not say no. Although I could barely contain my fear whilst near horses, the desire to remain in his company overcame my reluctance. "I would be delighted."

He took my hand in his own, then placed it in the crook of his arm, a most welcome gesture, and I allowed my hand to melt into his arm. He looked at me and smiled.

"I have the carriage horses, of course." He indicated six or so that were standing in the stalls closest to the coach house. Farther along we came to a number of large loose boxes, and he introduced me to some of his favorites.

"The gray mare was the favorite of a friend of mine, who's since posted to India with the cavalry," he said. The gray, along with most of the other horses, had come toward the front of their boxes, anxious to see the new person—me, I supposed.

"Is your friend a Hussar like yourself?" I asked.

"Yes," he said. "Our horses mean more to us than any person, and he trusted me to keep his girl safe for him in his absence. We who serve together in the military are deeply loyal to one another even once home," he said. "It's my pleasure to care for her."

He next pointed out a bay. "Mild-mannered, cannon-proof."

I recoiled. "You mean you'd shoot a cannon toward her?"

He laughed. "No, my dear Miss Ravenshaw. It means that if a cannon went off next to her, she'd likely not flinch. And this one"—he pointed to a large black mare, spirited, prancing—"is Notos."

"For the Greek god of the summer rainstorms," I said. "Is she stormy?"

His eyebrows rose. "Indeed she is. I am impressed you knew the history of her name."

"I am not completely bereft of an education, Captain Whitfield. In fact, my mother made sure I was well educated. Just not in the gentle arts of botany." I smiled wryly.

"I meant no offense, Miss Ravenshaw. You surprise me anew each time we speak."

Oh dear. I had come across like a defensive schoolgirl. What was it about this man that made me act so out of sorts? I was honest enough with myself to recognize that the image of him striding toward me in a slightly disarrayed linen shirt may have influenced me. In fact, in my mind the picture persisted.

I decided to make amends by offering a compliment to the thing he most loved. He brought us closer to Notos. The horse had beautiful silver threads plaited into her mane. "She is splendid and spirited. In some ways"—I pointed to the silver streaks against the black, which mirrored his hair—"she's very like you."

His ears pinked. "I'm pleased that you noticed. How very poetic."

"Thank you, Captain Whitfield." My slightly forward compliment had been, perhaps, even more bold than the fan tap in the garden. He recognized that, too.

He drew near and in a low voice said, "You're welcome to come closer if you like." To the man or to the horse?

Perhaps I should like to draw nearer to the one, but not to the other. "No," I said quickly to regain control. And then, "I was in an accident in India, at the end, involving a horse that fell with me upon her," I said. "I survived, though my foot was crushed. The horse did not survive, nor did the cavalryman next to us. I haven't ridden since."

"Ah . . . this is why you no longer ride. The cause of your slight limp?" he asked.

I nodded; he'd noticed. "You'd chided me once, remember . . . 'No riding, no piano playing.'"

He nodded. "Yes, I recall. And now I know the reason. Speaking of piano playing, did you enjoy the music at the soirée?" He turned away from Notos to escort me back past the standing stalls toward the coach house.

"I did."

"You hesitate," he said.

I nodded. "Everyone was perfectly lovely . . ."

"Even Lord Ashby?" he teased.

"*Especially* Lord Ashby." I kept my face straight and was rewarded with a troubled look upon his own.

"But . . ."

"I miss having people around me that I know. I have no mother, no father, no siblings, and my friends are far, far away. I feel alone." I wondered that I allowed myself to be so open with him, speaking, again, frankly to him though I'd told him it had been but a departure from the norm, for me. Perhaps the answer was in what I had just stated. I was lonely.

He responded with an admission of his own. "At Sandhurst, Miss Ravenshaw, the other cadets would return to their country estates, but Lord Ledbury felt that I was an unwelcome intrusion in his home. A distraction from his own son, Lord Frome, or perhaps a reminder that my mother had loved another first, before him. Until I became a Hussar, although often in the company of many, I most always felt alone." We reached the end of the stables and as we did he took my hand from his arm.

"Thank you for sharing that with me, Captain Whitfield. It blunts my pain."

"You're welcome, Miss Ravenshaw. So you can see how very important Headbourne is to me. It's no other man's home, no other man's family home. But it is my family home."

"Mine, too," I said.

He said nothing, for a moment. Then, "I've arranged for you to see someone whose company you may very well enjoy," he said.

I stopped. "Whoever could it be?" I saw delight on his face.

"Now, Miss Ravenshaw, you don't want to deny a man a surprise, do you?"

"Why, yes, actually, I do," I teased.

He grinned. "I've asked him to dine with us next week."

Ah, so it was a man who was coming to call. I'd wondered, as he'd mentioned that he'd often kept the company of many, how often that number had included the fairer sex. A prickle of envy arose, somehow.

"I shall look forward to it," I said. He bade me good day with a wide smile and took his leave.

I should have immediately walked back to the house, but I did not. *Come along*, I cajoled myself. *The horses are safe. I'll just visit the gentle bay.*

I walked back through the archway, past the standing stalls toward the loose boxes. I stopped before the bay's box and leaned in and called to her. "Here. Come, little one." Now that Whitfield was no longer with me, she seemed uninterested and did not turn around.

I had to overcome this fear somehow. I could not avoid horses for the rest of my life. I slid open the bolt to her gate and walked in, sliding the bolt shut again behind me. She backed up as I moved forward, but did not turn around. I took another step forward, close to the manger where she ate. She must have caught sight of me out of the corner of her eye, as she pivoted round and whinnied a shrill warning.

I'd scared her. She scared me! I decided that was enough for the day, cannon-proof or not. My heart pounded unmercifully, unrelentingly, in my chest.

I began to back up and, keeping my eye on the horse, reached over the gate, feeling for the bolt. Where was it? The bay stepped closer to me and tossed her head. There it was. I slid the bolt open to unlock the box but the gate would not swing open. I was stuck!

I kicked and shoved against the gate, twisting my ankle. The bay begin to rear noisily. She was clearly unused to anyone other than the grooms being in the box with her and sensed my anxiety. My heart pounded and I felt ill.

"Hello? Hello, Daniel? Anyone?" I called out. No one answered.

The horse was becoming more agitated and whinnied louder and came closer to me. I could barely breathe and dared not turn around and take my eyes off her. A memory of the cry of the soldier when his horse fell rang in my ears, and my ankle throbbed.

I finally turned around, and when I did I saw that someone, somehow, had braced a small crate filled with tack and other heavy items against the gate, blocking me from opening it. I pushed with all my might, slid through a small space, thanking God that I had decided to forgo huge hoops, and clanged the gate shut behind me.

The bay made her way back to her trough. I closed my eyes, caught my breath, and then looked down at that crate.

It was heavy and had been pushed there with a purpose. Why would anyone lock me in with the horse? Whitfield had been the only person I had mentioned my fear to. Would he have done this? I couldn't believe it.

But if it was not he, who?

After catching my breath I walked back down the stables, into the coach house, looking up and down for someone, anyone. Everyone had simply, unbelievably, vanished. I wiped my cheeks with a trembling hand, the leather gloves scattering rather than absorbing the tears, and hobbled back to the house.

Later that week I was still mulling over the event, though I had not mentioned it to anyone for fear of what they would think of me for suggesting sabotage. I myself wasn't certain if what I'd *thought* had happened had *actually* happened, and that concerned me. Could I have imagined it? Was the crate there all along? I sat at the bureau to rewrite the letters I had already written but lost, wondering if Mrs. Blackwood could have taken them after all. And if she had, to what purpose? Later, I asked Michelene if it was possible.

"Perhaps she did," she'd answered. "After all, if you prove to be Rebecca Ravenshaw, *vraiment*, then she will have to leave this grand house, and I am certain she enjoys serving here."

That was true. "But would she lie?"

"She is in the employ of Captain Whitfield, *non*? His interests are her interests. And she was quite taken with Mademoiselle Ravenshaw. I mean, the young woman who arrived first. All were. I was here then, and I hear them talk now. They don't like to think of you taking advantage of a young dead woman. Or perhaps," she delicately suggested, "you placed the letters somewhere on your own, and you've forgotten where that is."

"Absolutely not," I said.

She shrugged, unconvinced. "Did you ask the other servants?"

"I asked Landreth, who asked me in return if I'd made a query with Mrs. Blackwood. When I told him I did, he considered the matter settled and suggested it would not do for me to press beyond her inquiries. None of the staff, he was certain, would offer her a mistruth."

"His confidence is charming," Michelene said as she continued to arrange my hairpins.

I had at least one true friend at Headbourne, though I hadn't seen her for a day or two. A few minutes later, I inquired, "Have you seen the cat?"

She shivered with abhorrence. "*Mais non*. Ask the cook. They seem quite the pair."

So I decided to visit Cook, with whom I hardly ever spoke. I had noticed, once, when I was strolling through the gardens, that she had set a dish of milk out back, near the tradesmen's entrance. I, too, had suspected she had a soft spot for Kitty. I went to the morning room and rang for her. A few minutes later she came up, and I asked her to shut the door behind her.

"How can I be of service, miss?" She rubbed her hands together against her apron, hastily replaced, I suspected from the uneven tie, after hearing my call.

"I wanted to thank you for the extra work involved in providing meals for Mrs. Ross, Mademoiselle d'Arbonneau, and myself."

She fanned her red face a bit. "It's my job, and I'll do it well." There was no softening in her in response to my expression of gratitude.

"Having no family here, I've grown rather fond of the little housecat," I said. "Have you seen her?"

"Ah, Marie," she said.

"Marie?"

"I doona know what that Miss Ravenshaw called her, it were some Indian name. But when she . . . passed on . . . I decided to call the cat Marie. After the Blessed Holy Mother, but the French name for it, to irritate, er, the lady's maid. It seemed better than some heathen name," she said. "I wanted to take care of her pet. She were sweet, that Miss Ravenshaw. We all liked her."

I held my irritation back at the last comment. "Marie is a lovely name. Have you seen her?"

She shook her head. "No. She used to sleep in front of *her* bedroom door. And sometimes"—she lowered her voice—"I've seen her walk out toward the graves, where *she* sleeps now."

"The cat goes out to the graveyard?"

She nodded. "Will that be all, miss?"

I smiled. "Yes, for now."

She took a few steps, and then, before opening the door, she turned back and said, "It were a real shame he buried her at midnight, alone but for the two hired men, paid very well indeed, I heard. In the dark wet and all that. The ground was frozen, of course, but he didn't let that stop him. He was in a hurry."

"Midnight?" I stood up. "Why then?"

"It was his way of insisting everyone believe it was self-murder," she said. "Suicides must be buried without service, and at night."

"His insisting?" I asked. "Do you mean Captain Whitfield?"

She wouldn't name him. "All I say is that I'm a local girl, and my loyalty is not to him, but to my own self and those that I choose to give it to. I'll never believe she took her own life. Never."

I had become aware of hints that there was a possibility Whitfield had been involved with her death. But he was so charming, and in some way I grew more drawn to him each day.

Charm is deceitful, Scripture says.

I recalled the woman in Mr. Highmore's office saying that it *was said* that she'd died of self-murder. Not that, in the opinion of all, she'd implied. Whitfield was deeply attached to the house. He'd made that clear to me at the gardens and at the stables.

Perhaps he had locked me in the stall to scare me. To further destabilize me. The only person I had mentioned my instability to, in passing, had been Michelene. Had she told the captain? Were they somehow working together? I shook my head. If I should share these weak conjectures with anyone else, they would believe them to be mad imaginings, perhaps with warrant.

It had taken courage for Cook to speak up at all, so it must have been important to her. I thought I'd press on a little for more details. "In your opinion, was Captain Whitfield . . . close to the woman here earlier who'd claimed to be me?" I asked her. It was clear she refused to refer to the imposter by any other name.

She shrugged. "I'm sure I don't know, miss, I am not abovestairs often. But she talked of him, yes she did, when she came to fetch milk for the cat. And then after a few months, she did not." She pulled her cap down and lowered her voice. "He's keen on this house, isn't he? Perhaps he wanted bed and board and she turned him down. It's not for me to say, now, is it?"

That night, I took my dinner in my rooms, as usual. There were three courses, two of which were very rich, served on a garish red platter that I knew my mother would never have allowed to be used. It must have been a recent purchase.

That night, I told Michelene that I was having trouble sleeping and that I had aches again, probably a recurrence of malaria.

"Captain Whitfield said he would purchase some tincture for me," I said.

"Ah, that is good," she cooed. "And perhaps a little laudanum to help you sleep? Sleep makes all things right. It clears the mind for the next day, restores the body, allows one to eat." She glanced at the red dish of uneaten food.

My mother had given me laudanum as a girl, but only small doses and when it was truly called for, as our first mission doctor was not enthusiastic about it. He had seen opium misused in China, and indeed, it was banned there still. But I was weary and in pain.

"It will also help whiten your skin," she tempted. "Just the smallest amount."

I agreed. I needed sleep. Deep sleep, I knew, warded off nightmares.

She brought a small dose and left; a sleepy well-being coursed through me. The scratching of the ivy against the house didn't trouble me as it normally did. I still felt chilled, though, so I got up to close my curtains. There was just a sliver of moon in the sky, not enough to light a path and, as usual, the mists rose from the warm ground into the cool night air. Normally they obscured everything but tonight, the wind also blew, and so it swirled the mist like smoke, here murky, there clear.

I looked toward the guesthouse; it was dark and the curtains were pulled shut. Beyond it, well beyond it, I could make out the silhouette of the chapel and then two eyes glowing.

I shook my head to clear it and a shiver inched its way up my spine. *Who or what could it be? The cat, Marie? Was I imagining things now, as an effect of the laudanum?* The graves were much too far off for me to see the tiny eyes of Marie in the dark.

Perhaps, after all, the crate had always been in front of the stall's door. But how could it have been? I would not have been able to get in so easily then, would I?

Perhaps someone had tried to lock me in. Perhaps I really had misplaced the letters myself and cannot remember.

I took the Bible from the top of my bureau, pulled the curtains tight, and hastily returned to my bed, unwilling to think that, perhaps, reason truly had fled.

CHAPTER TEN

A few days later Mrs. Blackwood alerted me that a guest was coming to stay with Captain Whitfield, and would I please join them for dinner? I agreed. It must have been the person he'd mentioned in the stables. Perhaps it was someone local who knew my mother or my father. But why was Captain Whitfield eager that I should meet him?

Michelene did my hair in a lovely upsweep anchored by jet pins. I turned and looked at myself in the mirror. It was just right. I didn't look like anyone's governess, but I also did not look as though I should be rooming at the Swan.

"Very nice," I said. "Michelene, I'd like some cologne. Could we perhaps find me some scent that is a little less English rose and a little more reminiscent of India? Something warm and spicy?"

"*Oui*," she said. "I will order some when I order your riding habits."

"Riding habits? I don't ride."

"Every English lady rides." She snorted in a way that reminded me of the beasts themselves. "Are you an English lady or not?"

"Of course I am."

I went downstairs, but the gentlemen had not yet arrived. Not wanting to seem overeager, I sat at the bureau in the drawing room and took pen in hand for a fresh batch of letters. I had not yet received any in return—perhaps the post was still difficult coming from India.

Within a quarter of an hour, Landreth came to announce that the men had arrived and dinner would be served.

Their eyes were upon me as I set down my pen and walked to greet them. Captain Whitfield looked at the pen for just a moment longer than I would expect before looking at me. Was he wondering to whom I wrote? Perhaps he'd had some involvement with the loss of my other letters. Or perhaps I was letting it all un-settle me and suspecting everyone and anyone of everything and anything! In spite of my qualms, my heart quickened when he held my gaze.

"Miss Ravenshaw," he said, "how very lovely you look, as always. Lieutenant William Dunn, may I present Miss Rebecca Ravenshaw? Miss Ravenshaw, Lieutenant William Dunn."

Lt. Dunn looked to be just a few years older than me, perhaps twenty-six or twenty-seven years of age. Dunn's blond hair was rather closely cut for fashion and he had a neat beard; we had always kept current of fashions, in India, by way of secondhand ladies' magazines, which were craved and pored over. Penelope had never been keen for men with blond hair, whilst Violet had, though she did not prefer beards. I'd always preferred men with dark hair and beards.

Men like Whitfield.

I looked up and caught his eye and he winked. I quickly looked away. Dunn had wide, welcoming blue eyes and a ready smile even if I sensed a slight reserve. His eyes did not leave me.

"How do you do?" I held out my hand and he brushed his lips lightly against the back of it.

"How do you do, Miss Ravenshaw?"

Captain Whitfield led the four of us into the dining room. He seemed a bit taken aback when Lt. Dunn quickly made his way to hold out my chair, leaving Captain Whitfield to seat Mrs. Ross.

The soup was served and Lt. Dunn said, "I understand you have recently returned from India?"

"I've been back in England since the end of April," I replied, setting down my soup spoon after a sip or two, as Michelene had instructed me. "About two months."

"Tell me . . . what do you most miss about India?"

I closed my eyes for a moment. "Well, the people, firstly. I miss my parents and my brother, Peter."

A look flashed between Captain Whitfield and Lt. Dunn, for the briefest of moments, but neither had completely turned his face from me, so I continued.

"I miss the Indian people, who are warm and welcoming. Truthfully, I have not yet accustomed myself to seeing so many fair faces and not as many brown."

"Understandable," Captain Whitfield said.

"I miss speaking the languages common to the area we lived in," I said. "Mainly Tamil and Malayalam."

Captain Whitfield coughed and then recovered himself, indicating with his hands that I should continue.

"But, as it is June, I will tell you what I am missing now. I miss the rains. The rains start first in Kerala, near to where we lived, and move northward in great gray clouds, like flocks of birds. Before the rains arrive, the ground is dry and compact, like ground spices pressed together. The air is parched, and then suddenly you can smell the rain upon it. When the water hits the ground, the pent-up scent is released, perfuming the air with the smell of vibrant earth. People come out from their homes and huts, greeting one another, laughing. Minor quibbles amongst friends and neighbors are forgotten, stories are shared, smiles given. Life is celebrated again."

Although courses continued to be served, Lt. Dunn and Captain Whitfield had set down their forks and were no longer eating, and Landreth and the footman serving were listening to me rather than refilling glasses or replacing plates.

"Do go on, Miss Ravenshaw," Lt. Dunn urged.

"Then the peacocks begin to dance."

"Dance?"

"Oh yes," I said. "There are only two times when the peacocks dance: when the rains are about to arrive, and when they are seeking a mate. Their bright blue bodies shimmer on thin legs, green-and blue-eyed plumage carefully arrayed. In seeking a mate, the peacock wants to show himself to best advantage because that's what attracts." Mrs. Ross pursed her lips slightly and shook her head just a little. I tipped my head slightly while the flush of pink disappeared.

"Peahens, then, are little different from the fairer sex of our own species," Captain Whitfield said quietly to Lt. Dunn, while my head was down. "I entreat you. Show me a woman who does not marry only after display of title or money. You'll not be able to. She doesn't exist."

"But then, men marry for money, and for property," Dunn replied. "You yourself said—"

I put my head up, and Dunn stopped speaking, abruptly.

By then my face was flushing again for another reason. "You certainly didn't mean to compare women to peahens, did you, Captain Whitfield?"

"Perhaps my intentions were not well stated," he said.

"I see," I said with a gentle smile. "Then you can hardly blame us, can you? Perhaps you can show me a man who does not display his wealth and status to attract us."

I caught a glimmer in his eye, but he caught his smile just before it spread across his face. I ducked to hide my own as the conversation drifted back to polite chatter.

Soon the meat course was served and we chatted about Lt. Dunn's future departure. "I'm afraid I've kept a bit of a secret from you," he said to me.

Ah, yes. The surprise.

"I'm the son of missionaries who served in the West Indies."

"How delightful!" He regaled me with a story or two of his life with his sisters, who used to like to dress him in their clothes, and more somber tales of the hardship of the lives of those his family had served for decades. The meal was quickly coming to an end, so I said, "I hope I shall hear some of your stories another time. Will you be staying on for Captain Whitfield's dance next week?"

He nodded. "I shall. Whitfield has extended the invitation and I've accepted."

I looked at Captain Whitfield and grinned. It would be lovely to talk to another missionary. What a splendid gift to me, his arranging this! A handful of others might judge him wrongly, but I was beginning to believe I was judging him, and his goodness, correctly.

"And," Lt. Dunn seemed slightly uncomfortable, "I have met your brother, Peter. We were at Eltham together for a short period of time, he being older than me."

"Oh," I said. My heart lurched. I should so like to talk with someone who knew my brother. "Did you know him well?"

"No," he said. "But there were not so many of us that we didn't each have a passing acquaintance with one another."

I tried to hide my disappointment. "I shall very much look forward to being regaled by your West Indies adventure, and learning what the Lord has wrought through your ministries. I've not yet met anyone here who knew my family. Even a passing acquaintance is a blessing."

"No one?" Dunn asked. "Not even at church?"

"My carriages have just been made ready so that Miss Raven-shaw will be able to begin to attend the Methodist church," Captain Whitfield said.

I smiled. "This is good to hear."

Landreth cleared the meat course and presently brought in bowls of fruit, heralding the end of the meal. That day it was fresh strawberries in a pool of cream.

I put one in my mouth and let the tart and sweet explode. "I have always loved strawberries."

"Your brother did, too, as I recall," Lt. Dunn said in a low voice.

"Not at all," I corrected. "You must have him confused with someone else. Peter had a hypersensitivity to strawberries. He'd come out in a rash almost immediately upon eating one. Mother never served them. Perhaps that's why they are so dear to me."

"Mummy, please. Everyone loves strawberry trifle. Surely I've outgrown it and can eat it whilst in England."

I watched them speak to one another, spooning pudding into my own mouth.

"No, I'm sorry," Mother said. "But here is a pudding I've made you with molasses and spice. I'll give you the larger portion. You can eat other trifles at school, too."

"Well, all right then."

"*Promise me you won't eat strawberries when you've returned to England. Please.*"

"*Very well, Mama,*" he said.

"*I shan't like to think of you being ill whilst I'm not there to tend to you,*" she said softly, already mourning his looming journey home.

"Miss Ravenshaw?" Lt. Dunn called me back to the present.

"Yes, yes," I said.

"I said that I must have mistaken him with another," Lt. Dunn said, not meeting my gaze. I glanced at Captain Whitfield, busily examining his strawberries. I knew it was to avoid my eyes. I saw it, now. The first trap had been laid, but I'd neatly sidestepped it. *You've tipped your hand, Captain Whitfield. I'll be more circumspect henceforth.*

In bed that night, I could not sleep, or would not sleep, or feared to sleep, or perhaps all three. I put the lamp on the bedside table to keep the shadows at bay, and took Milton in hand, propped up against the pillows.

I leafed through the pages carefully, reading some, skimming others, and found a place that Father's hand had marked.

Satan, involved in rising mist; then sought
Where to lie hid; sea he had searched, and land,
From Eden over Pontus and the pool
Maeotis, up beyond the river Ob;
Downward as far Antarctic; and in length,
West from Orontes to the ocean barred
At Darien; thence to the land where flows
Ganges and Indus: Thus the orb he roamed
With narrow search; and with inspection deep
Considered every creature, which of all

Most opportune might serve his wiles; and found
The Serpent subtlest beast of all the field.

I closed the book and blew out the lamp. *Why had Father marked this passage?* I climbed out of bed and made my way to the window. Because of the mists, perhaps, which did rise from our grounds almost nightly, obscuring clear vision? I should not like to walk in the dark in that mist, though I did so, now, metaphorically. Indeed, I could well believe that Satan lay hidden there. Here. Waiting to see whom he could impress upon, or discourage enough, to serve his wiles.

Perhaps it was the mention of the Indus River that had brought him to this chapter, knowing India lay before them. It had been Eden, in a way. Paradise, till it had been lost.

Till it had been *stolen*, by the serpent, the subtlest beast of all the field.

I returned to my bed but was unable to sleep. I thought of the laudanum. *It will help me to rest. Ring for Michelene.* At the last, I refused to, but when those I'd loved and then lost came, in midnight dreams, and I awoke drenched in sweat and sorrow, I wished I had asked Michelene to leave the small bottle for me.

CHAPTER ELEVEN

That Wednesday Lt. Dunn sent a note asking if I would be available to walk in the gardens. I penned a quick reply and he arrived at half past two.

"I'm delighted the weather has accommodated our stroll," he said. He was an attractive man with a military bearing and he looked fine in his uniform. He'd either arrived with his own valet or had taken advantage of Captain Whitfield's valet, Thornton, because the uniform was impeccably brushed and pressed. We strolled round the green whilst Mrs. Ross sat on a bench, watching carefully, as she always did.

"Do tell me about your service in the West Indies."

He regaled me with stories, some funny and some poignant, and discussed how life in the West Indies was now very different than it had been in his father's youth, as slavery was long ended. "That's how Whitfield and I began our friendship," he said. "Over that issue. And I'd like to hear more of your mission work in India, before this"—he swept a hand toward the house—"all became yours."

I nodded. "I would have preferred it be Peter's," I said quietly.

He squeezed my hand lightly in sympathy. "I'm sorry for the loss of your family."

"I, too." Then, aware that it was impolite to remain melancholic, I continued. "It's all mine, as you say, once the mission in India replies to Mr. Highmore verifying my identity. There was another woman here earlier, claiming to be me, and of course all believed her, why shouldn't they? She passed away just before Christmas."

"Yes, I know," he said. "I was to have visited Whitfield then, but with the death, well, that was not a time for entertaining."

"Knowing the sacrifices that others make to serve, I feel like I don't deserve all this," I said. "Because I know you have been in the mission field, too, serving those who have so very little . . ."

"You mean the house?" he asked.

I nodded. "With so many in India having given up all . . ."

"It may be God's intended blessing, Miss Ravenshaw. All of us knew the risks when we took to missions." A mischievous look crept across his face. "The book of Numbers says, 'If a man dies and leaves no son, give his inheritance to his daughter.' That would be you."

"'If he has no daughter, give his inheritance to his brothers. If he has no brothers, give his inheritance to his father's brothers. If his father had no brothers, give his inheritance to the nearest relative in his clan, that he may possess it.' That would be Captain Whitfield, of course."

He took my hand from his arm and clapped. "Bravo, Miss Ravenshaw. I knew you'd know that passage."

I smiled. "What are your plans, Lieutenant Dunn? Will you return to the West Indies? Remain in the military service? Or stay here in England?"

"My commission is nearly up, and then I plan to minister in

China," he said. His eyes gleamed with excitement, what my mother used to say was Calling Fever. *It will temper with time to keep you warm or it will burn hot and then out within a few years,* she'd said. "The fields are white, Miss Ravenshaw. And having been a part of the harvest of souls yourself, you do understand!"

"I do," I said. "I know very little of the Far East, but I should love to know more."

He turned and looked at me, somber and, perhaps, a little more fondly than he'd looked at me before. "I'm certain you'd be a fountain of knowledge on the particulars of China in no time at all."

I dipped my head down for a moment. Had he meant . . . ? Perhaps. I gently turned the conversation. "It took me twenty years to figure out the particulars of India, and now I've yet to completely sort through England, not having had the advantage Peter had of returning home for school. I shouldn't want you to test my knowledge, though, in any case, as with the berries."

He smiled, but seemed lightly subdued.

"Do you mind if I ask . . . how did you know that Peter was unable to eat strawberries?"

"The answer ties back into the very schooling you've mentioned. He was the only one there who had to forgo pudding when strawberry trifle was served." He smiled. "Boys at Eltham live for pudding."

Dearest Peter. He'd obeyed Mother as he'd said he would. My chest hurt and I pushed away the thought of him till I could consider it more tenderly, in private.

"I'm sorry for participating in that deception," Dunn finished, sheepishly. It was a feeble apology, but kindly meant, so I smiled.

"I understand. Did you cross paths with Peter in any other way?"

He nodded. "In activities, mostly. He was a superb croquet player. Do you play?"

"A little. Peter was best at croquet, I was a better shot."

"May I ask, Miss Ravenshaw, if your parents sent your brother back to England for schooling, why did they not send you? It would have been very ordinary."

"Yes, that's true. But my mother built her ministry upon educating girls, and she wanted to show, I think, that she was capable. If she was willing to be the only teacher of her own daughter, then certainly the Indian mothers would understand that she was competent."

And she'd needed me to keep her whole and steady. I understood that implicitly; it had remained an unspoken truth.

"Did you resent that?" he asked. It was openly honest, but I was not offended.

"Not at all," I said. "I came to love teaching. Though I fear I disappointed her as a lace maker."

He put my hand pleasantly back in the crook of his arm. "I am sure you were never a disappointment."

Shortly, we met Mrs. Ross at the bench where we'd left her, and Lt. Dunn walked us up the steps, where Landreth opened the door to let us in.

"I shall look forward to seeing you on Friday evening," Lt. Dunn said. Then he stopped. "I believe the Methodist church is having a Bible meeting tonight, as it is Wednesday. Would you care for me to escort you?"

It might be better to attend for the first time on a Wednesday, which was usually less formal, at least in India. Also, I would not have to go alone. "I would enjoy that very much," I said.

The church was small; my mother had told me that the Methodists themselves had only been meeting in Winchester for about ten
years before my parents left for India. The Church of England was,
of course, the church of England, and dissenters such as Methodists,
Catholics, and those of the Jewish faith worshipped on the fringes.

"After you." Lt. Dunn held the door open.

A kindly older woman in a woolen shawl who had arrived just
before us turned to speak to me. "Hello. Are you new?"

I smiled. "In a way. My parents had attended here some years
ago before they went to India as missionaries."

She nodded warily. Could she, too, have heard?

"I'm sorry." I held out my gloved hand. "I'm Miss Rebecca Ravenshaw."

"How do you do? I am Mrs. Margaret Knowlton," she said. She
looked at me curiously, as one would appraise a pet whose domesti-
cation could not be trusted or, in that particularly English way and
which may have better applied to me, a foreigner. "I did hear that
you had returned to Headbourne House. I'd meant to call."

"Oh?" I inclined my head. Lt. Dunn made way for us to take a
place in one of the pews before they filled, and I nodded to signal
my thanks and agreement.

"Yes," she said. "Constance Ravenshaw had been a particular
friend to me."

"How wonderful!" Here, at last, was someone who'd known
my mother!

"You have the look of her," she admitted. "Though you have
darker skin."

I worked hard to keep from sighing aloud. "Please come to
call," I said. "I would very much enjoy that. Any day."

"I'm afraid I cannot," she said. "Lady Ledbury . . ."

"Lady Ledbury," I started, "Captain Whitfield's mother?"

Just then the minister approached from behind. "Mrs. Knowlton, I'm so pleased to see you. I know you've been unwell and unable to join us for quite some time. Have you brought a friend?"

She turned to make introductions. "Miss Rebecca Ravenshaw, may I present the Reverend Benjamin Bennetts. Reverend Bennetts, Miss Rebecca Ravenshaw."

The Reverend held out his hand, but his look was not warm nor his handshake firm. "I was not here when the Ravenshaws were commissioned to the field, but I have had the occasional report from friends and all *four* of them are greatly missed."

Four: Father, Mother, Peter, me.

"I'm glad to hear that, Reverend. I miss my mother, father, and brother as well. I hope you and your wife will find some time to call on me soon."

"It's a busy time, miss, but we shall try."

A busy time? I was not aware of a large number of ecclesiastical responsibilities stacking up in late June, but I was not going to plead for Christian charity, either.

"Thank you," I said, thinking, *By this shall all men know that ye are my disciples, if ye have love one to another.*

I took my seat and listened as Reverend Bennetts preached the Word. The lesson was quite good—not as good as Father's, of course, but deep and rousing nonetheless. I would return, even if I had to sit at the back alone.

As soon as he had finished, I stood and looked for Mrs. Knowlton. Why had she mentioned Lady Ledbury? And what about Lady Ledbury had precluded a friend of my mother's from calling upon me?

I looked to see where Mrs. Knowlton was. She had apparently left for home.

"Have you noticed that cakes are rarely served in this household?" Michelene asked me two days later as she prepared me for the dance that Dunn had mentioned earlier, at dinner.

"I had noticed," I said. "With the exception of the tea with Miss Dainley, I have not seen them."

Michelene pursed her lips. "That's because Cook favors Miss Dainley. I will wager that you will not see them this evening, either. No trifles, no ices, no tipsy-cakes. Just the meats and the breads. *Les fruits*. It's all very dull and perhaps now you are here, and will begin to hostess, you can request a change, *n'est-ce pas?*"

I agreed with her. Perhaps it was simply the way things were run when a man was in charge. But Lt. Dunn had certainly seemed to appreciate his pudding, had said most men do.

She finished fiddling with my gown, which was made of a light fabric that folded in deep, close ruffles from the bustline to the floor, although there was a flat panel in front adorned with becoming buttons. It was dove gray. As July and the end of the mourning period approached I was preparing to wear colors again, shortly. I was eager to have Michelene leave because I had something to practice in private.

"I shall see you after the dance," I said. "Enjoy your evening of rest."

She frowned at being waved away, but departed, and as she slipped out, Marie slipped into the room.

"Well, hello," I said, and stroked her once, which was all she would allow before slinking away.

I stood in front of the cheval mirror and began to dance. I made it through three or four steps, but then my ankle started to wobble. My foot had been healing nicely, and when I could walk in slow, even steps, I barely faltered, but dancing was another matter altogether. I wasn't fluid enough. I had no desire to become an object of attention or pity at the dance. I certainly did not want to be a distraction to others' enjoyment.

I tried again. Five steps. Falter. I heard the clock in the hall-way. It was just before nine and the guests would soon arrive.

I could not dance. I sat down on my bed, put my head in my hands for a few moments. Why had I tried to push open the inso-lent horse gate, twisting my ankle as I did?

I sighed. Reality being such that it was, I would not dance at all. There would be so many people in attendance that surely no one would notice if I declined, nor be ill-mannered enough to press if I said I was unwell. I would go downstairs for the socializing, then go to my room during the dancing, re-turning later for supper. I quickly swiped away the tears from my eyes.

Mrs. Ross was waiting outside my door for me, and we walked together to the ballroom, which opened out onto a ve-randa and the newly mending gardens. There were perhaps three dozen people already there, dotted about the room and porch; a string quartet played quietly in the background, in the minstrels' gallery, as people mingled.

"There's Lord and Lady Ledbury," Mrs. Ross whispered to me. Captain Whitfield's parents. I nodded. I wondered how she knew.

I watched as Captain Whitfield and another man, whom I could only see from the back, drew near to Lord Ledbury. After some minutes of talking, Lord Ledbury laughed, clapped the younger man on the shoulder, and walked away with him, leaving the captain alone in their wake. He was not alone for long; a swarm of young ladies soon enveloped him.

"Miss Ravenshaw!" Lt. Dunn made his way toward me. "I hope there is room on your card for my name?"

"I won't be dancing, but I'm so happy to see you. Please, don't let me forestall you from collecting other names." He agreed, though it seemed to be with great reluctance.

Soon, Miss Dainley came to take me by the arm. "Miss Ravenshaw," Miss Dainley said. "How I've missed you!"

"And I've missed your calls!" I left unsaid that she had distinctly asked me not to call upon her at her house, and I'd honored the request.

"Oh, Mother has been unwell and I've been occupied," she said. "But I shall be present for the shooting party next week . . . you'll ride out with us, I presume?"

A sick little pit quickened inside me. "I presume." Riding.

"Do allow me to make some introductions," she said. She was a confectionary froth in pink and it suited her well. She escorted me around and introduced me to all the ladies present, from the oldest to the youngest. Lord Ashby spoke to someone in the corner of the room, then caught my eye and smiled, and I smiled back, glad to have a friendly face nearby.

"Come now, I want to introduce you to Lady Ledbury." She fairly tugged me toward them. "She's delightful." We stood nearby, like desperate beggars, while Lady Ledbury finished her conversation. Then she turned with an overbright smile to Miss Dainley.

"Delia!"

The use of a Christian name did not escape me. It was reserved for intimates.

"Lady Ledbury, Caroline, allow me to present Miss Rebecca Ravenshaw."

Lady Ledbury turned her smile on me and held out a gloved hand, reluctantly, as one might do to someone suspected of infectious illness. "Miss Ravenshaw. How do you do? I've heard so much about you. I hope you don't feel quite out of place, although one imagines you must."

"How do you do?" I said. "I don't feel out of place at all. This is my home."

"My son, Captain Whitfield, feels much the same as you do, of course," she cooed, but her cold eyes made it clear she did not think it was my home, or shouldn't be, if it were. "And of course you know no one."

"I'm meeting more and more people each week," I replied. "In fact, I met a friend of yours a few days ago. Mrs. Margaret Knowlton."

Her face reflected a complete inability to place the name.

"Of the Methodist church in Winchester?" I prompted.

After a moment, she appeared to remember. "Oh, yes. Friends? Indeed, no. But Lord Ledbury and I have made it a habit to support her coal charity. Generously. How kind of her to mention me." She smiled, catlike.

I wanted to end the conversation, not leaving that privilege to her. "Please, enjoy the hospitality and the music. I'm delighted that you and Lord Ledbury could join us this evening."

She'd already half turned away, emphasizing that I was not the hostess, having the final word, nor anyone that merited courteous attention from her. *She wants Whitfield to have the house.* Of course. As I moved away, I overheard shards of her conversation, mainly about pennies from Honiton and how I might need some thrown toward me. What did that mean?

I looked up to find Captain Whitfield looking not at me, nor Miss Dainley, but at his mother. He stood alone. Some of the other men had made friendly overtures, but they were apparently superficial, as the men purposefully drifted away in groups that did not include him, and their talk and laughter became more boisterous once they'd left his presence. Once or twice I caught them pointedly looking at me and then at him.

Were they questioning my identity? Did shunning Whitfield tie into that somehow?

Perhaps if he had a home of his own, one with his family pedigree, *my* home, Lady Ledbury could comfort her conscience, if she had one, for abandoning him for a title and thirty pieces of silver; he had not yet regained his place in society. Maybe he thought the house would do that for him. I glanced up to the corner of the room and caught the eye of Dr. Floyd. He quickly turned away from me.

Miss Dainley soon rejoined me at my side.

"I wonder if I might ask a question," I began.

She nodded. "Certainly."

"Can you tell me what the significance is of pennies, in connection with Honiton?"

"Ah, yes, I'd heard your mother was originally from Honiton. From days way back, five hundred years or more, I believe, the landed gentry of Honiton would throw hot pennies at the poor in an annual celebration of sorts. The poor would then have some spending money, more than they'd seen in quite some time, one supposes. But the pennies caused burns as they struck or were picked up. Terrible, isn't it?"

I was horrified. "My mother had never spoken of that tradition. Is it still practiced?"

"Oh, yes," Miss Dainley said. "But the pennies are no longer hot."

"Thank you."

"My pleasure," she said before someone took her arm, and they departed amidst happy chatter.

So Lady Ledbury wanted me to be seen as mad, poor, and of low caste.

My thoughts were interrupted when someone tapped my shoulder. I turned to see a woman a few years younger than me, but still very prepossessed and expensively dressed. "We haven't met. How do you do? I'm Lady Frome." She held out a gloved hand, which was garlanded in pearls, and pearls very like those buttoned the front of her gown, which, although cleverly designed, could not hide the soft swell of a baby. "I saw you speaking with my mother-in-law." She raised a hand toward Lady Ledbury.

"Lady Frome, how do you do? So you are married to Captain Whitfield's brother?" Michelene had told me Lady Frome was an heiress in her own right.

She nodded. "The eldest of his half brothers. The others are not yet old enough to worry about mustaches or beards, much less wives."

She held out her dance card. "Did you receive one? If so, I'm certain it must be filled by now."

I shook my head as the quartet grew louder, signaling the beginning of the dancing. "I have not yet fully recovered from injuries suffered in India and cannot participate."

She fanned herself. "You understand they will say you do not know how to dance, either because you are not who you say you are or because you are ill brought up."

I appreciated her refreshing frankness. "I care not for gossip. An Indian proverb says that one who opens her mouth as wide as a crocodile's to speak ill of others is likely to be as unkind as a crocodile as well."

She smiled. "I like you, Miss Ravenshaw. I hope we get to know one another." She nodded at the man who had earlier been speaking to Lord Ledbury and the captain. I could see his face now; it was a slightly marred copy of Captain Whitfield's, so I presumed him to be Lord Frome.

Miss Dainley soon made her way back to me, dance card in hand, and she either didn't notice that I didn't have one or didn't comment. I glanced at hers and noticed Captain Whitfield's name as well as Lt. Dunn's. Captain Whitfield's name was written twice. The music grew louder and I sensed the dancing was about to begin so I nodded to Mrs. Ross and quietly slipped away to await an indication that there was a break in the dancing and supper was about to begin, whilst I enjoyed a quiet respite of an hour or so in my room.

Once there, I saw both *Paradise Lost* and the scriptures resting on the table near my bed. I opened up the Bible, drawn to Joshua, because my father had marked and underlined so many places in it.

> *Moses, my servant, is dead; now therefore arise, go over this Jordan, thou, and all this people, unto the land which I do give to them, even to the children of Israel.*
>
> *Every place that the sole of your foot shall tread upon, that have I given unto you, as I said unto Moses.*
>
> *Be strong and of a good courage: for unto this people shalt thou divide for an inheritance the land, which I swore unto their fathers to give them.*
>
> *Only be thou strong and very courageous.*

I was struck by sudden understanding. No one was going to give me my house, my home, my money. If I wanted it, my legacy and mine alone, my security, which no man could touch unless I married, and which meant all to me, I would have to take it. Room by room, account by account, gardens by shed by stable.

After a short while I closed the book and set it aside, newly determined.

Be strong and very courageous. Take the land.

"I was nae aware that the Lord enlisted malingerers or loafers, nor the proud at heart, as soldiers. To be on the field is to engage . . ."

I made my way out into the hallway. It was earlier than I had anticipated. Another song struck up so I tarried awhile instead of returning just then.

I would choose the first room to take back. Just down that long, cordoned-off hallway stood the entrance to my parents' bedroom, confirmed by my conversation with Mrs. Blackwood. I looked around; no one but Mrs. Ross, making her way from her room, was near. This was my house. If I chose to go into an empty bedroom, then I would.

I slipped under the cord and turned the handle to the bedroom door. I half expected it to be locked, but it wasn't. I half expected it to be emptied of the furniture, but again, I was wrong. There was a kind of holy silence. The clock had stopped. The desks, still and at the ready, sat side by side against one wall. I'd heard that the Queen and Prince Albert had desks that faced one another; I liked to imagine my parents working side by side on their letters, even as they prepared to depart for India.

There was a pair of wardrobes and a high tallboy; did any of their personal effects remain within?

I stood in front of the dressing mirror and then I sat down on the chair in front of it. I closed my eyes and I could remember standing nearby watching my mother sit in this very chair while her lady's maid—what had been her name? Florence. Yes, Florence—she'd brushed my mother's hair, and when I'd looked up at her, she'd brushed mine. I opened my eyes and jostled the small drawers in front of me. They were empty except for a few hairs, an oil stain, and, right in the front, a sapphire-tipped hair-pin stuck in the front of a drawer. I wiggled it out.

Mother's!

Carefully, I slid it into my upswept hair. I was flooded with gratitude to have found something personal that had belonged to her.

Then I stood again and turned. The bed. I recalled that Captain Whitfield had taken this room as his own and a flush crept over me as I realized that he had slept in this bed, very recently, in fact. As I had slept in his, in the guesthouse.

Did he always sleep alone? I let my thoughts tarry on that for a while.

As I shook the thought from my head, and as if summoned by my conscience to answer the charge, Captain Whitfield suddenly appeared in the doorway.

"Hiding, Miss Ravenshaw?"

CHAPTER TWELVE

I slowly turned to face him; his presence did not unsettle me so much as the thoughts I'd had about him mere breaths ago.

"Is there someone I need to hide from, Captain Whitfield?"

He smiled. "I noticed you did not dance. I knew that your father was a dissenter but I did not realize that you do not dance."

I was puzzled. "My family is Methodist, yes, but mainly because my father thought they best tended after the needy in missions. In everything, my father followed Scripture's lead. Scripture does not forbid dancing; in fact, King David danced."

He looked truly mystified. "Then why did you leave?"

"My foot is not yet healed," I said. "It would have been awkward and I did not want to draw attention to myself, nor discomfort your guests. But I assure you, Captain Whitfield, I love to dance."

He stood silent for a moment, his stance relaxed. "It seems I owe you an apology." His voice reflected true contrition; it had relaxed from defensive stridence to honeyed affection. "No, two."

"Two?"

"I regret my crude comparison at the dinner table, with Lieutenant Dunn, between peahens and women. I should have apologized immediately; if I was the man I believe myself to be, I would have, and I have regretted it since."

"Do you believe honorable ladies and peahens are alike, Captain Whitfield?"

"I've not met many of either." He sidestepped the question with a grin, unwilling to capitulate. I let him have it; his apology had been truly contrite.

"And now I have misjudged your motives for not dancing," he continued.

"You owe me nothing," I said. "After all, I misspoke about the portrait."

His eyes warmed. "Would you . . . could you wait here for a moment?"

I nodded. "Certainly." I would wait for him for much longer than a moment, but I could not let him know that!

He left, and as he did, I saw a sliver of Mrs. Ross's dress hem just outside the open doorway; she did not enter.

Captain Whitfield soon returned and the softest of violin music struck up in the minstrels' gallery not far from my parents' rooms. I looked at Captain Whitfield. "Johann Strauss?"

"I've asked the quartet to play a waltz whilst the others begin to dine." He extended his hand. "Would you?"

"What a delightful surprise!" I took his hand and he lifted me, lightly. I relished the feeling of him leading me. "With pleasure. Won't your guests miss you?"

"Perhaps," he said. We faced one another, and he placed both of his hands behind his back and bowed, I curtseyed in return, and then he reached his left hand out to take my right, and cupped me with his right arm, drawing me close. I reached up and rested my hand on his shoulder. It felt natural, and I longed to keep it there.

We fit together neatly, perfectly, perhaps. He stepped, and we began to dance. He wore gloves, I wore gloves, and yet I could feel a frisson of skin-to-skin energy through our hands. I wanted to remove my gloves, and his, and I suspected he would not have protested. His arm, around me, emanated strength. *It has been so long since I had anyone to lean against. And never anyone like him.*

After a few steps and a swirl, my ankle weakened and my foot faltered, but his eyes did not waver from mine as he held me even more firmly. As he held me more tightly I sensed his desire to draw me closer to him than was strictly necessary for the dance, and I fought my own inexplicable desire to yield and let him. In the end, I did, and I did not regret it. A scent could be drawn from his skin: spice, and musk, and warmth. I closed my eyes and inhaled it like a tantalizing vapor.

I wished for the tune to persist till morning; alas, it could not. As the music drew to a close he put his arm round me and lifted me before setting me down, gently, on the ottoman at the foot of the bed. He held both my hands in his and I cherished it. He did not bow as was required; for a long moment we held one another's gaze. Captain Whitfield stepped back and bowed. I stood and curtseyed in return.

"Forgiven?" he asked, his voice low and husky, his eyes still holding mine in an intimate manner.

"Forgiven," I whispered, and then finally looked away with a dip of my head lest my eyes reveal more than I wished them to.

Perhaps it was too late, and they already had.

I had been right about many things that night. I'd chosen the right dress, along with Michelene's assistance. I had been correct to melt away before the public dancing; my tender ankle told me that. The bedroom door had been left unlocked, after all, and the furniture rested as it was. I needed to be bold, to take back my home, and my life.

In one thing, though, my judgment had been badly mistaken. Captain Whitfield—trustworthy or disingenuous, innocent or murderer, tester or entrapper, gentleman or Hussar, I should have to find out which—still unsettled me very much indeed.

I left Michelene in my room mending and sponging my dresses a few mornings later, before we were to leave for the shops in Winchester. I went down to the morning room and rang the bell that would call Cook. She soon appeared, looking none too pleased.

"Yes, Miss Ravenshaw?"

"Good morning, Cook. I wanted to tell you what a splendid repast you and your staff provided for the dinner and dance last week. Every day is a treat with your food, but for that number in attendance, well, you excelled yourself."

She gave up a smile, though it seemed to be an unwilling one. "Thank you, miss," she said. "Mrs. Blackwood brought in some help from town, of course, for the maids, and some extra help for myself." She stood looking at me, waiting, I supposed, for me to proceed with the reason for calling for her.

"I imagine you have dozens of duties to attend to, so I won't keep you long. I wonder if there might be included, from time to time, some sweet dishes on the menu. Perhaps some trifles, a pudding, or some small cakes would be appropriate? I appreciated them so much when Miss Dainley called."

"Captain Whitfield, he was gone that day," she began.

"Yes, I do recall that," I said. "But even though he has now returned, I'd very much like to see them on the tea trays on Thursdays, and occasionally throughout the week, if possible."

Her face tightened. "If you say so, miss."

Perhaps her reluctance was due to the increased workload that might come with baking.

"Do you need additional help in the kitchen?"

"I should say not," she retorted. "And if I did, well, I'd be sure to ask Captain Whitfield, now, wouldn't I?"

A simple reminder of who was really in charge, whose household it was.

I continued. "I wonder if it might be possible to ask the vendors to procure some Indian seasonings and spices. I'd like to have curry now and again. Some dried mangoes or other fruits would be lovely, if you will."

Her face crumpled like a pug's. "I'll inquire. But I don't want anyone leaving the table complaining of foreign spices."

I kept a straight face. "Surely there has never been a complaint after one of your meals," I said. "And if I ever heard of one, I would put it right directly, myself."

She seemed satisfied and returned to her duties.

Michelene joined me, carrying my bonnet and gloves. She was dressed in a stunning blue lawn dress, her neckline gently scalloped with lace and a delicate crucifix resting on her collarbone. Suddenly, I felt rather twinned with the also-black-gowned Mrs. Ross, who trailed her.

"Shall we leave?" I stood.

"Yes," Michelene replied. "I asked Captain Whitfield if he would ask Daniel to drive us into Winchester for the day."

"I had planned to do so." The way she said Whitfield's name was familiar and friendly, although she did not use his Christian name. Why should that irritate me?

Why indeed.

"I thought to be a help to you, *petite.*"

Landreth let us out of the door and Daniel brought the carriage round. Captain Whitfield walked over from the carriage house to meet us.

"Good morning." He had on his riding outfit. I knew he'd been practicing shooting because I'd heard shots on the grounds and had inquired after it. My father had taught both Peter and me to shoot when we were young.

He helped me into the carriage first and I held his gaze as he held my hand. "Thank you, Captain Whitfield. Not only for your assistance but also for letting us avail ourselves of one of your carriages, and Daniel, for the day."

"My pleasure," he said. He next took Mrs. Ross by the hand.

"Thank ye, guid sir," she said as she heaved her considerable self into the carriage, which rocked and jostled in an effort to regain its balance after she'd sat down.

Michelene held out her hand, a dainty offering, and although she was the last person to enter the carriage, the verse *and the last shall be first* floated across my mind. She seemed, somehow, to claim preeminence. A look passed between them, some sense of familiarity. Perhaps simply because Michelene had served the woman who had claimed to be me. But the look seemed to hold more. Michelene lowered her eyes coyly. I'd not seen her do that before.

Captain Whitfield's expression did not change, except, perhaps, upon closer inspection, a blush of pink rose from under his shirt collar clear to his beard-line. He did not look her in the eye.

"*Merci,*" she whispered as he released her hand.

"*Je vous en prie.*"

I hadn't realized he spoke French.

A short while later, we arrived in Winchester; Daniel took the carriage to wherever carriage men go to wait out the day and we began to walk up High Street and several streets off it. Michelene and I went into the perfumery, and she explained that I was looking for a rather more exotic fragrance, one with sandalwood and spices but not too dear as I was watching expenses.

"I shall see if I can find something *appropriate*," the shop assistant replied. Her tone reflected that she considered essence of rose or violet more suitable, but I missed the balmy scents I grew up with. She came back with something reminiscent of sandalwood and cinnamon, alluring and different.

"This is perfectly correct!" I said. "Thank you kindly. Do you carry cinnamon oil by any chance?"

"Yes, of course."

"I should like to buy a small amount."

She disappeared, muttering peevishly as she tottered away, and finally returned with a small brown bottle, corked. I could tell Michelene was curious as to what I intended to use it for, but I did not share my thoughts just then.

Later that night, as she was assisting me for bed, I asked, "Did you do all this with the woman pretending to be me? Help her to buy clothing and shop?"

"*Oui*," she said.

"What happened to the Indian maid after the imposter passed away?" I untwisted my hair and Michelene began running the heavy brush through it.

"*Disparue.*" Michelene lowered her voice, and then she made sure the heavy door was firmly shut.

I stopped untwisting and turned to face her. "Disappeared? How could she? Where would she go?"

"It was chaos, *ma chère*," she said. "*Quelle horreur* to find Miss Ravenshaw dead, and all focus was on that."

"Who found her? You, I imagine, as her maid."

"*Non!* Most definitely not," she set the brush down and appeared flustered. "It was . . . I believe the Indian maid. Or maybe it was Captain Whitfield."

"You don't know?"

"I was not there," she said, looking confident again. "I had just left for Winchester for the day and evening, to stay with a friend who was unwell. I did not think this to be a problem, as she had two maids, *n'est-ce pas?*"

I nodded, but it was dreadfully convenient and coincidental.

"How could Captain Whitfield have found her? He was at the guesthouse, and besides, would a man enter a lady's bedroom?" Perhaps, I thought, if he'd been invited to do so before.

"Mrs. Blackwood could not rouse her with a sharp knock on the door. She quickly sent for Captain Whitfield. Maybe the Indian maid called for her. I do not know. No one has talked about it since the burial." She tapped her heart. "Bad luck."

Or avoiding revealing remarks.

She continued. "The doctor, he was called, and he pronounced her dead of the suicide. By the time I returned the next day, preparations had already been made to bury *la pauvre petite* at midnight, with no minister," she snorted. "As is your law."

The doctor, Captain Whitfield's friend. The constable—also Captain Whitfield's friend. "And the maid?"

"As I said, *disparue.*"

"Alone? In a country whose language she could not speak?"

"Perhaps she could speak English all along, but did not want us to know."

This was a thought I had recently considered. Perhaps the

maid had been an Anglo-Indian, a woman born of an English father and an Indian mother.

Perhaps the imposter had been, as well! That, certainly, would drive a person to desperate measures. One foot in each world, unwelcome and considered the lowest caste in both, brought to England as a child, desperate to make her way up as an adult. They'd said she was darker skinned. Like me. Though I was certainly not Anglo-Indian. I instantly felt ashamed at how quickly I had defended myself against that "charge," even to myself in my own thoughts.

I shook my head to clear the tangle.

Michelene nodded her head as I did. "It is strange. Perhaps someone wanted the maid taken away, very quickly, before she shared her secrets. That is what I think. After all, the day maid told me that the captain was quietly searching the young lady's room after she was buried. When there was no one left to protest. And then—he locked it up."

Did she mean the maid was dead, too? I was about to ask but she closed her lips tightly in that way she did when she was going to say no more. She worked for me now, of course, and I depended upon her to be discreet. In fact, her future as a lady's maid for anyone depended upon her discretion. If she was understood to tell tales on her former mistress, who was to say she would not tell tales on me?

Michelene returned to her room, but before I went to bed there was a knock on the door. "It's Mrs. Blackwood, Miss Ravenshaw," she said.

"Come in."

"Here are the accounts," she said. "We thought you may want to look them over, to see that all is right, before we ask Mr. Highmore to pay them."

"Yes, yes of course," I said. "Thank you kindly."

She handed a bottle over to me. "Dr. Warburg's Tincture," she said. "Captain Whitfield sent it over for you. He instructed me to tell you that you should begin taking it straightaway."

"Thank you," I said. "The instructions are on the bottle?"

She nodded.

I began to look through the paperwork. Goodness, there were more expenses than I had expected. The dressmaker's bill was high. I sat down on the chair next to the window to regain my balance. *I must consult with Mr. Highmore, soon, about what progress he has made in establishing the balance of my father's funds and investments. I'm certain Father would have provided well for me, but do not want to overspend.*

And what was this? I ran my finger against the paper. Peignoirs? That would make sense, robes to pull around oneself whilst dressing. But not the next item. "A *négligée*? That must certainly be a mistake, isn't it?"

Mrs. Blackwood was still standing there. "You don't hope to marry, miss?" she spoke up.

This was a slightly forward conversation! I thought for a moment. "I hadn't thought to marry." But, perhaps . . . I might like to marry. I took but a moment to envision myself with a man, wearing clothing that women wear only for themselves, for their husbands.

"No? Was there once a man in India, one that your father had intended you to marry, but you did not? He might have married a friend of yours? Perhaps the right man for you is here in England."

I blinked. "How do you know about John Mark?"

She froze. "We . . . don't. It just seemed . . . possible, of course." She was not telling the truth and was uncomfortable lying. I was certain of both.

"Thank you, Mrs. Blackwood," I said. "I will have the *négligée* returned, and I appreciate your close attention to detail on the accounts."

She nodded politely, reserve regained, and left the room.

How had she learned about John Mark?

CHAPTER THIRTEEN

Miss Dainley called on Thursday and we had a pleasant chat about the cathedral in Winchester and what kinds of clothing one would pack if one found oneself aboard a ship sailing for India. I knew her kind father had a meager budget and she would be expected to pay for her furniture and provisions aboard, so I offered a small list and said I would give it more thought. She clearly did not want to depart, and my heart stretched toward her as it put me in mind of my own dilemma, which was, as of yet, unresolved. She would, at least, have a brother to greet her when she arrived.

Lady Frome, Captain Whitfield's sister-in-law, called for just a moment, bringing a small gold box in which lay a perfectly beautiful lace handkerchief.

"Thank you," I said. "I shall treasure it!"

"You said your mother did lacework, and this is Honiton lace."

"Of course, I recognized it instantly by the pattern and bobbin work," I said. "You are so very thoughtful."

"I can act as your chaperone at the shooting party next week," she said.

Yes. I wasn't, of course, looking forward to it as I would not be able to ride out with the others.

"I suspect Mrs. Ross will be content to be relieved for that day and as I am"—she smoothed her dress over the sea swell that was her burgeoning belly—"*enceinte*, I shall not be riding either."

"I'm very grateful," I said. Lady Frome had provided an out! "But how did you know that I shall not be riding?"

"Luke told me."

Luke. That was, of course, the name I had come to use for him in my own mind.

We talked comfortably for a while, and after she left, Lady Ashby, Baron Ashby's mother, came to call. Landreth showed her into the drawing room. For a moment, I considered slipping through the secret door and into the breakfast room, having Landreth plead "not at home" for me. But I remained.

She handed a single peony to Landreth, who clipped it and placed it in a silver bud vase before handing it to me.

"This is from Lewis," she said. "My son, Baron Ashby. He ensured that the gardener protected the finest blossom until I could bring it to you today."

That melted me, just a little. "What a kind son you have raised," I said. "I have yet to meet anyone here as genteel as he."

"He will be gratified to hear that . . . as am I, Miss Ravenshaw." She smiled and accepted tea. She raised an eyebrow at the tiny dish of petits fours, but helped herself to one nonetheless.

We made polite conversation for a short while; she invited me to the local Anglican Church. When I told her I'd been to the Methodist church, like my parents, she stopped for just a moment. "You are welcome to join us should you wish to return to the fold."

"Thank you, so very kind," I said, hiding my smile. Then she took her leave. In spite of her stated reluctance, I had hoped for my mother's friend, Mrs. Knowlton, to call. Alas, she did not. As it was nearing the end of my at-home hours, I asked Landreth to join me in the drawing room.

"Please, have a seat." I indicated the sofa.

"I'd rather not, Miss Ravenshaw," he said. "It's not, it's not done." He pinked.

I sighed. "This is precisely why I've asked you to join me. I occasionally find myself quite out of place, like a person walking in somewhat familiar environs, but without a map. My mother took great care to raise me properly, but as we were in India, and not England, not every occasion arose in which suitable training might be offered. I hope this will not make you uncomfortable, but may I ask a few direct questions of you, Landreth?" I let my voice turn lightly pleading. "So I do not trip on a rabbit hole and stumble in full view?"

His shoulders relaxed. "Of course, miss. I am here to help."

"Was Lady Ashby calling on me simply to be polite?"

He nodded. "And, of course" —he coughed into a closed fist— "because you are an heiress of some means with a house that has been in your family for a considerable time."

I sipped my tea and he continued. "Her son, Baron Ashby, is from an old family which has fallen upon complications."

I see. Since he'd been so forthcoming, I decided to press on, but I knew I couldn't ask for too much without making him feel as if he were compromising his position.

"And Captain Whitfield? Is he, too, from an old family which has fallen upon difficult times?"

Landreth sighed. "His family is also that of your own, is it not?" He raised a skeptical eyebrow. "The captain has some quarters in London, of course, and he's been abroad and only recently began looking for his permanent country home. But, miss," he added, "it is one thing to *buy* a house, and another entirely, to move into and inherit *your* family home. Do you understand?"

Yes. After all, this was my family home. This was England and these things mattered.

His tightly drawn face told me that he had concluded all he was prepared to say.

"Thank you, Landreth," I said quietly, "for enlightening me on these small matters. I can ride an elephant and I can shoot a kite midflight but I have yet to master the intricate pattern of the English social web."

He relaxed into a smile. "My pleasure, miss."

In my room Michelene waited to help me dress, and as I entered there was not only the peony waiting for me, but a thin ivory box, beautifully wrapped. I'd open it before bed, privately, after Michelene had retired for the night. I should have been able to completely trust my lady's maid, but I didn't. Not yet.

The men, and some of the women, rode out to the area where we would practice shooting; Captain Whitfield had generously provided pistols to everyone, a newer model to try out. It seemed a bit odd to me, and at the house, before we rode out, I heard some muttering about Whitfield trying to buy his way in . . . or out. Lady Frome and I rode in a carriage, of course, she because of her delicate condition and I because of my foot. Well, that's what I'd told everyone.

She was a most agreeable companion. We chatted about India and my mother and I was delighted to find that Lady Frome was an experienced lace maker, something I did not expect to find in someone of her station.

"And you?" she asked.

I smiled. "I'm afraid I was rather a disappointment to my mother in that way. I was able to help her teach reading, writing, and penmanship as well as religious studies. But she found other girls more apt at the lace making than I."

"English girls?" Lady Frome asked. "Indian girls?"

"Both," I admitted. "English girls who were from the mission, or daughters of those working for the East India Company nearby. And many, many Indian girls. Some, although slave castes, had had practice with intricate henna designs and so readily picked up the skill."

"Your mother was from Honiton, you've said."

"Yes. I should like to visit sometime, after . . . after I'm completely settled. The Queen commissioned Honiton lace for the christening gown of the Princess Royal," I said with pride. "Which gave it great value. My mother remarked on it. It's been used with every royal baby since."

"And there have been plenty of royal babies since," she teased, and I smiled with her, which was easy to do.

"Perhaps we can steal the gown for your little one when the time comes," I teased.

"A stay in the Tower offers no appeal!" she answered.

Our carriage came to a halt and when it did, Lord Frome himself was there to assist his wife as she descended, and then he helped me, too, though I certainly felt as though I were an afterthought. I noticed his paunch, rather large for a man his age, a man who did not stay himself from the final courses.

Lord Pudding. I grinned.

An arm was at my elbow. "Would you be willing to share whatever it is that is making you smile?"

I turned and saw Lt. Dunn and smiled more widely. "Not that particular thought, but I will say that your gift of the pearl-handled pen in the lovely ivory box made me smile. Thank you for your kind generosity. I fear it is far too dear for me to accept."

"No, please, I insist. With no . . . expectation. I hope that while I'm away for a short while you might write to me, as I shall to you."

"Ah," I said. This would be socially acceptable, even with a new friend, especially as we had mission work in common; Mother and I had often written our letters together, so I was quite sure of this. I was not sure, however, what kind of communication he anticipated, but as he had said it was with no expectation, I could safely keep the pen.

"You're leaving soon?"

"After the dinner this evening," he said. "Although I shall return in a few weeks. I spoke with Whitfield about it, and he agreed, although I think he had only intended for the one visit this summer."

"The one to catch me out."

"Yes." He grinned with me. "I apologize again."

"No need. I know Captain Whitfield is interested in proving my identity to be true or false." For reasons of integrity or for darker, more personal motivations I was not yet sure. I left that unspoken.

He took my arm and walked me to the area where the guns were being loaded. There was a table upon which many of them rested, leather bags of ammunition beside them.

"They're all Adams."

Lt. Dunn looked bemused. "Why, yes," he said. "I'm surprised a lady would recognize the manufacture. You don't think Whit-field would shoot anything else, do you, as he owns the manufacture of them? That is, after all, why we're out here today. So he can show us his new model. Very generous of him, I might say, to offer to each a pair as a gift."

"Yes, generous indeed," I agreed. There was no muttering from Dunn about the largesse. Perhaps because he was not from Winchester? And I hadn't known about Whitfield and the Adamses. Perhaps this was the source of his fortune.

Apparently, all were to ride out around the property first, perhaps to look at changes made to the grounds, and were mounting their horses and beginning to ride out. Lady Frome and I stood near the table where the pistols, and the servants caring for them, had been left. Captain Whitfield had not yet greeted me, but as host, perhaps he'd been busy. He looked magnificent in his riding attire, and by the way he carried himself, he knew it. All of the other men had caps on, but Captain Whitfield let his longish hair whip freely behind him as they left walk for canter and I found I could not take my eyes off him. Notos looked splendid. Captain Whitfield, so vain, even his horse had silver leg gaiters . . .

Wait.

I looked several yards in front of the horse and saw something rise in the field. The horse saw it, too, and began to rear on her back legs just a little and then she screamed.

A snake.

Without pausing for thought I took one of the nearby loaded pistols in hand and shot.

In a second, the snake was dead on the ground. Notos had shied away and Captain Whitfield worked hard to get her under control.

I stood there, shaking, as the others pulled their horses to a halt and Captain Whitfield raced back to me.

"What in the . . . what do you think you're doing?" He stared at me, and then at the pistol in my left hand.

"You and your horse were in danger, sir. An adder." I set the weapon down and tried to control the shaking at my core. "Did you not hear your own horse scream?"

Soon after, Baron Ashby rode up with half an adder in his gloved hand. "I say, you are quite the shot, Miss Ravenshaw," he said admiringly. "And bravo for spotting that from a distance, too." He tossed the remains behind him, into some tall grass.

"Thank you, Lord Ashby," I replied. Someone brought a field chair for me to sit in and I sank into it.

Captain Whitfield dismounted and then pulled up a chair next to mine.

"I owe you a life. I was distracted and thought the shot came at the same time as the scream. I should know better."

"Your horse may owe me a life," I jested, "but you most certainly do not."

"How did you see it?" he asked.

"I'm well equipped to see a snake in the grass, Captain Whitfield."

He raised his eyebrows and I grinned.

He took my left gloved hand in his. "You shoot left-handed."

"I *am* left-handed," I said.

"You write right-handed. You eat right-handed."

He'd noticed?

"What does it matter? Surely you don't believe the superstitious nonsense that left-handed people are somehow evil?"

He shook his head. "No, I do not." Then he set down my hand.

"Every well-brought-up young woman is trained to use her right hand when she can. But as a left-hander, that's how I shoot. Each of us has a dominant eye, you see . . ." I began.

He smiled somewhat wryly. "Yes, of course I understand that." He looked to his guests. "I hope you'll excuse me, but I need to attend to the others, if you've recovered, that is." He hesitated. "However, I have something I'd like to discuss with you. As the evenings remain light until late now, would you be willing to walk round the gardens with me before dinner?"

"I'd be delighted," I said. "Is there a particular purpose?"

"Most definitely." He said nothing more.

The others waited for him and Miss Dainley did not remove her gaze from us the entire time we spoke. I sat and passed the time with Lady Frome for an hour or so, and even when the others returned from shooting I did not leave her company. "You're wilting," I said gently.

Lady Frome fanned her face. "I'm afraid so."

I called Daniel over. "Would you be so good as to take Lady Frome back to the house?"

He nodded. "Would that be acceptable to Captain Whitfield?"

"I'm certain he would not want his brother's wife to suffer discomfort any longer than necessary," I said.

"And you, miss, will you come back now as well?"

I rather liked the idea of being out in the open by myself, enjoying the rustle of the leaves in the occasional breeze, sounding much like crinolines swishing beneath the stiffest gown. "I'll wait for you to return."

They left and after a short time the others wrapped up their practice, Miss Dainley side by side with Captain Whitfield.

"Ah, Miss Ravenshaw, you look positively abandoned," she said, and I did not know if she was teasing me or drawing attention to my isolation.

"Not at all," I said. "I but wait for Daniel to return in the carriage for me."

The others hung about awkwardly, on horseback, and it became clear that they could neither ride back to Headbourne

House without me nor leave me on my own. Captain Whitfield pulled his horse up alongside me.

Please don't offer your horse to me. I do not want to be humiliated in front of this crowd.

He came close, so he could speak to me and hear my answer without the others overhearing, no matter how Miss Dainley might crane her neck.

"I'd be happy to have you ride with me. We can go slow, and it's not far. That is, if you're willing to ride behind me."

"I've never ridden behind," I said.

"Never?"

I shook my head.

"Why not?"

I smiled. "No need to." I allowed myself a slightly forward jest. "Or perhaps there's never been a man I've wanted to follow. In any case, my dress would not fit."

"In front of me, then, on the pommel."

I nodded my agreement, and he dismounted and then held out a hand to help me; I was glad I had insisted on having some fine dresses with narrower, smaller hoops, simpler dresses, as I'd worn in India, in spite of Michelene's tut-tutting. Once up, he leaned into me, our faces close enough to feel one another's breath. "I've never met a woman who can shoot like that."

It was the first admiring thing he'd said to me, in unabashed honesty. I was a little mystified by his almost instantaneous change in manner, though. There was no mocking, no teasing, no edge to his words. All because of one shot? He rode with one arm around me, the other held the reins. I leaned back into him as we rode back, finding myself wishing he'd extend his clasp into more of an embrace than a steadying hold. I could feel that he held himself like a soldier, steady and taut, but did not draw away from me. I relaxed and rested into him.

What would Mrs. Ross say?

But we rode in company with the others, and I was sorry to let go when we arrived at Headbourne. I'd never felt that way before, though I had, of course, kept chaperoned company with young missionaries and British plantation owners in India. Unlike Whitfield, they had, to a man, seemed placid.

I viewed my house on approach—crumbling, stately, tangled, distressed, splendid. It was, I believe, the first time I'd looked at it and thought, *Home*. Headbourne was a needy, long-neglected child requiring love and commitment, and I was now prepared to offer those without reserve. I looked at the statues and thought how I might add to them, glanced over the moldings and promised I would make reparations, apologizing for decades of inattention. I no longer had those I loved with me here on Earth, but here, on this particular piece of land, I could honor them and remain safely home.

Captain Whitfield rode into the stable and a groomsman helped me down. I shivered a bit as Notos turned her huge head, disdainfully flared her wide nostrils, and looked hard at me from beneath long lashes. Whitfield steadied her, then dismounted and took my hand in his own.

"I look forward to your garden surprise," I said before releasing his hand.

CHAPTER FOURTEEN

A short while later I made my way to the gardens. The evening light angled across the lawn so it was now half dark, half light, and as I looked at Whitfield in the distance I knew that was an apt description of the man, too.

Mrs. Ross settled herself on a stone bench, needlework basket nearby, as Captain Whitfield took my gloved hand and placed it on his arm as we walked. His hair was free, again; he did not wear a hat even when the other men did. His beard was well trimmed, which allowed an easy look at his lips. He caught me looking and looked at mine in return before speaking. A ripple of heat passed between us and I tipped my head down for a moment to recover. He feigned no such disinterest.

"I must admit to surprise and delight at your shot today," he began. "You are a most unusual woman. The military could use you as a sharpshooter!" He laughed and I smiled at him. "Is that how you dispatched snakes in India?"

I tucked my arm deeper into his. "We had several methods. Snakes often slithered around the house, or hung from the ceiling over one's bed."

"And shooting them was the easiest way to protect yourself?" He looked incredulous.

"No. We also had hooks we could wrap around them. But the easiest way was to call for Father." I smiled at the memory and he grinned with me. "And now, Captain, you asked me here to speak of something?"

"There's no delicate way to begin," he said. "Simply put, I believe you are who you say you are and I apologize for treating you with suspicion."

I drew in my breath as a rush of cold excitement prickled through me. It was so sudden, so unexpected. I had not anticipated this conversation at all. I exulted even as I strove to keep my composure. Within the minute, the initial rush of excitement melted into a welcome wash of relief. I would not have to wait until August! Salvation was here, at hand. "Please, sir, do explain."

We sat down on a bench next to a dilapidated statue of Flora, patroness of gardens, who looked over at us imploringly. Her gardens needed further tending. I would, happily, begin to think of that soon.

"I'd hoped Lieutenant Dunn would be able to help me ascertain if, indeed, you are truly Miss Ravenshaw. I knew that Eltham is a close community of missionary sons and that Dunn might know something about your brother."

"Very few outside of my family would have known about the strawberries. But that can hardly be enough to convince a man of your . . ." I was about to say *worldliness*. And then I thought, *motivation*. I settled on "skepticism."

He ran his hand almost unconsciously over the back of my right glove, in a soothing manner, and I did not withdraw my hand. "One day when Landreth and I were removing some boxes from the uppermost parts of the house, the attic, I came across some papers lying in a corner where some linens were stored. There were documents pertaining to the house so I sorted through some of them. I also found a letter your mother had written to her own mother despairing of the extra effort you would be required to put forth to learn to write with your right hand when you are, in fact, left-handed. I kept the letter to myself. No one else could have known."

"My mother was a natural teacher, and she worked with great care to help me," I said. Then I understood. I had been saved by a reflex—the shot. Nothing I could have planned or done had proved me true so well as an unaffected reaction. "So you saw me shoot today and knew I was left-handed after all."

"Yes. I couldn't be sure before then, although I erred toward not believing it because of the writing and eating. The truth set you free."

I nodded. "Was the woman who'd pretended to be me left-handed?" I thought that would be unlikely, as such a small percentage of the population was.

"I don't know," Captain Whitfield answered. "She was well into her few months here when I came across the box. I watched her thereafter, but of course she, too, ate and wrote with her right hand. And I did not see her shoot; I don't think she could shoot."

"And yet, there was some doubt about her early on?" I could see the guests begin to gather, preparing for dinner to be served, and I spied Thornton, Captain Whitfield's valet, trying to catch his eye.

He nodded. "Once in a crowd she raised her hand, quickly, to wave to someone as they approached. She used her right hand. A spontaneous gesture would demand the dominant hand, I would think. But I don't know. It caused me to look at things more closely."

Thornton was making his way to us now.

"I do apologize for my doubt, but it was my duty to the Ravenshaws, as the apparent heir, to make sure the property was
safely delivered to the right hands. Those hands"—he took mine
in his own again—"are now made clear, and I have done my duty.
If acceptable to you," he continued as he helped me to my feet, "I
should like to stay on at the guesthouse through the summer in
order to find an appropriate property for myself." He wrapped my
arm around his, rather than placing my hand on top as he usually
had. It was more intimate, and perhaps hinted toward possession,
though I could not be certain. Maybe I only wished it to be so. But
why make this gesture now? I let his arm remain for a moment,
then unwound it.

"I bear no ill will toward you at all; you've been most kind to
me considering the circumstances. You're very welcome to stay
through the summer." My voice shook with a mix of emotions:
gratitude, relief, joy, and then, strangely, longing and melancholy.
"I'd be most appreciative if you could help me oversee the improvements you've arranged. I shall repay every penny as soon as
Mr. Highmore has the finances in order. I expect to see him early
next week."

He nodded and then stopped walking. "Are you quite sure
you're willing and able to undertake this on your own? To retain a
house such as Headbourne might prove more difficult than to
gain one."

"It is my home, Captain Whitfield. It is all that I have left of
my father, my family."

He said nothing more, but what was left hanging unspoken in
the silence was that it was all that he had left of his father, his lin-
eage, as well. I remembered Whitfield's comments about being left
alone year after year, holiday after holiday, whilst his brothers had a

family and a home, and my heart was aggrieved for him. We passed by the firmly rooted wisteria in silence. He glanced at it in passing.

It's a devil to relocate, he'd said.

Michelene helped me dress for dinner. "Soon you will be wearing the colors, *n'est-ce pas?*" She pulled out a gray dress; the neckline was highlighted by tiny pearls which caught and held the candlelight.

"Are they real?"

"*Bien sûr*," she said. "Only the best for Mademoiselle." Like the best of lady's maids, Michelene noticed my altered mood.

"What has changed?"

"Captain Whitfield has admitted that I am, actually and truly, Rebecca Ravenshaw."

Michelene dropped the brush but then quickly concealed her shock with her normal look of disinterested sophistication. "What caused this admission? Has he heard back from the Missionary Society?"

"Apparently not," I said. "Through Lieutenant Dunn, my writing and shooting, and some information he's gleaned from my mother's letters, he just . . . knows. I must say, he's been very solicitous in the short time since realizing it."

All of a sudden, I realized he'd said he'd kept the letters. Had he somehow, perhaps through his staff, procured my lost letters as well? And if so, to what purpose? I would like to look for others of my mother's letters, ones he had, I assumed, left untouched.

"But of course," she said. "Now that you are the heiress, the wooing must begin."

I turned and my heart lurched because she'd spoken aloud the thought I had forbidden to take complete form in my own mind. Did I want him to woo me? She implied that the captain would be wooing the house, via me, and not me for my own sake. Perhaps I believed that myself.

"Why do you say that?"

"It would not do for Captain Whitfield to have a bought house with bought furniture, so *nouveaux,* when Lord and Lady Frome have the pedigreed property, would it?"

"Do you believe they would treat him poorly for that?"

"I do, *absolument,*" she said. "With the little cuts, *n'est-ce pas*? It is very much the English way. If he's forced to buy a property, it will be well away from Hampshire . . . and the whispers."

The whispers. I hadn't heard them, but I'd seen the whispering. And the dubious looks.

"Do you believe him to be the kind of man who would be troubled by bought property?"

She nodded. "Every man craves the respect of his family. And all men need love. Do you understand men? I do."

Mr. Highmore arrived for a visit the following Tuesday. I met with him in the morning room, which Mrs. Blackwood had prepared for visitors. A small table sat between two chairs deeply upholstered in a rose-scattered chintz fabric. It made me smile—this iconic English piece of furniture covered in a fabric drawn from India, the name itself Hindi. Now that I knew the room would be mine, forever, it seemed a little brighter.

"Thank you for coming," I began the conversation. "Have you heard from India? From the mission? It is, after all, July."

He shook his head. "It will have been too soon to have the papers arrive, be transported to Kerala, and then returned to me. I suspect by the end of summer. However"—he pushed his spectacles higher on his nose, to no avail, as the slick of sweat at the bridge sent them slipping down again—"I have spoken with Captain Whitfield. He tells me he is quite convinced that you are, indeed, Rebecca Ravenshaw, although I have no idea who the wretched soul is that lies in your grave."

A shudder ran through me. *My grave. It has my name on it. I should have a look at it.*

No. I've seen too many graves already and while I'm not superstitious . . .

"A lost person who saw an opportunity," I said, pulling my thoughts into a calm semblance, not wanting anyone who could have been me, for even a short while, to be as unstable and unbalanced as she must have been.

As I worry I, in fact, might have become.

"Charitable of you," Mr. Highmore answered, but his voice was not inflected with admiration. "I'd be more inclined to label her a criminal."

"*Imposteur,* Mademoiselle d'Arbonneau, my lady's maid, has said."

"How easily Mademoiselle d'Arbonneau has switched her loyalties." He sniffed. "I should like to warn you that I have not completely assessed the finances. It will take some time because of the complexity and diversity of your father's investments, and the various places he had money sent and spent." He stopped talking while Annie poured tea and then, when she withdrew from the room with a flickering glance in my direction, Highmore glanced at Mrs. Ross before continuing.

"My chaperone is completely trustworthy," I said, but even as I did, I wondered. How much did I know about her, really? I hadn't pressed for more information, as it would be uncharitable, considering that she was widowed. Her friends seemed to be confined to those who attended her kirk.

Mr. Highmore continued. "As you know, the house has been properly transferred to Captain Whitfield. I shall file the appropriate papers to have it transferred to you, which will just take a short period more, along with the conclusion of the audit of your accounts. But, as they will be uncontested, there will be no intervening problems."

"Captain Whitfield has been most understanding," I said.

He made motions as if to leave. I put a hand on his arm to stop him. Then I arose and closed all the doors around the room, leaving just the three of us within. I returned to my seat.

"One further question, Mr. Highmore."

"Yes?"

"I have an unclear understanding of what would happen to my properties, and my monies, should I marry."

"You mean *when* you marry," he corrected me.

It was not at all a *when*, not at this point, even if I was the only one who knew that. "I mean if, but please, proceed."

He looked surprised.

"Well, according to the law," he began, "once you marry, all your property becomes your husband's under the principle of coverture. As Blackstone said, when a man and wife marry, they become one, and that one is the husband." He chuckled at that but he chuckled alone.

"Except for the Queen," I noted. He did not respond. "So Headbourne House would become the property of my husband, at his disposal to do with as he pleases, whether or not I agree or approve."

"Yes."

"And my personal property, belongings and cash, and investments?"

"Your husband's. Your husband, should he so wish, could give you an allowance. Many husbands, indulgently, do. I do so myself, for baubles and such." His chest ballooned. I pitied poor Mrs. Highmore, whoever she was.

However, I began to see with clarity what was at risk, to me, in a marriage. Headbourne. My finances and the security of my home. I must marry a man with absolute scruples, an unquestioned character, or I should be in jeopardy. "What else must I know about this?"

"Once you have accepted an offer of marriage, everything you have would become his property at that point, even before the ceremony. You cannot deed nor gift or even give to charity because you will be signing away what a husband might reasonably expect to be his in future."

"And should he decide to pick up and take permanent residence in, say, the Outer Hebrides and leave Headbourne House . . . ?"

"You would follow, of course." Mr. Highmore became impatient. "'For whither thou goest, I will go, and where thou lodgest, I will lodge.' I expect you are familiar with that passage in Scripture, Miss Ravenshaw."

"I am indeed."

His demeanor softened a little. "Customarily, a young woman's father would have selected a choice of appropriate suitors for her. It may be more difficult for you, of course, on your own, but you would be well advised to find a worthy husband, and quickly. Lord Ashby—"

"Thank you, Mr. Highmore. You have been most attentive. Shall I have Landreth call for your carriage?"

He nodded. "Yes, please."

He left, but I remained in the morning room for some time. Every woman had to consider this, at some point, though most did not have the choice I had. Their fathers, like Delia's, made the final decision for them. Or there were not finances available to sustain them without a man, so there was no decision to be made, and, if a man was not at hand, one set sail on the fishing fleet to find one. Maybe one became a governess, always the old woman in another woman's household, even if one wasn't particularly old.

I spent the day reading, eating but little, and praying for wisdom and comfort and guidance.

What of Lt. Dunn? Surely he was a good man. A good man en route to China.

Lord Ashby? Perhaps. I was uncertain. Did he want me? My house, my fortune? That is, after all, what Cook had implied Captain Whitfield had been after with my imposter.

Captain Whitfield. My breath caught a little as I turned his name, and image, over in my mind. He was an unknown quantity, to be certain, or maybe not unknown but puzzling and complex. He was a Hussar. He had some kind of history with women, with weapons, and was not opposed to using the means at hand to get his way.

I saw, again, the look that had passed between him and Michelene as he helped her into the carriage. And he clearly wanted Headbourne. It was not at all clear how he felt about me. But when we'd danced I'd felt it in my body, my mind, and even in my soul, the gentle melting of the edges of two people into one, a comfort I'd never expected to feel. Perhaps I could unravel the mystery of the man.

I recalled my first day at home—the constable standing outside my door. The fresh grave near the chapel and Whitfield's reference to it.

I would call upon that constable once I'd gained enough local trust that he would be willing to disclose the truth to me, unlike, for example, the doctor, with whom, perhaps, I had rushed.

Later, on my way to prepare for bed I paused at Mrs. Ross's room and knocked at the door. She was, of course, in residence.

"Do come in, Miss Ravenshaw." I had no idea how she'd known it was me. Perhaps no one else ever visited her, which made me a little sad.

I entered and shut the door behind me. "You heard what Mr. Highmore said today," I began.

"I did indeed. It upset ye, did it?"

I nodded.

"My mother did not want to leave England for India. But she did because my father wanted to."

"Could it be that she came to love India, and her ministry was just as important as your father's? A missionary wife's often is."

"She could have been happy at home in England."

"She could have been." She nodded. "But she'd likely nae have done as much good. Perhaps your father knew what she was called to, in the long view. Perhaps they had conversations of which you were not a part."

Perhaps. Was she somehow suggesting Lt. Dunn for me, or simply comforting me that my mother's life had not been ill used? Furthermore, she spoke as a woman wise in the ways of marriage.

"If I am not interested in a man who shows interest in me, shall I let him know? Directly?"

"'Tis only fair to be honest, lassie. Ye don't need to make a proclamation straightaway, but once ye know the man is not of interest, then it's best to let him move on."

Yes, that was right. Then she offered a thought of her own.

"Ye know there are good men, that both do good and do good by others. By their wives." She smiled and I couldn't help but smile back. Perhaps she was thinking of her late husband.

"How shall I know if he's good or bad?" *He* could have meant anyone, of course, but to me, *he* immediately meant Dunn. Ashby. Whitfield.

She quoted the Gospel of Matthew. "'A good man out of the good treasure of the heart bringeth forth good things; and an evil man out of the evil treasure bringeth forth evil things.'"

I wavered. "I don't judge myself able to know the difference sometimes, especially where the heart is concerned. But I also do not want to be lonely." Did I dare admit to her, even to myself, that my heart was becoming entangled?

I finally decided to return her quote with one of my own, from Saint Paul's first letter to the Corinthians. "'I say therefore to the unmarried and widows, it is good for them if they abide even as I.'"

"Are ye instructing me, now?"

"Not at all," I rushed on. I was mortified, then left wondering if indeed this kindly old woman was seeking to remarry.

"Guid night, lassie," she said, then recalling my earlier concern, called out softly. "Remember, Mr. Milton said loneliness was the first thing which God's eye named not good."

I slipped down the quiet hallway, running my hand against the wall that was now *mine*! I could not be dislodged. I was safe. Security had been gained, and put right for good!

Michelene waited in my room for me, and, possibly sensing that I did not want to talk, did not press with questions or even relay mild gossip to amuse me. She removed my crinoline. "I've left laudanum in a small cup for you, near the bed," she said just before she closed the door behind her. "In case you have trouble sleeping."

Why, on this night, had she decided to prepare that for me although I had not asked her for it? She'd not done that before Captain Whitfield admitted my ownership of Headbourne. It beckoned to me, though. I admit it. I wished for it to pull me into its velvet embrace.

The dark approached and the silence encircled me, tomblike in its absolute hush; if it were possible to hear quiet, to hear absence, then I heard it. Marie broke the moment by leaping down and scratching at the door to be let out. I let her go rather than have her pitiful mewling keep me awake. She crept down the left wing, all the way down the right, and stretched out at the foot of the locked doorway. I saw naught but her eyes as they picked up a stray beam of moonlight through a hall window near the bedroom.

Her bedroom. Had Michelene provided laudanum for her, too? Perhaps too much laudanum? For what purpose—or working in tandem with whom?

Captain Whitfield? Very possibly. I suspected that was the reason why the others snubbed him; they suspected he had had a hand in the death. And the Indian maid? Perhaps she did speak English and Michelene had tipped her hand.

I should deduce who the maid was, how she died, *if* she died. To bring me rest. To bring her rest.

Come now, be honest. You mean to prove Whitfield either malevolent or true.

I woke early to the sun crowning the horizon. The laudanum had helped me sleep deeply, and all night. I slipped from the bed and padded to the window. Captain Whitfield, already up and on Notos, rode the downs, disappearing like a phantom into the rose-tinged mist.

CHAPTER FIFTEEN

That week, Captain Whitfield was in London, so it was with surprise that I noted Miss Dainley's card among my callers. She didn't usually call when he was not in residence.

"Miss Dainley." I hoped my voice reflected my delight as Landreth showed her in. "I'm so pleased to see you, and I hope we'll have time for a good chat before anyone else comes to call." I had understood that Lady Frome would be by, and I was most enthusiastic to see her again.

"Would you like tea? Cake or sandwiches?" I asked.

"Cake, please." Annie brought the tray to her.

We made polite conversation for a few moments, and then she came to the real reason for her visit. "I wondered, Miss Ravenshaw, did you have picnics in India?"

"Oh yes," I said, although I found the subject an odd opening salvo.

"Delightful! Would you be interested in having a picnic here, at Headbourne House? Perhaps in a month or six weeks' time?"

She must have seen a look of offense cross my face as she rushed on with the next sentence. "Our property is under . . .

renovation at the moment, so I cannot offer it for use. However, I thought you might enjoy something more entertaining. Perhaps to help ease the pain of your loss?" Her voice reflected genuine concern, and now that all believed me to be who I said I was, their compassion was palpable and welcome.

"That's very kind of you. A picnic would be delightful, less formal than a musical soirée, and the nights are positively lovely."

"I can help," she offered. "If you wish. I can assist you with the invitations, and discuss whom to invite. Cook and Mrs. Blackwood can help with the menu. Landreth can assist with tables and cushions and such. I'll draw up a plan and begin to execute it."

It was time to exercise just a little authority over my own domain. "In India, we often held moonlight picnics. It was a change from the usual, and if it were mid- or late summer, and it is, we could count on the weather. We'll also have a full moon in a few days, so there will be plenty of light."

Delia considered it. "It's unusual. It may even be inconvenient."

"Perhaps the novelty will repair for the inconvenience," I said.

"Perhaps." She tugged on her bonnet. "I can certainly make inquiries."

"Splendid," I said. "And we shall plan together. Perhaps Captain Whitfield can arrange for the music?"

She didn't answer right away. "Customarily, it would be for us two to arrange everything. I can help with the music. I do play." She looked longingly at the piano across the hall. From earlier discussions of her rather austere home life, I gathered that the piano she had wasn't quite as grand as the infrequently used one in my music room.

"Would you care to play now?"

"Oh." She blushed. "I hadn't meant to imply . . ."

"Not at all," I reassured her. It reminded me of the time I'd urged Captain Whitfield to play for me. I wished he would again. "Instruments are enhanced when played often and well. Please, it would be a favor to me."

She smiled and we walked into the music room, where she played a lovely sonata.

"Chopin," she said after she was done, as a way of politely educating me. I couldn't help but wonder if she was better suited than I to my music room, my country, and perhaps my house.

"I should like to know more about music," I said.

"Truly?"

I nodded. I listened attentively as she spoke for a few minutes, knowing it to be an important part of my life here and now.

"Thank you," I said. "I wish I could help you more, too."

"You can," she said quietly. She stood up from the piano stool and I led the way back to the drawing room.

"What shall I expect in India? Not that it's certain I'll be going. I'd prefer even Derbyshire, if need be. I'll have to cook, I assume? What shall I wear?"

I sought to reassure her. "You will not need to cook. There, just as here, you will have a cook to do that for you. In fact"—I hoped this would cheer her— "you are likely to have many more servants there than you do here. One, a punkah wallah, just to fan you!"

She smiled at that. "I did not expect to be a lady of leisure."

"You will have plenty of white cotton dresses, and you'll have servants to wash them for you. During the hot season you will not need corsets or crinolines, and you'll be finished with church by six a.m. on Sunday before the heat smothers all thought, secular and saintly. You'll have English friends with whom to play croquet and bridge. You can even have British magazines delivered, and there are many amusing book clubs. This was one way my friends and I understood what was happening 'back home.'"

I did not tell her about the social structure among the English abroad, how she would be expected to be submissive to the senior Englishwomen in her town and would not even participate in charities unless invited; I did not mention how she would stay home unless invited out, how her children might perish from unusual diseases. She probably knew that already and I did not wish to overburden her or provoke concerns about that which might not come to pass.

"Was this your life at the mission?" she asked, and I giggled.

"Oh no, a British lady of leisure's life is far removed from the life of a missionary. I helped my mother and father as they sought to share the Good News with our beloved neighbors, and to teach them to read and to write. Eventually, there were many Indian men who went to seminary and became teachers in their own right. Many others managed coffee plantations. I tried to help my mother with lace making, but . . . alas." I threw up my hands. She smiled with me.

"So you had no servants then?"

"Oh, we did," I said. "Everyone had to have some. Cooks and ayahs, bearers, which are like butlers." A memory shimmered forth in my mind and I closed my eyes but could not forestall it.

"Into the ditch, memsahib, into the ditch!"

Musa, who had been a bearer before the town had scattered, determined to help me and the young woman fleeing with me to escape, pushing each of us deeply into the side of the road, and then he threw his brown horse blanket over us and covered it with brush till we blended with the earth.

The soldiers rode up, and then Musa lied, swearing on his Koran for our lives. "There is no one else!" he insisted, and we dared not breathe but as if through a straw so as not to give ourselves away.

A spider slowly picked its way across the earth toward me. I blew, lightly, which did not dissuade it; it crept closer. Please, please, please stay away. What if it should bite me? Should I be able to keep from crying out? It was close enough, now, that I could see its bulging black eyes.

"Do you see anyone else? No! Are you seeing a mirage?" I heard Musa prod the others.

The spider, blobby and black, with a body nearly the size of a child's tea saucer, made its way toward my body, and then it inched onto my arm. I closed my eyes and swallowed my gorge. It made its way to my shoulder and then into my hair, where I could feel it entangle itself, my hair prickling from the scalp, the desire to claw it out almost overwhelming. My head shook with loathing and fear.

"Bah!" The men spoke angrily to Musa and I heard them ride off. He waited nearly an hour before allowing us out from the ditch. I choked because I could not scream or cry and desperately tore at and shook my hair, but the spider was gone.

I made the Namaste *sign to Musa, but then remembered, as a Mohammedan he would not consider himself polluted by my touch, so I reached out to embrace him. "You saved our lives. If they had known we were here, they would certainly have killed us."*

"It is nothing, memsahib," he said, but he was shaking and I knew what that lie had cost him.

"There is nothing so righteous as saving a life. Two lives," I told him. "Thank you is not enough but it's all I have. I shall pray for you every day of my life."

And I had.

"Miss Ravenshaw?"

"I'm terribly sorry," I said, blinking back to the present. "I was thinking of a bearer I'd known in India."

Miss Dainley raised her eyebrows. "I was saying, it seems you were so at ease in the East Indies. Almost as though you were born there."

"But I was not," I said sharply. I had done with defending my heritage.

Miss Dainley politely offered her hand. "Yes, I'm so sorry. I didn't mean to imply . . ."

I let her hold my gloved hand for a moment, taking it to be a sign of friendship. "Not at all. I've needed a friend, here, someone I could speak to."

She looked at me, torn, I thought. She had not considered me her friend. Did I have a friend here at all?

"You've said that you would like to revisit India some day. Why would you want to return to the kind of people who took your parents' lives?"

I looked at her sternly. "That's not who I would be returning to see," I said. "I'd be returning to the kind of people who saved mine."

I'd said I was going to take the land, metaphorically, but in actuality, I had not wandered very far out onto my own land at all. I recalled that Captain Whitfield had said there was a stream nearby, and a few days later I determined to find it and enjoy it whilst the weather was warm.

I made my way through the gardens, which were taking shape, save for a distinct lack of statues, and into the woods that edged the grounds. I soon found out that they not only lined it, they were thick and extended deeply. Although it was midday, I walked in relative darkness; although it was warm, I had a chill. Dead trees lay across the ground, forest carcasses, and I took care to step lightly over them so I did not trip. Unusual, gargantuan ferns flourished in the shadows, otherworldly, eerie. Rank vapors escaped from piles of rotting leaves. I heard some rustling, spotted a bit of black in the background, and stopped. After waiting a good minute, in silence, I moved forward again. When I turned, the black shadow was gone.

Was someone following me?

I soon reached the edge of a burbling river, fresh as a baby's laugh. I unbuttoned my boots and pulled them off, then the stockings beneath, and held my skirts in my hands as I waded out. So cool! So refreshing. I smiled. No crocodiles!

I stood there for quite some time, face tipped toward the sun. When I turned back toward the riverbank, there, to my surprise, was Captain Whitfield, sitting on a chair. There was another chair beside him, empty, and next to that, a wicker fishing creel and a net. Disquiet blended with delight as I made my way from the middle of the stream.

"Captain Whitfield! I thought I'd heard someone in the woods behind me, as I approached from the gardens, but I did not hear you arrive just now."

"You should not be out here alone," he said. "It's not safe."

I smiled. "There is no one, excepting yourself, for a mile or more."

"My point is proved." He smiled back. "It was not me that you heard earlier. You most probably heard a deer or a hare."

"How can you be certain?"

"I did not come by way of the gardens," he continued smoothly, "which are badly in need of new statues. Would you like to accompany me, in a few weeks' time, to select some? Or perhaps I am being overbold and you'd prefer to select them on your own."

"I would very much appreciate accompanying you to select the statues and will lean on your good opinion of the choices; you've not put a foot wrong with the house yet."

"I'd be delighted to assist," he said. "I'd like to purchase them, as a gift. May I say that you look beautiful, and perhaps carefree in some way?" He held out a fishing rod. "Perhaps it is because you no longer wear mourning?"

I smiled. He'd noticed what I was wearing! I was glad I had dressed with care. "Perhaps," I said, taking the rod in hand.

"I confess to making plans to fish only after I'd heard you'd gone walking. I wanted to be sure of your well-being." His voice softened. "And I desired your companionship. Do you know how to fish?"

I nodded, aware that my feet were indecently bare as I picked my way through the stony ground toward where he sat. "Indeed I do," I said, sitting near him on the chair near the bank. "My father's friend and fellow missionary, Mr. Mead, taught my brother and me how to fish." Dear, dear Mr. Mead.

I must have winced because Captain Whitfield asked, "What is it?"

I took the pole in hand. "Mr. Mead was a close friend to us. He eventually married an Indian woman, a Christian convert from the slave castes."

Whitfield nodded. "Ah. Yes. Ill considered. They threw him out?"

Perhaps it was the sun or the fact that my feet were now dry, but I felt immediately warm. "Yes, it's true he was no longer welcomed by the Missionary Society. He's kept ministering, though." I looked at Whitfield defiantly, as though he were the cause of Mr. Mead's situation, had personally dismissed him, and was not simply a callous commenter.

"And it was not ill considered, Captain Whitfield. Not by far," I continued. "A good man marries for love, forsaking all else if necessary. That is, perhaps, the best, and only, reason to marry. The Indians weren't too pleased, either. Anglo-Indian offspring are reviled, it seems, by both societies."

He looked thoughtful. "Yes, this is true."

"Do you know an Anglo-Indian?" I inquired.

"Perhaps," he said. "Perhaps."

"Someone you'd met whilst serving in the army?" I asked.

He shook his head. "No." But he would say nothing further. We spent some quiet moments fishing, and I eased into the day again. I looked beyond him, into the woods, and thought I saw a flash of black dress edged with white lace. Yes, yes, it was certainly she. How had she made her way here and why didn't she just come forward? Perhaps I should not have left without a companion, but I'd had no idea Captain Whitfield would follow me.

"Mrs. Ross?" I said aloud.

Whitfield turned. "She's here?"

"I thought maybe you'd brought her," I said. "As I should not be without a companion in your company."

He shook his head and looked bewilderingly at me. "I don't see her."

And now, I did not either. He looked at me as if I were unwell. Maybe I was.

"You've just come from London?" I asked, changing the topic.

"Yes, for the moment."

"You must return?" I set down my fishing rod to better enjoy the rest the scenery offered.

He nodded and his face clouded. "Someone has seen fit, I believe, to use a part of my weapons patent. My barrister will soon see this to a quick end and inflict financial measures such that the thief will wish he'd never undertaken the use of my property."

I recoiled, perhaps in fear, at the venom in his voice. "That sounds severe, Captain Whitfield."

"He should not have taken what was mine."

"Surely he thought there was some, some gray area, perhaps? Maybe he thought it was common knowledge? Or had an earlier claim somehow?"

"He may have thought so, but I do not. If he had made an offer to license or share, purchase the rights, cut me in on the deal, I could have acquiesced. But this?" He shrugged. "No. Severe consequences are in order."

We turned back to the river and he spoke more quietly, of the train journey, of how London was nearly abandoned now as people had fled the Great Stink to relax, ride, and hunt in the country for the summer.

"Captain Whitfield . . ." I began.

"Yes?" He turned and looked at me with curiosity.

"Speaking of riding . . . has anyone mentioned that the stable door to the bay horse might be, well, loose? In need of propping from time to time?"

He frowned. "No, not at all." He looked at me curiously. "Did you want to ride her?" he asked. "The bay?"

"No, no, of course not," I said.

"Are you quite all right, Miss Ravenshaw?" he asked. He looked concerned. "Perhaps you've been outside too long?"

"Oh, no, I'm fine," I said. I went on to make some pleasant conversation about the household and the gardens, but the atmosphere was now tense and unusual. I regretted bringing the topic up at all. Shortly, a drift of swans traveled up the river.

"Oh! I have not seen swans since I've been home." I turned toward him.

"We've got plenty as it's forbidden to hunt them, you know." Whitfield kept casting into the river, but well away from the swans. "And even if it weren't, you would not find me shooting one." His voice was now soft, no trace of the earlier acid remained.

"Why not?" I asked.

He set his rod down and came to sit near to me. "They mate for life. If one is killed, its mate mourns, alone, till it, too, is killed or dies. That wouldn't settle with me. Couldn't bring myself to do it."

I held his gaze and it was not teasing nor flattering, but boyish and pure. I took his hand for a moment and he willingly let it mold into mine. "It's a beautiful sentiment, Captain Whitfield, one I shan't forget."

"You're not the only one with romantic sentiments, Miss Ravenshaw," he teased. I assumed he referred back to my conversation about Mr. Mead. He grinned then, and after packing up the creel, held out his hand to assist me back to Headbourne. "I've very much enjoyed our time together," he said. "Would you care to join me for an early dinner. Fish?"

I loathed fish and it'd likely be served in a rich sauce. "I'd be delighted," I said. It had grown rather lonely, eating alone. I was beginning to doubt whether I wanted to do it for a lifetime.

CHAPTER SIXTEEN

He left after dinner. I watched as Michelene left, some hours later, by the second carriage, after I'd dismissed her for the evening. Where was she going? It was nearly dusk, but it was the start of her day off. I sometimes allowed her to use the carriage, but only with prior permission.

I dressed myself and went down to the stables, where Daniel's assistant was ordering things for the night.

"Hello?" I called from the door.

"Oh, good evening, Miss Ravenshaw," he said. He looked surprised to see me—as well he might. I did not frequent the stables and, of course, the carriage was customarily brought to me when I needed it. He, too, now used my full and proper name.

"I was wondering—do you know where Mademoiselle d'Arbonneau has gone?"

"To a friend's house, for her day off, I believe. A training driver took her."

"Thank you," I said. After a moment I turned toward him again. "Daniel, have you been with Captain Whitfield some time?"

He grinned. "Two years on, now, miss, since he returned from the army."

"So you were here when the woman claiming to be me was in attendance."

"I was."

"Did her maid take carriages, too?"

"I'm sure I can't say, miss," he said. His cap was off and I could see his ear tips pink.

He couldn't say, but he knew.

"Is that all, then, miss? I've got a bit ahead of me tonight before I can turn in."

"Yes, that's all," I said. "Please prepare a carriage for me, for Sunday, if you'd be so kind. I plan to attend church in the new landau, unless Captain Whitfield has returned and has need of it."

"Certainly, miss. I'll do that."

I'd find a way to get further information from him later, I promised myself.

The following Sunday Daniel had the carriage ready. I walked into the church, where, now confirmed as a missionary daughter who'd survived her parents' martyrdom, I was warmly welcomed.

"Miss Ravenshaw," Reverend Bennetts called out to me from the front of the church. "Welcome home."

To my utter delight, the congregation broke out in a refined but genuine patter of applause. I blushed with gratitude and raised my hand to wave my thanksgiving.

After conversing with some others after the service, I turned to the reverend's wife. "I do hope you'll come to call," I said to Mrs. Bennetts.

"If you're sure you'd like us to," she replied.

"You would be most welcome at any time. I would delight in your company."

She drew me aside. "I have to apologize for the, well, the cool welcome you initially received. Until we knew that you were who you claimed to be . . ."

I took both her gloved hands in my own. "I fully understand."

"No one likes to believe they've been duped," she said. "Not even ministers and their wives, perhaps we most of all."

I understood. It had been a common sentiment among the household, too. "If I may," I asked Mrs. Bennetts, "do you believe that Mrs. Knowlton was duped as well?"

She shook her head. "She alone never warmed to the young woman claiming to be you. I believe she knew that woman was not Constance Ravenshaw's daughter."

"Why will she not see me?" I asked.

"I do not know. I shall ask her to accept your call, but I do not know if that will help. She has a cancer and is often unwell."

"Please do." I adjusted my bonnet with an eye to the sun. "I would very much like to speak to her as well as bring her whatever comfort I may."

On Monday, I got dressed on my own. Michelene was in her room, ill, though I suspected she was being recalcitrant, as I'd reprimanded her for taking the carriage without permission. Once dressed, I made my way down the right wing. I had decided to enter the room. It was, after all, my home; no one questioned that anymore. The little cat followed me, keeping pace and rubbing against my leg. I gripped the handle firmly; it was locked. Why? My parents' room had not been locked. I tried again, but it would not jar.

I made my way to the sitting room and rang for Mrs. Black-wood.

"How may we help, Miss Ravenshaw?" A smile warmed the housekeeper's face. Her tone seemed warmer to me than it had before. I couldn't really blame them, any of them. They'd been living in an odd and upsetting déjà vu.

"I should very much like to see the storerooms on the top floor of the house," I said. "I'm looking for some of my mother's letters. I believe you have the keys?"

She nodded. "Just a moment or two to finish up with the day maids, and we'll be back to take you."

"Take your time, and thank you."

Mrs. Blackwood soon returned and we walked toward the stairs. She looked up at the portrait of my and Captain Whitfield's common distant ancestor.

"He looks very much like the captain, doesn't he?"

I agreed. "I mistook the portrait as being one of Captain Whitfield himself when I first arrived." I blushed at the memory of my false accusation.

"'Tis a mistake anyone could make," she said. "When you walk into Graffam Park, you'll see a portrait of Lord Ledbury's forebear above the staircase. A similar portrait, I understand, hangs in Lord Frome's home." She turned to lead the way upstairs and I looked up at the man. Determined. Insistent. Driven. Principled.

Like my father.

Attractive. Almost rakelike in his smile. Compelling.

Like Captain Whitfield.

She stopped on the landing to catch her breath, and as she did I glanced down to the right wing. "Do you have keys to all the rooms?" I asked.

She saw where I glanced and said, "All but one."

"And that one is . . . ?"

"Where the woman claiming to be you died. Captain Whit-field took it."

"I should like the key to that room as soon as possible."

She nodded. "I did ask for the key back. Captain Whitfield re-assured me that once the renovations have ensured the safety of the room, he shall return the key to me, and then I shall bring it to you."

That seemed fair. I had, after all, asked Whitfield to continue with the renovations, especially those with safety concerns. A week or two more would not matter. Would it? We began to climb again till we reached the hot and narrow top floor. She pulled out her great ring of keys, and without looking, selected the proper one. She slipped it into the doorway and pushed it open.

"Shall I wait for you?" she asked.

"No," I said quietly. "This is perhaps best done alone."

Her face softened. "I lost my mother some years back, too. She was a housekeeper in a house not far from here, and, unusu-ally, they offered lodging for my sister and me as well. She always told us that'd be the nicest place we'd ever live and it was, until I came here. All of us in service hope to serve in a fine house and now I do. Take your time, Miss Ravenshaw, and I'll lock up again when you say." She turned and made her way down the stairs.

The windows were caked on the inside and out; it had been years, perhaps decades, since they had been cleaned and only the thinnest light seeped through. I kept the lamp lit to cut through the gloom. I somehow felt the steps, the presence, the hopes held high and dreams dashed of the many generations of my family to have trodden here before me.

To the left were trunks stacked one upon another; the ones on the bottom had ragged straps that had been pulled and perhaps nibbled away. I walked over to one and lifted it open; it was empty.

The one next to it was stuffed with disintegrating books. The pile next to that was forbiddingly laced with webs. I did not wish to come face-to-face with the makers of such, even if it held a trove of gold, and left it alone.

On the right-hand side of the room were newer trunks and the wardrobes of which Captain Whitfield had spoken. One trunk was ajar; I lifted it and found a letter casket filled with fragile yellowed papers. My father's handwriting was on many of them and I traced them just to feel something that he had once touched. A long dark brown hair lay in the middle of another one. His?

No, that was impossible. His hair had been black, but never this long. Mother's hair had been fair.

It was the color of my hair. Of . . . Michelene's hair.

Or the imposter's hair, which had also been dark, like mine! I thought upon whose it could have been, and how it had come to be here. Perhaps it had been laid to deceive.

I turned back to the other papers, which seemed to be deeds and other business matters, but there were also chapters of Scripture written in Father's hand. There were letters in Mother's hand addressed to Honiton. Why had they not been sent? I took the small packet and closed the trunk. I read of their day-to-day lives, of their ideas for ministry, the names of some who would be working alongside them in India, and what Mother hoped to bring with her.

Then it struck me. Letters, yes, letters! That must have been how the imposter had found out details about our lives. She'd read letters my mother had written. Perhaps she had taken them. She could have learned enough about our lives to perpetrate her deception. After all, that was how Captain Whitfield had ascertained that I was left-handed. She had, apparently, not found *that* letter. Or perhaps he'd taken it first. Mr. Highmore had said she'd presented something from my mother to the London Missionary Society to prove her identity. It may well have been that she'd found it in this attic, too. Where had that gone and what was it?

I recalled that Mr. Highmore's secretary had suggested that I'd learned of the events from the newspapers. This, certainly, was as plausible for her as it was for me. Where could I find old newspapers? Perhaps if I found that they were commonly available, I'd understand what happened, see what facts had been published. Perhaps I could ascertain the first half of this equation, how she came to believe me dead, now that the second half, how she'd learned so much about my family, had been solved.

I moved to the first wardrobe, breathing heavily; the July air was pregnant with humidity but my lungs had already accommodated themselves to England. The hinges squeaked open and dust motes flew into the air, descending slowly, then drifting sidewise, gracefully, like the gentle ballet of jellyfish off the Kerala coast.

The wardrobe corners were stitched with spiderwebs! I gasped for air, closed my eyes and prayed away the spider memory, and quickly closed the doors again.

The second wardrobe, when I opened it, had but one lone garment, wrapped in a kind of tissue. I touched one corner, and it fell away, fragile with age. I pulled a little more, and it began to unwind like shroud clothes until there before me was the most beautiful wedding dress I'd ever seen. The edges were laced, Honiton lace, and I recognized the work as belonging to my grandmother. I could not remember her, of course, but my mother had her lacework on some linens we'd brought with us to India.

I could see why Mother had not brought this beautiful dress with her. I shook it out and held it up against myself. Pity there was no looking-glass at hand. I closed my eyes and tried to imagine what she had felt on her wedding day. I felt her, somehow, near me. Urging me? Warning me?

How could she be? Foolish. I shook my head to clear my thoughts.

"Mmm-hmm." A throat cleared and my eyes flew open.

"Mrs. Blackwood." I kept a hold on the dress but let it drop to my waist.

"Miss Dainley is here to see you," she said.

"It's not my at-home day, is that right?"

"Intimate friends are allowed to call on one another at other times," she said. "She's here to continue the planning for your picnic. That'll be your first event as hostess, albeit jointly with Miss Dainley. You'll want it to go right."

"Oh yes," I said. I began to wrap the dress and she came over to me.

"You go visit with Miss Dainley and we'll do this and have it brought to your room. I've already asked Annie to prepare some tea."

"Thank you," I said with especial tenderness for the care as well as the suggestion. "I'm indebted to you, Mrs. Blackwood."

She smiled. "The dress looked lovely. It'll make a fine wedding dress for you."

"Thank you," I said. "But as I mentioned once before, it's not certain I shall ever marry."

Her countenance dropped then, and I wondered why it was such a particular concern to her. She turned back to her work as I descended the stairs.

Miss Dainley waited for me in the drawing room, and as I approached she stood.

"Miss Ravenshaw, I do hope you don't mind my calling."

"Not at all," I said. "And as we are friends, please call me Rebecca."

"And I must be Delia to you," she replied. "I hope I didn't interrupt?"

"Oh, not at all. I was just looking at a wedding dress."

She went white and fairly plopped backward on the sofa. "Oh!"

"It's my mother's," I rushed on to say. "I was going through her things."

She began to revive, taking a cup of tea from Annie and then handing it back, quickly, for a refill. "Ah, well. Then. She didn't take it to India with her?"

"No, we had little trunk space. If she'd planned to be married there, she could have, though. You can't be an Englishwoman and not be married in an English wedding dress. It isn't done. The best gowns, of course, have Honiton lace because it was used on Her Majesty's wedding dress." I smiled. "My mother had Honiton well before the Queen!"

Delia's face looked so sorrow-filled and abject then, perhaps thinking of her own future wedding in India to a man she'd have known but weeks, that I pushed the small silver cake tray toward her. "Please, take one."

She did and within a few minutes had recovered. "These tea cakes are superb. It will be difficult for you to replace Cook, indeed, this household, when Captain Whitfield leaves."

I had the idea that it was more a question than a statement, but I did not feel compelled to answer any questions, spoken or not.

"I shall have some difficulties, that is certain." I thought about Michelene leaving to Winchester without permission. "How to gently address concerns with one's staff. I should need insight on that, too."

She set down her teacup. "Anyone currently in mind?"

I was not ready to confide in her to that level yet. "There are ongoing concerns," I said.

"The perfect person to assist in these matters would be Lady Ashby," she said. "I can think of no one better suited to help you, and she would be most eager to come to your aid, I'm certain of it."

"Lady Ashby?"

"Of course. I saw her when I mentioned the picnic to Lord Ashby. He is most enthusiastic, and so is she." Every time she brought him up her face grew bright—as a matchmaker's might, not as a potential lover's would. She wanted me with Ashby. For my sake, possibly, but more likely for her own. To free Whitfield from whatever she assumed might be between us. She had not, I suspected, the financial resources to attract Ashby and his mother on her own merits even if she'd wanted to.

"Shall we begin?" She turned back to the small sheaf of papers she'd brought. Should she have wished it, I was certain she'd have made a fine governess. I did not want to mention such an idea to her. However, for the time being, I would strive to be an apt pupil. I knew I had much to learn and I wanted the picnic to go perfectly for my sake . . . and for Whitfield's.

CHAPTER SEVENTEEN

I'd looked forward to our garden outing and had been concerned that the day would be very much like the one before—wet and gray as a hunting dog—but I was delighted to be wrong. Michelene helped dress me, of course. I requested a dress I'd always found especially flattering, and had been waiting to wear, made of ivory with roses scattered upon it. The waist was becomingly tight and yet I could comfortably walk in it.

"*Très jolie,*" she said, tugging gently at the lace sleeves. "It is enjoyable to wear the colors again, is it not?"

I'd eased out of mourning and back into life. I missed my parents still, of course. And yet I was young and I was certain my mother would have found extended grief to be a waste of my youth, given that I knew where they now were. The ruffle at the back went all the way up to the top of my neck, but dropped into a slightly daring scalloped cut in front. I handed a bottle to Michelene. "Please blend some of this into my pot of gloss."

She opened the lid and sniffed it. "Cinnamon?"

"*Oui,*" I teased in feeble French. "For *le* puffing of *les* lips."

She grinned. "Ah, Miss Ravenshaw has some Indian secrets of

her own. I shall have to steal this idea. With your permission, of course."

"Of course," I said with a wink. "As long as you don't use it for the benefit of anyone with whom I am in competition."

"Which competition?" She grew unusually pointed.

"Oh," I said coyly, "you yourself brought it up months ago. Any at all I might find myself in, I suppose."

"But you hold all the most important cards, as they say," Michelene responded. "Headbourne. Your fortune. Your beauty . . ."

"There are others here more beautiful than me," I replied. She did not refute me.

"Some gentlemen prefer the dark hair, as I well know," she teased. I suspected it was to make me feel better, but her reference to that made me understand that we were both thinking of Delia and her fair skin and sunlit hair.

Michelene returned a few minutes later with my tingling gloss. I was now ready to meet Captain Whitfield. I hummed downstairs, where the good captain awaited.

The care taken had not gone unappreciated.

"I am at a loss for words, Miss Ravenshaw," he said. "And I promise you, that does not often happen. You are lovely. I would say unmatched, but having once been chastised for comparing you with other women, I hesitate to risk it again."

At that, I laughed aloud. And then I stopped.

"What is wrong?" His face grew somber.

"Nothing is wrong," I said. I looked up and smiled. "I just realized that was, perhaps, the first time I have laughed aloud since I've been home."

"I could not be more delighted to be the one to have teased that out." A tender note, hitherto unheard, undergirded his voice. "Shall we?"

I nodded and placed my hand in the crook of his arm. He wore lightweight black trousers, a linen shirt, and high black boots. I remembered one thing Michelene had told me about Hussars. "Their uniforms are vivid," she'd said, "but they truly need no color. The men themselves are the *panache*."

Ah, yes, indeed. I was falling under the spell of the man and his panache and, for the moment, had no desire to wake from it.

We took the carriage to Winchester—the day was bright and I was especially proud to be riding in a carriage fitted with such beautiful glass.

The town bustled and Daniel neatly wound his way through the streets so we could enjoy the view of people shopping and walking, and there were quite a few who tipped their hats, from street or carriage, to Captain Whitfield as we passed by. He seemed to know nearly everyone, but I noted most greeted him with reserve, perhaps even suspicion: a slight raising of the hand followed by a quick tug of a hat to cover the eyes, or a nod with a nearly instantaneous turning away. Whitfield flushed just a little and grimaced after quickly releasing forced smiles that appeared to cause him both embarrassment and pain.

Hadn't Annie said that both the doctor and the constable were his great friends? But when we passed the doctor he turned his back to Whitfield after the briefest of acknowledgments. The doctor had grown awkward with me, too, after I'd asked questions. Perhaps I imagined those instances, but if not, I wondered that Whitfield should want to stay here.

But his family was, after all, here. Perhaps he'd thought owning Headbourne would change how people felt about him. But Headbourne was now mine.

"If you . . .when you choose to buy another property," I began, "will it be here in Hampshire?"

He shook his head. "No, I do not think that would suit. I have a friend, Captain Chapman, who will soon return to England and his family's estate, which he's just inherited in Derbyshire. He's almost convinced me to take up residence there as well."

"Derbyshire! So far?"

"It's far enough," he said quietly, but he seemed thoughtful and there didn't seem to be an appropriate follow-up so I said nothing more about it. I considered where I'd last heard Derbyshire mentioned; it had not been long ago.

Ah, yes. Delia had said she'd prefer to move to Derbyshire, if need be, than depart for India. I thought it hardly coincidental that was the county she'd named.

"Here, then," Whitfield said as we pulled up to a lovely building, by the side of which was a large lawn with a pretty paved path.

"Finest Quality Statuaries To Be Found Near Or Far," I read on a plaque near the doorway. "Marble and Other Fine Materials." My delight to be on such an outing, with such a man, must have shown because Mrs. Ross squeezed my hand and said, "Don't go overboard, lassie."

Captain Whitfield had already descended from the carriage so I leaned over and whispered to her, "With the purchases or the man?"

She grinned back. "Both!"

Whitfield helped me down, then her, and we proceeded through the gardens whilst she sat nearby.

I felt attached to my Flora statue, so, rather than replace it, I asked the proprietor if he could make some improvements to it instead.

"Of course." He looked rather downhearted.

"I'm delighted," I said.

"And now," Captain Whitfield spoke up, "perhaps we may look at urns and other statues you have. New ones, for purchase."

The proprietor's smile returned. "Yes, I remember the statues you purchased for the other lady. You have fine taste, Captain Whitfield. Follow me!"

I turned to him inquiringly.

"My mother," he responded smoothly to my unanswered question. His mother. Lord Ledbury did not accompany her for her purchases? It seemed unusual.

After selecting some urns and a few Greek statues that would make noble companions to the ones we already had, I stopped in front of a large statue of an imposing angel, not at all cherubic, but a warrior, with a drawn sword and a ready stance.

"You like this one?" Whitfield asked.

I nodded. "I-I think so. It reminds me of something, I'm not quite sure. Perhaps because I felt that, somehow, the Lord must have sent angels to surround and protect me in India. Or maybe, well . . . I'm reading *Paradise Lost* once again."

"I see." He took my hand and placed it on his arm, comforting and friendly but not forward. "You feel as if in the Uprising you lost Paradise?"

He'd understood it was not the book I was speaking of, but my life. I nodded and held back tears that threatened. I hadn't cried for some time and did not wish to spoil the day.

"I understand, Miss Ravenshaw." He put his arm around me, protectively. "I've been at war and seen its ravages; I'm afraid I grew quite callous to death, and even to the taking of life in the pursuit of a necessary cause."

A troubling sentiment.

"Perhaps Paradise once lost cannot be regained no matter how one wishes it might." He looked downcast.

He next ran his finger along the sword. "This was cast by a man who has held a sword in battle. It's not for show." He turned to me; I looked at it in awe. "Would you like this statue for your gardens?"

"Yes," I said. "Yes, I truly would."

"Then I shall see to it that it is yours," he said quietly, and indicated to the owner of the business that he should mark that one as sold.

A thrill ran through me, yes, because I truly wanted that statue in my gardens and was overjoyed to see it come to fresh life. But also, I drank in the feeling of having a man stand beside me, strongly, protecting me and looking out for my interests, one who could be both warm and cool. Strong and affectionate. One, yes, in honesty, whom I could not completely understand and, therefore, control. But was he trustworthy? This I did not yet know. What, after all, did he find to be a necessary cause for taking a life?

After we placed our final order with the proprietor, he invited us to sit for tea, which one of his men delivered to a delicate table placed under a jasmine vine that climbed around a pretty arbor. I looked at the men gently removing my new statue to be wrapped and then delivered within a day or two. "Do you believe in angels, Captain Whitfield?"

"I must, mustn't I?" He looked at me for a long moment; the look in his eyes was hungry and I could not decide if it thrilled or scared me. "At least, now that I've come to know you, I cannot deny that there are angels on earth."

"You flatter!" He may have been trifling with me, but he lifted my spirits and made me feel wanted; somehow, he alone was able to coax forth joy in me. Perhaps it was not Headbourne alone over which he tendered care. The jasmine was now blooming and the blossoms sent a heady, intoxicating scent into the air between us, which was already heady with unexpressed emotion. Some of the buds had unfurled, showing white petals, as beautiful as the finest pearls. "Shall I tell you a story of white petals, and India, Captain Whitfield?"

"I should like nothing better." I looked him full in the face, and he didn't flinch; his gaze was open and I believed that in this, at least, he did not trifle with me.

"Many people believe that India was a land untouched by Christianity before the missionaries arrived, but that is not true." I reached up and plucked a white blossom from the tree above us. "Actually, Saint Thomas arrived in India fewer than twenty years after the crucifixion, well ahead of the faith's arrival in Europe. Thomas was eager, as were all the apostles, to share the Good News."

"Like your parents," Captain Whitfield said.

"Yes." I reached for one more blossom, the only other one within my easy grasp. "One day, Thomas walked among the Brahman as they threw water into the air as an offering to their god. 'Why does your god reject your offering?' Saint Thomas asked. 'If it falls back to the ground, surely he cannot find it pleasing. My God would not reject such an offering,' he said. He then scooped up a handful of water and threw it into the air."

"And it disappeared?" Captain Whitfield asked. I could not tell if he was mocking.

"No. The droplets hung in the air but for a moment, and then fluttered back to earth as white flower petals." At that, I threw open my hand and released the jasmine petals into the air above us. Some landed on my head, but in the main they came to rest on Captain Whitfield's dark hair. I laughed at the sight of it.

"It's worth the humiliation to hear you laugh twice in a day," he teased. He shook his head, but several petals remained. I reached up and gently plucked them from his head, placing them into my open, cupped hand, which I had earlier ungloved. He reached out and took them from my hand, then placed them in a shirt pocket before kissing the inside of my palm, where they had rested. My palm burned.

Oh, Mrs. Ross, I've succumbed to that which you warned against. I'm not only overboard, I'm drowning. I remembered a passage I'd just read in Joshua. *So the sun stood still in the midst of heaven, and hasted not to go down about a whole day.*

If only the sun would stand still to stop this day from passing.

Whitfield set my hand down. "I, like Thomas, am a doubter," he said softly. "A skeptic, as you yourself said. I cannot afford to believe what I cannot see."

"What happened to Saint Thomas was a miracle, Captain Whitfield. A miracle is a sign that something is happening, even though we cannot understand it all. The Greek word we translate as miracle is *sign.*"

He took my hand in his again, for a brief moment, but did not reply. The earnest look on his face, though, told me that he very much wished for a miracle he would not speak of.

On the ride back to Headbourne I asked him, "Is that why you do not attend church very often? You've left God because you cannot see?"

He shook his head. "A person cannot leave God, but God can, if He chooses, leave a person. I believe that, perhaps, He left when my father died. Certainly when my mother left me He fled me as well. I have not heard from God since, not in any way that I can discern." He looked slightly alarmed after freeing this thought, and I could well understand why. Many have doubts; few voice them. The silent tended to quickly condemn those honest few who air misgivings dormant deep within us all. Somehow, knowing his tender points enmeshed me with him as much as knowing his strengths.

"Do not be afraid to share your doubts. He freely entertains them, and says He shall never leave nor forsake us."

"You may henceforth refer to me as Thomas, the doubter," Whitfield jested, but his voice shook and I did not press him further.

The next afternoon, Landreth asked me to come to the hallway. On the hall console table stood a creamy porcelain vase. In it was a large bouquet of white jasmine branches, thick with buds just beginning to unfurl and release their perfume. A small card was attached. It said simply:

A Sign.

CHAPTER EIGHTEEN

⚜

Delia and I were to put the finishing touches to our picnic plan, which would be held in about a fortnight. I waited for her near the foyer; Captain Whitfield's valet was moving about in the main house, too. It appeared that Thornton was preparing for another journey to London but he took a moment to rearrange the jasmine bouquet, now beginning to wilt and shed petals that drifted silently to the floor.

"White petals forever remind me of India," I said.

"India sounds marvelous," Thornton replied. "Except for the, er, maid that was here earlier, I've never met an Indian person and have only read of the place in an improving book."

"There are no other Indian servants hereabouts?"

He shook his head. "I've never heard of it outside London."

He bowed slightly, but politely, and took his leave just as Delia's carriage pulled up. I had never watched her alight from it, having always greeted her inside. It was weathered around the edges, and the coachman looked tired and perhaps older than a man should be who is still required to drive. He helped her to step down, taking more than a moment to uncoil his back, which never did completely straighten. I backed into the main hallway to save her any discomfort she may have had at my observance of the worn state of her man, horse, and carriage.

"Delia!" I kissed her cheeks at the door, and she kissed mine in return. "I'm thrilled to have the day together."

"I, too." She looked me over carefully; I wore a lavender-colored dress with mother-of-pearl buttons. "No longer a raven." She carried a small sheaf of papers, which, I assumed, included not only the names of those we had invited but details such as menus and music. We walked arm in arm out into the garden. "It is coming along nicely." Her voice held real admiration. "You've done well!"

I surveyed it along with her, and yes, I agreed, the gardens, after a faint and fallow era, were well and truly reviving; a renaissance was under way.

"I must admit," I said, "Captain Whitfield has done well. The planning is mostly his and I have only been here to see that his arrangements have been properly carried through." But I'd done that with care and concern, and as I looked over the gardens, I thought that I now loved this landscape as much as India's. The soft green and delicate blooms had begun to wend their way, like ivy, around my heart.

Delia sniffed. "Yes, Captain Whitfield has done well. You might take a bit more care with the roses."

I looked up and saw said Captain Whitfield striding toward us across the long lawn. Delia saw him, too, and immediately loosened her bonnet.

"I must have been born under a lucky star." He took one of each of our arms in his; we flanked him. "Two of my favorite ladies blossoming right here in the gardens. To what do I owe this fortunate encounter?"

"We were finishing the plans for our picnic. Would you like to help plot where the cushions should be placed?" I teased.

"I shall leave that to the experts," he said. "A picnic in mid-August could be quite warm. Perhaps I might suggest under the trees?" He looked at the jasmine vines wrapping their way round a garden arbor. I admit, I had come to think of it as our flower.

"I've suggested a moonlight picnic," I said, as we three strolled toward where Landreth had set up a small table. "It should have cooled by evening."

"A moonlight picnic, what a wonderful idea!"

I was sure that settled it in Delia's mind. She'd ensure that the other guests would find the idea irresistible as well.

"Would you care to join us for a light lunch?" I asked.

"The table is set for two," he said.

"Mrs. Blackwood will not mind adding a third," Delia offered. I thought it rather forward to direct someone else's household, but the suggestion was sound.

"Please do," I said. "It will sustain you ahead of your trip to London."

"I capitulate, as there are only two ladies I could not bear to disappoint." Landreth brought out another chair and Mrs. Blackwood rose admirably to the addition, her adaptability really never in question.

"Does your business in London involve your time in the army?" I asked.

"In a way it does," he said. "I've got a partnership in an arms manufacture. I've always been fascinated with weapons, and my years in the army only sharpened that. Due to my experience in war I came to see that the weapons we were using didn't have quite the immediate . . . stopping power we needed for a quick kill."

I squirmed a bit at that, and, out of the corner of my eye, I could see that Delia did, too. The captain quickly offered a rationale. "Slow deaths cause unnecessary pain. I pulled together with an engineer friend and another man, who was a lieutenant at the time, to design a revolver which allowed for quicker, firmer action."

"I'm sure it's been a great success in every way," I said, wondering just a little if death was ever a success.

"Well, Colt has completely shut and left London, so that says something, doesn't it?" He grinned, but it was tinted with a bit of insolence. "Happy to have British arms in British hands." Delia had recovered from a near swoon which was not, I was certain, from the heat, which was mild, but from the thought of the pounds sterling she imagined Captain Whitfield's hard-fought and well-defended licenses brought in.

"I shall have to depart shortly if I'm to make my train," he continued. "I'll be calling at Southampton again, Miss Ravenshaw. Will you need more of the tincture?"

"That would be very kind," I said. "I do believe it's helped, as I am feeling much better now."

"It works best if you take it without pause," he said firmly.

Annie brought out sandwiches a few moments later. "Please bring the cakes soon," I said. "Captain Whitfield will have to take his leave very shortly."

She looked at him, and then at Delia, and then at me, before bobbing and returning to the house. She was back in an instant with a tray of shortbread biscuits and small cakes. She held it out to Delia, who, remarkably, passed. Captain Whitfield also declined a sweet. Annie held the tray to me. I had asked her to fetch them, so I knew that I must take one, and I did.

"Is there some other kind of biscuit or cake I could have had prepared that would better meet with your enjoyment?"

Delia answered, but not for herself; rather proprietarily, she spoke for the captain instead. "Captain Whitfield does not eat sweets."

The shortbread went dry in my mouth and I took a great swell of tea in order to wash it down. "I'm sorry."

He smiled and responded softly. "Do not chide yourself. You could not have known. I stopped eating them some years ago due to the slave trade in the West Indies, origin of much of our sugar."

"Slavery has long been outlawed, is that not so?"

"In name," Captain Whitfield responded. "My stepfather, Lord Ledbury, still has considerable investment interests there, so I am perhaps better informed than many on some of the practices which prevail to this day. I find they've ensured I've lost my taste for all things sugared."

With great restraint I did not inquire as to Delia's notable and sudden onset of disdain for sugar. I nodded to Annie and had her take the tray away.

"Please, continue to enjoy them," Captain Whitfield looked as if he were about to call Annie back.

"No, no. While this remains your home, too, I shall ensure that they are not served."

"Speaking of which, I understand you've made specific inquiries on several properties," Delia said. "Some near, and some quite far away."

I had not heard this news. Lady Ledbury, no doubt, had passed it along to Delia.

"Yes, I have," he said smoothly. "But perhaps that is news for another day as I know my partners will be quite cross if I miss my train tonight. Ladies, this has been a rare pleasure."

He stood, and indicated that Delia and I remain seated. His gaze flickered in a friendly manner toward Delia, but then settled on me. "I will look forward with unrestrained enthusiasm to your picnic."

"I shall miss your company," I said, surprised to find a large void begin to hollow my insides at the thought of his absence. We bade him good day, finished our preparations, and then Landreth called for Delia's carriage to come and fetch her.

Later that evening, I climbed the stairs to Mrs. Ross's room, then knocked. "Mrs. Ross?"

"Come in, lassie."

I opened the door and shut it behind me. A tea tray rested on the table next to her window, and she had a small stack of shortbread on it. "Have one. Ye know they're guid," she said with a bright grin.

I smiled back. I had no mother, but I did have this gentle woman to speak to in confidence.

"Perhaps . . ." I began. "Perhaps Delia is better suited to life in Hampshire and I to life in India."

"For a young lady who is the daughter of a preacher, the daughter of a teacher, and a teacher herself, that doesna sound very promising. Self-pity is the enemy of joy."

"I wish I could find out who the imposter might have been," I said. "And I wonder where she might have found an Indian maid. I've made some inquiries, and I've even asked Annie, Landreth, and Delia, who each said they'd never met an Indian servant round here before. Delia and I seem to have become friends so she's got no reason to lie."

"Seeming to be friends is not always the same as being friends," Mrs. Ross said. "You'll learn the truth. It always outs." She set down her teacup. "Miss Dainley and you have made great arrangements for your picnic. Will Lieutenant Dunn return to attend?"

"I believe so. He's a lovely man, but I . . . hadn't given that much thought."

"I'm certain *he* has." She popped another shortbread into her mouth. "And given you much thought, too."

I considered it a moment more. "I don't think I'm cut out to be a missionary wife. I'd know what to do, of course. But my heart isn't in it. Not in China, in any case."

"The heart might be turned if you loved the man. Or felt a calling," she said.

I nodded. "I'll pray about it. But for now, neither is true."

She brushed crumbs off her ample lap. "'Tis wise. And now, lassie, it's off to bed with ye as we both have church early tomorrow."

I turned to leave, and then turned back for one last question. "Had you noticed, when we three went to Winchester for statues, how the people who recognized Captain Whitfield seemed to treat him with reserve?"

She nodded. "I did. But I doona believe it was always that way."

She'd lived here much longer than I had. She'd know.

I said good night to her, and went to my room, where I took supper with an extra serving of leftover cake. After the conversation about weapons that did not stop advancing enemies, I began to feel the memories of the journey to the Residency creep around my mind, and told Michelene so when she came to dress me for sleep.

"A little poppy will help you sleep without those memories," she reassured.

It seemed lately she offered it too readily. Yet as I thought back on it the nights I had taken laudanum had been more restful on the whole, with fewer dreams, even if they'd been more vivid. I wanted to be fully refreshed for church and so, reluctantly, I agreed. She poured a dose for me, thickly spiced with cinnamon, and left after I drank it. Almost immediately the welcome warmth coursed throughout me, spreading from my center like a bottle of spilled ink. I grew a little frightened at how much I appreciated its comforts.

I should not take it again.

I walked to the window and looked out at the guesthouse, fully dark, and wondered how far along in the process Captain Whitfield was in the purchase of his new home. I looked just beyond that and saw, again, a tiny flash of light near the graveyard. *How could that be?* Soon even the flash was obscured by the mists, rising, as they always did, almost like breath exhaling from an open grave.

Another flash of light. Perhaps from the chapel? I was immediately more alert in spite of the laudanum.

After slipping into a dressing gown and a long robe, I tiptoed down the hall. I wanted to see what was causing those flashes by the chapel.

CHAPTER NINETEEN

I was not yet prepared to look upon a grave with my name on it, so I did not take the direct route, but I thought to take the back path and enter through the side door if it worked. I stopped in one of the rooms near the library where Captain Whitfield stored some of his weapons and took a pistol for safety, as I would have in India. After loading it, I walked along the corridor, quietly slipped out the door, and silently made my way round the stable and then toward the chapel.

The moon was but a shard in the cloud-clotted sky, but it reflected off the rough path, slick with mist, which massed around me. I picked my way down that path; the night birds had gone quiet. I stepped on a loose stone and lost my balance, twisting my ankle, which caused immediate shooting pain. Because it had recovered, though, it righted itself shortly and I was able to move forward. My eyes adjusted to the dark.

The ground smelt of powdered earth and the must of moss; enormous, surreal mushrooms peopled the path on left and right. I beheaded one with my foot and it rolled down the hill till it rested against a decomposed tree trunk with a tiny *thwack*. I walked again, and was soon at the chapel, and yet, there was no discernible light on either side—grave side or dark side.

What had I seen, then, from my window? A specter? I did not believe in them.

Come have a look at the gravestones, came a slithery voice from inside my head.

No, but I shall just pry open the side door to the chapel. My breath came shallowly, quickly, and it made me light-headed. I kept the pistol in my left hand and with my right, I shook the door loose. It was not the main door, but a side one. I'd expected it to be sealed over with growth from being so long underused, but it wasn't. It opened neatly, almost as if it had been recently tended to. I stepped inside the chapel.

Some windows were broken and the pews were eaten with rot, legs unsteady as a newly landed sailor's. The floor was strewn with rushes and dried weeds of all sorts except for . . . in one far back corner, it looked as though someone had cleaned the area out. There was a fairly steady pew, cleaned off, and a stand that looked as if it had been used for candles. I moved back there, slowly. Then I stopped to listen. A noise. Distant, but present. My heart pounded in my ears and in my throat.

"Hello?" I called out. "Who is here?"

I inclined my head but there was no additional sound. I shivered, though it was warm, and when I paid attention I noticed my gown was drenched in sweat. *From the laudanum.*

I caught a glint of something in the corner on the floor, thoughtfully illuminated by a ray of moonlight. I moved slowly, and when I was very certain no one hid in the shadows nearby, I bent to pick up the item.

Once in my hand, I could clearly see what it was. A hairpin made of mourning jet and diamonds. Very costly, very expensive indeed.

Whose was it? My own mourning jewelry had not included diamonds. As I slipped it into my pocket, I heard another noise. Or had I? Had I really seen the light from my room or was that a laudanum fancy, too? Had I heard something just now?

Yes, yes I had. I kept my hand on the pistol in my pocket, knowing I could shoot, effectively, without ever withdrawing it from my gown if need be.

"Who's there?" I called out. The door squeaked open and I placed my finger on the trigger. "Who is there?" I demanded.

"*C'est moi*, Michelene," came the answer.

I sighed with relief and removed my finger from the trigger. "Michelene! Whatever are you doing here? I could have shot you!"

"*Quelle horreur!*" The color drained from her face. "I am very thankful that you did not. It is late. I returned to your room to see if I might remove one of your gowns for mending and found you gone. When I looked for you in the house and could not find you, I looked out of the window and saw the hem of your dressing gown before it disappeared on the path. *Et voilà*. Here I am." She looked at me with a strange look on her face. "Are you quite well?"

I nodded. "I . . . I thought I saw a faint light out here. I wanted to see . . ."

Michelene looked around. "There is no light except my lamp."

I nodded. "No, it's quite dark, I agree, now that the moon has gone behind the clouds again." I held out my open hand. "I found this here. Do you know who it belongs to?"

She looked at the jet and diamond hairpin before closing my hand softly around it. "It is yours, little one. It belongs to you."

"Mine?" I was confused. I didn't recall ever wearing this. And I hadn't been in the chapel before. Had I?

"Come, *petite*." She put her arm around me. "You need sleep. We shall leave by the door that opens smoothly, and not the one that does not?" She shepherded me out of the chapel and back to the house, extracting a promise that I would not make any more late-night visits to the chapel, insinuating by her choice of words that this had not been my first.

It had been. Hadn't it? Had she really seen me, and followed? Or on this night, in which she had given me a large dose of laudanum, had she been planning to visit the chapel herself, for some reason?

On Monday, we took the new landau to Winchester. This time we took Mrs. Blackwood with us so she could procure some ingredients for Cook. Daniel ran errands, as he often did, and planned to take the carriage to the coachworks to purchase some grease. He said he would be back for us in two hours.

"I'll be at the poulterer's," Mrs. Blackwood said. "And then I've other errands. I'll meet you back here." She popped up her black umbrella against a sudden summer shower. We headed for the milliner's, but on the way passed the china and home-goods shop. I drew close to the window.

"Let's go in," I said, and Michelene smiled and opened the door for me. We wandered around for a bit, and I looked longingly at a lovely tea set, which I did not purchase, and also at some lace linens that reminded me of my mother. On the way out, I spotted a dish—a fish dish, to be precise—in garish red. It was the duplicate of the one Cook had used some time before. I brought it back to the counter, and asked the assistant, "Do you know if one of these was sold to Headbourne House?"

The matron switched feet, fidgeting, and finally said, "Yes. It went with a large order, many months ago, last year, in fact. There were few dishes in service and the mistress of the house, er, at the time, ordered quite a few from us."

"I am the true Rebecca Ravenshaw of Headbourne House, returned," I said gently.

She nodded. "My sister told me."

"Delightful!" I smiled. "Who is your sister?"

She nodded and coughed into a small handkerchief. "She's your cook."

My eyes widened. "Ah, I see. And she, she directed the woman claiming to be me to your shop for purchases."

"It's not like all that, then," she protested. "There aren't many shops in town which sells dishes and such, now, are there? She, Miss Ravenshaw, the first one, I mean, and my sister, well, they were close."

"Oh, I didn't mean to imply . . ." It would have been most unusual for a servant to be "close" with her cook.

The woman hesitated. "She reminded my sister of her daughter."

"I see," I said. "And is her daughter nearby?" Perhaps the daughter had known the imposter!

The proprietress shook her head. "No, miss. She was murdered in Ireland. She was an actress and fell in with a bad lot of men and married one of them. So when the young thing came to her, my sister took her under her wing. She didn't want her to marry a bad man, too."

"Oh, I'm terribly sorry," I said, and I was. Poor Cook! "But . . . was the, my, imposter thinking she must marry?"

"That, I don't know. I do know that when she arrived, well, my sister thought, here is someone I can mother, someone who needs attention. She couldn't give it to her own girl now, not anymore, could she? Then this one was murdered, too."

"Self-murder," I said.

She shrugged. "It would seem."

"You don't believe it to be so?"

"I have no opinion at all, Miss Ravenshaw."

None that she would share, anyway. "Thank you for your time," I said. "I'm sure I'll be back some day."

She nodded her approval, and we left. Well, Cook's daughter could not have known the imposter, but it did explain why Cook was so protective, so reluctant to admit the woman who'd claimed to have been me could have done wrong. I recalled her comment about Whitfield's proposing bed and board—marriage—and perhaps having been rejected. Had that been based on reality, or Cook's protective imaginings?

We left and began walking toward where we were to meet with Daniel. I could see Winchester Cathedral in the background, imposing and beautiful, stately. My head was up, though, and I wasn't watching where I walked, so I bumped into a small lad.

"Oh!" I said as he fell to the ground. "I am so sorry, it's all my fault." I looked him over. He was nearly smothered by two armfuls of women's clothing, some pieces stained and with torn piping, some dresses actually in good condition but in an outmoded style.

Michelene sniffed. "Thief."

"I'm not a thief." He drew himself up to his full height—which reached to about our chest level. He pushed his blond hair from his face, leaving a small trail of grime to mark the path of his hand. "Mum cleans the old clothes shop, you know, where the rich ladies sell their old clothes. I'm helping her carry these. That's what she's paid with."

"Understandable," I said. "I'm so sorry, I was looking at the cathedral and not where I was walking. You're not hurt, are you?"

"I'm tough," he said, and grinned. "The cathedral, well, I can understand that. It's so pretty from the outside."

Something in his voice prompted me to question more. "And the inside as well, no doubt?"

"I wouldn't know." He pointed downward. "I ain't got shoes. No church is going to let me in with bare feet."

"Surely not!" I said. "Why, Jesus washed the bare feet of his disciples and they had on, at best, sandals."

"I've tried, miss, and not just that one. That's the thing about the churches. They don't want you if you ain't rich."

I turned to Mrs. Ross. "Is this true? About the shoes?"

"I'm afraid it is in most churches, lassie."

"We really must be going. We do not want Daniel to be waiting, *non*?" Michelene looked impatient and tried to move farther away from the young boy so his armload of filthy clothes would not touch her.

"What is your name?" I bent down.

"Matthew. And what is yours?"

I grinned at his boldness. "My name is Miss Rebecca Ravenshaw. Matthew—I would like to give you some shoes. I remember what it was like to only have one pair, and those ones too big, not long ago. Would that be all right?"

"Oh yes, Miss Rebecca, I would like that." I ignored his charming use of my Christian name.

I looked around. I had no money. I carried no money. Daniel pulled the carriage up.

"Matthew, you tell your mother that I shall send around my driver to arrange a day for you to visit the cobbler and then come to my house to receive your shoes. She works at the old clothes shop?"

"Yes, miss," he said. "You won't forget, will you, miss?"

I shook my head. "I shan't forget, Matthew. I give you my word."

Daniel helped us into the carriage. Mrs. Blackwood was already inside with her packages. We shortly took off for Headbourne House.

"Really!" Michelene said. "This is most irregular. You can't invite all sorts of people to your home or the right sorts of people won't come."

"Perhaps he is the right sort of people." To be chided by a lady's maid on social propriety was a bit beyond what I was willing to overlook. I looked down at my parasol, my costly parasol, and was stricken with guilt. "What is most irregular is that there is a young boy who would like to attend church, but cannot, because he has no shoes."

"I hope Lady Ashby does not hear of this," Michelene said.

"Why ever would you mention Lady Ashby?" I asked rather crossly.

"She's invited you to her dance, just after the picnic, *non*?" Michelene said. "She'll want to introduce you to the best people. Not to old clothes shop cleaners." She sank back into her seat and closed her eyes, feigning sleep. We arrived at Headbourne a few minutes later and I could see that the other carriage was being wiped down.

"Captain Whitfield back?" Daniel called to one of his grooms.

"Yes," came the answer.

It was awkward, really, how both Michelene and I looked toward the guesthouse at the same time, hoping, I supposed, to see him. I noted her interest. I was certain she'd noted mine. We stayed in the carriage for a moment while the packages were unloaded and she never took her eyes away from the guesthouse.

"The conversation in the shop made me wonder, have you ever been married?" I asked Michelene after the others had removed themselves to the house. I knew some ladies' maids, if widowed young, returned to their former profession.

"*Non,* not married," she said. "But in love . . . *oui.* With a man in France, a *comte,* a member of the *noblesse.*" She looked sad. "He was not a man who would defy convention to keep me. Like some Englishmen would. For example, your Mr. Mead and his Indian wife."

My eyes widened. "How do you know about Mr. Mead?"

"You told me, *petite.* Do you not recall?" She looked at me as one might look at a fevered or confused child.

I shook my head, and then stretched into my memory to bring to mind when I might have mentioned such a thing. The only person I had, with certainty, mentioned Mr. Mead to was Captain Whitfield. Had he discussed this with Michelene? Or had I truly brought this up with her and completely forgotten the incident?

CHAPTER TWENTY

Wednesday was my day for calling; Daniel had the carriage ready.

"Have you made any inquiries about the shoes for that young lad?" I asked him.

"Yes, Miss Ravenshaw. The cobbler is currently making them, and I'll let you know as soon as they are ready."

"Thank you, Daniel. You are so dependable about running errands, and I appreciate your help in this matter, very much indeed."

"How will . . . how will you let the boy and his mother know?"

"Would it be impolite, or an imposition, to send you round with an invitation?"

He shrugged. "I will do it." His voice quieted. "It is a kind thing to do, miss. I was once an orphan, you know."

"I did not know," I said. "I'm so pleased you're in a happy situation then, here."

He nodded. "Captain Whitfield saw to it that I was offered a job. His father had known mine in the military." Daniel said no more but clucked and the horses took off.

I made a few quick social calls, to Lady Ashby, to a new friend at church, and one longer one to Lady Frome, which I most enjoyed, before stopping to drop my card off for Mrs. Knowlton, the friend of my mother.

I sent Daniel to the door with the card, expecting that she would not be ~ home, but he came out with a grin. "She'll see you!"

I nearly tumbled from the carriage in my rush to see her, making my way up to her tidy brick cottage, finally standing on the humble doorstep. Her man opened the door and showed me into her bright parlor. She sat in a corner, a blanket draped over her feet. She looked frail; her eyes were opaque with pain, cloudy white like the thick of an egg white covering what must have once been bright blue.

"I'm delighted to see you." She indicated I should settle in a chair near her own.

"I shan't stay long and overtire you. But I'm so very appreciative you've seen me."

After a few moments of light conversation she said, "I knew within moments of your arrival at church that you were Constance Ravenshaw's daughter as surely as I knew that the earlier young woman, God rest her soul, was not."

"How?" I asked.

"You've the look of her," she said. "The way you carry yourself, the tone of your voice. Your confidence and poise. There are not many of us left from the early years in the church. We were small in number and many of the founders were aged. It is not surprising that there were few who remember you . . . you were a wee child when you left. But Constance was a particular friend to me and we were of an age. She wrote to me for many years, both before and after the . . . darker years."

I nodded. "Those years are not secret."

Mrs. Knowlton set down her cup. "I'm afraid, my dear, that I've done you a disservice. After the first young woman arrived, Lady Ledbury called on me."

"You're friends?" Lady Ledbury had not thought so.

She cackled and looked around her modest environment. "Oh, no. But she is a liberal contributor to our coal charity. She made it clear that she would prefer her son, whom she believes to be the rightful heir of Headbourne, to take possession. She intimated that should I be in touch with the first woman, or with you, later, the coal money would come to an end. I was concerned for those who might go without on a cold night."

She took my hand in her own bony one. "Can you forgive me?"

"Oh yes, yes, dear Mrs. Knowlton," I said. "Do not give this another thought. I'm sorry to have delivered such trouble your way."

"Thank you, dear, but you did not deliver the trouble." Mrs. Knowlton looked at me, her eyes clearing for a moment. "Lady Ledbury's son did seem to focus on your imposter with a steady eye, and of course would have had cause to have been pleased to receive the house in the end."

"At the cost of her death?" My heart raced. Did she question Whitfield, too? Did they all?

"That, my dear, I couldn't know," she said. "I do not know him. Only his mother." She sipped a little tea, then sat quietly for a moment before saying, "Lady Ledbury has spread word, quietly, that you suffer from some . . . imbalance. She knew your mother had melancholia."

I sat there for a moment, silent, sipping my tea.

"Mummy!" I banged on the small door that separated my par-

ents' room from the main door. "Mummy, please let me come in and help you."

The crying quieted for a while but then it brewed again and I stopped knocking. Peter brought a small bowl of rice to me that ayah had made. "It'll be all right," he murmured. Our ayah clucked over both of us and drew us near to her bosom before returning to her own home that night.

Late, after Father had returned to the house, there was a loud, sharp disagreement about living in India. In the morning, Mother pretended nothing had been awry, hoping we would too, one supposed. She picked up her needlework and later showed our ayah how to begin with bobbins. That was the end of the beginning, I remember, and the start of something new.

I'd never forgotten the wailing, though it was the last time she'd cried out. It echoed, still, in my ears.

"Miss Ravenshaw?" Mrs. Knowlton drew me back to the present.

"Oh, yes. Sorry." I remembered the occasional question or implication inquiring as to whether I was well. But I hadn't imagined the gate having been blocked in the stable yards, or the theft of the first packet of letters, or the lights by the grave, or Mrs. Ross in the woods. Had I?

"And now," she said, "before I nod off, please tell me of the last years in India. Your mother wrote regularly for a time. Then she stopped."

"Might I ask why? If you know? I hope I'm not pressing."

"Not at all, dear." She patted my arm. "She hadn't wanted to be in India at first, as you know. I suspect news from one who seemed to have all that she wanted, a life of peace and comfort in England, was too painful to bear for a while. Once she found her feet, she wrote again, and then it was my turn to fence with envy as she accomplished so much, and, sadly, I let my return letters dwindle."

"Oh yes, I see." This was perhaps why I hadn't heard from one or another of my English friends in India—it all made sense now. They envied the calm of my situation, or of being home, though they certainly could not have envied my parents' death or my loss of family.

I obliged her, sharing the happy parts, and most of the later years were profoundly happy. I promised to call again. "Mrs. Knowlton," I began, pulling my gloves on, "you've spoken of my imposter, and I should like to find out what I may about her. Do you know anything further?"

She shook her head. "She said but little at church, very often did not attend, claiming illness, and in general, after but a month or two, kept most often to Headbourne. She wasn't here long before . . ." She cast her eyes downward and sipped her tea. "Before her life was taken."

"Taken? Not a suicide?"

"Perhaps it happened exactly as has been said, that she took her own life. But to what purpose? Had she been truly suicidal, there would have been no need for an elaborate deception first. She apparently had no family to come looking after her."

I recalled anew what the woman at Mr. Highmore's office had said to me upon my arrival. Perhaps that would provide a clue. "Where should I find archived newspapers, of the entire year of the Mutiny?"

She tilted her head. "The library at Winchester, I should think, dear."

"The constabulary is also in Winchester, is that not right?"

She nodded. "A fairly new building of a decade or so."

I bent to kiss her powdery cheek, chalky with age like her front steps, and took my leave. All the way home I wondered how

I could sort things out to make sense of it all, prayed to find out the imposter's identity, and hoped I would not yield to the tar pit of melancholia as my mother often had. The fear of it stalked my mind.

A few days later Daniel drove us to the library at Winchester. Michelene came along, wishing to stop at the milliner's and pick up a hat that was being repaired.

"Daniel, do you know where the constabulary is, in Winchester?" I asked.

Michelene bent forward. "The constabulary?"

"Yes," I said, "I should like to stop by for a moment."

She pursed her lips. "That is not done."

I looked to Mrs. Ross, who nodded her approval, and not to Michelene. "Please proceed," I informed Daniel. Half an hour later, we arrived at the tall, rather new building. We three ladies got out of the carriage, and made our way inside. I stopped at the desk.

"Hello, I would like to speak with the chief constable, if he is here," I said.

"Certainly, I'll fetch him," the young officer said. "Who shall I say is calling?"

I handed a card over. "Miss Rebecca Ravenshaw. I'd like to speak with him, if I may, about the death of the woman who had pretended to be me."

The man disappeared up the stairs. Michelene kept her head down, under her bonnet. Some minutes later, the young man reappeared. "I'm sorry, he's not here after all," he said. "I'll leave your card."

He would not meet my eye. *We who serve together in the military stick together even once home,* Whitfield had told me. Most of

Whitfield's true friends seemed to be former military men, like Dunn, who had run to do Whitfield's will in testing me. Unsettled, I bade this young man good day.

As we got in the carriage, I noticed Michelene tipped her head back and up, looking at the outside of the building. From one window I saw the face of a man looking down at me, and then at her, intently, before disappearing from view. It was the constable who'd been at Headbourne upon my arrival. I was certain of it. So why would he not see me?

"Do you know the chief constable?" I asked Michelene as we got into the carriage.

"What a thought," she replied. "The milliner's next?" I looked at her pointedly, but her countenance remained serene.

I nodded and Daniel left her there before taking us to the library. Happily, I arrived during the public viewing times and the librarian was most solicitous in helping me find what I was looking for.

I paged through paper after paper, smudging my gloves, but I cared not. There, in the *Hampshire Telegraph*, was a fully developed article of several pages that thoroughly detailed the Mutiny. I found another article in a later version that listed information about my family, including our names and deaths, as well as our connection to Headbourne House. Relief flooded through me as I leaned back and closed my eyes with gratitude for the closure that this knowledge brought. I might never know exactly who the young woman was who had claimed to be me, but I knew, with certainty, how she had acquired the information, both public, in the papers, and, private, in my attic.

Once in the carriage on the way back home, Mrs. Ross asked me, "Did ye find what you were looking for?"

I told her of my find, and she nodded, but did not smile or agree with my conclusions.

"Do you not agree with my supposition?" I asked.

She smiled, finally. "Ye'll find the truth, lassie, you will at that."

I sighed and turned toward the window. She was a kindly old lady, yes, but I was growing a little tired of her Scots muddle. I was satisfied with this answer; it all made perfect sense.

I had nearly nodded off into a nap when a thought intruded. *But how, and why, did she die? And where had she found an Indian maid?*

P icnic day arrived, and Landreth began setting up as soon as the sun dipped below the horizon. Delia had arrived early and was working with Mrs. Blackwood on the final touches. I briefly went to the kitchen to thank Cook.

I looked around at the spread awaiting service. "The food is simply unsurpassed," I said. "I count myself blessed to have you in the kitchen, and don't know what I shall do when the time comes for you to move on."

She smiled at me for perhaps the first time. "Me sister says you talked with her in town."

I nodded. "I'm very sorry for the loss of your daughter," I said. "I understand what it is to lose those you love."

She stared at me for a moment and then her eyes welled with tears, though she did not let them spill. "You do know, don't you?"

"I do," I said softly. "It can be lonely without family about to bring the comfort of home." I recalled how Cook's sister said she'd looked upon my imposter as a daughter. Surely that meant they'd been close. "Do you know where that young woman pretending to be me found a maid, her Indian maid?" I asked. "Since you are from hereabouts as well, I thought you might know."

"So you'd like someone from yer other home, too, eh, for comfort? I'm sure I don't know, but you might ask Daniel."

"Daniel?"

She nodded. "I can't be certain what happened to that other young lady's Indian maid, but if my eyes didn't fail me, I thought at the end Daniel drove her off in a carriage."

I should ask him as soon as it was feasible.

Cook came closer. "Be careful, miss, that's what I say. Just be careful. There's been enough loss around here."

"I shall," I promised, though I did not know if she spoke in general or had a specific thought in mind.

I shook the gloom from my thoughts and made my way back upstairs.

"You look verra beautiful," Mrs. Ross reassured me as I stood, useless, in the hallway.

I turned toward her. "I just wish I knew what to do."

"Here arrives Lady Frome," she said. "Her husband will no doubt go to the guesthouse and speak with Captain Whitfield. Perhaps ye should welcome everyone as they arrive, make them comfortable, conversing. Mary"—she nodded to Delia—"to her Martha."

"Yes, yes, that's right," I said. "Thank you, dear Mrs. Ross."

Lady Frome's grand carriage did indeed pull up in front of the lions, which were now tidied and recently restored so they looked fierce again and not frail, as they had when I'd first returned to Headbourne. And, as Mrs. Ross had predicted, Lord Frome strode off to see or provoke Luke, the elder brother.

"Here, let's not even go inside." I took Lady Frome by the arm. "I've had a nice cushion set up on a sturdy frame for you right in the center of the gardens. You should be able to participate without disturbing yourself."

"Thank you, Miss Ravenshaw," she said. "I've so been looking forward to this. I've still some months to go before my confinement but I can barely do anything but dine and nap, one after the other in regular rhythm!"

We walked arm in arm across the smooth lawn, and I settled her on her cushion and drew a table near. "I'll have Annie bring some chilled ginger beer to you. I'll be back once I've greeted everyone else."

Across the way I could see Captain Whitfield and Lord Frome dueling—thankfully, with swords and not pistols. I couldn't imagine that Lord Frome had ever used a sword for anything other than picking his teeth.

"Goodness me," I said. "I do hope they won't hurt each other."

"They don't duel to harm, my dear," Lady Frome said. "It's a matter of satisfaction. Of proving, one way or the other, that each is willing to live, or die, for his honor."

"They seem intent," I said.

"Those two always are. Honor is always an issue between them. Captain Whitfield is always more proficient with weaponry, but I'm afraid that my husband has the upper hand in several other manners."

I appreciated her forthright manner, borne, I suspected, by confidence in her position. "A father?"

"Yes. A father. A title. A home." She looked at the men, exercised now, sweat-drenched, grimacing and calling aloud. "Neither," she noted, "is afraid to draw a little blood."

I could not wrest my eyes from Whitfield; perhaps, having grown up with a father who had been in the military, I could be attracted only to a man who had a strong bearing and stance. Whitfield certainly did. He caught my eye and grinned, but as he did he lost his focus and Frome pinned him.

I'd caused him a loss. I was struck by the irony of this—I'd caused his loss of Headbourne, too. He waved toward me as if to say it was worth it, and I waved back, pleased by the gesture.

Several other carriages pulled up: the Ashbys, Delia's sister, a neighboring man, two ladies I'd met at church and many others I had not yet met. Lt. Dunn arrived—resplendent in his uniform, his blond hair neatly combed—and sought me out.

"I'm so glad to have been able to join you," he said enthusiastically. I recalled what Mrs. Ross had told me—if I knew there was to be no future, I should let him slip away to someone else. "I'm so glad you could come as well, Lieutenant Dunn," I said. He was about to speak, but Delia caught my eye and I excused myself.

"Did you plan for entertainment of any sort before we dine?" she asked. "We'll need to pass an hour or two before the food is served, and Captain Whitfield has arranged for music after dinner."

I'd thought Captain Whitfield was not to have been involved with the music! That was the impression she left with me when I'd suggested it.

"One moment," I said, thinking quickly.

I returned to the hallway where Landreth found me wringing my hands.

"Can I help, Miss Ravenshaw?"

"The pre-meal activity," I whispered. "I'd quite forgotten I was supposed to have thought of something. And now everyone's arrived. I'm not certain what the proper activity would be. What should I suggest?"

"Perhaps croquet would amuse," he said. "I've taken the liberty of ensuring that the bats, pegs, and balls are polished and the hoops straightened. You have only to command me to bring them out and we shall get the games under way."

"Thank you, Landreth. Whatever shall I do without you when you leave?"

"I'm sure I don't know," he said. But he pinked and looked pleased.

"Please bring the croquet set." I made a great show of instructing him and he smiled in return. I quickly repaired to Delia. "The croquet equipment is at hand. Landreth is having it brought outside just now."

"What a splendid idea," she said. "I have finished in here as well. Let's go outside." We strolled past the coach house; all of them could not fit inside, of course. "I believe that Lord Frome has a new carriage," she said. "It's quite as nice as Captain Whitfield's."

We walked by her carriage without a word; it was well past its bloom, as was, surprisingly, Lord Ashby's. We met and mingled with the others on the lawn. After greeting those with whom I had not yet spoken, I felt a gaze upon me. I looked up and saw Captain Whitfield staring at me from across the lawn. He smiled in a warm and personal way. I do believe he even winked! I offered a little wave—pointedly with my left hand—and he broke out in a wide grin. He waved next to Lady Frome, who waved back with honest delight.

"I do enjoy him," she said. "He's always made me most welcome."

"Shall we play cards while the others are at croquet?" I asked. Her husband and his brother had disappeared, to change before dinner, I assumed. I withdrew a deck of cards I'd brought for the occasion and moved the cribbage board I'd placed on the table just between us.

"Thank you, Miss Ravenshaw," she said. "You are so kind."

I dealt the cards and after some time looked up to see if the rest of the guests were content and engaged, and they were.

Delia had partnered herself with Captain Whitfield, who had returned; he looked happy and relaxed in her company, which unsettled me just a bit. He stood behind her as she maneuvered the bat, and when her ball went directly through the wicket, he led the cheers. I could see, even from a distance, she blushed with pleasure. She didn't miss a turn, though, and was able to ensure that everyone else on the lawn was in high spirits. I saw Captain Whitfield speaking with another man nearby, looking jovial at first. It was clear by their facial expressions that the man soon said something cutting to Whitfield, who visibly flinched and then coolly tipped his head and walked away. Two young ladies simpered their way to his side, each taking one of his arms, though he had not seemed to have proffered them; an older man—their father?—looked on with concern. Whitfield was never alone for long.

Lady Frome and I made small talk about babies and Hampshire, and the kinds of picnics held in India. "But of course you didn't ride," she said.

"Oh no, I was quite a good rider," I said. "Until the end, and the accident."

She nodded. "I see." She played another hand. I looked up and saw Lord Ashby in a small group gathered round a peg. He smiled at me and I waved, but my eye was drawn back to Delia and Captain Whitfield, now advancing toward another couple a few strokes ahead of them. I turned back to my cribbage game, which was nearing the end.

"I do hope you win, Miss Ravenshaw," she said. "It's just that till the end of the game, it's never entirely settled, is it?"

She turned her head toward Delia and Captain Whitfield, and then, bluntly, back to me, clearly connecting the points to ensure I understood.

. . .

Within an hour, deep gloaming beckoned and Landreth had the outdoor torches and candles lit. Annie began to bring out dishes of food. Cook had prepared cold duck, some ham, and several joints of beef. She'd shredded nearly fifteen lettuces and we had small carafes of oil and vinegar on each table that might be liberally sprinkled at will. There were sliced cucumbers and stewed fruits, cheese of every sort and smell, and jam puffs. Bread, refined and coarse, was sliced at each table along with a ramekin of softened butter. There was lemonade and ginger beer to drink, and, of course, tea.

Lt. Dunn had been kind enough to reserve a place for me at one of the tables. I took a deep breath; he was a charming man, a godly man, but I did not maintain the level of affection for him that he did for me. Perhaps we should have put out place holders so I could have avoided giving him false hope. The conversation was lovely; I enjoyed everyone present and felt very welcome and warm. Within another hour or two, the tables were cleared and a silver bowl of cut melon was set in the center of each.

"No pudding?" Lt. Dunn asked.

"No pudding," I responded.

"Whitfield?"

"He did not request it as such, but as this is still his home, too, for a few months, I thought it was kindest to accommodate his principles—which are fine ones, I believe. And the strawberries are well past their season." I grinned.

"I'm sorry about all that," he said. "I feel bad about laying the trap."

"I'm not sorry," I replied. "And I do not bring it up to cause you any further distress, just to jest. In any case, I do not know who was pretending to be me, God rest her soul, but I'm glad you were interested in finding out the truth of it."

"I suppose you shall never know."

"Perhaps not all of it, but some. I've deduced that she read my family letters, in the attic, to learn enough about us to pass as me. I've also read some archived newspapers, which is how she must have found out about our deaths. Mrs. Ross had told me she was certain that the truth would out."

"Mrs. Ross?" His voice and eyebrows rose. "I shouldn't have thought she'd be an amateur sleuth."

We both laughed at that thought. "Nor I," I agreed.

"Perhaps she was just quoting Shakespeare," he said. "'Truth will come to light; murder cannot be hid long . . . at length truth will out.'"

"Murder?" My voice must have risen, because several around us turned to look at me as I used the shrill word, including Whitfield and the man he'd flinched from earlier. Both stared at Dunn and me. I lowered my voice. "Don't you mean self-murder?"

"I was simply quoting," Lt. Dunn said. A sheen broke out on his upper lip and it quavered some before he rectified it with a smile.

The tables were cleared and I could see three musicians making their way from the guesthouse to the lawn. They must have arrived much earlier and Captain Whitfield had accommodated them in the guesthouse.

"I shall depart for China soon," Lt. Dunn said. "I am fortunate that I will be able to return regularly, at least at first, and I should be happy indeed if I could write to you whilst I am away."

The time was now. I took his hand in my own and held it softly. "I should be glad to hear from you on occasion. As a friend of my brother, indeed, as a brother in Christ, I will look forward to hearing of your time abroad. I myself have no calling to China, such as you yourself do, and it will be a pleasure to experience it through your eyes."

He looked crestfallen. He knew exactly what I'd meant. "I see."

"I know from my own family's experience, as perhaps do you, that missions work best when both man and wife are equally yoked in calling. As your friend, I shouldn't like you to be unequally tethered. I am certain you will find a delightful young lady who might already be dreaming of both China and a dashing military man. She shall pinch herself that such a man as you exists and can bring both dreams to life."

He lightened a little, and then laughed as he let go of my hand and prepared to take his leave. "I shall bank on your confidence, Miss Ravenshaw, I shall bank on it." Although he still looked mildly disappointed, his smile had returned and the lines on his face smoothed. Perchance he was a little relieved as well, as every man, I suspected, wanted to be the sole and focused object of his wife's affections.

Every woman, myself included, wanted that, too.

Dunn slipped away into a group of others, the violinists struck up, and I felt a familiar hand clasp my elbow.

CHAPTER TWENTY-ONE

"The elusive Miss Ravenshaw." Whitfield's voice sent a shiver through me though I couldn't yet see the man. *Just be careful,* Cook's recent warning whispered in my mind.

"I am in no way elusive." I turned to face him. "I thought perhaps you'd been avoiding me."

He reached his hand up toward the sky. "Could someone avoid the moonlight?"

I grinned. "I suspect you used an equally honeyed line with Miss Dainley some hours ago at croquet." Then I chided myself for letting him know I'd noticed.

He smiled back but did not answer. "Dunn has left your company looking rather low."

I nodded and thought back on my mother's early, difficult years in India. "He is a good man, and he deserves a wife whose dreams match his own."

"You have a kind heart, Miss Ravenshaw." His voice was downy with tenderness. "Would you be willing to stroll the grounds with me?" There it was, that boyish note in his voice that caught my heart as firmly as the deeper, rougher notes did. He looked so eager for me to be pleased. I wanted to please him.

"Delighted," I said. I took his proffered arm and we began to stroll around the vast gardens.

"This is not the typical Hampshire Noah's Ark picnic."

I shook my head. "I'm afraid I don't know that phrase. A fancy picnic? In animal skins?"

He laughed. "No, lovely Miss Ravenshaw, it's two-by-two. You know. Matchmaking."

I brought my hand to my mouth and then down again. "Oh, I see."

"I prefer moonlight."

"For matchmaking?" I pulled my dress, midnight-blue with crystals, up just a little to step over an exposed root; he held his hand out and helped me over it.

"In all cases," he said. "There is a proverb, 'Work by sunlight, love by moonlight.' "

"I have not heard that before." My voice and flesh weakened.

"Maybe it's not so much a proverb as an invitation." He spoke quietly. "If it were an invitation, would you answer it?"

"It is good manners to respond to every invitation, Captain Whitfield, although the answer need not always be in the positive."

He laughed aloud and squeezed my hand for a moment. "You are delightful, you really are. It gives me great comfort, happiness, and peace to know you live so nearby for now."

Happiness and peace, the two things I believed I must sacrifice to guarantee my security—my house. Hearing him say I brought those things softened me like wax that had long remained unlit, now tipped to gentle flame.

I turned the topic. "Talk of animal skins reminds me of India. And shooting for pay."

He settled us on some cushions on the ground. "Do explain!"

"There are, of course, all manner of exotic creatures in India, exotic to Englishmen, that is," I started. "Of course, there are elephants, which can trample a hut as quickly and flatly as a man might step on an insect. My mother, for some reason, never feared them and they knew it. She rode them with ease and command."

"Your mother rode elephants, no, commanded them!"

"Indeed she did," I said. "There were also jackals. We did fear them, really we did, as they seemed evil. Their wails sound like a woman in travail, or, if you like, siblings fighting over a sweet."

He grinned and moved closer to me. I felt his presence deep in my bones; I inhaled deeply of the manly spiced scent that had perfumed the guest room the night I'd slept in it. I had not taken laudanum for some time but that familiar and welcome warmth began to spread from my center outward again, this time a warmth without an edge to it. This comfort was, I decided, much better.

"Most feared were the large cats. One night, when Father was gone making rounds with other missionaries, we heard a noise in our small back garden. Our cow was tied there; she gave us milk but was also like a pet. I heard a dangerous purring and knew it was after our cow." I grinned. "We'd named her Bessie. See how English we are?" I swallowed hard. "Were, I mean."

He caught my mistake and my temporary sadness and gently urged me on. "Go on, Miss Ravenshaw. Do not leave me in suspense."

"Mother was not a good shot, so I took my gun, which was mounted above the door, and killed the leopard before she could get the cow. Our bearer had someone skin it and we let him keep the money for delivering the skin to the dewan."

"Now that I've seen you shoot," he said, "I know the leopard never had a chance. You are unlike any Englishwoman I have ever met." The affectionate look in his eyes told me that was a compliment. "Mademoiselle d'Arbonneau came close to losing her life at the other end of your pistol."

I sat up, alert. "Did she tell you that?" I had no idea they talked personally, or perhaps even frequently.

"Servants talk," he said soothingly, by way of a nonanswer. "Thornton mentioned it to me. You should be more cautious," he said. "Mistakes can be made." He withdrew his hand from mine for a moment and looked into the distance. "Even if you had killed her by accident, Miss Ravenshaw, she would still be dead and there would be consequences, both outwardly and inwardly. It would be on your head. Taking a life . . . that is not something you'd want to live with."

His distressed tone and the sharp turn in the conversation alarmed me. Was he speaking about me and Michelene? Someone else he knew? Perhaps he spoke of himself and, as the rumors had darkly suggested, the fate of my imposter.

"Do you speak from firsthand knowledge?" I asked quietly.

At the sound of my voice he turned to face me again, his composure mostly returned. "I've been on battlefields" was his response. Sound, but unsatisfying.

I caught the man Whitfield had seemed to quarrel with earlier looking at us, Whitfield in particular, with disdain. "Who is that man?"

He looked up. "Sir Alan Halford."

"He looked curt, earlier," I said.

A sad look crossed his face and he just as quickly replaced it. "Perhaps. I'd offered to help with a training and charity initiative which Lady Frome had just told me needed further assistance. By the time I made it to Halford minutes later, he coldly claimed they no longer needed help."

"But why?" I reached a hand out to his arm.

"It's been that way since last December," he said. December, when my imposter had died. "My father, even with his humble beginnings, would not have had to brook an insult like that. Shall I tell you something of my father?"

That boyish tenor underpinned his voice and I believed, once again, in his innocence and honor.

"Please do." I impulsively tucked my arm further into his and he drew me near him, possessively, and I did not mind. I was glad for my many layers, which formed a barrier between us. It enforced a physical discipline from temptation.

"I was but a lad when my father died. Indeed, I have no memory of the sound of his voice. Landreth was a young footman in our household and he says my voice sounds very much like that of my father. When I learned that I had inherited Headbourne"— he wouldn't meet my gaze—"I found Landreth again, unhappily in service to someone else, and asked him if he'd like to come to Headbourne."

I nodded agreeably. I'd come to feel very affectionate toward Landreth, who was the perfect combination of encyclopedic knowledge and grandfather. I'd miss him.

"My father died of wounds inflicted on the battlefield, and he left me naught but his uniform, his steady shot, and a diary."

"Oh, a diary, what a pleasure," I said.

"There was little written in it but military direction, insight into his strategic thoughts, but also hope that, once they'd been married a while, my mother's kinder nature would overcome her crueler one. I regret that I have not seen that kind nature. I take it that he did not, either. I do not know what drew them together. Married in haste, one suspects."

"Someday you will have a son to pass the diary and the uniform along to," I said. "And he will surely treasure them as well."

He looked pensive, perhaps hopeful, but did not answer directly. "A son or a daughter," he said. "I'd be pleased with either or both. But I've come to believe, of late, that the kind of woman to mother a child is not the kind of woman to marry a man like me."

I protested. "I have found you to be principled and kind." *Attractive. Complicated. Desirable.*

"You are overgenerous in your assessment," he said, holding up his hand against my forthcoming objection. "And I do mean that."

"Your father would be proud of you. For your pistol patents and other weapons work you've done. For the kind of man you are. How you've turned Headbourne House around." Whitfield had surely hoped even for a day or a week that it, too, might be passed to his son.

He took both of my gloved hands in his own, holding them and not letting go. "I've heard Miss Dainley call you by your first name."

"We've become close friends."

"So have you and I," he said with a grin.

"Hardly!" I laughed with real glee.

"We're cousins." He held my gaze and I caught my breath.

"We're 'cousins' so far back in the family as to be watered down to the place where the title scarcely counts. I may be cousin to the Queen that many generations ago."

He laughed, and it, too, was filled with joy. His comments flowed with the sort of teasing only found between a woman and a man with intentions. I thrilled to that. "Cousins are allowed to call one another by first names." He leaned near and whispered, his lips touching my ear, "Rebecca."

I half closed my eyes when he said it. I wanted him to say it over and again. I had heard my name spoken thousands of times over the course of my lifetime, in loud voices and quiet, conversational tones and private ones. It had never had an intimate feel until now.

"Go on," he said, backing away. "Try it."

"Rebecca." I teased. "It sounds lovely!" He laughed again.

"I'll bargain with you. You use my Christian name in private, and I won't ever use yours in public. Fair enough?"

I nodded. "Fair enough." He had no way of knowing that, since the day I first knew his name, I had turned it over and again in my mind, my heart, and on my lips. His face softened and he squeezed my hand, gently, and then quietly quoted, "'Speaking, or mute, all comeliness and grace attends thee; that what seemed fair in all the world, seemed now mean, or in her summed up, in her contained and in her looks; which from that time infused sweetness into my heart, unfelt before.'"

"*Paradise Lost*," I whispered in awe. "You've memorized that!" I flushed with delight and near exultation.

"It's a gift," he said, and took my hand in his own then kissed the back of it with tenderness. "From me to you."

"It's a gift I shall cherish." No man had ever declared such feelings toward me—nor had I ever wanted a man to. Until now.

"I have yet one more surprise for you," he said. "From India."

"Not someone who knew my brother? Come to test me further?" I jested.

He smiled. "Indeed not. This comes courtesy of one of my friends. It's a way of thanking you for allowing me to remain in the guesthouse while I complete the purchase of my own."

I noted that he did not say "home." And, having declared his affections for me, even in a veiled manner in verse, he had not, apparently, diverged from the path he'd set upon. To leave Hampshire. It bewildered me. It might be he meant only to have a harmless gentleman's flirtation, fine country manners. Perhaps that was the modus operandi for Hussars. Maybe, as he'd intimated, he did not feel he would do well by me for some reason.

He had brought me to highest high, like a kite flying into the air, and then wound the string that brought me quickly back to earth, but I did not detect any spite or cruelty in his actions or his words. I had thought I could live life, happily, with my house, not requiring the love of a man. Hadn't I? Now I was not sure. Perhaps he was equally conflicted.

One moment with him, the sun shone and I allowed myself to imagine a life together. The next, dark talk of killing, and distance placed, and leaving.

I grew cold, and perhaps a little frightened. If I allowed myself to fall in love with him, what of my house, my property, my only security, my safety! Whitfield himself had intimated that he was untrustworthy. I had seen no evidence of that myself. If it was there, it was well hidden.

Like a snake sleeping in a mazy fold?

I refused to believe it. Perhaps I, like Captain Whitfield, was a skeptic. I needed to see evidence of his bad character with my own eyes before I'd believe it.

"The gift will be here shortly, but I wanted you to have something to anticipate," he finished, bringing me back to the present. "I hope you'll like it."

We approached the others, so I kept my voice low and ignored my head and let my heart speak. "I'm certain that I will, *Luke.*" I whispered the beloved name into his ear with the caress I'd intended it to deliver.

. . .

Within a few days I made my way to the coach house. I wanted to speak with Daniel in private.

"Cook says that you may know where I can find an Indian maid," I began. "I'd be grateful for your help."

His face lost its color and for the first time his swagger wilted. "I have no idea, Miss Ravenshaw, where you might find an Indian maid, nor why Cook would say that, either."

"She said that you drove away with the Indian maid of the woman who had been claiming to be me."

"Her eyes have gone old and her brain soft. I know nothing of it."

"How did the maid leave, then?"

"Someone must have picked her up."

I didn't believe it and raised my eyebrows. Finally, he spoke.

"It was Christopher. He was the head driver then, not I. When he left, then I became head driver."

"What happened to Christopher?"

"Captain Whitfield fired him for mistreating the horses. He left with his pay and we've not heard from him since."

His mouth was firmly set, and I knew there would be no more information from him, if indeed there was any to be had. I nodded and he walked away. If my imposter had been murdered, I'd deduced, it had to be someone with one of three motives.

First, perhaps the young woman was local, had enemies, and changed her identity to hide. However, she would certainly draw a lot of attention to herself, claiming a grand manor and inheritance, so it wasn't a good place to disappear. Also, if she were truly local, she risked someone coming forward to say they'd known her. And how would they have made their way into the house to kill her?

Second, perhaps the murderer was the woman's Indian maid. Or someone had used the Indian maid to kill her. But Michelene had said they'd seemed close, almost intimates. So it was unlikely she had been put to the task, though intimates, of course, could be fooled if one was too trusting . . . or bought. If only that maid could be found!

Last, I admitted reluctantly, there was one person with a motive, the means at hand, and a number of people perhaps willing to help conceal the crime, or at least turn a blind eye. Luke. I just did not want it to be him. I truly did not.

Shortly thereafter, Mrs. Ross joined me and we left for the dance. "A wonder Captain Whitfield did not want to ride over with us," I said, as the footman helped us out of the new carriage.

After we'd alighted from the carriage, Mrs. Ross leaned toward me and said, "I doona believe Lord Ashby invited Captain Whitfield. Competition, ye know."

We made our way up the steps, which were carefully tended, but even I could see that the great house struggled with ill repair and was in need of attention. Once inside, we were warmly welcomed and I accepted a dance card.

"May I be the first to ink my name?" Lord Ashby came up next to us and I held my card out to him, now that my foot had healed enough to dance.

"I would be delighted."

"I'll claim three dances," he said. "More than that would draw attention, though I should not mind." He left me to attend to other hosting duties, but ensured that his household made certain my glass was never more than half empty. His mother took me by the elbow and introduced me to some local notables I had not spoken with before. At supper, Lady Ashby sat me near her.

"I remember your mother," she said.

"You do?" I set down my fork. "It was so very long ago that

she was here and I've been quite surprised that so few, if any, re-called her."

"We are a small community, Miss Ravenshaw, and a very few of us do remember our own, though it's been decades and we've had many incomers dilute the pool. I know she danced beautifully—as do you. And I remember her stunning lacework. She would have been a credit to our circle had she been able to remain, as she wished."

Ah. A clue that others knew India had not been my mother's first choice.

"I think she was a credit to her work in India, as well."

Lady Ashby smiled benignly. But she flinched, just a little, at the word *work*.

"Of course, my dear. How could she not?" She toyed with a tiny piece of roast duck and then set it down again. "We do have some charitable doings here as well. Some to help provide winter coal for the poor. A benefit is held each autumn. Would you like to be involved in arrangements, perhaps organizing decor?"

"Oh, yes," I said. "I'm happy to help in any way. I've heard that Lady Ledbury works with the charity."

"She's no longer involved." One eyebrow rose and she cut into a piece of fowl.

Due to Mrs. Knowlton? I could not ask Lady Ashby, though.

She put her hand over mine, briefly. "I knew you would be willing."

After supper, she led me round to chat with several other ladies, who warmly welcomed me. Lady Ashby treated me almost maternally. I hadn't realized how much I'd longed for that until it had, astonishingly, been offered and gratefully accepted.

Lord Ashby saw me out and waited with me and Mrs. Ross whilst the carriage was brought round. It took a while, as there were several leaving at the same time.

"I've been on a shoot this week," Ashby said.

"Splendid!" I said. "As you know, I like to shoot, too."

He tucked my hand in his. "Ah, yes . . . Captain Whitfield's snake. Seems apt, somehow."

I didn't respond to that, not knowing if it was personal and, in any case, not wishing to gossip.

"Perhaps it's the shoot," he continued. "But I'm put in mind of the plover. Do you know much of them, Miss Ravenshaw?"

I shook my head. "I'm afraid I don't."

"The birds are very good at what is called broken wing syndrome. They feign having an injury, to court sympathy in onlookers if only for a moment, in order to divert attention from something important but which they wish to remain hidden. A nest, perhaps. Birds, like people, are defensive of their homes."

He was speaking about Luke, I knew, by his tying the two topics together, suggesting that Luke was courting my sympathy through deceit.

Could he have been correct? It was indeed possible. Could this have been why the people in town had been cool and wary toward Whitfield? I simply did not know what to believe. When I was with him, I felt him to be true and good. Away, and under the suggestion of others, I was not so certain.

Just then Daniel arrived. "What a splendid outfit," Ashby said, and as I looked down at my gown I realized that he was talking about the carriage and not my dress. I couldn't help but be amused by my mistake. Ashby helped me up.

"Thank you for your gracious presence," he said, signaling to Daniel that we were settled. "Give thought to what I said about the plover."

"I will," I promised. "I certainly will."

CHAPTER TWENTY-TWO

"Mr. Highmore." Landreth announced the solicitor into the morning room. I set my correspondence aside, put my pen where it could not blot my letters, and stood to greet him. "Thank you so much for coming out. I've been looking forward to your visit."

He'd taken off his hat and gloves and took a seat on the sofa. The clear September light shone through the freshly cleaned windows; the leaded light pattern made a lovely design on the wood floor and carpets. A few leaves fluttered against the window as a breeze picked up outside.

"I've had final news from India," he said. "You'll be pleased to know that they have unreservedly confirmed your identity and authenticity. There were questions and concerns that only the legitimate Rebecca Ravenshaw could have answered. Captain Whitfield was correct."

"Of course, I've known all along who I am," I said. "But it is indeed a relief to have all suspicions put aside as far as the others are concerned—and settle the legal issues. Although I do wonder who the poor woman buried in my family graveyard is."

He grimaced. "It is a measure of your kindness that you

trouble yourself on their behalf, but in honesty, Miss Ravenshaw, she sought to exploit you without second thought. She's spent your money and as no family is looking for her we can only expect that she's come from the worst sort."

I nodded. "How is the state of my financial affairs?"

He fiddled with his glasses. "That, I'm afraid, is the bad news. I've had some difficulty untangling your fiscal concerns, and I'm not quite finished, though I will be soon. The main expense, over many years, was that your father had funded his mission with his investments, and had paid for others, such as doctors, printing presses for translation, and other ideas. It took some time to gather all the information, but I have it mostly in hand now."

Oh dear. I felt quite ill. Very pleased that Father had put his money to serving the Kingdom, and had lived frugally himself. Frightened that I could still be turned out.

"Your imposter spent quite a fair amount of money on clothing. The repairs on your home have not yet been added up."

"Captain Whitfield has already paid for those, correct, and I am to reimburse him?"

"Yes, that is true, Miss Ravenshaw. Which, when reimbursed, will be a further draw on your frail reserves." He continued, "My father was authorized to diversify your funds and did so with all fiduciary duty. However, some of them may have underperformed. Because there are many investments, because much was spent overseas, because the properties and funds have been transferred three times in a year, this is taking some months to calculate. All will be clear soon, rest assured, within the month, two at most, I should think. Until then—economize."

He left, and after he did, Annie came into the room. In her hand she held a packet of sealed letters. "These came for you from India."

"Thank you," I said with a little surprise.

"I wanted to make sure you got them."

I riffled through them with dismay. "Not the ones I'm looking forward to the most." I turned toward Annie. "Thank you for bringing these."

She nodded in return. "Miss . . . I just wanted you to know. When you first came, that first night, I stood outside your room and then outside of your chaperone's room, for a while, then in the parlor."

"You did?" Great relief settled over me. I hadn't imagined those footsteps after all! "Why?"

"To hear if you'd be plotting together," she said. "We thinking you were the imposter and all."

"And the next morning, when I had to push the furniture from the door . . ."

"I was a little ashamed, miss, to tell the truth. I'm sorry I frightened you."

"It's all right," I said. "The situation is confusing to me, too. Please don't concern yourself with it any longer. You were doing right by Captain Whitfield."

"Yes, miss. Whatever that might be." She nodded a little and left the room. She didn't read others' letters, but she'd implied by her tone someone else did. I knew of one person who had—Luke. He'd told me so himself.

The next day, an hour or so before my at-home hours, I went out to the coach house to see if Daniel had heard from the cobbler. I walked out to the stable yards for a moment, and then stopped in front of the cannon-proof horse. I put my hand out and she drew near to the edge of her box. I willed myself to be steady, to not flee. She came closer to nuzzle me, and just as her nose and lips touched my hand, I jerked back.

She pulled back and whinnied loudly. I still scared her. She still scared me.

I waited for Daniel to finish his work and then asked after the shoes.

"Oh yes, I've just had word," he said. "The cobbler, he's done," he said.

I smiled. For the first time, perhaps, since I'd been home, I sensed a renewed purpose and I blossomed into it. "I shall have an invitation drawn up for the boy and his mother to visit shortly, for the afternoon. Will you please deliver it to them, and then fetch them on the appointed day?"

As I turned to leave, Captain Whitfield rode in with Delia and her sister. "Miss Ravenshaw! I had not expected to find you here."

And I had not expected to find Miss Dainley here, I thought, well ahead of visiting hours. But I kept my peace.

"I thought I might come down and look at the horses," I said. "I know when you leave I shall have to purchase some of my own. I thought perhaps just two, sturdy enough to pull a carriage."

"I'd be honored to help you select them." Captain Whitfield grew subdued.

"Thank you, I shall need help."

I looked at the two of them. He owed me no explanation, of course, but I wished for one anyway.

"The horses need more exercise than I can provide them," he offered feebly. "Miss Dainley has generously offered to assist as often as possible."

"How very kind of her," I said. "I can see that she is an excellent horsewoman."

"Would you care to join us some day?" Delia asked. Her smug smile indicated that she knew I would decline. *"Seeming to be friends is not always the same as being friends,"* Mrs. Ross had said.

"I shall certainly give the offer every consideration it deserves," I said. "I do hope you'll join me for tea shortly, Delia, and your sister, too. I know that Cook has prepared your favorite cake."

She said nothing, Luke seemed to hold back a smile, and I turned and walked back to the house angry with myself that I'd let them rile me and then was petty enough to point out that cakes would be served.

One thing was certain. Captain Whitfield's charm had lulled me in a way that nothing save the laudanum had, and it might be best, perhaps, if I could find the strength to resist both.

Within a few minutes Delia had refreshed herself and joined me in the sitting room. Her sister, whom she'd referred to as Mrs. Dewhurst, accompanied her. Annie brought in extra cups.

"You have such a lovely home," Mrs. Dewhurst said.

"Thank you," I replied. "Our home in India was delightful, too. Cozy."

"My sister will leave for India in just a few weeks." She nodded toward Delia. "I do hope she finds the trip gentle."

"Just a few weeks?" I looked at Delia with surprise. "I had no idea the time was upon us so quickly."

"Perhaps," Delia rushed on. "It's *nearly* settled, but not completely." She rubbed her first finger over her thumbnail in an anxious motion; I noticed that the cuticles were ragged; she was normally so well composed.

She had been both kind and unkind to me. "I shall miss you," I said, sympathetic to her plight and the rough life I knew was ahead of her. I suspected she thought I held the remedy to that plight, and it was all tied up with my falling hopelessly and immediately in love with Ashby, thereby placing Headbourne out of Luke's reach. "I have received a first packet of letters from India, and I would be delighted to correspond with you as well."

"Did you have many friends there?" She looked hopeful. I know she worried about being marooned. "Tell me about them."

"Many friends," I said, and focused on the English friends, as I knew that was her concern. "Some are wives of commissioned soldiers. One of them used to sew with me, or I should say, I talked while she sewed." I closed my eyes and remembered. "My friend Lillian married well into the East India Company. I've just had a letter from her, finally, and can make an introduction if you'd like. Violet and I spent much of our girlhood together until she moved to Ceylon and a coffee plantation with her parents, though sadly, her mother later died, and her father . . ."

Oh, dear. This was not the place to bring up that her father had taken up with an Indian woman and had the family cast out from regular English society.

I turned the conversation back to pleasanter matters. "We girls saved up the money we earned from lace making—she more than I—and bought pretty polished stones at the marketplace."

I thought back to our moonlit picnic. "I loved moonstones best. The Romans thought they were solidified moonbeams. Violet liked cat's-eyes best, as she thought they brought good luck. My mother liked peridot, and while my father did not spend indiscriminately, he did buy her jewels from time to time and gave her some as a wedding gift. Perhaps you shall receive one as a wedding gift, too, as they are quite common in India." *I wish I had Mother's. Perhaps I could write to India and have them sent.*

Suddenly Delia choked, seeming to have inhaled her tea, and I looked at her with alarm until she was able to breathe clearly again. She set her teacup down and looked a little unwell. I signaled for Annie. "Could you please bring some mint tea for Miss Dainley?"

Delia shook her head and placed her hand over her teacup but did not speak. Her sister looked on with alarm.

Delia seemed to recover. "Do go on," her sister said.

I picked up the thread where I'd left off. "Weddings are the merriest time of all." I wanted Delia to look forward with enthusiasm to her wedding in India if she must leave England after all.

"The newly arrived to India bring news of home, and those long installed copy current English customs. Always, there is champagne and a favor table with little cake baskets and sometimes tins of oysters. The bride is beautiful in her dress, of course, as you certainly will be."

Delia stood. "I'm so sorry, please excuse me, I am suddenly unwell and I fear I should leave immediately."

I got up and helped her to her feet as her sister rushed to her side. Had something been wrong with the tea? Perhaps it had been the talk of weddings? I'd been trying to help her look forward to it but had, instead, set a foot wrong by bringing up a tender topic. "Landreth, please call the carriage for Miss Dainley and her sister, Mrs. Dewhurst."

I saw them away and had not a moment to recover before Lady Ashby arrived for a quarter of an hour with a friend from the coal charity. Two visitors later and the house was at rest again. But I was not.

Later that night, Michelene helped ready me for bed.

"You seem apprehensive," she said. "Was it the visit from Lady Ashby?"

"Oh, no," I said. "She was perfectly lovely, and has invited me to be a part of the coal charity fund-raiser . . . the one Lady Ledbury has left. I shall play some small role at first. It was that . . . Miss Dainley seemed so strange today."

"Riding with the captain?" There was an edge to her voice. Was she concerned for Delia's sake? Mine? Perhaps for her own, somehow.

"That," I said, "and, well, I think she's just perhaps overwrought to be going to India." A thought occurred to me. Perhaps she could not afford a wedding dress, and here I'd been carrying on over several visits about them.

Michelene's fingers eased then; I could feel it as she ran them through my hair to ensure she'd removed all the pins. "Ah well, assisting the coal charity is one thing, but you cannot solve all the problems of the world, n'est-ce pas? Miss Dainley will have to solve her own problem. It is September. Her fishing boat sails soon."

"She's trying to solve her problem here," I said grimly. *With Luke.* There came a knock at the door. I hurriedly pulled my peignoir around me and Michelene opened the door. I could hear that it was Thornton, Captain Whitfield's valet. Michelene returned with a tray, and on the tray was an envelope with my name written across it.

Miss Ravenshaw.

"Shall I read it to you?" Michelene attempted to liberate the card from my hand, but I held steady.

"No thank you." I refused to open it while she remained in the room.

She left and I turned my lamp up higher, slit the envelope, then pulled out the card.

Rebecca,

Would you honor me by joining a guest and me at dinner tomorrow evening? He is transporting the afore-mentioned surprise, and I think you'll find his conversation, in particular, a delight.

Ever yours,

Luke

I ran my hand over the card, knowing he had touched it. I tucked the card in the small drawer in the back of my bureau, where I kept the recent letters from India and the small packet of my mother's unsent to Honiton. Then I penned my reply.

CHAPTER TWENTY-THREE

"I think the green dress would be best," I said.

Michelene stood in front of my primary wardrobe. "All right." She arranged my hair in a big sweep in the back and fastened it with pins.

"Ooh la la," she said. "Cinnamon gloss as well?"

"Perhaps." I wondered about her. She was clearly attracted to Captain Whitfield, and, truthfully, her experience with him predated mine. And yet she seemed given to making me as attractive as possible tonight. Perhaps that was professionalism. Maybe she flirted with everyone. The French way? I did not know.

Mrs. Ross and I descended the stairway and I noted, at the bottom landing, that the door to the music room was fully shut. Odd. Perhaps the carpets had been cleaned? Still, that should have been finished before guests arrived. I wondered, with a pang, if this was the last time I would dine with Luke and his guests, perhaps the last of his prearranged social events, as he would surely not invite any more now that my ownership was firmly settled and he was preparing to move.

Luke, in full uniform, waited at the foot of the stairs. I stopped two steps from the bottom and took him in, though I tried to be discreet. Neither he nor his guest bothered to do likewise. They looked me up and down, the guest seeming to be pleasantly surprised. Luke looked like a man considering me as a first course. It was not a wholly unwelcome feeling on my part.

Mrs. Ross cleared her throat. "Perhaps introductions are in order, Captain?"

"Oh, yes, thank you. Mr. Anthony Breame, Miss Rebecca Ravenshaw. Miss Ravenshaw, Mr. Anthony Breame."

"How do you do?" I held out my hand. My silver silk gloves reached halfway between elbow and shoulder and shimmered in the candlelight. "To what do we owe the pleasure of your visit?"

"I've just returned from India," he said. "Captain Whitfield thought it might amuse you for me to bring some stories—some happy stories. We'd been corresponding on official business. He made a personal request, I was intrigued, and here I am."

"I'm intrigued as well!" I said.

We were seated at the table, and the first course was brought out. Although Cook took great pains for the cooking aromas to remain confined to the kitchen as much as possible, I detected a familiar and welcome scent. I was proved correct when Landreth served.

"Curry!" I clapped my hands lightly.

"Cook thought it apt, given Mr. Breame's level of comfort with spices," Landreth said. But he'd pinked, and I could tell that he was pleased that I was pleased. How I would miss him! And dear, dear Cook!

Mr. Breame spoke of his time with the East India Company, and how things would change now that matters would be officially under the Crown and not the company. He was well groomed and his refined clothes and manners spoke of a man with both family and money. He was attractive in his own way but missed the vein of vitality that I always sensed in Whitfield.

"You speak Malayalam, honored miss?" he asked me in that language.

"Yes, respected visitor, I most certainly do," I answered likewise. "Where did you learn to speak Malayalam so well?"

"I have an Anglo-Indian friend of many years who was originally from Kerala," he said. "She taught me. A bit of Tamil, too."

Ah. *She.* He saw my recognition, and also that I did not press for further details, as no lady ever would. I wondered if this was perhaps the Anglo-Indian Luke had spoken of during our time fishing. "It's a delight to speak in what is, in many ways, a native tongue to me and one I miss hearing."

We reverted to English, and after the final course, Mr. Breame spoke up. "Captain Whitfield asked me, if at all possible, to return with a gift. I'll have you know, Miss Ravenshaw, that the gift was difficult and cumbersome to transport. It must be that he holds you in high esteem."

"I'm eager to see what it is," I admitted, standing up. Then I realized that was probably unseemly and continued. "Whenever the time is right, that is." I sat down again. Luke winked, seeming to approve of my eagerness and curiosity.

"The time *is* right." Luke came around and pulled out my chair, placing his hand on the small of my back, for just a moment. Even after he removed it, a slow, resonant burn remained at the place his hand had rested.

We walked toward the music room. Captain Whitfield opened the door, and there on the floor, surrounded by cushions, was a sitar.

"Oh, my goodness!" I impulsively wrapped my arms around him in thanks, and he, caring not for propriety, embraced me in return. His thumb stroked my shoulder blade, a welcome and intimate gesture. Then, wanting to smooth things over, I also quickly hugged Mr. Breame and Mrs. Ross.

The sitar had a long neck, and the split gourd base of it was perfectly shined. "Teak?" I asked.

"Burmese teak," Mr. Breame agreed. "Whitfield mentioned that your father had served in Burma and I thought this would be particularly apt."

"Oh, yes, yes it is." I eyed it.

"Would you like to play?" Luke asked me softly.

"I would love to play," I answered as I held his gaze and lowered my voice. "For you."

"It's strange that your parents allowed you to learn," Mr. Breame said.

I shook my head. "It's only been in the past few years that Englishmen have been discouraged from learning about the culture they came to live in. Missionaries, in particular, are interested in understanding the people they came to serve. My parents felt that they came both to share the Gospel, teach and provide, but also to learn and to understand."

"Besides"—I ran my hand up the neck and as I did, I saw Luke place a hand to his own—"there are several famous women sitar players." I tuned the sitar, lightly.

"There are typically six or seven strings on top, and many more underneath." I touched each string in turn.

I closed my eyes.

The hardwood floor that my mother had just swept was beneath me. The fringes of the cushion I'd embroidered, badly, tickled my leg and I smelt the heat fused with the rains of the monsoon just past. Hookah smoke floated across the air and through our window. My mother did not care for the scent of it, but I loved its

*musky woodiness. A lizard skittered across the corner of our house.
I plucked some strings.*

*There was a tinny jangle, a tangy note, like yogurt stirred into
curry. Then the swaying melody that most sitar songs lent themselves to, deeper, softer, quicker. I could visualize elephants tread-
ing. People walking, baskets on their heads. An unrest of color and
a chatter of language.*

Soon enough the song was over and I opened my eyes back to
England. My home now, beginning to be beloved as well. As I sat
for a moment, I noted that, while I'd still had a few night terrors,
when I spoke of India aloud, mostly to Luke, or shared a moment
of India with him nearby, like now, the memories often came in
pleasant waves instead.

"Your song makes me want to set sail on the next ship back
home," Breame said in Malayalam.

I smiled. "Do you consider India your home?" I asked in Malayalam.

"Yes," he replied. "But that's a secret between us."

I smiled. I turned to Whitfield, who had said nothing aloud
but whose eyes held unconcealed pleasure and tenderness.
Awe, even. I was delighted that though, as Michelene had
pointed out, I was not the most beautiful woman in Winchester, nor a pianist, I could delight him in some unusual way.
He'd called me a most unusual woman. I strove to keep that
title. "I hope I shall be able to play once or twice more before
Mr. Breame leaves?"

"The sitar is yours, Reb . . . Miss Ravenshaw." Luke's voice was
rough with emotion and he cleared it twice.

"Mine?" I caught my breath and looked at him, hoping, but
not able to accept such a gift. "Oh no, that is too generous." Burmese teakwood, carried here from India!

Captain Whitfield shook his head. "For your hospitality these many months . . . for saving Notos from the snake. You might just yet save me."

"From what?" I asked.

He laughed to lighten the mood, but I saw the seriousness behind it. "From myself."

We were in the company of others, so I turned back to the sitar and ran my hand over the wood again to refocus. "This is truly, genuinely, absolutely mine. Yes?" Even Breame beamed at my enthusiasm.

"It's yours," Whitfield said. "Truly, genuinely, absolutely. I hope, when I've moved on, you'll think of me each time you play it."

The air thickened with intimacy. "I shall," I said, already mourning the loss. "Depend upon it."

We said good night and then I took my leave. Michelene came and helped me undress. "I could hear the music," she said. "It was enchanting. I see why they say that is the music to charm the snakes."

I laughed. "That's not snake-charming music."

"Isn't it?" She pulled my hair out of its arrangement and brushed it to a shine. "They seemed charmed to me." I glanced at her in the mirror, just above my shoulder. We were of the same age, same build and coloring, almost. She was definitely the prettier of the two of us, exotic even. And yet she served me. Could she have been jealous?

"Why do you think Mr. Breame and Captain Whitfield are snakes?" I insisted. "It could not have been a better evening."

"There are prey animals and predators," she said. "One or the other."

"And men are predators?" I asked.

"Not all of them," she admitted.

"Women can be predators, too," I said.

"*Touché*." She smiled and left for the night.

I closed my curtains, looking for just a minute across the way to the guesthouse. Although I could see into its sitting room, there was no movement present. No lamps were lit in the bedrooms, either, as far as I could judge.

I went back to bed, and as I was falling asleep Marie meowed. She'd been under my bed, and now she crawled out and clawed at the door.

"Oh, all right, then." I got out of bed, kept it dark, and slowly opened up my bedroom door. She tore down the hallway like a bolt of lightning, all the way down to the dark right wing. A door was open. It was *her* bedroom.

I pulled my peignoir around me, quietly closed my door, and walked partway down the hallway, which was usually dead, and now, at the end, was a pulse of life and light. Voices murmured. Men's voices. I could not hear what they were saying, so I crept a bit farther down. The floorboards squeaked and I thought I would be discovered. But the men were too busy talking to pay attention. I became aware that I was, in fact, dressed indecently to be seen by two men. But what were they doing on this floor now, at night, anyway? In my home!

I had not seen anyone in that room since I'd returned to England. Why did Captain Whitfield still have the key? I would insist on having a complete set of keys for myself, immediately. I should have acquired them long ago; indeed, I'd asked Mrs. Blackwood for one and it seemed to have slipped her mind, too.

I crept down the hallway, one step at a time, wanting to go far enough to hear what they were saying but no farther and be caught out. I stopped when I could hear them.

"I can't read it well," Mr. Breame said. "I cannot make out

much. This . . ." There was a pause and then he spoke again. "This is the word *evil*."

"Evil!" Captain Whitfield's voice rose. "Can you read no more of it, man?"

Some time elapsed. "No, I cannot. Why would someone write this?"

"I should have had it scratched out," Captain Whitfield's voice came again.

"Why?" Breame's voice sounded suspicious now.

"It's . . . difficult to explain, might cause discomfort. I . . . I shouldn't like to leave it for Miss Ravenshaw to find. It could distress her. I shall do it soon. Let's leave."

At that, I turned and fled. I quietly closed the door to my room and leaned against it, panting with effort and concern. Fear, perhaps. Who had written *evil*?

I would speak with Mrs. Blackwood, promptly, about the keys. Before Whitfield could return and scratch out whatever it was they'd been trying to read. Did it implicate him?

The next morning I rang for Mrs. Blackwood.

"How may we assist?" she asked, arriving in the breakfast room.

"Are there several sets of house keys?"

She shook her head. "Just the two—the one we have and the one Landreth carries."

"I'd like one made for me, if possible. And, if it's not too much to ask, I'd like the key to the bedroom where the woman posing as me stayed, today."

"That's the one key I do not have," she said. "I gave it to Captain Whitfield and he has not yet returned it."

"Can you ask for it to be returned, presently?"

She nodded.

Of course. He'd been in there with Breame. "I'd like it today, if at all possible," I pressed.

Mrs. Blackwood nodded. "Yes, I will speak with the captain after breakfast." Then she said, "We understand Captain Whitfield will be taking his leave shortly. To India."

"India?" I stood.

She blushed, unusually. "We shouldn't have said anything. It is, after all, a new discussion, since Mr. Breame arrived and invited him into his business dealings there. We were told only as the household was inquiring after our new positions, if we'd be expected to move to Derbyshire."

"New positions?" Michelene looked up, alarmed. She looked shocked. "This is possible for me, too?"

"Unfortunately, perhaps so. If economies demand it. I should certainly hope not," I said.

For once, she lost her cool reserve and seemed shaken.

I turned back to Mrs. Blackwood, shaken myself, but for another reason altogether. "So he's leaving?" The room felt a little like it was spinning, and I focused on a portrait on the wall to center myself. Derbyshire was one thing. India something else! I desperately did not want him to leave, and yet he apparently did not as desperately want to stay. I knew not what to make of it just yet.

"It's all just talk, miss." She did not address my concerns, but rather, perhaps, her own. "Please don't mention it. We should hate for him to think us indiscreet. We just thought you might want to know."

I understood. If there was something that needed to transpire between the captain and me, there was not much time. She was warning me as plainly as she dared. I truly believed she wanted him to stay for my sake, not only for her own. "I shan't say anything."

CHAPTER TWENTY-FOUR

An hour or so later, I stood by the sitting room window, watching; I walked around the room, stood up and then sat down again. I composed a letter to Penelope and John Mark but was so distracted that I wrote nonsense. Finally, the carriage appeared in the distance at the beginning of the long drive. Landreth polished the silver salver in the hallway once more. I went to wait for my guests at the top of the steps that led to the front door, aware that they might be ill at ease and that it was my duty to put their uneasiness to rest.

Daniel stopped the carriage and as he did, the carriage door flew open and Matthew jumped out, bare feet sending a small powder of dust into the air.

"Ho, there, young man." Daniel came round and steadied the lad. "You're to wait for someone to open the door and assist you as you come out. You'll see, here, I'll help your mother."

He reached his arm into the carriage and I could see a female foot with a well-worn slipper appear on the silver step meant to help passengers alight.

As a woman stepped out I was relieved that there was some

distance between us, because it masked my shock when I realized that she was little older than myself. That would have made her perhaps fourteen when Matthew was born, as I'd placed him to be about ten years old. She carried herself well, but her shawl was frayed and much too heavy for summer. Her dress had once been a lovely lawn, but it had been faded into bleached white with passage of time. She carried herself with dignity.

She nodded as she saw me, but Matthew streaked up the stairs. "Miss Rebecca!" Then, seeing Landreth standing there like a statue, Matthew halted. He took his hat off and bowed. "Pleased to meet you, sir."

He turned to me and whispered loudly. "Is that your husband?"

Landreth went red and disappeared into the hallway. I nearly burst out laughing.

"No, he's not." Just then, his mother reached the top of the steps. "Thank you very much for visiting today, Mrs. . . ." I was at a loss. I did not know her name.

"Miller," she said.

I nodded. "Please, come through to the drawing room."

I led them to the sofa so they could sit together and I took a nearby chair. I signaled to Annie. "Would you care for tea?" I asked Mrs. Miller.

"Don't mind if I do."

"Don't mind if I do!" Matthew chimed in. Annie brought teacups round and then the trays with cakes and sandwiches. Matthew took a sandwich and popped it into his mouth and then put another in his hand before seeing a stern look from his mother. It reminded me of my own mother, who never let us take more than one at a time.

"Thank you very much for accepting my invitation," I said. "It means a lot to me."

Mrs. Miller cleared her throat. "I'm very grateful for the invitation, and Matthew had a lovely ride in your carriage. But I have employment, Miss Ravenshaw, and we do not need charity."

I sipped my tea in order to take a minute to think. I hadn't thought that she might be offended at my offer. Perhaps my plan had been ill conceived and high-handed.

"I don't think that at all." I revised my idea as I spoke. "Matthew seems such a bright boy. Curious. He reminded me of my brother, and I thought, well, if there is some way I can help . . ."

"Your brother?" she said.

"He passed away in India."

"In the Rebellion?" she asked.

I shook my head. "No, but my parents died then."

She slowly sipped her own tea, then, perhaps revisiting her understanding and intentions as I had mine. "I'm sorry for your loss," she said.

"As am I," I replied gently. Matthew helped himself to another small sandwich. Annie had turned the tray so he'd have the best selection and I caught her eye and smiled before changing the subject.

"Do you mind if I have Matthew's shoes brought out?"

"Not at all." She smiled.

I rang for Landreth, but he had apparently been just outside, and he brought the box to me. I opened the lid, saw it was the lad's shoes, and quickly closed it again before handing it over to Matthew.

"I do believe these are too small for me," I jested, "and it would cause some comment if I wore men's boots, in any case. Here." I handed the box to him.

He eagerly took the box, and opened the lid. He inhaled and held his breath as he withdrew the first caramel-colored boot from the box, then the second. He looked at me, and I nodded, and then at his mother, and she nodded, too.

He slipped them on and stood. I was certain they fit perfectly, because the cobbler had measured his feet, but Matthew seemed to totter just a little. It occurred to me that he had not often worn shoes of any kind and would need some time to get used to them.

"They, they are beautiful, miss. I hope I never grow any more after this so they will fit me always."

"The cobbler will be happy to stretch and then replace them as you grow," I said. *Because I'll pay him to, even if it means I do without for a season.*

"Truly?" Mrs. Miller asked.

"Truly," I said.

"Miss Rebecca," he said. "We've brought something for you, too!" He handed me a gently worn fabric bag and I opened it to find a pair of clean, but fragile, gloves.

"Yellow, my favorite color for gloves!" I immediately took off the pair I wore and pulled the new ones on, to his delight.

We made small talk as Matthew walked in mincing steps all around the drawing room. When thirty minutes or so had gone by, twice the average time for a call, I stood up. "I do hope you don't mind, but I've some correspondence to attend to."

Mrs. Miller seemed relieved. "Not at all. This was a wonderful visit, and I can't thank you enough for your gift to Matthew."

"It's been my pleasure," I said, and we walked down the steps and toward the coach house. Matthew walked very carefully, stopping occasionally to dust his boots.

"You're going to have a hard time finishing your chores if you must clean your boots each minute," I teased.

"I don't mind, miss," he said. He turned and walked back toward me. "Can I visit any church now?"

I nodded. "You can," I said. I knelt down to him and spoke softly. "Jesus loves you, Matthew. With boots and without boots. It matters not to Him." I gave him a gentle hug and stood again. Daniel saw them both into the carriage and before he mounted to the driver's seat I pulled him aside so I could speak without the others hearing.

"Do you ever take on apprentices?" I asked.

He shook his head. "Not here, miss. And, well, with things unsettled about where Captain Whitfield will move to . . ."

Ah. So he'd heard, too.

"Would you be willing to make inquiries with others, at good houses?"

He nodded toward the carriage. "For the young lad?"

"I don't think he has much chance otherwise."

"I'll ask," he said. He turned back to me. "Someone gambled on me when I was a lad."

"And here you are." I smiled.

"Here I am," he agreed.

I watched as the carriage drove off and, as I passed the guest-house, saw a curtain drop. I turned toward my home and made my way up the outside steps. Mrs. Ross waited for me in the sitting room.

"I'm so sorry I didn't think to invite you down." I repented of not keeping her in mind more often, and not just when I needed her.

"I'm fine, lassie, no need to concern yourself." She smiled and I smiled back. "Have ye heard of Mr. John Pounds, then?"

I sat down. Rare was the occasion when she initiated a conversation.

"I confess I have not," I said. "Is he a friend of yours?"

"Mr. Pounds has passed away. However, he is, in a manner, a friend to all who look after those who have a more difficult way to make."

"How so?"

"Your gift of the shoes put me in mind of him. When Mr. Pounds was but a lad, he was apprenticed to be, I believe, a shipwright, living nearby in Portsmouth."

"Go on," I said, and waved to Annie to bring tea and shortbread.

"The poor boy fell and became a cripple, and so was no longer fit to be on ship. Instead of pitying himself, he trained himself to be a cobbler, and before he was verra old, owned his own shop. That fall, and the difficulties it brought, gave the man a kindly heart toward those in difficult circumstance."

She stopped for a moment and bit into her shortbread. "He sometimes bribed the lads and lasses with a hot baked potato, but then they were able to learn their sums and to read and make a life for themselves. With persistence in learning, they earned shoes from him as a reward in due course."

"What a fine story," I said. "It's too bad he is no longer with us to help those children."

"Ah, lassie, but his schools are. There be many ragged schools, which is what they've come to be known as, all about England. There's one in Winchester, in fact, though I think 'tis not well staffed with teachers."

I stood up, struck by a thought which was both new, here in England, and familiar. "I could help with that, couldn't I? In truth, one needn't travel to India to find children in need of food or clothing or an education . . . or hope. Isn't that right?" It had been some time, perhaps before we'd left the mission to travel north, since I had felt that touch of purposefulness.

I felt warmth. As my mother had a calling to the underserved in India, I had a calling to them here, in England. She would be so pleased!

Mrs. Ross nodded. "I thought ye might be interested to hear of it. 'There is that scattereth, and yet increaseth . . .'"

"'. . . and there is that withholdeth more than is meet, but tendeth to poverty.'"

She clapped. "I knew you'd recall that scripture."

"It reminds me of a Tamil proverb," I said. "They who give have all things; those who withhold have nothing." I allowed my tears free fall, not really understanding why they came just then, but feeling that, like the house, something that had once been mine, truly mine, was being reclaimed.

"Will you help me find out with whom I should speak?" I asked. "To help with the ragged schools somehow, perhaps with small donations, perhaps with teaching?"

"I shall make inquiries." She lumbered to her feet. "I'll be taking forty winks if you need me," Mrs. Ross said as she rounded the corner and went up the stairs.

I read, and wrote, and napped, and waited all day for Mrs. Blackwood to arrive with my key, but she did not.

CHAPTER TWENTY-FIVE

The next morning broke clearly with a sharp shot. From my window, beyond the autumn mists, I could see Captain Whitfield shooting. Michelene, who was planning for a day off after helping me dress, was already at my door and caught me looking out the window.

"Enjoying the view?" she teased.

I smiled. I'd been caught out. "Yes," I admitted.

"Let us hurry, then," she said. "You have not had the occasion to wear the beautiful tartan dress, *n'est-ce pas*? A casual day for a girl to shoot, I would think. And if she happens to run into someone unexpectedly, well, then, she's hit the bull's-eye." She pulled the beautiful red/blue/green-checked dress from the wardrobe. It went well with my coloring, and would allow me to wear the pretty white muffs I'd been waiting to show off.

"It's not as though he won't suspect why I'm out there," I said.

"Everything does not need to be said to be conveyed," she huffed. "Women can be subtle." She fussed with me for another minute. "The captain is leaving. For Derbyshire, or the East Indies."

I did not allow my face to show my pain. "Yes. It seems certain now."

She made a particularly beautiful high arrangement of my hair before fastening a hat. "Perhaps Michelene can assist you, *non*?"

If all it took was beautiful hair, Delia would have been Mrs. Whitfield by now. But I appreciated her sentiment.

I went downstairs for a quick cup of tea and Mrs. Blackwood was there, waiting for me. She held out her hand and in it was a key. I took it.

"I'm sorry it took a day longer. I didn't want to draw attention to the fact that you wanted it in your possession. So I did mention that a complete set would need to be made instead."

Mrs. Ross and I then made our way to the room where the guns were stored. I selected a shotgun, handed it to a servant to carry for me, and headed out past the stable yard, Mrs. Ross trailing well behind. She sat at the very edge of the lawn.

Luke turned after a few moments and saw me. His smile was wide and he came to greet me.

"May I shoot with you?"

"I'd like nothing better," he said. I watched him first, and then he looked at the rifle I had chosen. "Would you like me to show you how to best use that?"

"Please do."

He came round behind me, his left arm stretching across my back and left shoulder, his right arm helping me to steady till I saw where to best place the sites to hit the posts he'd set up along the edge of the greenway. He drew me much closer to him than need be but I relished the feel of leaning back into him, and him pressing forward to me. I should have thought of this shooting practice much sooner!

"Have it?" he asked.

"Not quite," I said, unwilling to let him step away from me. He moved the weapon again till I held it, and myself, firmly. I wished that the gun were not there, and Mrs. Ross were not there, which would mean that we were, actually, married.

I drew in a sharp breath. *I've admitted it. I want to marry him.*

"Is all well?" he asked, alarm in his voice.

"Yes, thank you," I said, and he stepped away. As he did, I steadied the rifle and shot, splitting the target cleanly down the center.

He came near. "Splendid shot! And with so little guidance." Then he took a step back and eyed me with skepticism. "You didn't really need my help, did you?"

I blushed and hoped the pink in my cheeks from the morning chill hid it well. But I answered truthfully. "No."

He smiled, and I laughed, and he came alongside me and we sat on the bench near the shooting range.

He reached out for my hand, his warm skin cupping mine. "I watched you, through the window, with that young boy yesterday," he said. "It almost makes me wish I were a troubled young lad. I could be sadly ensconced in the Society for Wayward Boys Not Yet Convicted of Criminal Offence and you could come and rescue me."

A little corner of me wondered, for the smallest portion of time, if there was a criminal offense he was not yet convicted of, and I retreated just a step from my desire for marriage. "I would certainly rescue you, Luke," I said with a soft, teasing smile.

He smiled when I used his name. "Would you have bought some new boots for me?" He looked down at his own.

I laughed. "Unquestionably."

He squeezed my hand, for a moment, and then withdrew his own. "I do believe that you would have saved me, Rebecca. You are good. Innocent. And good." His face showed admiration and held a steady smile, but his eyes reflected pain.

"Surely you are good, too," I said.

He lay his gun across his lap, protecting it from the damp ground. "My brother, the illustrious Lord Frome, has publicly stated that I am a man who has used my talent for killing to further my own goals." Was Luke warning me?

I gasped. "What did he mean? Is it true?"

"The guns," he answered. "My modification to the weapons, which kill more quickly. And which has made my fortune. So I suppose it is true."

I coughed. "Who gives credence to Lord Pudding, anyway?"

"Lord . . . who?"

"Your brother, excuse me." I was horrified. "I don't mean to insult your family."

A smile tickled the corners of his lips. But then it disappeared. "You cannot deny that I have made it easier to kill. And did so with intent."

"For a greater good," I offered weakly.

He nodded slowly, but not convincingly. "As I saw it." He stood. "Come, let us go to the stable."

A little fear pinched inside me. "Stable?"

He nodded. "I need to check on Notos, and I'd like to give her another chance to meet you."

I followed. Unwillingly. The early-morning fog had cleared and the coach house and stable bustled with heat and laughter and the sharp command of instructions, sometimes in strong language, which stopped as the grooms saw me approach.

"Good morning, Miss Ravenshaw." Daniel took his hat off and bowed and I grinned at him. It was unbecoming, I knew, but I'd begun to think of him as a younger brother.

"Daniel is a good driver," I said.

"He is."

"Has he been the lead driver long?" I asked.

"He's been with me awhile, but only lead driver since I fired a man for mistreating the horses," Luke answered smoothly. He didn't meet my eye, but didn't purposely look away, either.

Luke then took my hand in his and walked to Notos while Mrs. Ross trailed far behind, busying herself by looking at the horses in other stalls to give us some time nearly alone. Luke called softly to his horse, opened her box, and led me in.

She was huge. Her flanks could undoubtedly crush me if they rolled on me. But she gently walked toward Luke, looking askance at me with one big brown eye as she passed. Her mane was glossy and well cared for, and he whispered to her as he might to a lover.

He beckoned me and I came close, slowly. "There now, there is nothing to fear, is there?" he said gently, and I knew not whether he spoke to me, to Notos, or to both of us.

I tentatively reached a gloved hand up and put it on her neck, and after the lightest flicker of pulling away she allowed me to touch her.

"I believe you'll overcome this," Luke said, turning to me.

"You do?"

"I do," he said. "It is, perhaps, the last fear you have to conquer."

I nodded but thought, *Perhaps it's the second to last.* Could I trust a man, specifically him, enough to risk my house and the security my inheritance brought in exchange for that chance of a life of love and family?

I stroked Notos's side for a moment, speaking gentle words, and she seemed to accept them. I felt the anxiety bleed out of me, replaced by something less than confidence but stronger than fear.

"Let's ride her," he said, and this time, it was I who flinched. He reached out to steady me. "I'll hold the reins. We'll just walk her out onto the grounds for a bit, and back again. I'll control her the whole time."

I nodded my reluctant agreement. "Has Miss Dainley ridden Notos?" I asked casually.

He shook his head no. "No woman has ever ridden Notos, not Miss Dainley or any other. And in any case, I thought I'd mention . . . I shan't be riding out with Miss Dainley anymore."

"No?" I asked.

He shook his head but said no more, a gentleman in every way. Daniel soon had the horse saddled and then helped me up on her. After letting Notos get used to my presence, Luke clucked twice and led her, and me, out.

I held myself stiffly at first but then relaxed into the saddle and the animal. Notos seemed to accommodate herself to me, too, both of us trusting Luke, and when the ride was over a few minutes later I was sad.

Luke reached up, took my hand, and then put his arm around my waist, lifting me down again.

"I'm proud of you," he said.

"You are?" I looked straight up at him.

He nodded. "I've known many war veterans unable to overcome their fears."

As I moved away from the horse but closer to the man, Luke reached out and took one of the long curls of hair at the side of my face in his hand and wrapped it familiarly around his finger, binding me to him. He touched me in only one place but I felt it in a dozen others.

I allowed his hand to remain for just a moment before I took it in mine and carefully unwound my hair from his finger. "That is perhaps a little too intimate," I said, wishing I did not have to.

"I should apologize." He kept his voice low, too, but the husky sound had returned.

"I could not accept such an apology." I held his hand for just a bit longer. Then I smiled. "Scripture requires repentance before forgiveness can be offered. And you are not sorry."

He smiled back. "No, indeed, I am not sorry that I've touched you. Nor are you."

Indeed no, I was not.

When I arrived at my room sometime later, Michelene was there, mending a dress. "How was the shooting?" she asked.

"*Parfait*," I said, teasing her by speaking in French, and then, more to myself, "yet so much is still unknown."

She shook out the curls from my hair, pulled the pins, and set them on the tiny china hairpin tray on the dressing table. "Perhaps one is happier when one doesn't know everything," she offered. She seemed tired, or distracted, and I was in a hurry for her to leave so I let her comment lie where she'd left it. *The truth will set you free.* But did I truly want to be freed? Would the truth imprison me in loneliness? Or would it keep me, and Headbourne, safe?

"Perhaps," I said. I turned to her with a genuine smile. "Please help me think what should be appropriate to wear to the theater night that is coming up very soon." She nodded cheerfully, and whilst I could not completely trust her, I relied upon her and, in truth, liked her quite a bit. I should be sorry if I could not keep her in order to make further economies. There is much I could not have done without her assistance. "I will help you in many ways, *chérie.*"

After she left, I went over my room. Several of the drawers looked to have been jostled, and it seemed to me that even the tiny hidden drawer in the top of one of the bureaus had been opened and shut—it wasn't squarely closed. I looked inside, but all seemed to be as I'd left it.

After waiting half an hour to ensure Michelene was well and truly gone, I made my way along the dark wing. Far in the distance I saw eyes. Marie waited by the door I would shortly open.

I tiptoed down the passage, avoiding floorboards that I already knew squeaked when stepped upon. I walked past my parents' bedroom. Would it ever be occupied again? That would be, perhaps, my own decision. I closed my eyes for just a moment, savoring the memory of our dance, Luke's and mine, before moving on.

Finally, at the end of the passage, I reached the imposter's room. Who had she been? Had Luke danced with her, too?

Had he twirled her hair around his finger?

Had he feigned to love her, when really, he loved the house?

I slipped the key into the lock and, as it had been recently used, the lock turned easily. Marie followed me into the room and I closed the door behind us. I lit and then turned the lamp up against the autumn gloom and looked around.

I felt her spirit there, familiar, almost like perfume that lingered long after one left the room.

But that was nonsense. The familiarity was that she had, in some way, *been me*, if only for a time. She now lay dead, in *my* grave. She'd plundered *my* family and poached *my* heritage. The room was quiet but not at rest, if a room could be thus described. The linens were upon her bed; I assumed they had been washed and replaced. How had she died? Had they been bloodied? *I'm not sure I should like to know.*

There was nothing personal left in the room, no dresses nor shoes: Michelene had seen to that. I walked over to the small table by the window, which seemed to have served as a desk of some kind. Had she written letters here, authorized bills, pretending to be me?

I brought the lamp close to the desk and could see, faintly, written in Tamil on the desk itself, a proverb.

தீய மற்றவர்கள் தீய யார் அவரை நேரிடும்.
Evil will befall him who does evil to others.

It had been brushed on in henna by a practiced hand. Was the person who had pretended to be me part Indian, an Anglo-Indian? Or had it been the maid? "Why did someone write this?" I whispered. "And why in Tamil?"

Because no one else here can read Tamil.

But they clearly wanted, expected, some Tamil-reading person to find it.

I heard what I thought was a voice, a whisper, so I turned the lamp as low as it could go without putting it out altogether and sat steady in the chair. I motioned for Marie to come to me so I could keep her quiet, too, but she faithfully remained on the bed of the young woman who had first taken her in as an orphaned kitten.

Who had done evil to whom? Had evil been visited upon the woman who had impersonated me? Or was someone promising justice in the end to whosoever had done evil to an innocent woman? The possibilities traveled through my mind. The imposter. Her maid. Someone unknown. Someone known.

Luke? I had to face that real possibility.

He had, in every other way, seemed so honorable to me. I had heard innuendos from others, but had not yet seen evidence of it myself. I could not believe that of him, still, in spite of his own admission of waywardness.

Could not believe or would not believe?

Would not believe.

I wish my mother were here, Lord. I wish for guidance. I do not want to make a terrible mistake and give myself and my house, my legacy, to an untrustworthy man. But equally, I do not want to live my life in loneliness, and Luke is the only man who has ever quickened my heart. Why would You take my parents and brother from me but not provide someone else to love me?

After a few more moments, I heard no more voices and turned the lamp back up. I quietly opened the wardrobe, but saw nothing, as I'd expected. There was most probably little else to see in the room but I wanted to open the remaining bureau drawers, just to be certain. I pulled them out one by one. All were empty. One, however, stuck and did not smoothly return to place. I jiggled it a little, then harder, and it loosened and slid back, but as it did, something clanked against the frame behind the drawer. I reached my hand to the back, only able to do so because my arm and hand were thin, and unstuck something from the farthest reaches. I pulled it out.

A bottle of Dr. Warburg's Tincture! It was capped, but a sticky ooze surrounded the neck of the bottle, which is how, I supposed, it had come to be stuck to the drawer. I set it down and replaced the drawer. Captain Whitfield was the only one who'd ever mentioned the tincture, and had, in fact, procured it from the military hospital he frequented.

I picked up the bottle and prepared to leave the room, gathering the cat in my free arm as she would not leave otherwise.

Luke had brought some tincture to me from the military hospital. He'd brought some to her, too, it seemed. She'd have had to claim malaria if she'd been posing as someone who'd lived in India.

Once in my room I tucked the key and the newly found bottle into the travel dress deeply hidden in my wardrobe. I wished in some ways that I was still the simple, hopeful girl who had worn that thin dress sailing to what she'd thought would be a peaceful future six months earlier. I was home, yes, but now in love with a man I was uncertain I could trust. A man who would shortly leave for Derbyshire or, more probably, for India.

I looked at my bureau, at my own half-empty bottle of Warburg's. I determined to take it no more. It was, perhaps, not safe, not if Luke was who I feared he might be, doing what I feared he might do, and may have already done. Could he have given her a bottle that had been . . . amended, somehow?

Poisoned.

That night, I slipped into an edgy sleep.

"Here," a voice soothed; a hammered silver cup was held out. "Take it. Drink. It will make you well." I closed my mouth firm against it but the cup was pressed against my lips anyway. It was not laudanum, this time, but tincture.

CHAPTER TWENTY-SIX

Several days later I was reading in the drawing room when Delia's carriage pulled up. I stood up and straightened the gazettes, expecting Landreth to announce her, but no announcement came. I walked to the window and waited, wondering if all was well. Within twenty minutes she and her sister rode out with Captain Whitfield, exercising his horses again, apparently.

This was most strange. Luke had said he did not intend to ride with her again. I had not asked why, though he had implied that perhaps it was to emphasize to her that there would be no further relationship between them. Perhaps I had assumed to be true what I wanted to be true.

Perhaps I should walk in the autumn gardens?

I could go near the riding areas. But not too near.

I put on my cloak and walked down the sweeping front steps, past the lions, and toward the riding area, pretending to casually inspect the plants that were neatly grouped throughout the damp green grass of the gardens. All of a sudden in the distance their horses turned, faced the house, the grounds, and *me*—and then stopped.

I did not wish to be seen as spying on them. I looked to my left, a long walk to the house. And to my right, an old stone house—once a pump house, Landreth had told me—a garden shed. I had not been in there yet.

Inside, the walls were crumbling, and though it was dark a bit of light seeped in through broken windows. Webs claimed those windows, corner by corner, from the inside.

Luke and Delia began to ride toward where I stood, though they could not see me, I believed, through the tall trees. I had no choice. I pulled open the door to the storage shed and slipped inside.

It smelt of dry dirt and when some flew up with the movement of the door, I sneezed. My eyes adjusted to the light, and I crept close to a window. There were those webs, gauzy, and thready, and everywhere. There was one spider, a small one.

I swallowed my gorge and squeezed my eyes shut, pushing away the memory of the behemoth making its way toward me. In my mind's eye, it faded.

Be strong and courageous.

I opened my eyes and ignored the spider and the temptation to flee. A flood of pride filled me for a moment. I had, in part, overcome *this* fear!

Voices approached. Delia and Luke were clearly arguing as they rode toward the shed. I could not hear distinct words, only heated, pleading tones. I peeked out of the window. Delia's face was quite flushed. She tried to ride near Captain Whitfield, and he turned and seemed to speak to her in an uncommon anger and then he rode on ahead of her. She caught up, spoke again; her face looked pleading once more. He rode ahead of her, again, then, seeming to change his mind, turned his horse full around and came up behind but clearly not alongside her. Her sister, chaperoning, followed at a distance.

Delia then rode toward the stables and Luke followed as they passed by me.

After some minutes, Delia's father's carriage rounded the bend away from Headbourne House. She'd not even stopped for a quick greeting.

I'd see her the next night, at the theater. Perhaps I could pry from her what was amiss without letting her know that I'd seen it transpire.

My eyes had adjusted to the light, and I could see that the shed was not very big and, now that dust had settled, all it consisted of was a few shelves with tins of herbicides and paint. Some garden tools, rusty. An old wheel.

I turned to leave, but something under a shelf caught my eye. It was a glove, brown, which is why it had blended into the ground so easily. It was hatch-stitched in an unusual manner.

I recognized it instantly as one of Luke's.

Underneath it was a black bottle top, which, with my gloves still on, I picked up and examined. I was certain it was the cap to a bottle of Dr. Warburg's Tincture.

Michelene had said the day maid had told her that Captain Whitfield had been rummaging through the room after the lonely, midnight burial of the dead woman. What had he been looking for? The bottle I'd found? Why had he not wanted the Tamil inscription read? Perhaps he was worried it would incriminate him.

I returned to my room. Once there, I compared my bottle with the cap I'd found, and discovered that, indeed, they matched.

I had said I wanted to see some proof with my own eyes. Luke's glove, expensively made and individually patterned, had lain under a shelf with tins labeled *arsenic*, a tasteless poison, all knew, normally used to kill rats. Near that glove had been a cap which fitted the style, perfectly, of Dr. Warburg's Tincture, which Whitfield had been the only one, in my experience, able to procure.

My heart beat faster, in fear, and it was no longer due to the presence of a spider.

In spite of growing circumstantial evidence, I didn't want to believe that Luke had had anything to do with her death. I had seen nothing at all in his manner toward me that would suggest that he was capable of such a thing.

But there was the nagging question—why did others around him, some of long standing in the area, act so coolly toward him? Who else would have motive to kill her? Or why had she killed herself if she believed me dead, as, clearly from my own experience, did all.

I looked at the bottle. *It means nothing. Yes,* I admitted to myself, *I desperately want it to mean nothing. It is circumstantial, certainly. But significant. I will say nothing, but I will, as Scripture exhorts, in all things, guard my heart. I need to withdraw, for a time, from Captain Whitfield. From Luke.*

I wasn't sure I could withdraw. He was like the finest laudanum to me—he comforted me and brought me rest and joy and happiness. And yet he could confuse me, too. When I was with him, all seemed clear and easy. When away, I considered that perhaps it was best we remain apart.

I went into the armoire to pull out the key, to return it to Mrs. Blackwood, and the bottle I'd found in the imposter's room. I reached to the back, pulling aside gowns till I found the old one, and reached into the pocket.

The key was still there. The sticky bottle was not.

Sweat broke out. Who had taken the bottle? How could they possibly have known it was there? Whoever had been in my room had known just when I'd be gone, and had no compunction about stealing from me. It had been done, clearly, with intention. To protect herself? Himself?

Within an hour Annie appeared at my door, silver tray in hand. On it was the most exquisite embossed envelope I'd ever seen, clearly made with linen threads. The embossing read *Miss Rebecca Ravenshaw*.

"It's from Lady Ledbury," she said before I could ask.

"Thank you," I said, taking it in hand and placing the key on the tray. As she turned to leave I spoke up once more. "Annie—was anyone in my room whilst I was out?"

She shook her head. "I don't believe so, miss. I've been on this floor cleaning for the past few hours."

"Michelene, perhaps?"

"She's gone to Winchester, as you'll recall," she said. "You gave her permission?"

Yes, yes I had. "Has anyone else been about?"

She thought for a moment. "Thornton. He's been looking for table linens in advance of Captain Whitfield's guests, soon to arrive."

Thornton, Whitfield's valet. What guests? It would be impolite of me to ask, of course, as I'd told him to consider the guest cottage to be his home till he moved out completely. I was surprised that he hadn't made his way over today to tell me, though.

"Will that be all?" she asked.

I nodded and she shut the door behind her. I pulled the invitation from the envelope; it was for the illustrious ball the earl and his wife held each autumn. The theme was Heritage. I knew from Delia that guests were expected to bring a unique gift to share and that I would have to commission a costume to be worn. After I'd considered what that costume should be, I'd go to Winchester, with Michelene, and have it made.

I went to bed that night thinking about the Ledburys' grand event, and how they had treated Luke so poorly from when he was a small boy, very much left alone.

I arose and looked out of the window, hoping for a glimpse of him, but the guesthouse was dark. Beyond it, I could see the graveyard. The mists were out. I'd come to learn that, as the year turned darker, from summer to autumn, the mists thickened. My angel statue, sword held high, guarded the entrance, but behind him, plant and bush skeletons, brown and spindly, rattled in the breeze. Dead leaves clung, fruitlessly, all vitality drained. A sudden gust came and a flock of them spiraled to the ground like suicidal birds, golden and red, the remains of which would be blown away and forgotten, never to live again.

I let my eyes be drawn to the headstones. I could see a few, though not clearly, of course. I knew moss would have overtaken most of them; they'd be thick with green and brown, black perhaps with mold.

Mold grows well in the dark.

You have to visit it, you know, I told myself.

Yes, I will, I answered.

When?

Soon. Very soon.

CHAPTER TWENTY-SEVEN

We three left for Winchester late the following afternoon, spending a short time in the dressmaker's shop in order to commission my outfit for the Ledburys' ball, an outfit that was to be very unusual indeed. After a refreshing tea break we walked to the theater, which was already thrumming with chatter. Michelene looked yearningly at the gathering and I wondered what it would be like for her to have the door closed at almost every entertainment simply because she was a maid. I should not like that very much. She did not seem to, either. Daniel would be around shortly to collect her.

Lady Ashby, alighting from her carriage at nearly the same time as I, broke out in a delighted smile when she saw me. "My dear, what marvelous timing," she said, as her son Lewis soon appeared.

"Do sit with us." Baron Ashby took my arm and steered me inside. I was fairly resigned about the whole matter; sitting with them was better than being a social orphan. As my carriage pulled away, I saw Lady Ashby and Michelene catch each other's eyes. Michelene pulled the curtain over the carriage window. Lady Ashby turned away in disgust.

"Do you know her?" I asked Lady Ashby. "Mademoiselle d'Arbonneau?"

"Certainly not." She popped her parasol shut.

The interior of the theater was rich with claret-colored velvet trimming the walls, which were highly polished dark wood. The suggestion of cigar smoke lingered; perhaps many of the men had congregated in the smoking parlor nearby before meeting for the speech. One could barely see several feet ahead of oneself, for the crowd, and the collection of tall black hats. Baron Ashby and his mother ordered steadying sherries; I declined, and disentangled myself from them long enough to slip through the crowds to greet Delia.

I tapped her lightly on the shoulder; her sister was in attendance with her. "Delia?"

She turned toward me, and as she did a man bumped into her in the crush; when he had made his way past her I noticed that he'd dislodged a small piece of her elaborate hair. It was one of, apparently, several false pieces holding up her magnificent arrangement.

"Oh, Rebecca, hello."

"I missed seeing you this week," I said. "I hope you're well. I received my invitation to the Ledburys' ball just a short time ago. I'm eager to learn more about it from you. Perhaps you and your sister might join me for tea sometime?"

Her eyes filmed. "I'm afraid I won't be attending. I'll be sailing to India soon."

"You're leaving, for certain?" I asked.

Her sister spoke up with both sorrow, for her sister I supposed, and anger, perhaps with me? "Our father said that time enough had passed, our brother is expecting her, and she'll sail before November. Our brother has already arranged several promising introductions."

Enough time had passed to catch a fish in England, as Michelene would say. Was that what their horseback argument had been about?

"I'm very sorry," I said. "I hope that we will be able to take tea of an afternoon together before you leave."

"I should like that, but I expect to be constantly occupied with packing and preparing," she said. The gold flake of social kindness hid cold steel beneath. I felt as though she'd slapped me. She clearly felt she had lost and that I, in some way, had won. If only she'd known. I withdrew with equal coolness, my feelings wounded.

Shortly thereafter, Lord Ashby made his way over to me. "The best seats will be taken if we don't move into the auditorium." He looked to Delia. "Good evening, Miss Dainley. I've heard you're shortly leaving for India. Best of luck to you."

Delia took a deep breath, the breath of a woman frustrated with a man who need not worry about finding a wife, his title surely bait enough, though perhaps he'd had to look for one richer than was easily attained. Suddenly, she looked wan and old. "Thank you, Lord Ashby."

He took my arm to steer me away. I wanted to reach over and fix her fallen hairpiece, but to do so would be to call attention to it. Instead, I prayed that her sister would spot it shortly and tuck it in.

The speech given was rousing and interesting, and all present seemed glad to have been in attendance. My parents had not neglected to educate me in the natural sciences, though it had been unusual for girls. I was glad, once again, that they had undertaken to teach me rather than send me back to England, where my hours might have been more art and less astronomy. I quietly looked around for Captain Whitfield. I was certain that he caught my eye from several rows away. I cheered, immediately, and smiled and waved. He waved briefly, but coldly, and did not smile. Then he turned away without further acknowledgment, back to the elegant woman claiming his attention.

What had happened? I sank into my chair, distressed, confused, disheartened.

For the second time that day I felt cut, once by Delia, now by Luke. Why was he suddenly cold toward me? *Perhaps I had misinterpreted his turning away just now. Or . . .* had Delia said something? Before they'd gone riding he had been increasing in his attention, affection, and, though he hadn't said it, love for me. After their meeting he was a changed man. A pang of pain ran from my heart down my left arm.

"He puts me in mind of a snake," Lord Ashby said, noticing the focus of my gaze. "You'll be well rid of him." He tucked my arm closer to him, possessively, and I gently unwound it. "I understand he'll be moving to his new home soon?"

"Yes." I nodded. "To India."

"I'd heard India, too. I'm extremely surprised that he hasn't insisted on continuing at your guesthouse, but"—he seemed to offer a begrudging compliment—"he is a gentleman born in spite of it all. You'll do right by ensuring he takes all of his personal effects with him. There is a phrase, Miss Ravenshaw: When a snake sheds its skin you know it's been there even though you no longer see the serpent itself."

I smiled politely but honestly couldn't turn away fast enough. Luke had said that perhaps I could save him. What did he mean? Could I prove him to be the man I thought he was, no matter what others believed? I did not know what to make of his sudden coldness to me, but it wounded me more than Delia's sharp words. Maybe *this* was the true man, and not the one I had, perhaps, overimagined.

After the speech, everyone mingled and I tried to make my way over to Luke. He looked up at me, and I smiled, but he did not smile back. Instead, he turned his back to me.

I had not imagined it and I hadn't misinterpreted it. He was avoiding me altogether. Baron Ashby saw me safely to our carriage, but we waited for quite some time, to the consternation of the other drivers, for Captain Whitfield to arrive; he had not traveled out with us but we would return to Headbourne together. When Whitfield did arrive he was accompanied by another soldier.

"Miss Ravenshaw," he said. "Allow me to introduce a fellow officer from my regiment, Captain William Chapman, of the Eleventh Hussars."

Captain Chapman took my hand in his and gestured a kiss on the back of the glove. He met my eyes with a slightly flirtatious look, and I smiled warmly, but impersonally, toward him. Captain Whitfield, to my surprise, did not make any personal conversation or eye contact with me but for a moment. In that moment, his eyes seemed guarded and hurting. I wanted to reach out and touch his cheek and chase that sorrow away.

"Chapman is in town for a visit and I've offered him use of my accommodations, in the guesthouse, if that is acceptable to you?" His tone was even and friendly but impersonal.

"It's yours to do with as you wish while you remain, Captain Whitfield," I said. Perfectly polite. Perfectly gentle. Perfectly awful. Why were we talking like this? It was clear by his posture and tone he did not care for Chapman and yet he was offering hospitality.

A gentleman born.

The carriage jostled and I lost my balance, momentarily. Whitfield instinctively reached out to steady me. He held my hand a moment longer than required, and love, truly, frissoned through our hands, but he said nothing and would not meet my eye again.

We made painfully superficial conversation all the way home, which made me want to cry. Apparently I was not the only person who had decided to be guarded. Either that, or Luke had had a change of heart. If he'd ever really intended his heart for me.

Soon we arrived at Headbourne House. Captain Chapman pointed to the two stone lions. "You know what they say, don't you?"

I wasn't sure if he was talking to me or to Luke, but I answered, to be polite. "I'm not aware of any colloquialism involving lions."

"Captain Whitfield has passed through them, I presume?" He fairly bubbled with mirth.

I nodded.

"The saying is, Miss Ravenshaw, that when a Hussar who is able to be faithful to one woman passes between two stone lions, they shall spring to life and run away." He began to laugh, and I wondered if he'd had one too many sherries at the theater. "You'll note that this has not yet transpired."

Whitfield looked as though he was about to speak, but I retorted more quickly.

"Perhaps you should walk through them, then, Captain Chapman," I said, "and we'll all have the chance to see them in flight." He again burst out laughing, and, for a moment, I saw a hint of a smile on Luke's face. I did not smile back. It seemed an appropriate response for his recent coldness toward me.

"Whitfield has kindly agreed to host some small parties and social gatherings while I'm in residence," Captain Chapman began. "To reacquaint myself with people I don't see often, and it should be a merry time. Perhaps you'd like to attend?"

This time, Whitfield stepped in. "I don't think they are the kinds of occasions that Miss Ravenshaw would find to her taste," he said.

"Thank you for the invitation," I said to Chapman. "I have a great deal to attend to, so I shall have to regretfully decline." A memory of our summer picnic floated forward.

"It is good manners to respond to every invitation, Captain Whitfield, although the answer need not always be in the positive."

He laughed aloud and squeezed my hand for a moment. "You are delightful, you really are. It gives me great comfort, happiness, and peace to know you live so nearby. . . ."

Daniel helped Mrs. Ross and me down from the carriage and I made my way up the stairs and into my room. I'd dismissed Michelene earlier that evening, preferring to prepare myself for bed instead. I watched as two carriages arrived, and several men and ladies, including older chaperones, arrived at the guesthouse. The presence of chaperones meant that at least one of the young women was unmarried. I lay down on the bed, curled on my side, and let tears slip from my eye, roll over my cheek, and slide onto the pillow where they pooled before I fell asleep. After some time I awoke and realized I had not undressed, though it was well past midnight.

I reached into the drawer in the small bureau next to my bed, feeling for the small packet of Mother's letters, which I'd placed there to be near me. I undid the thin ribbon holding the letters together. I wondered why they hadn't been sent. They looked to have been written shortly after her marriage, well before Peter or I was born.

Dearest Mother,

Things are lovely here at Headbourne, only I miss you so. It has been a difficult adjustment, but Charles is constantly attentive and charming; I have only to mention the desire for something and he'll see it done for me. He's been

speaking to me about attending the nonconforming church,
and I readily admit it is a strange new thought. But I trust
his judgment implicitly. I have no reason to question him,
for anything, at any time. He is straightforward and true
so I believe he will properly lead our little family in this
way as well.

Do give my love to Papa, and tell him that I am happy
and that he has chosen well for me. I shall write again soon
when I am feeling better. I've been unwell of late . . . ????
Yours,
Constance

I read the other three letters; by the end, it was clear that she knew that she was expecting a child, my brother, Peter. I closed my eyes and let the tears slide down my face again at the sweet voice of my mother. I could hear it, in the words on the page, in my heart and mind. I felt her hands on my little arms as a girl and kissing my cheeks as a young woman. I recalled her crying out in melancholy during our first years in India, her hair falling out. I remembered how it grew back, lush and thick and beautiful, only to turn stark gray in the year following Peter's death.

I opened my eyes, wiped them with the edge of my sleeve, and whispered, "Dearest Mummy. Things are not lovely here at Headbourne any longer, and I do miss you so."

I folded up the letters, running my hands over each one before tying the ribbon back around them, and thinking how she trusted Father implicitly, even when she could not understand. I stood to prepare for bed, but as I did, wandered over to the window. I wondered if I should see Captain Whitfield and Captain Chapman, but I did not. The additional carriages were still there, but there were many rooms on offer in the guesthouse, and perhaps Chapman's friends were staying for a night or two.

Whitfield's business is his own, I thought, *and not mine. Though I'd wished it would be, had hoped it would be.* It did not make sense. I could not have so mixed up his intentions, nor the way we'd felt when we were together. Could I have? Perhaps this was yet another skill I'd missed whilst growing up in India.

It was, for once, a night in which no mist rose from the ground, which was equally cold with the air. The late-September moon was full, and I could see, clearly, all the way to the graveyard.

Wait. There was a man in the graveyard!

I blew out my lamp so I could get closer to the window without being seen, and so that the light from my room would not blur my vision.

It was Luke. Without a doubt. I had studied him, I knew him from afar. He had moved so that he faced the only perfectly straight grave in the graveyard; the others were leaning a bit to left or right, as graves did, when the ground heaved with age.

It was her grave. The woman who had claimed to be me! Luke knelt before it, head resting on it. He pulled his head back to look at it from farther away, and then rested his head against it again. After two minutes or so, he began to turn around and I quickly drew my curtains so he would have no idea, I hoped, that I had been watching him.

I undressed and slid beneath the bed linens. In earlier days, when I'd thought we were affectionate and close, I might have gone to him and asked. But not now. Things, after Delia's ride with him, had somehow changed. I wasn't sure what he intended for me, for us.

What had he been doing out there?

· · ·

The next morning at breakfast, I asked Mrs. Blackwood, "Do Captain Chapman's guests remain at the guesthouse?"

"Yes, I believe so, for another day or so." She looked at me pointedly. "Perhaps he's catching up with acquaintances before leaving for foreign shores. Like Captain Whitfield."

After breakfast, I walked upstairs, where Michelene finished my hair. "I shall need some steady walking shoes," I said. "I am going to visit Headbourne Chapel today."

Michelene dropped a pin. "Why is that, *chérie?* So sad, *non?*"

"It is sad," I agreed. "But it's time."

She removed some of my clothing from the wardrobe. "To alter, in my room, and sponge press," she said. Before she left, she replaced, in my chest of drawers, some gloves she had already mended and cleaned, including the beloved yellow pair from Matthew. I'd wear them, for courage.

The autumn air was chill and I drew my shawl around me as I made my way down the steps and between the two stone lions. Had Chapman's comment about the lions, and Luke, been but a jest? Dry leaves swirled around my feet as I passed the coach house, where Daniel laughed with some of the younger grooms. I should miss them, all of them, when they left. Perhaps they would want to stay on. I did not know how many I could afford to keep. It was probably high time I began to look into hiring my own small household. I'd send for Mr. Highmore and ask for his recommendations, and also for an accounting of my father's investments. I needed to know what I had to live on.

Several minutes later I arrived at the edge of the graveyard, which preceded the church, itself built of chalky stone. I was on the precipice of discovery, and, I somehow knew, at the point of no return.

I moved forward, and touched a gravestone. I ran my finger over the name and date; it startled me to see my father's name on a grave, Charles Ravenshaw. But of course it was not his, but that of a long-dead relative, perhaps his great-grandfather.

I touched a few other stones and was relieved that I did not feel horror and darkness, but connection. They were my people. I was theirs. They belonged here. As did I.

One did not.

I walked just a little farther and finally faced the straight grave, not old enough yet to be subject to the freeze and thaw of the ground. The grass grew sparsely over it; it had had but one season, after all. The ground was flat and someone had planted a few small flowers to the side of it. I found that touching, someone had cared enough to see it was light and pretty. Cook, perhaps.

But nothing could have prepared me to see the stone itself.

REBECCA RAVENSHAW, 1834–1857

DAUGHTER OF GOD, DAUGHTER OF INDIA,

DAUGHTER OF HAMPSHIRE

REST IN PEACE

I ran my fingers over the name. Who had this woman been? Why had she died?

For Headbourne, came a sharp whisper inside. *She died for Headbourne*. I knew that was right, fully believed it was truth with a certainty I could not shake.

Below the name, I found something truly startling. The headstone had been somehow defaced. Something just below it had been scraped out. What had it said? Why had it been scraped out? Defacing a grave, even the grave of a suicide, was most unusual and strange. The back of my neck prickled.

I walked into the church. The side door had swung open to the elements; leaves had blown in, to gather and clot and rot together. The stone crumbled here and there, leaving a chalky residue on the floor. The altar bowed with neglect. *I should repair this*, I thought, *even if I continue to attend church in Winchester. I owe it to my family.* Luke, who had done so much to complete the house renovations, had done nothing to the church. *Call me Thomas*, he'd said.

I sat down on a pew. "Thomas, Thomas . . . Luke!" I whispered. "I loved you. I love you. Let me see your goodness with my own eyes.

"His welcome when I first arrived, that was good," I answered myself in the hush of the chapel. *Or, perhaps he'd meant to trap me. Time and again, in actuality.*

"The sitar, that was goodness." *Ordered early on, as a test to prove you could not play.*

"The statue. The new carriage so I might attend church." *Both of which you might as well pay for*, came the voice from the mazy fold.

"The flowers, the blossoms, the hard kisses, our sign." *Charm is deceitful*, Scripture was quoted.

The laughter, the dance, the touch of his hand against me, the taking of my hair in his hand, gently.

What about the glove? The tincture? The evil proverb written in henna? I turned my thoughts heavenward into a silent prayer. *If it's there, then, Lord, let me see, without a doubt, his dark, troubling character to which so many allude. Open my eyes so I may clearly see.*

Outside, I paused at her gravestone once more, reaching out to touch and trace. Dust came off on my finger. It had been defaced recently or the rain or mists would have washed it away.

Last night, the night Luke had knelt before her gravestone, had been unusually dry.

CHAPTER TWENTY-EIGHT

I sent a note to Mr. Highmore asking if he could come soon to meet with me, and his secretary replied that he was on holiday but could visit in a week's time or thereabouts. I had slept restlessly since visiting the graveyard, I told Michelene a few nights on.

"That's to be expected, *poupée*," Michelene cooed. "It's very troubling to see one's name on a grave. To then know that someone was . . . left life too early. Well"—she snapped her fingers—"that would cause ill rest for anyone."

I nodded, unwilling to share with her the true nature of my unease. Did anyone else visit the graveyard? Unlikely, with the exception of, perhaps, Cook. So no one else would have noticed the scratchings. Had Captain Whitfield's guests seen him leave for the chapel yard, so very, very late at night? Surely Thornton had noticed.

Chapman's guests were back again tonight; I'd seen two carriages arrive and Cook had sent over supper baskets.

"Perhaps a little laudanum?" Michelene poured the golden cup nearly to the brim and handed it to me, waiting, it seemed, for me to drink it in front of her. "As I shall leave for my day off as soon as you are settled."

I set it down on the bureau and stared at it. "I'm not sure," I said. "I'll consider it later."

"I think it would be best." Her voice was gentle and motherly, and she picked the cup up and handed it to me. "I'll be back to-morrow evening."

"I'll take it in an hour's time." I had no intention whatso-ever of taking the laudanum, in fact; in spite of its beguiling soporific charms, my mother's warnings about not overusing laudanum had come back to me, and I felt the pull to drink it perhaps too often. *I must push away now or begin to be ruled by it.*

"All right, then," she said, brushing out my hair. "Make certain you do. And then soon, very soon, we shall return to Winchester together to pick up your fancy outfit for the ball, *n'est-ce pas?*"

I nodded. Attending the Ledburys' ball was much less entic-ing now that things had cooled between Luke and me. He had not dined in the house since his ride with Delia. There had been no socializing at Headbourne, no invitations extended to me. He'd had guests, and was busy preparing to depart. He had, in the main, kept out of my way. I would do likewise.

I'd attend the ball. I supposed I needed to maintain my social relations with everyone in the area and this was as good a way as any to do it. I realized, too, that Luke would be required to be there and it might be the last time I'd see him. I wanted to see him, to say good-bye.

I read some ladies' magazines for a while, and then a section of Scripture, before turning out my light. I turned this way and then that, tangling myself in the linens. I could not sleep. Finally, near midnight, I slid out of bed and returned to the bureau, which held the laudanum, and also was near the window that faced the guesthouse.

It was misty again but the moon was still nearly full and it lit the area. I looked out the window, hoping, to my chagrin, for a glimpse of Luke in the windows of the guesthouse, but I did not see him, though I could see the lights were on in the valet's quarters, and there looked to be a guest carriage nearby.

I looked beyond, to the graveyard. There, in the midst of the dark stones, shadowed by the dim lamp she held before her, was a woman.

A woman!

My own lamp was off, so I moved to the edge of the window where I could continue to watch while hiding behind the thick velvet curtains in case she looked up at me as well.

Oh, the mists! I decried the fact that they were back and I couldn't see the woman more clearly. Her dress was dark, and expensively cut. She kept her face turned from the house and the window but turned, regularly, toward the guesthouse, keeping her back mostly toward me and the main house. She tarried a few minutes more, then turned the lamp off and began to walk toward the guesthouse before I lost track of her in the dark mist. A few minutes later, back still turned, she lit the lamp again, very softly, and made her way toward the chapel. Was it some kind of signal? To whom?

I was about to put on my cloak and go out and look—or at least call for Landreth to investigate—when I saw someone new, a man. He left the guesthouse and began to walk quickly. I pressed close to the cold pane and its chill seeped into my skin, firming the flesh, and then into my jaw. Was it Thornton, Captain Whitfield's valet? It was hard to tell.

Then I could see.

It was Luke.

He came from behind her, wrapped his arm around her intimately and protectively, and they went together into the church. All went dark.

I returned to sit on my bed, squeezing my head in horror, pain shooting from my center through every extremity. A sob stuck in my throat, shock weakened my limbs. Tears came and I did not stop them, though I held the counterpane to my mouth to quiet my sobs. In my mind's eye I saw, again, his arms around her, but I felt them around me, as I wished them to be, in an embrace of love and desire; knowing I'd never again truly feel them around me made the pain intense beyond the point of easy bearing. I got up again, pressed my face against the glass—the coolness of it calmed my hot skin and soothed me a bit—but I saw nothing further. I pulled the curtains shut and returned to bed.

Perhaps I'd imagined it. As I'd imagined the stall shutting behind me when I'd first arrived home? How about seeing Mrs. Ross in the woods whilst Luke and I had been fishing? She'd never claimed to have been lurking. That memory brought an ache, the two of us together, at the beginning of all things good.

I knew, though I wished I could dismiss it as fantasy, that I had well and truly seen Luke and the woman together just minutes earlier, and she was in his embrace. I'd asked to see the truth with my own eyes, and I quite literally had.

Who was she? Perhaps Delia had found out the truth about him and another woman, and had confronted him with it. Maybe she'd threatened to tell me and that's why he'd withdrawn. Perhaps she had arrived in one of the guest carriages still present and they'd met in the chapel to avoid the eyes and ears of the servants and other guests. I could pull on my boots and walk to the chapel and see who it was. But, the truth was . . . I did not want to see him *in flagrante delicto*. I did not want to provide my mind with fresh nightmare images. I promised myself, though, that he would answer for it, for the way he led me, and left me, in the end. Had he done that with my imposter, too? Had she "caught" him? I'd insist on an answer in cold daylight when I was quite prepared.

I cried, off and on, planning, in calmer moments, for a quiet life of good deeds and charity, usefulness, till wan light wriggled through the small spaces between and around my curtains. Then I fell asleep.

I couldn't have been asleep long when I heard a sharp knock at my door.

"Michelene?" I called out.

"No, Miss Ravenshaw, she's got the day off as you'll recall."

"Oh, Mrs. Blackwood."

"Captain Whitfield is here to see you, miss," she said. I heard the hope in her voice. "Shall I tell him you'll be down soon?"

I hurriedly got out of bed and looked at my clock. It was nearly noon! I glanced in the mirror. My hair was tangled and my face puffy and swollen from crying. I would not be able to master my hair in a short period of time, not alone, and it would take several hours and cold compresses to smooth my skin. I would not let him see me so discomposed. That would not give me equal footing at all.

"Please let him know I am slightly unwell, and shall call upon him soon," I said with finality.

"But, miss . . ."

"Thank you, Mrs. Blackwood," I insisted. If she could see me, she'd agree, I was certain.

Later that afternoon, when I'd gotten myself assembled and put on one of my better dresses, I headed downstairs. I gently waved away an offer of tea and pulled my gloves midway from elbow to shoulder. I allowed Landreth to assist me in putting on a warm cloak and I slipped my hand into a white fur muff. I realized, with a pang of pain, that I'd last worn it when we'd gone shooting.

Midway through the gardens between the house and the guesthouse, I noted a large pile of brush, mostly dead twigs and leaves, branches that had been pruned. The stack appeared to await the gardener for autumn clearing. Strangely, though, there appeared to be a ribbon atop it. I walked closer to inspect.

There, gently set on top, rested a small bouquet, still fresh, of white blossoms clinging to cool branches. Jasmine season was months past, but white autumn camellias had just come in. They alone bloomed when all else was dying.

Who but Luke would have gathered a white bouquet on the property, and for what purpose other than to give it to me?

"But of course," Michelene had said. *"Now that you are the heiress, the wooing must begin."* Had he been wooing me or Head-bourne? When I was with him I felt his love and affection emanate from what seemed deep inside him. But when we were apart, the doubts rained down steadily, unstoppable. He'd been warm. And then cold. Now, perhaps, warm again?

I let the flowers lie for the moment and made my way to the guesthouse.

There were all sorts of strange persons milling about, people I did not recognize, carriages and carts that were unknown. When I got to the front door, a man unknown to me was conducting an orchestra of servants going in, boxes coming out.

"Is Captain Whitfield available?" I asked. "I'm Miss Rebecca Ravenshaw."

He shook his head. "I'm sorry. Captain Whitfield has left for London."

London. I could not believe it. In the span of only a few hours since he'd come to call? "Has Thornton accompanied him?"

"Yes." He was not very forthcoming.

"When will he return?" The wind began to blow around me; I felt cold coil at my legs atop my boots.

"He won't be returning, miss."

I gasped. "He's not coming back?"

He shook his head. "No, miss. Lord and Lady Ledbury sent us to finish packing his belongings."

"Oh." I stepped aside so a man with a large trunk could get by me. "Thank you for your help." I kept my voice steady. He bowed, and made his way back to directing the flow of personnel.

I walked slowly back toward the house; on the way, I stopped to claim the white bouquet. I took it in hand, fingering the ribbon, knowing his hand had likely tied it. I touched the cut tips of the stems. They were damp, had been freshly cut. I held a blossom to my lips.

I had, perhaps in pride, set aside the last chance for us to talk at length; he had, perhaps in pride, set aside his last gift to me without leaving a note. He had been cool to me, and I to him. *I do not know whether to pray to see him at the ball or not. So I ask only Your will be done.*

CHAPTER TWENTY-NINE

On a blustery day soon after, Mr. Highmore arrived.

Landreth let him in and tried to take his cloak, but the solicitor held up his hand. "I wondered if, perhaps, Miss Ravenshaw—and of course Mrs. Ross—would join me for a walk outside to enjoy the brisk autumn air?"

I looked out the front door—it was beginning to grow misty, from the sky and not the ground this time—and the wind was picking up. I imagined that a nice cup of tea near the fire in the drawing room would be far more amenable. But Mr. Highmore was nothing if not a practical man, and so, if he was suggesting this, it was for some good cause. We bundled into warm outer wear and off we went down the steps and between the stone lions. Mr. Highmore offered his arm in a fatherly manner as we made our way through the weather. We came to a bench in a fairly sheltered area and there we sat.

"I am sorry for this unusual suggestion," he replied. "But I thought you would like some privacy whilst we discuss the issues of your accounts." He smiled but it was tinged with seriousness. "I'm afraid I have bad news."

"Go on," I urged.

"The funds—well, I'm sorry to say that the money in your father's investments are nearly depleted."

I stood up, and then, aware that there were likely to be eyes peering from the house, sat back down again. "Oh no! Depleted. How can that be?"

He sighed. "It's taken some time to work through the records; there were many investment accounts and they had been directed to various sources. The bulk of the money went to the support of the mission in Travancore."

I shook my head. "We lived so simply . . ."

"Yes, you did," he said. "But additionally there were medical expenses, and doctors to be brought, and the educating of your brother. Supplies."

"I suppose I thought some of that was funded by the Missionary Society," I said.

"It could have been, but it was your father's implicit request that he fund as much of it on his own as possible, freeing funds for other mission works. I'm certain that he thought Peter would have his own profession . . . truly, Miss Ravenshaw, I suspect he had little idea how much of the funds had been spent and he, we all, thought there would be more left once it was sorted."

"I see."

"He certainly thought that you would marry. There are some funds set aside for a dowry, and small amounts in current accounts. The woman claiming to be you spent a good sum on millinery, dresses, and the like. But mostly, it went to the mission field," he said softly. "You could not have known. I would have had to write to him shortly, informing him, had he not passed away."

"The repair of the house and gardens?"

"Captain Whitfield paid for them, all necessary, I might add."

"If my dowry fund needed to be liquidated for that, would it cover the expenses?"

His eyebrows drew together. "Perhaps. But it would deplete them, and you will need funds to operate the house, complete the repairs, upkeep, taxes, and such like." He put his hand back on my arm. "Headbourne is a large house, Miss Ravenshaw. It consumes quite a lot of money just to keep it running. Laundry bills, entertainment and food. The coal bills alone . . ."

I smiled. Perhaps I could be listed on Lady Ashby's coal charity. Which brought to mind the ragged schools. I had already made some commitment to assist, by teaching, mainly, but had considered helping financially as well if it were possible. Likely it was not.

"Is there money for charity?" I asked.

"You *are* a charity, my dear Miss Ravenshaw," he said. "Or you will be very shortly." By now the wind had picked up and I feared that Mrs. Ross's tightly tied bonnet might not hold. Mr. Highmore had been right—I would not want this discussed where ears could pry.

"Household staff?"

"As you'll have noticed, staff salaries are small compared with the other expenses. But you must economize. There are other options."

"Please tell me. What are these other options?"

"You could always marry, of course," he said. Luke's charge— *Show me a woman who does not marry for title or for money. You'll not be able to. She doesn't exist*—rang in my ears.

"No, marriage is not an option just now. Even if I wanted it to be. . . ." I trailed off sadly. He looked surprised, but only for a moment.

"You could sell Headbourne. I'm sure we could find a suitable buyer."

I sat with my hands in my lap. "My family. My father's legacy." The family, and the legacy, had once been lively and blessed, like the gardens around me; had thrived and had shown such promise and beauty. And now, it seems they were dead, brown, lifeless and crisp, ready to be blown away for good. "I'd meant to steward that which had been left me, and to find and keep financial security. I've done neither."

He waited a moment before speaking. "Your family's legacy is not in this house, however lovely and ancient it is. It is you, and those they served."

I looked at him and blinked back the tears. "Yes, thank you, Mr. Highmore, for that kind word of exhortation. Do I have time?"

He nodded. "Some months. End of the year."

I nodded and stood, deeply chilled in spite of my wool layers. "Thank you, Mr. Highmore. I shall take your concerns with prayerful reflection."

He repositioned his tall black hat. "I am always here to help, Miss Ravenshaw."

We walked back to the house, and once inside he gave me a small leather envelope with some cash and a folio of information on my account.

I handed the accounts book to Mrs. Blackwood, who had been assisting me with financial matters, and kept the leather envelope with cash in my room. "Please keep this in confidence. And, soon, I would very much appreciate your going over the household expenses with me so I might properly adjust. You'll know better than I at this point how to best economize."

"Certainly. I'm here to assist you in any way," she said quietly, and, I thought, with great compassion.

I blinked back tears and nodded, then she turned to go.

Luke was gone. My house was gone. I had thought to lose one or the other, but not both. I must think, now, push aside grieving for a moment. *What shall I do?*

I looked through my wardrobe. Perhaps Matthew's mother would be able to sell some of these fine gowns. I laughed, not wanting to cry. I touched my mother's wedding dress. It was so beautiful and now, I was certain, I would never wear it.

What would my mother do? After some time, I had a growing conviction. *But I say unto you, Love your enemies, bless them that curse you, do good to them that hate you, and pray for them which despitefully use you.*

I knew what I was being pressed to do, a first step, anyway. I did not want to do it at first. But in the end, I was convinced that it was right.

I waited beside the coach house till Daniel finished up the task at hand. He saw me and came over. "Do you need me, Miss Raven-shaw?"

I nodded. "Would you have a footman deliver this box to Miss Delia Dainley, today, if possible, with all speed?" I handed over a small wooden trunk.

"I can have someone leave shortly," he said. "It's a slow day." He grinned and I had the idea that, had we been social equals, he would have winked at me. I liked him.

"Thank you. Do let me know that it's safely delivered."

I went back to the house and into the music room. I sat at the piano, and lifted the lid. I ran my hands over the keys. My father had played; surely he had played tunes on this one. Had they had musical evenings together? Did my mother sing to his playing, as she sang without accompaniment in India?

Soon I could see the little heart-shaped carriage approaching the drive. It was Daniel, and he stopped in front of the house rather than drive all the way to the coach house. I met him at the top of the steps.

"She's gone," he said. "Miss Dainley is on a ship, waiting for the convoy to gather before leaving for India."

The same fleet Luke was to leave on? Was she going to meet with him in India?

No, that could not be possible. He was in London, not Southampton. The idea of them being together, though, in India gave me pause. It made me wonder if I should carry through with my plan, because if I did, and if they married . . . I could not imagine that pain.

I had a moment to change my mind, a second chance. I pressed forward.

"The fleet tarries?"

He nodded. "For now."

"Can you take me all the way to Southampton?"

"Of course." He stopped for a minute. "Is it important?"

"Yes, it is."

I ran up the stairs in a most unladylike manner, not knowing if the ship were to leave in fifteen minutes or ten days. They waited till there were enough of them to sail safely together, and till the tide was right, and then they set out through the Solent.

"Mrs. Ross?" I pounded on her door. "Can you come along, please? Quickly?"

"Aye, lassie. I'll be right there."

Daniel helped us each into the carriage.

As we clattered down the drive and through the town, I thought how very much this drive reminded me of my trip to Headbourne some months back. I'd arrived at the docks, ready to embrace unknown England. I'd been fearful and plagued with anguish over the loss of my family, and my home. And now, I rushed toward Delia, who was making my journey in reverse. It was late afternoon, and I hoped that we would reach the docks before darkness descended. It could be a sordid, somewhat squalid place by daylight and I had no desire to be at the wharf in the evening.

I smelt it before I saw it and it brought back powerful memories, the tang of salt preserving the rotting green scent of seaweed. Daniel slowed the carriage and then stopped it completely, asking for directions. There were many ships anchored in the harbor, swaying and bobbing, sails furled. My stomach lurched a little, remembering.

Daniel looked back at me. "I've called out to a few people asking about the ships for India, but no one will respond. They're all occupied."

"Drive closer," I instructed him. At one part of the dock, I could see that there were more Indians nearby. I leaned forward toward the front of the carriage. "Lascars?"

Daniel nodded and called back. "Yes, miss. They're most likely sailing to India to work the ships, but many of them live here, now."

He spoke with a confidence, perhaps borne of experience, that I had not expected. I remembered anew Cook's comment about Daniel taking the Indian maid away.

"Daniel, please help me alight."

He came near the carriage door. "I don't think it a sound idea, miss," he said. "We're at the docks."

I smiled at him. "Yes, I recognize that. Please help me alight."

He held out his hand. I looked back at Mrs. Ross, and she nodded her approval but called out, in an unusually strained voice, "Doona stray far from the carriage, lassie."

"I won't." I stepped out and, with a woman in their midst, the men slowed down.

"Esteemed seamen," I called out loudly in Tamil, certain that some among them would speak it. "I am in need of assistance."

Two Indian men came closer to me, and Daniel moved closer yet, looking at me with a mixture of horror and awe.

"Lady, you speak our language as if you were a woman of India," one of the men said, looking at my fair skin and English finery.

"I am," I said quietly.

They nodded politely. "How can we be of help to you, respected lady?"

"I am looking for a friend, kind sirs. An Englishwoman sailing to India, and I have a crate that it is very important that she receive. Her name is Miss Delia Dainley. Would any of you be able to check the manifests and see if she is on one of those ships?" I pointed to those lingering in the harbor. I opened my purse and withdrew a coin.

"I can find out for you, miss," one man said as he took my coin.

I turned to Daniel, whose mouth was agape. "You speak heathen!" he finally choked out.

I laughed. "Oh, Daniel. It's Tamil."

He closed his mouth.

We passed a few quiet moments and I watched the workers load crates onto the ships. A growing part of me wanted to board one myself. But there was nothing for me there, really, anymore. Was there?

Shortly, one of the lascars came back and spoke, again in Tamil, to me. "Yes, Miss Dainley is indeed aboard one of the ships. If you'll give your package to me I'll see it reaches her."

"Thank you. I'd prefer you row me out instead."

"I cannot, miss. You'd have to climb a rope ladder."

I saw that this was quite impossible. "Thank you, kind sir." I held up the wooden crate to him, glad that I had tucked a note of explanation into it for Delia, in case I should not be able to present it to her myself. "This is very dear to me. Please treat it carefully. I shall await your return to know that it found its way safely to Miss Dainley." He seemed honest, but one could not know. "Please ask her to send a note of acceptance." I put two pieces of silver in his hand.

"I will care for it as tenderly as I care for my son," he said.

"*Kadavul unnai aaseervadhippaaraaha,*" I said to him.

"May God bless you as well," he replied as he gingerly eased the crate from my arms.

I watched him walk away with my treasure and prayed for safe travels and that it would accomplish all I hoped it would. Daniel helped me back into the carriage.

"It'll get there safely," Mrs. Ross reassured me.

"Thank you for your encouragement," I said. "You're always so encouraging."

"It's my responsibility, lassie."

That was thoughtful. I was certain that most chaperones did not believe their job included being encouraging. None I'd come into contact with, in any case.

Within the hour the lascar returned with a note. The handwriting was indeed Delia's.

Thank you, Rebecca. This gift is far too generous, but knowing what it cost you, personally, I should not think of returning it. I shall be married as a proper Englishwoman; rest assured it will be treated with honor. I am truly sorry for the manner in which I handled our last exchange, and beg your forgiveness. I have done you a turn in friendship, too, though you may never know of it. I am, now, especially gladdened that I did.

> *Your friend,*
> *Delia*

I wondered, on the ride home, what that friendship favor had been. Perhaps it had to do with Captain Whitfield. Perhaps she had, somehow, frightened him away from me, knowing that he would prove false.

CHAPTER THIRTY

Some while later we arrived home. Michelene was in my room.

"I noticed the wardrobes were in a disarray," she said. "I went to put away some new dresses . . ."

"New dresses?" I stood up. "I haven't ordered any."

"*Calmez-vous*," she said. "I meant the, er, saree, for the Ledburys'. In a moment, we shall try it on, *non*?"

"Oh, very well." I hadn't shared my financial situation with anyone else yet, hoping to pray and think my way to a solution first.

"Your wedding dress. It needs some work? It's missing."

I quickly shook my head. "No. I . . . I gave it to Miss Dainley."

"Oof!" she gasped. "That belonged to your *maman*, *non*? Why ever would you give it to Miss Dainley? She was a friend, yes, but . . ."

"Amongst the English in India," I said, "a traditional English wedding is highly prized. Wearing an English wedding dress is among the most important statements of all. Some women buy used wedding dresses in India. But I knew Miss Dainley would not have the . . . wherewithal to do that. I did not want her to be ostracized. She helped me, and I wanted to help her."

"But a gift so dear . . . you could have bought her the ready-made dress, *non*?"

Non. But I did not share with Michelene my conviction about loving your enemy.

"Dresses trimmed with Honiton lace are most prized, since that was what Queen Victoria chose for her own dress," I said instead. "The dress will give Miss Dainley a great push forward into the society she must live in."

And I hoped for her sake that Delia did find affection and acceptance, not only with the other wives, but with the man she would marry after having met him perhaps three or four times first.

"You will not need the dress?" Michelene inquired quietly.

I shook my head. "No, I believe I shall not."

She clapped her hands. "Well, if you do, you can buy another one with Honiton lace, *n'est-ce pas*?"

I nodded. But not one that had lace made by my grandmother's hands. This was no time for regrets, though, and I didn't have any. It would do Delia far more good than me.

She chattered with me for a few more minutes, and I was glad when she took her leave. Her presence troubled me more as each day went on. She was pleasant to talk with, but perhaps too directorial. She'd taken the carriage without asking, purloined my gowns. Something nudged me, troubled me, at the edge of my mind. I reached but could not quite grasp it.

She had not mentioned Luke's absence. It was odd.

"I warn you, I do not know what to do with these henna things." Michelene had shaken the henna I'd had sent from London into a small wooden bowl, so it wouldn't stain the china.

"I do know," I said. "Not as much as an Indian woman, especially those of the castes which practice the art of henna, but more
than anyone else likely to be at the ball tonight."

We mixed in lemon juice and a little of the cinnamon oil I'd
been using in my lip pomade. I'd asked Cook for molasses, and although she grumbled, she acquiesced once I told her what I was
using it for. "Wish I'd had me a bit more fun when I was young,"
she said, and handed over a copper tin filled with the molasses,
which would help the dye adhere to my skin while it dried. Mrs.
Blackwood had readily offered up some needles when I'd asked
her for some.

"It smells like the stable!" Michelene pinched her nose and I
laughed in spite of myself.

"It smells like the clay soil of India to me," I said. Once the
paste was the proper texture and we'd let it rest till the dye released, I used my left hand to draw a pattern of dips and swirls
and trails that crossed and crossed back over again upon my right
hand. I wrapped the henna around my wrist like a bracelet and
then let it snake slightly up my arm.

"*C'est très joli*," Michelene breathed out a sigh of admiration.

"Now, you just copy, as best you can, the same design on my
left hand. I have done lacework and you've done sewing, so it's not
as though we do not know how to bring forth a design with a
needle. It's just for a different purpose in this case."

She used the needle to gently apply the henna to my left hand,
and after I'd let it dry, we peeled it off, saw where there were gaps
in the design, and added a bit more. An hour or so later, I was
done.

"You will certainly be, er, different from anyone else at Lady
Ledbury's tonight," she said. "I wish I could be there to see. Oh!
Wouldn't Miss Dainley be shocked."

I giggled at that. Yes, Delia would certainly have forbidden me from doing this if she'd known. I had a little pang, knowing that she'd sailed.

My sari was edged in peacock blue with a pattern in gold running all along it. As the fabric rose up my body it became deep indigo, and then sea-green. The pallu edge, which wrapped around my neck and then down my arm, was also trimmed in a gold patterned fabric. Had I been a real Indian woman, and married, I would have boasted of all my gold jewelry by wearing it all at once. The household gathered to look at me, openmouthed. No one spoke, and Mrs. Blackwood soon hustled them back to work.

Daniel pulled the carriage up. "I'm sure Lady Ledbury will be surprised by your outfit!" he said.

I grinned. I was a daughter of Hampshire, born and bred here. This was my family home, and the Ravenshaws had lived here longer than even the esteemed Lady Ledbury. I had little to lose at this point. As Mr. Highmore had pointed out, I was nearly a charity case. A little more pity or scorn would not matter, because I was a daughter of India as well.

Michelene came up behind me. "Do you remember what I said to you about the Hussars? That when they arrive, everyone runs, the women to them and the men away? Tonight, it shall be the opposite. When you arrive in your lovely costume, the women will run away from you but every man shall wish that you were his. You look beautiful."

"Thank you for that," I said. There was only one man I wished to run to me, to wish I were his.

Once in the carriage I watched the route carefully, not having been to Graffam Park before. It really was quite a short journey through the back way, but the roadways were smooth; I was surprised. Within twenty minutes we had arrived.

Daniel pulled the carriage up along the long drive, which had been lined with lanterns; still more lanterns lit the steps to the main house, which was made entirely of red brick. The windows were white-framed, tiny little squares warped by time, often seen in grand houses in England, and which I had come to love as confirming a sense of place and home. The lights glittered and shimmered through the windows; some of the panes were wavy with age, which only added to their charm.

As we walked up the steps, and then inside, under the forbidding portrait of an early Ledbury, there were whispers and nods, and a few smiles. I was dressed exotically, yes, but it was a costume ball and there were many others in unusual attire. I made my way through the crowd of men in historic uniform and the ladies in patrician clothing of years gone by. One person, in particular, made me smile. Lady Frome, full with her baby, stood in the center of the room in a shepherdess's costume.

I went to her first. "Oh, my dear, you look absolutely charming," she said. "And I mean that in the best sort of way. Wherever did you find an Indian dress?"

"I commissioned the sari made," I said. "I'd thought of having my nose pierced, too, but perhaps that would have been one step too far."

"Next year!" she teased, and put one hand to her back.

"I cannot believe that you have descended from shepherds," I said, pointing at her exquisite and expensive country attire.

"No," she agreed. "But I wanted to be different. And my family owns land upon which the sheep meander."

Lots and lots of land, I thought, *with lots and lots of sheep*. I knew, too, that her grandfather had made a fortune from wool. But she was genteel enough not to refer to it, and bold enough not to have to wear a costume that tied her, feebly, to some Hanoverian or his courtiers, like many others present.

The room was edged in gilt—the door frames, the floorboards, the windows, tastefully done, of course. In the far corner a quartet softly hummed. Someone came by and handed a dance card to me. So there were to be dance cards, then. I saw, just outside the great hall, a table spilling over with boxes and bags.

Lady Frome saw my eyes drawn to it. "The gifts?"

"Oh," I said. "I'd nearly forgotten." I started to walk toward the table, which was guarded by two footmen.

"Let me come with you," she said. "I'd like to look the offerings over before deciding whom to invite to our Christmas ball."

She had a pleasant, happy look on her face and I knew she teased. "It would be my pleasure, Lady Frome."

"Please," she insisted. "Call me Jennie."

"Jennie," I said, aware that this was a new step in our friendship. "Then you must call me Rebecca," I said. I set my gift down on the table.

She looked at it, took it in her hand. "Honiton lace, of course. But what is inside?"

"Pennies," I said with a grin. "But not hot."

She grinned back.

Pride wrestled with desire. Desire won out. "Your brother-in-law, Captain Whitfield, is he here?" I asked.

"Somewhere, I believe," she said, a twinkle in her eye. I wondered how she had kept her sense of humor alive whilst being married to Lord Pudding. "Though he's preparing to take immediate leave to the East Indies for a year or two, to attend to his business accounts, and perhaps make some strategic investments now that India is firmly under the control of Her Majesty."

"Seems wise," I said softly. She had not mentioned Delia or another woman.

"Perhaps, perhaps not," she answered. I saw her husband moving toward her. To my surprise, when he arrived he took my card in hand and scrawled his name on one of the lines before taking her arm and moving away.

Baron Ashby came over and said a cool hello. He signed up for one dance on my card. "I'm sorry to hear of your recent misfortune."

I inclined my head. "Which misfortune is that?"

"Your father's investments, unraveled." How had he heard that? Certainly not from Mr. Highmore? Perhaps Highmore's milk-faced secretary had lost a sense of discretion and disseminated the unwelcome news.

"It's not all yet settled, Lord Ashby," I said. "But thank you for your concern." He made small conversation and then offered a feeble excuse to withdraw. No fortune, no suitor, apparently.

"Guid riddance," Mrs. Ross said, and she didn't seem to care who heard her. Several other young men came to put their names on my dance card, and many were very attentive—even without my fortune—as Michelene had predicted.

I looked up and, in a suspended moment, saw Luke make his way toward me.

CHAPTER THIRTY-ONE

He stood near me seconds later and I looked him over; he was dressed in a vintage uniform. "You served for many more years than I'd thought," I teased him. I wondered if he'd worn it to taunt his mother, or Lord Ledbury.

He smiled, and I saw that it was in spite of himself. "It's my father's uniform."

"I'd thought so. You look striking in it."

"And you look incomparably beautiful. I pity the other ladies present." He nearly moved toward me, leaning to take me in his arms, I could both see and sense it, but he stopped himself. "I thought that, having been denied a dance when we were at Headbourne, I would claim one now," he said. "Before I leave for India."

He was unfailingly polite and devastatingly handsome in the high white collar that brushed against his jaw, but he made no overt move to be more personal to me than anyone else had. I sighed with disappointment and resignation, inwardly, and put on my own cool mask of feigned indifference, though I wept inside.

He marked down his name, once. "I couldn't leave without a dance, though it would be easier, perhaps, for both of us if I did."

Across the room, Lord Ledbury held up a finger and motioned for Luke.

"I'll see you shortly," he said softly, and kissed the back of my bare, hennaed hand.

The dancing began and, I admit it, I counted them down till my dance with Luke. He found me; we formally bowed as the music began and then he took me in his arms. I fit perfectly.

He looked at my hennaed hands, so unlike the carefully gloved ones of the other women present, and an amused, appreciative smile crossed his lips before he caught it.

"I've heard that you might be leaving for India," I said.

He nodded. "Yes. Breame—you'll remember him—says that the time is ripe for investment now the Rebellion is settled. British are flocking to India in great numbers, and for those willing to gamble, there may be lucrative days ahead."

"I suspect you're willing to gamble," I said.

"There's not much to keep me here," he replied.

"I noticed that nearly everything has been removed from the guesthouse and that Mrs. Blackwood had sent some day maids to begin cleaning it." He let his hand slip a little lower, until it rested on the small of my back. I felt his touch resonate all the way up my spine.

"I've been staying with Lord and Lady Ledbury as I'll be leaving very soon."

"You didn't say good-bye," I said softly.

"I could not," he admitted. "Though I tried."

"About that . . ." I started, and he put his finger to my lips to hush me.

"Later." Neither of us spoke until the end of the dance. It wasn't for lack of something to say, it was so as not to disrupt that which was being said through touch and movement, which was

We fit, I miss you, don't leave, ask me to stay. I still had much to ask, and to say. Why had he been so cold? Why was he not, now? I would wait until supper, when we could speak together at length in a private corner. Later.

There was a break in the music, and champagne was circulated along with pleasantries. I danced with two other perfectly well-mannered men, one of whom was quite attractive. But there was no spark. As I rested during the next dance, that thought brought Scripture to mind.

"Yet man is born to trouble as surely as sparks fly upwards. But if I were you, I would appeal to God; I would lay my cause before him. He performs wonders that cannot be fathomed, miracles that cannot be counted."

I thought back to our conversation about the blossoms. "It was a miracle, Captain Whitfield," I'd said. "The word miracle means *sign.*"

I need a sign, Lord. Please send one.

I glanced at the next name on my card. *Viscount Anthony Frome.* Lord Frome came and found me, took my hand in his gloved one, and sneered slightly at my ungloved, hennaed hands. He bowed and I curtseyed and then we began. The particular song and dance kept us apart from one another more than I had been with Luke, but we were still able to converse.

"Your wife is beautiful and charming, one of the loveliest women I've met since I've been home," I said. "You must be very proud of her."

"I am," he said, and I was somewhat surprised to hear the softness in his voice when he spoke of Jennie. "My only hope and prayer is for her to come through the birth of our child with all speed and safety."

"I shall pray to that end as well," I said. He was a practiced, technically perfect dancer, but there was no give or emotion in his movements.

"Are you quite at home at Headbourne House?" he asked.

"Oh yes," I said.

"My brother has recently repaired to Graffam Park, leaving Headbourne House. It was quite a shock, I'm sure, as he had all but moved into his 'family' house." He smirked.

"Why, it is his family house, isn't it?"

He laughed. "It cannot be, by definition, Miss Ravenshaw, if it's yours."

The music slowed and we were able to talk a bit more. His mouth was close enough to my ear that I could both hear what he intended that others did not, and also feel his damp breath rim my ear.

"Perhaps it's better. It's a pity Miss Dainley has sailed for India. Mother liked her. She was so very fair. And English." He glanced again at my hands, and then, in a leering way, toward the top of my sari. "He didn't prefer her; Mother feels he never makes the right choices. I'm afraid my brother is a bit of a mercenary," he said. "Can't blame him, really, not having a father to put his foot down with him when he was a boy. Fooled around with women and weapons. Neither got him far."

We parted for a moment in the dance. "I was under the impression that his weapons manufacture did very well."

"If one must earn a living of some sort, I suppose I would just as soon choose one that did not involve human bloodshed." His voice was both sharp and bloated with condescension.

Of course. Lord Frome would never have had to dirty his hands.

I remained parted from him, although we were at a juncture in the dance where we should have joined again. I felt my voice rise and did not heed the memory of my mother's earlier advice toward temperance in speech. "I assure you, Lord Frome, that if you'd been in the midst of a battle, and I have been, and a man wielding a sword with intent to cleave your skull was fast approaching, you'd be happy to have an Adams in hand to stop him. But you haven't, and you won't, so it's nothing to you and your country life of quiet disdain."

He looked shocked. And then I realized that there were shocked faces all round me, because the music had stopped and there was a small crowd who had heard me speak so brazenly about weapons and murders and take to task one of the evening's hosts. Lady Ledbury, I could see from across the room, looked as though she'd just bitten hard on an unripe berry.

The music started up again, but I slowly made my way to the door. It was polite to remove myself then, so the others could enjoy the rest of the evening without an issue arising, sides being taken or rounds of awkward gossip squelched. I did not see Luke anywhere. *He will think I left him, not wishing further conversation. Perhaps I could send a note on the morrow. If he's still here.*

I did stop to say good-bye to Jennie.

"I'm so sorry," I said. "I fear I've made a terrible breach of etiquette. And I've insulted your husband. I apologize and do hope we can still be friends."

"It was a bold thing to say." She drew me near and kissed each cheek in turn as a response. "Fortune favors the bold, Rebecca." Then she made her way back into the crowd.

"Back to Headbourne?" Daniel asked. "So early?"

I nodded and held out my trembling hand for him to lift me into the carriage. He stared at the henna.

"The henna troubles you?" I asked. He'd not been bothered by it earlier.

"It's just that, well, it makes me recall that the-the woman who had pretended to be you, her maid had that kind of heathen paint on her hands, too." He quickly added, "Not that you're a heathen, miss. But while I'm speaking of them . . ." He looked down and kicked the ground once before looking up again. "I do know what happened the night Christopher drove her maid away. I want to be honest with you now."

"Why now?"

"I . . . I want him to stay, miss. And you, too. I know you've heard the rumors about him and that woman pretending to be you; we all have. How she died. If he had a hand in it. My loyalties always are with the captain and he said not to tell anyone where she'd gone, for her sake. Christopher took her to the lascars, in Southampton, the dock to India, because none of us speaks heathen now, do we, so we could hardly help. She was scared—being a foreigner, an Indian just after the Rebellion—that she'd be blamed, and just wanted to run away. But Captain Whitfield gave her money to pay for someone to assist her. He thought, being her countrymen and sailors all, they could help and they promised Christopher that they would. Don't be angry with me, miss."

He lowered his voice and looked back at me earnestly, as if he were entrusting a secret to me. And maybe he was. "Captain Whitfield wanted to make sure she were taken care of and not followed by toughs. So that means he couldn't be, well, guilty of anything. Isn't that right? No matter what the gossips say?" Even faithful Daniel had his doubts.

"Taken care of? What does that mean?" I kept my voice soft. "That he was looking out for her best interests? Or getting her out of the way as quickly as possible?"

"Oh, he's a good man, miss," Daniel continued. "You can be sure of it."

I had never thought the Mutiny would have occurred, that my parents would have been murdered. I would never have guessed that someone would steal my identity. I could not believe that Luke might be a murderer, nor that he was completely play-acting only to gain my home. His home. But perhaps I had lost sense of what men, or a man, could do and what they could not. I could be sure of almost nothing.

Daniel continued. "I think he sent her back to India."

I shook my head. "How could that have been arranged?"

Daniel looked at me. "I don't know, miss. But I know there's lascars, Indian sailors, that end up in London at the Strangers' Home. At least that's what they say in Southampton, when I've been waiting there for the captain on his military business an' all."

I'd toyed with an idea the past few nights, but first I wanted to make sure Luke was, indeed, worthy of what I planned to offer him. This might be my final opportunity. "Do you think there are Indian women at that Strangers' Home? Maids?"

"I can't say, miss."

"Can you take me to those lascars?"

"Now, miss? There won't be anyone there this late. And we don't speak their language . . . wait, you do."

"Perhaps if I can find a man who helped this maid I can somehow help solve our very difficult problem and clear the captain's name."

He looked hopeful, and then scratched his head. "I would take you in the morning, but I don't see what you hope to do. The maid has long gone back to India. It's been months and months."

"I don't know either, Daniel. But I need to follow this as far as I can. Please be ready to leave at first light."

CHAPTER THIRTY-TWO

Early next morning I told Mrs. Blackwood that we were leaving to go to Southampton and that she should not expect us until late that evening. I assured her that Daniel would come along to protect us. Strangely enough, Mrs. Ross raised no objection at all to our going into a rather rough neighborhood; instead, she seemed to relish the adventure. It must get dull, I thought, sitting in her room or waiting upon the occasion to accompany me someplace. Perhaps, being more local, she understood that the locale was gentler than I knew.

Once at Southampton, Daniel went to find some lascars. I spoke with one in Malayalam and he told me that, yes, there had been an ayah delivered here late last year, which was most unusual and why he'd noted it. He would make quick inquiries.

A few minutes later he returned. "The woman you seek was taken to London. We don't have many Indian women here, you understand, so it was easy to remember her." He called over another Indian man, who spoke only Hindi, which I spoke haltingly. It was enough for me to understand that there was indeed a home in London, near the West India dock, for Indians who were stranded here, and that all were helped with food, money, and arrangement for work to earn the money to return home if they so chose. It was called the Strangers' Home. I thanked him and returned to the carriage.

"Can you lodge the carriage and horses in town overnight?" I asked Daniel.

He nodded. "For a fee."

I withdrew my leather wallet from my account folio, which Mrs. Blackwood had given me before we left, and went to purchase train tickets. Before closing the folio I noticed new papers had been slipped into the accounts. I would look at them on the train.

I paid for a note to be delivered to Mrs. Blackwood so she would not worry.

We made our way into the carriage. The seats were softly upholstered in supple leather that hissed in exhalation as Mrs. Ross settled her considerable self upon one. The train began to pull away from the station, and I wondered, as Daniel had asked, what I hoped to achieve.

I want to know who the maid was.

I want to know who impersonated me.

I want to clear Luke's name from the whisperings and innuendo that he had a hand in her death. For his sake. For mine.

The train chugged through the Hampshire countryside, autumn clear churned to autumn fog and smoke. I opened up my wallet: an invoice from the dry goods store, marked paid, and one from the poulterer; the invoice behind it was attached to a note from Mr. Highmore. I withdrew it, too, and as I read, was stunned. I read it twice, just to ensure that I had not made a mistake, but I had not. The enormous cost of repairing, remodeling, and bringing Headbourne current, as well as this year's taxes, had been paid in full by Captain Luke Whitfield. All other monies due him as a matter of course had been duly and permanently discharged.

My breath caught and my hand trembled. I had asked to see the truth of the man with my own eyes, and I had.

Luke had paid my bills expecting nothing in return. I would have at least a year, perhaps two or three, now, to discover how I might acquire enough funds to keep Headbourne. Or, perhaps having paid for it, Headbourne deserved to be his. My heart swelled with love and urgency to complete my mission and return to him. "Luke," I said softly.

"Ye'll not find another one like him," Mrs. Ross said from across the aisle.

A short while later we pulled into Waterloo Station. It was my first time in London—that I could recall, anyway. I longed to explore the city, but at the moment, I was on a mission. Daniel met us and we commissioned a hackney carriage.

"I'd like to go to the Strangers' Home," I said. "West India Dock Road. Do you know where it is?"

"Yes, miss," he said. "The Prince himself laid the cornerstone for it. It's not . . . not a place for ladies, miss, if you don't mind my saying so."

I let out a big puff of air. "There aren't women there, then?"

He shook his head. "No, ma'am, it's a home just for men. India men, other sailors who be far from their home. The London Missionary Society runs it."

Pride surged; I, of course, had come from a family that had given its life to the work of that organization. "But what about the women?" Had we come all this way for naught?

"They'd be at the Ayahs' Home," he said. "That's not too far away, neither. In Whitechapel. On Jewry Street."

"Take us, please," I said. He cracked his whip and his team took off toward the Ayahs' Home.

We soon turned down Whitechapel, a street of mismatched buildings; tidy homes, crumbling bricks, bakeries that sent out sweet smells, breweries that sent out bitter ones. There were women loitering, dressed in garish makeup and evening wear so early in the day. My heart went out to them, for when they had no other means by which to make their way, they sold themselves. It happened in India, too.

"Shall I wait here, then?" the carriage driver asked me as he pulled in front of a tidy brown terraced house. I knew it would be costly to have him wait but there was no other place for Daniel to remain, and I was not at all certain that another carriage for hire would come out here to get us.

"Yes, please," I said. "I shall pay your complete fee upon our return to Waterloo."

He nodded and we walked up the steps to the narrow house. It looked to have about four floors, typical for London, I'd heard, but it was much tidier than the other houses in the area. This being Saturday, I would have expected more activity, but there was little going on outside. We walked up to the door, and I knocked sharply. A young Indian woman opened the door.

"May I help you?" she asked in thickly accented English.

"Yes, my name is Rebecca Ravenshaw," I said. "Is there a house mother here?"

She shook her head. "I'm sorry—speaking too quickly. Please, try again?"

I switched to Malayalam and hoped she spoke it. "My name is Rebecca Ravenshaw. Is there a house mother I might speak with?"

"Oh, memsahib speaks Malayalam!" I knew that most English women stationed in India never learned the local languages, pre-

ferring instead to learn only the few words required to communi-
cate with their servants. My mother, and indeed most missionaries,
had been exceptions.

She suggested we sit down in the front room. It was but steps
from the door, and sparsely, but comfortably, furnished.

"Here we have ayahs who traveled from India with their English families," she said. "The families normally purchase tickets
for the return trip and hand them over to the Missionary Society,
which keeps them until the ayah can be engaged with a family
leaving England for India," she said. "But because of the recent . . .
trouble . . . not many families have returned to India in the past
year. So"—she waved her hand toward the upper floors—"about
forty of us still remain, although many are sailing soon, now that
English people are returning to India. There are a few of us," she
said in a hushed tone, "whose family did not buy them a return
ticket. They must hope for someone to engage them who is willing to do so."

Forty ladies and a house mother lived in this small house?

"I see," I said. "No, I am not in need of an ayah." Her face
dropped. "But I have come to see if there is anyone here who
knows an ayah who would have come here last winter, in December. The girl would not have been coming from a ship, but from a
home in the country."

The woman carefully rearranged her hands. "There were one
or two women who were in a situation like that. It happens, sometimes, the family brings an Indian servant to England but one or
the other doesn't adjust."

"I would guess not many people were arriving during those
months," I said. Because there were fewer ships leaving India
during the early months of the Rebellion.

She shook her head.

"Would there be anyone here that was attached to an English lady who died unexpectedly?"

"There is no one like that here," she said, and now it was my face that dropped.

All this way to find nothing!

"But there is a woman, her name is . . . Sattiyayi. She was friend to a maid like this."

Oh! "May I speak with her?"

She shrugged. "We are not friends, and I do not know her well, as she keeps to herself. I can go upstairs and ask."

"Thank you very much," I said. She left, and I looked at the room around me—pretty and personal, with books and scriptures in many Eastern languages.

In a moment, the woman came back down the stairs. Alone. I took a deep breath.

"She says she will join you, please, in the garden at the back?" She continued to speak in Malayalam. "Alone." She nodded toward Mrs. Ross.

I nodded. Mrs. Ross nodded and remained in the sitting room.

I followed the young woman out to the small area at the back, which was chilly, but in a protected area, and there were some well-worn chairs to sit in. A few minutes later, a beautiful young Indian woman came out.

The first thing she did was look at my hands, which I had un-gloved for a moment to fix my hair.

"Henna?" She spoke Tamil, and she sat down across from me. She was beautiful, her eyebrows newly shaped and threaded, her hair gently curled in a traditional style. She had a thin gold ring through her nose and a ready smile, although she looked wary.

I nodded and responded in Tamil. "Yes. Thank you for speaking with me. I am looking for someone who may know the ayah to a woman who called herself Rebecca Ravenshaw. The one who claimed that name, that is, who died by her own hand last December."

"I knew this maid," she confirmed. Her face remained serene. "We were friends."

"Oh, that is wonderful," I said. I could not believe that, through fortune, boldness, and certainly divine intervention, I had made my way to someone, somewhere, who knew the maid connected with Headbourne. "I am the actual Miss Ravenshaw."

At that, her eyes opened wide and although she worked hard to contain her shock, I could see that she was stunned.

She swallowed hard and then spoke. "The daughter of the missionaries?"

I smiled. She had indeed known the maid! "Yes, yes, that is me," I said. "I arrived back in England in the spring. My parents, unfortunately, died, but by the grace of God I survived."

She took all this in. "The house mother told us all about the Ravenshaw family when this maid arrived, as the London Missionary Society supports us as well as the missionaries in India, but we thought all were lost. I am certain that the ayah in question would have been delighted to hear of this. All of us connected with the Society will be."

"I am hoping to find out more about who the young woman was who pretended to be me," I said. "And also to learn, well, if the man who was to have inherited my house, if he was involved in her death in any way."

Sattiyayi shook her head vehemently. "Oh, no, memsahib," she said. "Of this I am quite certain. The man who was at the house, the captain, he did not try to harm that English lady. It was very much the opposite. He didn't know it, but *she* was attempting to murder *him.*"

CHAPTER THIRTY-THREE

"Murder him!" I pitched forward in my chair. "How do you know?"

She backed up and crossed her arms. "My friend, she told me everything. Do you want to know this?"

"I'm very sorry for startling you," I said. "Yes, yes, please do go on."

"My friend is from Ceylon," she began. "She was an ayah there. Last year, her mistress went to Kerala to visit friends, and after they arrived there, they learned some missionary friends had died in the Rebellion. There was, as you know, considerable unrest in the north, but in the south, ships were regularly sailing still. My friend's memsahib said she wanted to go to England, to visit, and needed an ayah. There were other English women traveling who could serve as chaperones for the trip. My friend agreed. She was promised a great sum of money and a return ticket to India. My friend does not speak English."

I nodded. Many English ladies in India did not like to employ English-speaking maids so they could keep their personal discussions private.

"Did your friend know what this woman's name was?" I asked her.

She nodded. "She did not speak English, but when they were arranging for traveling papers and tickets, she heard her called Violet many times."

"No," I breathed out. No. Could it have been a coincidence? It could not have been. Could not have been my friend, my lifelong friend, my Violet. And yet it must have been. Violet had known every detail of our lives. She had nothing to lose, really, as she had no family nor a future of any value, as she could see it, in India.

My skin prickled and I squeezed back the tears. "Please continue."

"I'm sorry, I do not mean to upset you." Sattiyayi looked nearly as distraught as I felt.

"You have done nothing wrong," I said. "I can listen without interrupting you again."

She pulled her shawl more tightly against the wind. "So my friend came to England. They went to the grand house and all was well for some time. Although she didn't speak English or have any time alone, she did begin to notice that at first people were very warm to the young miss, but then began to treat her oddly. Especially the captain began to treat her with . . ." She hunted for the word.

"Skepticism?" I offered and she nodded. "Yes, I'm sure he would have begun to notice things," I said. I recalled the left-handedness.

"And then soon, my friend began to notice that people were calling the memsahib 'Rebecca' and not 'Violet,' if not 'Miss Ravenshaw.' She said the memsahib began to take the sleeping medicine more and more, that the French maid had brought her quite a bit but only because memsahib was asking for it and the French maid seemed to think it helped to calm her, which it did. Violet was much agitated during the day. One night, my friend noticed that the memsahib had two bottles of malaria preparations. You know of it?"

"Dr. Warburg's Tincture," I said.

"That's it. One day she came upon her in the shed where the cutter tools for the trees and shrubs were kept and it looked as though the memsahib was putting some powder into one of the jars."

The glove. She had taken one of Luke's gloves and used it so she would not poison herself by touching it. Then she must have been startled and left one glove behind.

Sattiyayi continued. "The memsahib was very angry with my friend and told her to leave, immediately. She slapped my friend's face. She was very upset."

At that, the maid touched her right cheek and flinched in sympathy. "This tin the memsahib had been taking it from looked like the same powder my friend had seen the cook in the kitchen use to kill mice. The lady became upset when she saw that my friend had noticed her doing this, and appeared to be frightened. I now know she was scared they would find out she was not you. And perhaps that my friend would find some way to tell the captain."

I drew my shawl around me.

"And then?" I asked.

"And then memsahib spoke with the French maid, pointed to one of the bottles, and said the captain's name. The maid took one of the bottles. Earlier, when the memsahib had left the room, my friend saw that the bottles looked to be the same, but one of them had a little mark in the label, like that left by scraping a fingernail. That was the one that was taken."

How could this have been Violet, *my* Violet?

"The French maid, she did not know that memsahib had put something into the bottle so she might have given it to the captain. My friend took that bottle and hid it away in a bureau drawer that memsahib never used, planning to retrieve it later, when memsahib left the room, and dispose of it where it could hurt no one. My friend said that the memsahib became more and more melancholy after the captain, he told her that a friend of her brother's was coming to the house to visit. My friend told her that she should be happy, but she screamed that she didn't have a brother. She was greatly distressed that the captain had mentioned something about a constable."

Violet knew Dunn could find her out, she'd be caught, she would have nowhere to go; worse, she would most likely be imprisoned for impersonating a dead person and stealing money and lands. I could imagine her despair; I'd seen her despair when her own mother had died, when her father had moved her to Ceylon and taken up with a native woman, ostracizing them from English society. She had no hope after that. No friends, no suitors. Could not even be taken on as a governess. Her letters in India had not indicated the depth of her pain, but perhaps I could have questioned more, reached out sooner.

"She did not have time, now, to poison him. It drove her to desperation," Sattiyayi continued. "Shortly, my friend found her, arm hanging off the bed. The whole bottle of the sleeping poppy juice the French maid had given her had been drunk as well as one from the housekeeper. She was dead."

Oh, Violet. Violet! I grieved for her, for me. Tears streamed down my face.

"You knew this memsahib?" she asked.

"Yes," I said. "She was my friend." I knew Violet had taken my money and tried to take my home, but she thought I was dead and could not have imagined it would do me harm. Suddenly, I was very, very glad she was buried on my land. It was a family plot. "She was like family."

Now Sattiyayi looked truly horrified. "I'm sorry to have told this to you."

"I am not. But I have a very important question. Why didn't your friend dispose of the bottle, later?"

"It was shortly after the memsahib had self-murdered and the household was distressed. The captain's driver took her to the station, with some money and a note, and he forced her to leave immediately. Later, when she arrived here, she asked someone what the note said and it was instructions to help her travel back to India with another family. But the lascars and their English friends stole the money before leaving her here and there was not enough money for passage. And no families returning for some time, due to the Uprising."

"There was a proverb, in henna, in the room."

She nodded. "My friend wanted to make sure that people understood that Violet's own evil, wanting to kill a man, taking what did not belong to her, had brought this on herself. But she does not write in English."

"I'm very sorry this happened to your friend."

"I, too," she said. "But there are also good English people. An Englishman, the captain, made sure she got quickly away. Very often it is the stranger, the foreigner, who is blamed for these things. People mistrusted Indians, especially after the Troubles. We know that now, since we have lived here, at the Ayahs' Home, with many other Indian maids. The home is provided to us by caring English people. So there are good people, and bad people, everywhere, Miss Ravenshaw."

I nodded. "That is true. Will you return to India, like your friend did?"

She nodded. "Very soon. I have been saving some money, I have some valuables to sell, and there is a family who would like me to come with them on the ship to India. The memsahib speaks Malayalam, just a little, not like you." She smiled.

I stood, feeling a compelling need to return, immediately, to Hampshire and talk to Luke. She walked me to the door, where I joined Mrs. Ross and opened my leather wallet.

"Please, do not sell your remaining valuables," I said. "I cannot help the maid who was hurt in my home, by my friend, but I can help you." I handed her a sum of money, realizing, now, how foolish and naive I'd been to travel with that much money, but thinking it had been perhaps divinely appointed. I could afford it now, because of Luke's generosity. "Will this be enough?"

She tried to push it back at me. "It is too much."

"No. It's what I want to do."

" தே வில் க்நொவ் யு பி யுவர் லவ்," she said.

"I hope that is true," I said, pleased that she knew the scripture.

"Many of us have profited by your father's work. My brother, he has a good job and their house has a roof and they have food because of your father's work in teaching them to read and to keep accounts, and he now has a situation with the English tea planters. His life, your mother's life, it was not in vain."

I was warmed by her reassurance and glad to have provided her passage back to India and we offered the *Namaste* sign to one another.

We met Daniel at the hackney carriage. The driver assured us that, if we hurried, we could take the train from London to Hampshire that very day. I told him, "All speed," and extra if he could get us to Waterloo in time. He took me at my word.

As we blazed through London, I mentioned my giving the maid enough resources for her return trip. Mrs. Ross put her hand on mine. "That was a nice thing ye did," she said.

"She needs to get home," I said. "I understand that more than anyone."

She nodded. "They'll know ye by your love."

I turned toward her. "Why, yes, that's just what the young Indian maid said to me, too! In Tamil. Were you . . . did you serve in India, Mrs. Ross?"

She grinned and nodded, and then turned aside to watch London fly by. Well, much more about her began to make sense. I should speak with her of this later. For now, I looked out of the window, consumed with grieving for Violet, both resolved and distressed to know at last who lay in my grave.

I needed to get to Luke before he sailed.

Some hours later we pulled into Southampton. Daniel left us there on a bench, while he went to fetch the carriage. It took some time longer than I expected before he returned.

"One of the horses is not well," Daniel said. "We shall have to travel slowly, and I will attend to her once we return to Headbourne House."

"Thank you," I said. I wanted, if at all possible, to speak with Luke that very evening. He had said he was leaving soon. Not the next night, or the night after, but soon. However, he had been vague and I didn't want him to go without knowing the truth.

Actually, I simply didn't want him to go.

We made our way home from the station, though it took hours. Time seemed to have stopped for me and I wished to urge the poor horses on.

"Fear not," Mrs. Ross said, echoing the angels in the Bible, before being swayed to sleep by the carriage.

But I did fear. I feared being too late, too wrong, and perhaps having misunderstood many things all along. When we arrived, I asked Daniel to pull directly into the carriage house so he could attend to the lame horse.

It was all but empty. There was one horse still, in the back.

"Notos?" he said with surprise. "She was not here when we left. Perhaps Captain Whitfield is here?"

Oh! But that he were. My breath and pace both quickened. I went directly to the house and Landreth met us at the door.

"Is Captain Whitfield here?" I asked.

He smiled, and by his smile, I knew that my enthusiasm for Luke had shown through. Landreth shook his head. "No. But he was here earlier, inquiring after you. We told him you'd gone to London and didn't say when you'd return." He looked at me with a reprimand. "He left Notos, though." By his expression I knew he found that unusual. As did I.

I went upstairs and changed into the velvet riding habit Michelene had ordered for me but that till now had gone unworn. I rued, now, the extravagance of the cut. Perhaps I should have known to economize more even then. I did not ring for Michelene; I did not want to speak with her just then. Instead, I made my way back downstairs, not stopping to talk to Mrs. Ross, either, as there were not two mounts.

"I shall ride to Graffam," I said.

"Alone?" Mrs. Blackwood was in the hallway with Landreth now.

I nodded. "I'm a grown woman who has made her way through the murder of her parents, through a journey from the Indies, to face an imposter trying to steal my home and heritage.

One ride will not undo me nor my reputation, and Lady Ledbury is sure to be at home."

I turned and walked into the dusk, hoping that the dimming light would conceal my shaking. I made my way to the stable yard, where Daniel was attending the lame horse.

"Would you saddle Notos for me?" I asked. "A saddle with a pommel?"

"For . . . you, miss?" His mouth was agape.

"I do know how to ride, Daniel. And, at present, I do not see another mount which is not ill or tired. Do you?"

"No, miss, I do not. Where are you going?"

"To Graffam Park."

He gave me some simple directions, but I felt certain that I knew the way having traveled it only two days before. And, if I went astray, Notos would certainly know the way.

"Miss Ravenshaw?" he said. He looked toward the horse boxes, then looked back to me. He went white.

"Yes?"

"I have one more confession to make. Early on, miss, when you first came. I . . . it was I who locked you in the stall with the bay."

"You? Daniel, why?"

He looked shamed. "We didn't like you, I'm sorry to admit. We thought you were an imposter and I wanted to scare you. Please forgive me, and don't tell the captain. We all like you now, we really do. I just didn't want you to be afraid, now, as you take up riding again."

I softened. "Thank you for telling me, Daniel. And I won't tell him. Now—get my saddle!"

I came close to Notos, patting her side before presenting myself near her head. She shied away.

"I'm afraid, too, girl, but we have to do this." I waited another few moments till she got used to my presence, then Daniel saddled her and helped me on and I rode, slowly at first, and then more quickly, down the drive and toward Luke.

The dark closed in around me like a tunnel; it was deep October and the mists came early now and blew in my face as I rode. I prayed there were no snakes, no holes in the ground, no tangling vines, but mainly I prayed I would know what to say and how to say it. We raced through the night. I soon recognized the ornate drive that led to Lord Ledbury's estate. I slowed Notos down, and she seemed relieved, too, at the familiar place. I rode her to the stable, where there were several grooms present. One of them helped me down.

"Are you expected?" he asked me, eyeing the familiar horse.

"I know not," I answered. "I shall find out, shan't I?"

I straightened my dress but the velvet was damp. I tried to pull my hair into a neat arrangement after having ridden in the mist. I walked up the front steps, feeling a bit out of place, and before I could knock, the butler opened the door. His face screwed up as he looked, in vain, for a carriage or a chaperone. "Can I help you?" he finally asked.

"I'm here for Captain Whitfield," I said. "Is he in at present?"

"I'm uncertain, miss. Please, come in." He ushered me into the great hallway. "Who shall I say is calling?"

"Miss Rebecca Ravenshaw."

He nodded. "Wait here."

CHAPTER THIRTY-FOUR

A few minutes passed before Luke entered the hallway from one of the long wings. "Rebecca." He took my arm and led me into the library, to a set of large leather chairs placed before a huge fire in an ancient fireplace. "Your riding habit is damp," he said. "Shall I ring to see if there is something you could change into? And where is Mrs. Ross?" He looked toward the hallway.

"I came alone," I said quietly. "The fire will help dry this quickly." Warmth was already seeping through me—starting with the arm he had so tightly held. He drew our chairs near one another so we could speak quietly, but of course, the library door had been left open.

"I hope you don't mind," I said. "I rode Notos."

"I knew you would," he said. "Since you'd asked for her to be left."

"Asked?" I gently inclined my head. "I've been in London all day."

Now he looked askance. "Mrs. Ross herself asked me to leave her for you earlier this afternoon."

"But Mrs. Ross was with me," I said. Then I softened. We could sort that out later. That was not why I had come and I did not want to be distracted. "One of the carriage horses was lame and . . . I wanted to reach you. Quickly."

He took my hand in his own. "I was very concerned when Mrs. Blackwood told me that you had gone to London."

"Daniel and Mrs. Ross went with me," I reminded him. The skeptical look on his face shared that he did not believe that to be enough. *Wait till he finds out I went to the docks and Whitechapel!*

We sat there quietly for a moment. "I have a proposal for you," I said.

He looked up, hope on his face. "I hope it mirrors the proposal I have in mind."

I took a deep breath. "I wondered if, perhaps, you'd like to buy Headbourne House. I'd like it to go to someone who will cherish it and you would, certainly . . ." I stopped speaking as the color drained from his face and then he flushed again with what looked like confusion and sorrow. He ran his hand through his hair, looked at me with a crushed expression, stood up, and walked away from me. Then he looked out of the window for some time before coming back.

"Your proposal is that you should sell the house to me?" His voice conveyed disbelief and grief.

I stood to face him, my heart sinking, and then crying out for me to tell the man how I felt, honestly, to risk all, to explain why I must only offer my home and not my heart. But I could not. "You'd paid for the renovations, which I thank you so much for . . ." My voice faltered.

Fortune favors the bold, Rebecca.

I closed my eyes for just a moment before proceeding. I was Flora, the garden statue, pleading and still, but crumbling round the edges, in need of rescue. I needed to be immediately forthright with the main concern. Now. Now! Speak of it. "I saw you pull another woman into the chapel with you," I whispered. "I didn't want to interfere in your personal concerns. So . . ." It was all too much. I blinked back tears. "I just thought, well, I just thought that we were, you and I, that we'd . . . I misunderstood. Then once I knew my financial position I realized I could not keep Headbourne. Who better for it to go to than you? And then, someday, to your children."

By another woman. I choked on the thought.

He ran his hand through his black hair again, silver streak falling stubbornly out of place, then pulled the second chair closer and leaned in toward me.

"That woman at the chapel was Michelene."

"Michelene!" Not that it made it better; in fact, it was, perhaps, much worse. Betrayed on two sides.

He put his finger to his lips and then to mine. "Let's not involve the household, shall we?"

I nodded my agreement. "I'm sorry."

"That night, I heard a noise at the window of the guesthouse. I looked out and thought I saw a woman. When I looked again a few minutes later, I saw that it *was* a woman. I believed, or perhaps hoped, it was you, grew concerned, and wanted to make sure you weren't in need of help. I thought there was something, perhaps, you wanted to share with me away from prying eyes and ears. Where better than the chapel?"

I could understand that. "Why did you believe it to be me?"

"You'd been to the chapel late at night on your own before. She was wearing your dress—the midnight-blue one that has crystals scattered about. And her hair and face were hooded."

I savored a thought. "You remembered one of my dresses."

He kissed my cheek. "I remember all of your dresses," he said after pulling away.

I smiled at that. "What . . . what did Michelene want?"

"I'm sure you can guess. Once she'd tricked me into coming to the chapel, it became clear that she was interested in further . . . discovering if we had mutual interests. It was something she had subtly suggested earlier, when the imposter had engaged her as a lady's maid."

"Do you understand men?" Michelene had asked me. *"I do."*

I couldn't believe it. "But she's wanted me to look pretty and . . ." Had I been deceived all round? She most certainly *had* taken one liberty too many.

"She couldn't very well stay at the house as a lady's maid if there was no lady, now, could she?" His tone was still gentle, his face open and honest. "She wanted a liaison and also thought if she could persuade me to stay with you, then you'd have the resources for a maid and she and I could . . . I left as soon as I understood."

Impulsively, I reached to touch his open, honest face. I was so, so very glad he had not been with another woman of his own accord, I practically bled relief. I cupped his chin, feeling the brusque beginnings of whiskers graze against my soft palm. I left it there for a moment, exulting. "I cannot take it in that not only are you still here, in England, I am touching you." I quickly took my hand away. "Forgive me."

He took my hand in his own and placed it back on his face. "I can't," he said simply. "That would require your being sorry."

"And I'm not," I replied.

He laughed aloud and then I did, too. "I shall never tire of that sound," he said. "Why did you go to London?"

"After reading the Tamil inscription, and learning that you'd instructed Daniel to send her back to India, I needed to see if I could find someone who knew the Indian maid," I said. "And I did. I found her friend, and she explained all to me."

"You read the writing in the room the imposter had slept in?" He looked downward. "I worried it implicated me in some way. That she'd written something in revenge."

"It did not implicate you," I said. "And her name was Violet."

"Violet?"

"The imposter. She was my friend."

He stood and stirred the fire himself so that no one would have an excuse to disturb us. I was astonished he had no reaction until he spoke. "I knew that."

"You knew it was Violet?" I had thought to surprise him but instead, he had surprised me!

"I did not know her name. But I knew she was your friend." He sat back down. "One day you had been speaking with Miss Dainley and had shared how you and a friend had a love of stones whilst growing up together in India. Yours, you said, was moonstone. One of your friends loved cat's-eye. The woman who was here pretending to be you loved cat's-eye; among her few possessions she'd brought some. Once I'd buried her, and realized she had no family or anything personal, I went through her room looking for them, found them, and had them affixed to her gravestone."

The lights I'd seen flickering on dark nights would have been moonlight hitting the cat's-eyes. So very much like Violet's little cat, Marie. "So you removed them from the gravestone after Delia told you." This must have been the friendship turn Delia had mentioned, though, in light of her other offenses, it hardly seemed noteworthy.

"Yes," he said. "I did not want you to know you'd been betrayed by a friend. You—you had so few friends and I wanted to protect your memories."

"Thank you, Luke," I said, looking into his eyes. Our chairs were side by side but for a small table between us that I suddenly wished was gone. The fire had warmed me through by now. Or perhaps it had been the man who'd done that. His mentioning Delia brought another question to mind.

"What were you and Delia arguing about when I saw you riding from the downs toward the stables?"

"She told me that everyone knew I'd had a hand in your imposter's death, that she could overlook it because she understood what the house meant to me, and that my character was good in spite of it all. She made clear, though, what you've likely noticed. I can have no life in Hampshire. Everyone suspects me, and I and mine would always be under a cloud of distrust." He stood and stirred the fire again. "She said it did not matter to her, and we could move to Derbyshire and start fresh. She said you'd never forgive me if you knew I had a hand in the death of your childhood friend."

Oh! That I might go and retrieve my mother's dress from her. I pitied the man who would receive her in it.

"I'm sorry," I said. "She was unkind, at the very least."

"I am sorry, too," he said. "I never wanted to marry her; she is much like my mother. But at that moment, I realized once and for all that you and I could never live happily here. People would always suspect that I had killed your friend, even though I know she killed herself. They'd been thinking that for months. I'd have lived in dread that you would find out it was your friend and hate me for it. Even now, people will think I married you for Headbourne. I'd made it plain how much I desired it. After Miss Dainley made it clear that everyone still suspected me, and I knew by their reactions to me that she was right, that there was no way to clear my name, I knew what I must do."

"Which was?"

"Withdraw from you," he said, pain in his voice. "This would be no life for you after all you have already undergone and lost. People wondering if I wanted you or the house, making you the target of insinuations, the focus of looks in the streets as we drove by. I did not want you to live under the stigma of it all. Did not want the . . . suspicion attached to your children. Our children."

Our children. I relished the sound of it. He sat down again and I knelt before him and took both his hands in mine. "Once, many months ago, you cleared my name as you declared me the rightful heir. I can clear your name from any wrongdoing," I said softly.

"You cannot," he said. "There is no one left to prove that I did not have a hand in it. Because, even though she took her own life, I pushed her toward it, not realizing how fragile she was. I am culpable. I said things I shouldn't have said."

"That you would inform the constable of her duplicity?"

"How did you know that?"

"The Indian maid's friend told me."

He looked miserable. "She knew I suspected her, the left hand, and that I was having a friend of your brother's come to the house. It was that last fact, I suspect, that pushed her to the edge. If I hadn't done that, perhaps she'd still be alive."

"You tested me, repeatedly, and I did not harm myself."

He cocked his head. It seemed to be a new realization. "That is true." I returned to my seat and leaned in close and shared what Sattiyayi had told me about the Dr. Warburg's Tincture and Violet's intent to murder him by switching his Warburg's with the bottle she had poisoned as soon as she knew he'd suspected her to be an imposter. "Perhaps when you were to force the last truth, with Dunn, she knew you'd be wary or perhaps she didn't have it in her heart to kill you when it came down to it. Knowing her, that is what I believe."

His eyes widened and he stood up abruptly before sitting down again. "Murder me? I would never have suspected she'd try that; I'm thankful it didn't get that far. If *she* hadn't died . . . *I* might have."

I nodded. "It is possible, and I shan't ever understand it completely. And I shall never fully be able to get beyond the fact that Violet tried to kill you. She grew cold when her father took her and her mother to Ceylon, where her mother died, and then he took up with a Ceylonese woman. Although Violet had returned to visit India several times a year. She hadn't had a mother for some time—would not, perhaps, have even been aware how important it would have been for her to have a chaperone here."

"She didn't have one," Luke said. "Mrs. Blackwood tried to look out for her. She suggested a chaperone. The young lady declined. That was a first clue."

"Perhaps she worried that with a chaperone she'd be caught out," I said. "She heard that our family had perished, and believing us all dead, began to weave her facade. She probably thought no one would be hurt—I was dead to her—and then became entangled beyond her ability to cope."

I knew, now, who lay in that grave. I should have to write to her father.

"I am not to blame." His face took a wry and sad twist before he composed himself again.

"You are not to blame, in fact, you did a generous thing in ensuring her ayah would not be accused and in giving her money to leave England."

We were inches apart. He leaned toward me and kissed my top lip, and then my bottom lip, and then both of them at once. He stood and then pulled me to my feet before embracing me, which said, *I shall protect you*, and then stroked my hair, which said, *I adore you*, and then kissed me in a way that conveyed *I desire you*. My mind swirled away and I could hardly breathe, but I wanted to, because when I did, I breathed in his breath, his essence, and it bonded us.

The library door was open, but in the face of convention I kissed him back, unreservedly, before he whispered in my ear, "And into all things from her air inspired the spirit of love and amorous delight. She disappeared, and left me dark; I waked to find her, or for ever to deplore her loss, and other pleasures all abjure: When out of hope, behold her, not far off, such as I saw her in my dream, adorned with what all Earth or Heaven could bestow."

"*Paradise Lost*," I said, pulling back a little in wonder. "Had you memorized that section for me, too? You'd thought we were to be no more."

"Mostly," he said. "But for the first time in many years, I allowed myself a flicker of hope. I had hoped to speak with you at my mother's ball. I knew I should utterly forsake you for your own good but I found that, in spite of my best efforts, I could not."

"And I am very glad of it." Then I blushed. "I'm so sorry for what I said to your brother at the ball."

He took my face between his hands. "I am not. I knew then that you loved me as I love you."

"You love me," I said in quiet wonder.

"If I haven't made that quite clear, then please accept my apologies, Miss Ravenshaw. I love you. I unreservedly, undeniably, unconditionally, uncontrollably love you."

"And I, you." I reached up to touch his face, too. "I have become quite expert at reclaiming what is mine, Luke. My house, my land, my name. My man." I smiled before jesting. "Shall you depart for the East Indies, then?"

"By no means." He pulled me toward himself once more. "But I will not stay at Lord Ledbury's long, either."

I smiled. "Other accommodations can be arranged. But not an irregular union." At that, he laughed again. "And I shall need my chaperone to attend me at all times until . . ."

"Until we are wed," he said quietly. "If you'll have me."

"Until we are wed. I will have you."

Oh, Lord. I have my house, my security and peace, and happiness. You have truly restored it all. Thank you.

Luke had a coach take me back to Headbourne House. I went directly to my room and closed the door tightly. I did not want to speak to anyone, especially Michelene, until I had gathered my thoughts. By morning, I was prepared to confront her.

CHAPTER THIRTY-FIVE

I called Michelene into the drawing room then closed the door.

"Are you ill?" she asked. "You did not call for me for two days." She came over as if to observe me for signs of disease.

"Please, have a seat," I said. She chose the chair farthest from me and eyed me suspiciously.

"It has come to my attention," I said, "that you have been wearing my gowns."

"Oh!" she said. "You mean the lettuce one and the yellow one that you had given me."

I had forgotten about those. "No, not any I had cast off." I regretted, now, not insisting that they go to charity. "I mean the blue one encrusted with crystals."

Real fear crossed her deep brown eyes. "What do you mean? I have it for mending."

"You wore it to meet Captain Whitfield," I said. "At the chapel."

"Ah." She raised her eyebrow. "Yes, yes. He requested the *rendez-vous* with me. I did not understand—until I arrived—what exactly he had in mind. Once I arrived, and realized that he wanted me to accompany him through the tradesman's entrance to the guesthouse, I fled."

The most effective lies are always truth based. But my eyes were open, now.

"Captain Whitfield and I are to be married," I said.

"*Félicitations!* I can help with the most beautiful wedding dress."

The utter gall! I held up my hands. "I'm afraid your service with me has come to a swift conclusion. Unfortunately, I will not be able to offer a recommendation, as most women do not prefer that their lady's maid press her case with their husband, or husband-to-be, nor provide regular laudanum to the lady of the house in an effort to make her more pliable, or, perhaps, bring on sleep so they may dally with men or take the carriage at will. You said you wanted to help!" I tempered my voice.

"I was helping. You wanted him to stay, *non*? I was giving the extra incentive to that." I remembered the look that passed between her and Lady Ashby. Had she perhaps tried this trick with others?

I would not shoot this snake in the grass, but I would wrangle it with a snake hook and fling it far from my home.

Her eyes darted left and right, not able, apparently, to remain steadily in my gaze.

"With your dressmaking abilities, I'm certain you'll be able to secure work in another town. London, perhaps," I said. "Certainly not around here. Mrs. Blackwood is, even now, packing your belongings. Any dresses, even cast-offs, you procured while in my employ will remain with me. Except the blue crystal-encrusted dress. You may take that with you as a reminder, as I shall never wear it again. Daniel will take you to the train station, or anywhere nearby that you like." I held out an envelope. "Your final settlement."

I softened my voice. "You have talent, and skill, and the ability to make a fine living honestly, Michelene, if you choose to. You could marry."

"A tradesman, perhaps? Or the chief constable, who pursued me? *Non.* I am above that."

Ah. The constable. Now I understood.

She sneered at me and stood up. "*Bon courage* in your marriage, mademoiselle. You shall perhaps need it." Trying to plant doubt to the last, but I had none of it.

I stood and saw her to the hall. Mrs. Blackwood arrived soon thereafter with two small trunks and I saw Michelene down the walk. As Daniel drove away with her, I turned to Landreth.

"Who removed the lions from the pillars at the foot of the steps?"

He repressed a smile, barely. "Captain Whitfield ordered it done, miss, early this morning. Sent for the stonemason from Graffam. Said to tell you Whitfield walked through them and they ran away."

I grinned.

"He asked, miss, that you not return to the chapel till he brings you himself."

I nodded my agreement and thanked him. For the first time in memory, Landreth smiled, too, a genuine, wide smile, bowed slightly, and then held his hand out for me to make my way, first, into my home, where he handed a package to me. "This was delivered by hire carriage this morning."

I took it in hand. It had no return address, and was addressed simply to Miss Rebecca Ravenshaw, Headbourne House.

"Thank you," I murmured, and went upstairs to open it.

I slit open the side of the package with the ivory letter opener in the top drawer of my bureau. A card fell out first, and then I was able to see what was inside: a delicate bag that held yards and yards of white Honiton lace. I gently took the lace out and held a stretch of it between my hands.

Mother.

It was clearly worked by my mother in a pattern she had designed herself and had used, often, in the past. I held it to my cheeks, then to my lips, then set it down before my tears stained its snowy perfection. I opened the folded card. It was written in Tamil.

Dear Miss Rebecca Ravenshaw,

I am enclosing this gift to you. I had not wanted to sell it; I'd thought I would bring it back to the mission in India because I knew how valuable it was. But then I thought I must sell it, or there would be no way for me to return home. Because you provided the gift to me I was able to purchase my return trip ticket without doing so.

We had been to the mission to visit when news came of your family's death. Violet was grieved, but also, I believe, saw her opportunity. When we left India, Memsahib Violet took some papers which I believe she thought would prove she was you, and this lace, which I kept so the French maid could not take it. I know now that this is your mother's handmade lace and Violet had kept it in case she needed further proof of her identity. As you may have guessed, I was the maid to Violet and not the maid's friend, but given that the other memsahib had lied to me, I did not know if I could trust you and therefore did not tell you the truth right away. I am sorry for this.

I hope you enjoy many long and happy days in your homeland. I hope I do, too, in mine.

Blessings and peace be upon you,

Sattiyayi

Oh, yes. Deep inside, I'd known. The touching of the cheek, and flinching, upon further reflection, confirmed it in my mind. The detailed knowledge of what had gone on, even the explanation about the hennaed warning. I held the lace in my hand like the treasure it was.

My mother's hands made this. The release of peace, so long awaited, spilled forth in my heart and spread throughout my body in every kind of warmth. I had, for a moment, regretted giving her dress to Delia, but charity had won out. Charity, in turn, had returned something more precious to me; not my grandmother's lace, which was dear, but my mother's, which was priceless.

A knock came at the door. "Miss Ravenshaw?"

It was Mrs. Blackwood. I got up and opened the door, leaving the lace across my bed like a joyous streamer, a banner of goodwill and affection.

"Yes?"

"I'm sorry to bother you," she said, and I remembered the day when she did not want me in her quarters.

"Not at all," I said. "Please come in."

"I've heard, while . . . though, we don't gossip, miss, as you'll know, but Landreth has said that there is to be a wedding." She grinned, which was quite a sight to see on her bright face, lightening her of a dozen years and perhaps twice as many cares.

"Can you arrange for a wedding breakfast, planned for and prepared in about six weeks?"

"Oh, oh yes," she said. She glanced at the bed. "Is that for your wedding dress, then?"

Wedding dress!

"Just what is taking place here?" Mother walked into the room and scolded in jest. *We girls had wrapped ourselves in yards of*

lace, around our heads and draped like veils, around our bodies like shrouds.

"Playing wedding," I said, with a small curtsey.

"Where are the grooms?" Mother asked, looking about her, playing along. I could see her suppress a smile.

"They've not yet arrived," I answered. "But they shall. Very soon indeed."

She drew me to her and kissed my head, through the lace veil. "You make a lovely bride, Rebecca."

"Miss Ravenshaw?" Mrs. Blackwood's voice brought me back to the present.

"Oh yes," I answered, blinking back happy tears. *Mother.* "Mrs. Blackwood, what a stunning idea. Of course, yes, it must be." I stopped. "But, well, Michelene is no longer in my employ and . . ."

"Might I suggest Annie?" she said. "With a bit of training, she'd make a fine lady's maid."

"Indeed she would! No more French maids. But the dress . . ."

"Lady Frome is certain to know someone who can make a fine dress, quickly," she said.

"Indeed! Jennie will help, I know it."

"Jennie?" she asked.

"Oh, I'm sorry, yes, Lady Frome," I answered. "Lady Frome and I use our Christian names with one another now."

She smiled. "All will be well, then." She turned to leave the room, and as she did, her keys jingled. "When I was packing Michelene's room, I found several of your dresses hanging in her wardrobe. I also found some of your letters in her bureau." She handed them to me. They were held together by three hairpins, all jet and diamond. Of course the pins had belonged to me, in that she'd spoken truly. She'd taken them from Violet, who also had been in mourning and worn them, who knows when, in the chapel.

"Now that I realize she took your letters, I see where she found some information she shared with me. She'd told me you had wanted to be married in India, but your friend had stolen your intended."

"Never!"

"And she suggested we encourage you. I was glad to do it, Miss Ravenshaw, once I knew what a lovely woman you are. I thought I was doing good, but I see now, I'd been ill used for her purposes."

I drew near. "We all were. Please do not give it another thought. And it's certainly worked out well, hasn't it?"

She grinned and nodded before leaving my room.

I unclasped the packet—the letters I'd meant to send, and some I was to have received. One letter was from Mr. Mead, one from Penelope, several from others at the mission. That mystery was solved. Michelene had wanted knowledge to taunt me with, perhaps, to help me fear the dreams or my sanity. That certainly was where she'd learned of Mr. and Mrs. Mead, where she had learned about Penelope and John Mark, and the fact that she had married him, not I, which she'd shared with Mrs. Blackwood.

I turned back to happier thoughts, gathering up the lace in my arms and hugging it close.

I had six weeks to prepare for my wedding. My wedding!

The December day was a gift; cold, clear, beautiful, with the lightest powdering of snow, like crystal talc on a lady's face, which made even the mundane and ordinary sparkle. Although it was against protocol, Luke came by the house early so we could have some time to talk and walk together before the late morning wedding. He had a surprise for me, he'd said, and wanted to show me privately before the ceremony and wedding breakfast. I met him in the drawing room.

"Good morning, darling." He kissed both of my cheeks in turn. He smiled at Mrs. Ross. "This will be your last official duty, then?"

She smiled back. "I doona ken about that," she said. "But I shall take my leave right after the breakfast."

It was the only cloud cast over the day. "I will miss you terribly," I said.

"I will be nearby," she replied. Winchester wasn't very far away.

Luke bundled me into my warm coat and we walked down the stone steps. We walked the path past the stable yard and coach house; Luke had already begun the process of bringing his horses back to Headbourne. By the time we returned from our honeymoon in Europe his personal effects would be completely reinstalled. I'd ensured that the master bedroom had been refreshed, too. How lovely it would be to share it. Shortly, we came to the graveyard, where he stopped in front of the newest grave.

The stone had been smoothed, and the cat's-eyes reapplied. Violet's name had been carved where mine had been, just above the line *A friend loveth at all times.*

"Oh, thank you," I said. "I know she has done some horrible things, but I will rest easier believing she rests, too."

"I know," he said. "I had the stonemasons attend to this. You are a true friend. But this is not the gift I have for you. Turn around."

I did, and I was astonished that the church had been completely renovated. I knew that Luke had planned to complete the work because I'd said I wanted Reverend Bennetts to marry us there, but each stone had been cleaned, grout and mortar attended to. Inside, the pews had been replaced and the windows mended and polished; one had been replaced entirely with a stained glass of the garden of Eden.

"So this is why you did not want me to enter the chapel till you could bring me yourself," I said in awe.

"Even the good Lord found that love is a risk. Paradise lost. Paradise regained."

I hugged him. "Luke! This is the best gift you could have given me. When did you think of it?"

We sat down on a pew, Mrs. Ross several rows behind us.

"The morning you'd gone to London, I came looking for you, to thank you, to love you, for speaking up for me with my brother."

"I recall," I said with a little shame.

"Do not be ashamed; it was then that I knew I could not let you go," he said. "When you were not at home, I came to the church to pray."

"Truly?"

He nodded. "And in the midst of it, I knew I had to restore the chapel, whether I won you back or not. It was, perhaps, a bit like you. Placid and cared for on the outside. A bit undone inside, at the heart. I wanted to change that . . . for it, for you."

He reached over and slipped my gloves off my hands, then removed his own gloves so we could hold hands, skin to skin.

"Henna?" he seemed surprised.

"Just a little," I said. "Not enough to make a spectacle. In India, a bride has an intricate design created on her hands or feet before her wedding day. The design is meant to have no clear beginning and no end, like the relationship itself." He turned my hand over in his own to verify that he could not see a termination in the design. I used my other hand to point out a tiny *L* and *R* in the design.

He traced it, then reached over to kiss me, firmly enough that our cheekbones pressed together, and we did not part.

Mrs. Ross cleared her throat. "The ceremony has nae taken place yet, ye know."

We looked at each other and laughed before standing up, closing the church door behind us, and running joyfully in the snow.

The wedding service had been beautiful and everyone had made their way back to the house for the breakfast. Mrs. Knowlton sat in the place of the bride's mother, directly across from Lady Ledbury, which amused me. I'd asked Mrs. Blackwood to ensure that there were swans carved of ice in the middle of the buffet.

"Swans," I said, and Luke smiled.

"When you first shared why you wouldn't hunt them, perhaps that was when I began to fall a little in love."

"Not when we first danced?" he teased.

"I admit that provoked, perhaps, a more natural response."

He grinned and pulled me to him for just a moment before mingling with our guests. I'd kept on my white dress, and even the veil, though I'd pulled it back across my hair. I went to meet Mrs. Ross in her room just after the tables were cleared so we could say our good-byes in private.

"Are you sure?" I asked. "Do you need a carriage ride?"

"I doona need a ride; it's best this way, lassie," she said.

Someone from the kirk must be shortly arriving to take her back to town.

"You are married to a guid man." She looked at my veil, trimmed in my mother's lace. "Your mother and father are content, I'm sure."

I looked her in the eye and asked softly, "Do you think they know?"

She nodded and took my hand in her fat warm one. "They know," she said. She hugged me and then opened the bedroom door to walk out. I started to follow her down the stairs, but, stubborn Scotswoman, she held up her hand and indicated that she wanted to do it alone.

I looked around her small, neat room. On the small bureau next to the window was a bottle of Dr. Warburg's Tincture. It must have been the one that had disappeared! I went over to inspect it. Empty, clean, dry, and the only thing left in her room. She had wanted me to find it. How had she known it needed to be removed, to keep others safe from its consumption?

I stood at the top of the stairs just as she closed the great door behind her. I walked, as quickly as one could in a billowing, binding white cloud, down the flights and into the main hallway hoping to catch and ask her.

I opened the door and stepped out onto the landing, but she was gone. I walked farther out but there was no sight of her to be found. No footprints nor carriage tracks marred the freshly fallen drifts.

Luke came up behind me and wrapped his arm around my waist. "Come inside, darling. It's cold out here."

I looked up and down the way once more, seeing nothing. And then, an extra shimmer in the snow, which reached heavenward and was met by an extra shimmer in the clouds.

Then I understood. Mrs. Ross was no ordinary chaperone, overseeing my comportment and guarding my reputation. She had been sent, protecting and ministering to my very being by divine decree, as Scripture claims—and I, unawares. It was why she felt so familiar; she'd been with me all along.

Thank you, Lord.

I melted into my husband's side like a snowflake on a warm hand and we walked together into our house. Our home. Headbourne.

EPILOGUE

SUMMER 1863

Annie helped me close the remaining trunk. It was stuffed beyond capacity, really, and a testimony to her industriousness that everything had been accommodated in the cases Luke had allocated for the trip. Annie had, at the last moment, plucked out Marie, who had been making an attempt to stow away. Daniel brought around the carriage, and Matthew helped me in.

"You'll help Daniel take care of everything in our absence?"

"Yes, ma'am, Miss Rebecca." He still called me that, and I did not chide him, because it brought back lovely memories from the time before he was a member of our household. I stepped up into the carriage first and then Peter was handed to me. Mercy, at four, followed, then Luke, and lastly, Luke's valet, Thornton.

"Better than the improving book?" I teased.

"Oh yes, ma'am, infinitely," he said, barely able to contain his boyish excitement at the trip.

Shortly after we'd boarded ship and were settled, we pulled away from the harbor, at sunset. I stood on deck, two-year-old Peter in one arm, and holding Mercy's hand.

"I shall ride a painted elephant, shan't I, Mummy?" She jumped up and down. "Or shall I shoot a tiger?"

"We'll see when we arrive," I said with a smile. I had longed to return to India, and now we were going back together.

"But then we shall return home to Headbourne, is that right?" Mercy asked, a bit anxiously this time. I squeezed her hand. I, too, had once been an anxious, eager young girl pulling away from Southampton on my way to the unknown.

Her father gathered her in his left arm. "Yes, dearest, you needn't fear. We shall return home." He put his other arm around my waist, drawing me near. The water shimmered its release of day and embrace of night as gentle mists floated above the land in the distance; I closed my eyes in thankful bliss as Luke whispered Milton in my ear.

"Joy, thou, in what he gives to thee, this Paradise, and thy fair Eve."

AUTHOR'S NOTE

I love Gothic romances, a little creepy around the edges, the kind of book wherein you devoutly hope the hero is who you want him to be, not who you suspect he might be. I especially love those with a historical and British bent, with a heroine who is both vulnerable and strong. I've fond memories of sharing Victoria Holt's books with my grandmother.

My interest in this particular story ignited when I read a biography of the first wife of William Carey, the man often considered the Father of Missions. Dorothy Carey was an unwilling missionary. She did not want to leave England, but her husband persisted and planned to take their eldest son with him, perhaps forever, leaving her home with the younger children. Dorothy was finally convinced to accompany her husband (or perhaps was bullied into it). Suffering first from what we would call depression, she was an unhappy woman who was locked inside, crying, while her husband baptized their son and his first Indian convert. Her illness progressed and she ended her days in paranoia, psychosis, and misery after the death of their son Peter from dysentery, which she herself suffered from throughout her life. Carey, who seemed to have been both driven and a man seeking relief, as well as confinement, for his wife, went on to marry another woman after Dorothy's death, a woman suited to mission work. They lived and worked together happily.

This interest next led me to the Mault family. Among the earliest missionaries from England to India, sent from the London Missionary Society, both Charles and Margaret Mault were admirably, happily suited to missionary work. They joined Margaret's brother, Charles Mead, and his wife in South India. Mrs. Mead and Mrs. Mault worked together to open schools that taught both academic and practical subjects to girls in a state where girls never went to school. Mrs. Mault, an accomplished lace maker from Honiton, shared her skill. Lace making offered Indian girls financial freedom, dignity, and the ability to climb the social, if not the caste, ladder. Their lace was proudly displayed at the Great Exhibition of 1851 in London and sold throughout the world.

Although I drew from hard history and inspiration from those named above, conflating them in some ways, my story is (and my characters are) purely fictional. I did keep Mr. Mead's true name, rather than fictionalizing him, to honor him. He was removed from the London Missionary Society after marrying an Indian Christian woman some years after his English wife's death. He remained in India, serving, and died there.

There is no better lead than that to show the complexities of nineteenth-century missions. Many missionaries gave up lives of comfort and ease to follow a call to share their faith and their God, very often at great, lifelong, and final cost to themselves. And yet when you read the history, there are also serious cringe-worthy moments: the marking of others as "heathen" and high-handed paternalism among them. Sometimes missionaries arrived before, with, and after colonialists, which further complicated interpretation of motives. The story of missions is the story of Christianity writ small, striving to achieve and do good to others, and for God, often succeeding but also succumbing from time to time to the clay feet we all have.

To place in context the redeeming work of nineteenth-century missionaries to India, I offer some insight from Indian Christians of the twentieth and twenty-first centuries.

In a 2014 interview in *Christianity Today*, Gary Gnidovic talks with Dr. M. A. Raju, who presides over an Indian hospital founded by Christian missionaries. Gnidovic acknowledges, "When it comes to the history of missions, we often think in terms of all the mistakes that have been done, in India and other places where there's been cultural insensitivity." Raju responds, "The missionaries came on the backs of the colonists. When the missionaries arrived, they didn't find a unified India. They found nearly 70 major kingdoms, warring against each other.

"How did India get a new identity? Missionaries mastered the languages of India. In eastern India, William Carey and his associates mastered Bengali and Sanskrit. German missionaries mastered Tamil. English missionaries mastered Malayalam. American missionaries mastered Marathi. The first dictionary, for example, in Tamil and Bengali was written by missionaries. And they did it because they wanted to master the language in order to translate the Bible into the language. But they were also interested in teaching people to read and write."

Raju continues, "So they taught Bengali. They taught Tamil in the south. They taught Malayalam in the south. In the west they taught Marathi. The languages developed, and people learned to read and write. They needed people to read the Bible, so they started schools. And they taught English, and the result was a highly Anglicized community of higher education of regional communities of language learning, codifying the script. So language and education went together."

Later in the article, Raju says, "Christians also spoke against the caste system. Abolishing the caste system is a big blow to Hinduism, because if you abolish caste, you're basically saying there's no rebirth, and you're allowing people to go up and down the social ladder. Low-caste people weren't allowed to go into Hindu temples, but now they are allowed to go into them. There were all sorts of reforms to Hinduism because of Christianity."

Finally, he highlights the "impact their [Indian Christians] missionary forefathers had, on language, education, Indian identity, health, and the treatment of women, outcasts, the poor."

In *A Forgotten History*, by Joy Gnanadason, Dr. K. Rajaratnam proposes the following insights: "The entry of the Brahmins [in the tenth century] coupled with feudalism caused dissensions among the people. The oppression of the so called 'low caste' by the upper class people started. It was only by the end of the 19th century when the missionaries infused into them the spirit of dignity and courage through education and the Gospel message that they could shake off their bondage. Ironically, it is the same race of people who had enslaved India through the East India Company, who also helped the exploited to free themselves!"

Even before Protestant missionaries arrived, Catholic missionaries arrived, in 1510. Still earlier, it's been reliably claimed, Jesus' disciple Thomas arrived in Malabar, where he ministered and was later martyred. The miraculous story of the petals, as told in the book, has been faithfully handed down through the ages and can be found referenced in *National Geographic* magazine's March 2012 issue, among other sources. Syrian Christians in India spring from Thomas' ministry.

In the nineteenth century, many Indian people found their way to England, and most were in difficult circumstances upon arrival. According to the Open University on its website in its Making Britain section, the Ayahs' Home "had been founded by a committee of women who had resolved there should be a place to house stranded ayahs in England." The Ayahs' Home appears to have been founded in 1825 in Aldgate by a Mrs. Rogers (according to an advert in *The Times* on December 1868, although there are conflicting reports about the exact date and manner of foundation). "It provided shelter for ayahs whose employment had been terminated upon arriving in Britain, and found employment and passage back to India for them with British families who were travelling there. The employer who brought the ayah to Britain usually provided the ayah's return ticket, which was surrendered to the Home. The matron then 'sold' the ticket to a family requiring the ayah's services and in the meantime, before the travel date, the Home would use the money to pay for the ayah's board and lodging."

The Home was mission run for a number of years.

Poor Delia Dainley was in good company. There really was a fishing fleet of young women hoping to reel in a respectable husband, usually one posted to India, an area parched of young English roses. Women in the Victorian era were still dependent upon fathers, brothers, and husbands unless they were women of their own means or widows. Happily for our heroine, she caught the heart of Captain Luke Whitfield. Whitfield was loosely based on Lieutenant Frederick E. B. Beaumont, who was granted a patent for improvements to the Adams revolver.

Nineteenth-century India was a time and place of tumult, and there were indeed missionaries killed in the Uprising of 1857, though not the families I loosely based my book on. I read many accounts of the Uprising, but the one that most impacted my book was *The Memsahib and the Mutiny*, a firsthand account by R. M. Coopland. Although my book is fictional, I drew heavily on her writing, not only for accuracy but because I did not wish to imagine and then impute violent acts to any person or people who did not commit them. There were villains and heroes on both sides. I retained the name of the real Muslim bearer (butler), Musa, as well, in order to honor, these many years later, his selfless actions.

The Hussars have a reputation as horsed ladies' men, but I must credit Sir Arthur Conan Doyle for the observation, put in the mouth of Michelene, that the men run away from them and the women toward them!

There really was a large-hearted man named John Pounds, of Portsmouth, who despite his own difficult circumstances reached out to impoverished and overlooked children. His actions led to the foundation of the "ragged schools," which provided food, lodging, schooling, and trades for hundreds of thousands of the poorest children.

Finally, the portrayal of dear, shortbread-eating Mrs. Ross was inspired by my own interaction with who I believe to be a guardian angel in London (complete story on my website, www.sandrabyrd.com). In spite of my firm belief in the angels of Scripture, without that encounter I might not have had the desire to write one so directly on the page.

ACKNOWLEDGMENTS

I feel thankful and blessed to have a number of wonderful people who graciously contributed their many talents to this book.

Jenny Q of Historical Editorial twice brought her pen and insight to the completed manuscript and I can't envision writing an historical novel without her fine insight into story development. Special thanks to Dr. James Taneti, author of *Caste, Gender, and Christianity in Colonial India: Telugu Women in Mission*. Dr. Taneti offered guidance as the book was developing and read the manuscript to ensure the material was handled with accuracy and sensitivity. A huge thanks to Dr. Alex Naylor and Finni Golden, historical advisers and residents of Portsmouth, England (in a house dating to 1600!), both of whom were instrumental as I wrote and developed the novel. They not only helped keep my history straight, they helped me keep my English English, and not American.

Danielle Egan-Miller, Joanna MacKenzie, and Abby Saul of Browne and Miller Literary Agency are among the rare agents who are also great editors and this book was a skeleton of itself before they came alongside with excellent advice. Thanks, too, to the entire hardworking team at Howard Books who help bring these books to life and to market, including the careful attention of Senior Editor Beth Datlowe Adams.

Friends Serena Chase, Debbie Austin, Renee Chaw, and Dawn Kinzer deserve a healthy and thankful shout-out for their focused comments as the book developed and their friendship in the difficult patches. My newest editor-in-residence, Miss Parnel Bennetts, native of Hampshire, read the book both as a lover of Gothic romance and as a local expert. Special love and thanks to Ben Bennetts and the late, lovely M.M. Bennetts for all their help.

I could never have written this book without my wonderful husband, Michael, and all THREE of my children now that we've added a wonderful son-in-law to our family.